USA Today, and *Wall Street Journal* bestselling author, Nina Levine, lives in Brisbane, Australia, and is the author of more than thirty romantic suspense and contemporary romance novels, including the international bestselling Escape With a Billionaire and Storm MC series.

CONNECT ONLINE

ninalevinebooks.com

🄾 ninalevinewriter

🅕 AuthorNinaLevine

ACCIDENTALLY, SCANDALOUSLY YOURS

USA TODAY BESTSELLING AUTHOR
NINA LEVINE

Andrea,

Thank you for teaching me to love all my parts.

PART I

1

KRISTEN - TWENTY YEARS OLD

I WAS eight when Cinderella convinced me I wanted to find my very own prince. To be saved and loved by a man was a fairytale I wanted in on because I didn't feel loved or cherished by the man in my life, my father. I also wanted the beautiful dress and shoes, but mostly I dreamed of the prince wanting me, searching for me, choosing *me*.

Everything my mother taught me as a child perpetuated the story that little girls should spend their lives preparing themselves for their prince. I learned how to look, how to walk, how to smile, how to think. As I got older, I learned about the right clothes, the right makeup, the right social circle. I watched and listened to how other girls attracted boys. I perfected the art of flirting, deferring, flattering. And all along the way, my mother reminded me with everything she said and did that marrying the right man was my goal in life.

I was nineteen when I began questioning the fairytale. The princes I'd met were far from what I imagined as a child. My experiences were clumsy. My boyfriends weren't attentive. And they didn't stick around if I didn't sleep with them.

Where was my prince who wanted me, searched for me, chose me?

A year later, and my doubt is strong.

"It wasn't supposed to be like this." I yank my necklace off and dump it next to the sink of the restroom I'm in as I stare at myself in the mirror. "I've spent the last month preparing for this ball. Running my heart out, attending every spin class I could find, barely eating, and agonizing over my dress and hair, and he does *that*?"

My friend looks at me in horror as I pull at my hair, removing pins and freeing it from its perfect braided low bun that my hairdresser assured me was romantic and classy. *He'll love it, darling.* Ah, no, he didn't even notice it, let alone love it. The only thing my boyfriend loves about my appearance tonight is the sparkling silver dress I'm wearing. And not because of its beauty, but because it hugs my body like it wants to suffocate it. I imagined Jeremy whispering sweet nothings in my ear all night. Instead, he's whispered nothing but the filthy things he wants to do to me after he gets my dress off. Well, that was before I angered him. He hasn't been whispering anything in my ear for the last hour since I did that.

"Kristen, stop. What are you doing?" Lesley shrieks, eyes wide with panic as she watches me ruin my hair in the middle of one of the biggest balls of the year.

I don't stop. I can't. It's not only my dress suffocating me tonight; it's everything. My hair, my jewelry, my makeup, my shoes. My *expectations*.

I need it all off, but since I can't strip every piece of it from my body, I'll settle with removing my necklace and liberating my hair.

"Did you see the way he's been leering at Susie?" I continue tugging at the pins holding my hair in place. "We've been together for six months. Six months! I've been the perfect fucking girlfriend, doing everything he wants, and then the one time I don't fall into line, he starts ignoring me and checking out other women."

Lesley frowns. "What do you mean you didn't fall into line?"

I meet her gaze in the mirror, almost finished freeing my hair. "He wanted me to suck his dick." When she doesn't stop frowning, I add, "Here! At this ball." I finish with the last pin and fluff my hair out as I turn to her. "I am never going to get on my knees in a public place, and I've told him that. Sex is a private thing. I don't understand men who want it outside of the bedroom."

"Umm, I think they all want it outside of the bedroom. You may have to give it to him in other places."

My eyes widen and I stare at her with disbelief. "I don't have to *give it to him* anywhere I don't want to." It's my turn to frown now. "Do you really believe that?"

"Everyone I know believes that."

"Not everyone. I don't."

"Well, that may be where you're going wrong."

My eyes flare even wider, and I'm lost for words. I'm not the one in my relationship *going wrong*.

She receives a text and immediately checks it. "That was Martin." She eyes me with uncertainty. "Are you okay if I go and dance with him?"

Lesley has spent the last three months chasing this guy. I might need a friend by my side right now, but I would never stop her from dancing with him. "I'm good. Go. Dance." I smile. "He's been watching you all night, Les. He's into you."

Her eyes light up. "Really?"

"Really."

"Okay, I'm going." She's halfway to the restroom exit when she glances back at me. "Text me if you need me."

I nod. "I will."

I won't.

No, I've just decided I'm going home. I'm not putting up with Jeremy's bullshit and I'm absolutely not giving him a blowjob here.

I leave the bathroom and make my way back to the ballroom to let him know I'm leaving.

"Where did you go?" he asks, wrapping his arm around my waist and resting his hand on my ass.

"I went to the bathroom while you ignored me in favor of Susie."

Displeasure flashes across his face and he lets me go. "Fuck, you're really going to do this now?"

"If you mean, am I going to refuse to suck your dick and then acknowledge that you've been an asshole ever since I did that, then yes, this is exactly what I'm going to do. I don't appreciate you openly checking out another woman while ignoring me during a sulk."

"I wasn't sulking."

"You were, and I'm not impressed with it, so I'm going home."

The displeasure on his face intensifies. "Yeah, you should go. I'm not interested in spending the rest of the night listening to your insecurities over me supposedly checking some other woman out."

I stare at the guy I've been dating for half a year, wondering how I missed this side of him. But then, a tiny voice pops up. The voice I do my best to never hear because she always turns out to be right when I desperately want her to be wrong. *You didn't miss this side of him. You chose not to see it.*

"There was no 'supposedly' going on tonight, Jeremy, and you know it. Be a man and own your actions. And yeah, I know I have insecurities, but they had nothing to do with any of this."

With that, I turn and walk away from him.

What a dick.

A dick I think I'm done with.

My mother will have to change her expectations of this relationship. She almost peed herself when I began dating Jeremy. His family is the perfect family as far as she's concerned. He comes from old money. His family has all the right connections and are well respected. *A match made in heaven.* Those were her exact words about a month ago when she casually dropped over some bridal magazines for me to peruse. Actually, scratch the word "casually." Nothing my mother ever does is casual when it concerns a potential husband.

I'm in the middle of thinking about my mother changing her expectations and what that will mean for me (read: a fresh round of *attend this gala*, *wear this dress*, and *you should really consider a date with so and so*) when I exit the ballroom and come across a sign that tells me there's a Moonlight Soirée on the rooftop of this building.

I love the stars and could happily spend an entire evening staring up at them, getting lost in my thoughts. New York isn't the place for stargazing, but since I could really do with some thinking time tonight, I make the spontaneous decision to join the soirée.

A few minutes later, I step out of the elevator onto the rooftop and into a magical party that's filled with laughter, candles, beautiful floral decorations, and twinkle lights strung everywhere. Music plays at just the right volume and I smile as I weave through the crowd to an old song I love, "Kiss Me" by Sixpence None The Richer.

I head for a corner and when I reach it, I rest my arms on the railing and gaze up at the night sky. I don't know what it is about the sky, but it never fails to help me pause. To help me sort through the layers of thoughts I often feel trapped under.

I close my eyes for a moment and inhale a long breath. I filter out the noise of the party, of my brain, of life, and try to just *be*.

The minutes pass. I'm not sure how many, but enough for me to get lost in just being. Enough for the tension in my body to ease to a much more acceptable level.

I'm in my bubble of peace when a smooth, deep voice comes from beside me. "Have you ever spent a night stargazing in the Hamptons?"

I open my eyes and look at the owner of the sexiest voice I've ever heard.

Bradford Black.

We've never met, but I know all about him. Everyone in New York does. The Black family is synonymous with power and the kind of old money that needs no introduction.

"I have. It's amazing." I smile as I let my gaze slowly cover every inch of his face. I take more time with it than I've ever taken with a face.

Bradford is breathtakingly handsome. I could imagine him gracing magazine covers or the silver screen with his tanned skin, strong jaw, full lips, and thick dark hair that begs to know fingers. And those blue eyes of his. They're deep, expressive, unfathomable. I get the sense I could spend hours staring into his eyes and still not reach the depths of him.

He angles his body so he's facing me and rests his arm on the railing. "You ditched the ball too?"

I glance down at my dress that is more suited to a ball than this party. It's likely the giveaway that I came for the ball. Just like his tuxedo gives him away. "I did. I had to."

He leans in a little closer. "*Had* to?"

"Well, it's almost midnight. My coach will turn into a pumpkin any minute now."

His lips twitch with amusement as he looks at my feet. "I'm glad to see you didn't lose either of your glass slippers."

"I always make it a point not to leave my shoes behind. I might be searching for my prince, but that doesn't mean I'll rely on him for things like returning my shoes."

"Smart choice."

My breaths slow at what he says. Men use words like *beautiful* and *sexy* with me; they don't use *smart*. Not even my father has told me he thinks I'm smart, which is disappointing because my grades have deserved that kind of comment. But no, he says things like *good girl*. Two words I've grown to detest.

"Why did you leave the ball?" I ask.

"I was also concerned my coach would turn into a pumpkin."

I smile at that and at his super straight face. "So, we're both avoiding the real reason we left. I can appreciate a fellow avoider." It's my turn to lean in closer. "But tell me, was it a girl? Did she break your heart?"

"Maybe a little." He cocks his head and narrows his eyes at me. "Did he break yours?"

I point at my hair. "This doesn't give it away?"

"Your hair looks beautiful. It was the first thing I noticed about you."

"I don't believe you."

"Which part don't you believe?"

"Neither part."

"You think I noticed your dress first."

"Isn't a woman's body the first thing men notice?"

"For some guys, I guess, but not always for me." He pauses, searching my face. "I'm drawn to whichever quality is screaming the loudest."

Oh, this man has all my attention now. "My hair was screaming the loudest? You're going to have to explain that."

"Your hair is uncontrolled and wild. I'm drawn to that. To the freedom of you, because when I look around the world, all I see are women with perfect hair, perfect looks, and perfect lives. I'm exhausted by perfection."

"I feel like you've just described me. I'm that perfect woman, not the free one you think you're seeing." The pure honesty that just came out of my mouth stuns me. It's not that I'm a dishonest person, but I usually try to hide the parts of me I'm unsure of.

He takes a moment with what I said, and I see it in his eyes that he's processing and contemplating. "If you were, there's no way you would have come here with your hair like that."

"I didn't. I arrived at the ball with it in a romantic, perfect bun."

"He really did a number on you."

"You have no idea."

"So, you pulled your hair out, left him, and gate-crashed a party. I think you're freer than you think you are."

There's something about being seen differently than the way everyone else sees me. Than the way *I* see me. I've never experienced this with anyone, and I like it. *It's* freeing.

Bradford glances around the party for a moment before looking back at me. "How are your feet coping in those glass slippers?"

"They're slowly killing me."

"There's a couch in the corner if you'd like to sit."

"I'm enjoying this conversation too much to leave it for the couch." I'm almost certain Bradford intends to sit with me, but I don't want to chance our conversation coming to an end.

His sexy smile reaches untouched parts of me. "I'm not going anywhere." With that, he takes charge, his hand coming to my waist and sliding around to the small of my back so he can guide me to the couch.

My pulse picks up from his touch faster than any man has ever caused it to. We might be in a crowd of people, but I'm only aware of him. And I know that's wrong since neither of us are single, but I feel all of it so strongly that I'm helpless but to just go with it.

This might be one of the biggest surprises of tonight to me.

I am not a spontaneous person. I'm a planner and I stick to my plans. I don't cause waves with my boyfriend; I don't leave balls early; I don't go to parties I wasn't invited to; I don't speak so honestly with someone I just met. And I *never* just go with a feeling. Tonight, I think I want to let loose.

The couch we find is barely big enough for both of us. It's a cozy fit I'm good with. I get the impression Bradford is too.

While I'm settling in next to him, I momentarily think about the partners we left behind at the ball. It's a fleeting thought, though, because Bradford wipes it away when he leans in close to ask, "How do you breathe in that dress?"

If I thought I was aware of him a moment ago, I knew nothing. Now, I'm *very* aware of him.

His voice that's like silk.

His divinely masculine cologne.

His proximity.

His suit jacket brushing my bare shoulder.

Our eyes lock and the connection we share is undeniable.

I smooth my dress while trying to get a handle on the thrill running through my body. My voice is a little breathy when I answer him. "That is a good question. One I often ask myself."

His brows pull together. "You always wear clothes you can't breathe in?"

If only he knew.

Normally, I wouldn't ever get into a conversation like

this with a guy, but there's something about Bradford that makes me feel okay with being vulnerable. He's twenty-four but seems older than his years. Wiser. More thoughtful than any guy his age I've met.

"Clothes, shoes, makeup. You name it, I feel strangled by it."

"It's your life, Kristen. Fuck what *they* tell you to wear."

My heart beats faster at his use of my name. "You know my name?"

"Of course I do. Every guy in New York knows your name."

I blink. *What*? I want to challenge him on that, but I quickly move on because really, all I care about is that *he* knows it. "Okay, so imagine you arrived at this party and looked around and saw me wearing loungewear. And very little makeup. Would you have come over and started a conversation with me?"

He doesn't even hesitate. "Absolutely."

"I call bullshit."

"That's because you don't know me yet. If you did, you'd know that I would have wanted to get to know you because you were doing your own thing, not following a crowd. And just so you're aware, you don't need an ounce of makeup to catch a man's attention."

Warmth spreads across my face and neck. It's not often that a man causes me to blush. Compliments about my looks don't usually affect me like this. However, there's far more than a compliment being exchanged right now. Bradford isn't just saying words to me; he's telling me in so many silent ways that he's attracted to me. And my blush only highlights to me that I've never been as attracted to a man as I am to him.

"I see that the Bradford Black charm I've heard about is a real thing."

His eyes light up when I reveal that I also know his name. "I hope my reputation doesn't precede me."

"Do you want me to lie and tell you it doesn't?" He has a reputation for going through women. Not in a player type way, but rather in a *he's a great guy but never stays for long* kind of way. From what I know, his current relationship is the longest he's ever had.

"I always prefer the truth."

"Let's just say that you've broken hearts you haven't even met yet."

His brows arch. "That seems unlikely."

"That's because you don't think like a woman."

"You'll need to enlighten me."

"Every woman in New York wants to date you, and that's not an exaggeration. We're all sure we're the one who will change you. But your track record really doesn't lend any credence to that, so broken hearts lie scattered through the streets of this city."

"*We're* all sure?"

My use of that word was a slip of the tongue, but the way he's asking, combined with the way he's looking at me like he really wants to know the answer causes my reply to tumble out of my mouth without hesitation. "Yes, *we're*."

He likes my answer.

A lot.

That's written all over his face.

"It's a shame you're pining over another man."

"Because?"

"Because I would have liked to know what you had in mind to change me."

I have to work hard to keep my hands to myself. I've never wanted to touch a man as much as I want to touch Bradford right now.

Deep down, I suspect tonight will be all we have together. The timing is off for anything else. While that makes me sad, it also forces me into action. We've got one night to feel this spark, and I want to make the most of it.

"Do you know what I think?" I ask.

"I'd like to know as many of your thoughts as you'd like to share."

That statement gets me bothered in the kind of sexy way that no flirting or foreplay ever has. Not one guy I've dated has been this interested in my thoughts. "I've got no plans for the rest of the night and would like you to change that. I want you to show me your favorite parts of this city and I'll show you mine too. And when my glass slippers become too much for my feet, I want you to carry me home on your back before we say goodbye and go back to our lives."

The smile that spreads instantly across his face lets me know how much he approves of this idea. "I'll say yes to all of that so long as we add food to our list of things we need tonight. I'm starving."

I stand, pulling him up. "Deal. But just so you know, I've barely eaten for a month, and I intend on rectifying that tonight. I may break your back when you carry me home."

He looks stunned. "A *month*? Jesus. We're getting food first."

With that, he takes my hand in his, holds it firmly like he doesn't intend on letting it go anytime soon, and leads me out of the party.

My last thought as the twinkle lights fade from my vision is that maybe princes really do exist.

2

BRADFORD

Kristen Blaise is a beautiful contradiction. I've now spent almost four hours with her and am bewitched by her beauty, but even more than that I'm captivated by her mind. To the world, she projects a cool confidence, seemingly indifferent at times, but she's showing me a different side. One minute, she's keeping it light and laughing easily with me; the next, she's going deeper and offering thoughtful opinions on a variety of topics. Anything and everything from movies, to books, to politics, to climate change, to existential dilemmas.

We've walked a great deal of Manhattan since leaving the rooftop party and she's taken me to some of her favorite parts of the city. Tacos from a food truck were first on her list of favorites. I struggled to take my eyes off her as she devoured a chicken taco, a pork taco, and chips with guacamole. The joy that covered her entire face as she ate was the kind of joy I don't see often enough.

When she realized I was doing more watching than

eating, she tilted her head, and said, "You're looking at me like you've never seen a woman eat."

"That's because I've never seen a woman inhale her food like you are," I'd replied.

Barely skipping a beat, she'd taken another bite of her food, grinned at me, and said, "You need to up your dating game. Switch the fancy restaurants for taco food trucks."

"Your boyfriend takes you on dates to food trucks?" I'd asked. It astounded me just how much I wanted to know the answer to that question.

She'd rolled her eyes. "My boyfriend would never bring me here, which is truly disappointing."

I liked the roll of her eyes when I mentioned her boyfriend. Possibly a little too much.

After we finished eating, she'd taken my hand and pulled me with her to wind our way through streets so she could point out community gardens she loves, cafes that have the best coffee, tucked-away dress shops and tiny art galleries she frequents, and the buildings that house charities she supports.

Book stores rank highly on her list too and we're currently sitting outside her *most favorite of favorites,* her words not mine.

"It may not be eighteen miles of books," she says, referencing the bookstore I'm surprised isn't on her list of favorites, "but it has the best collection of lesser-known books that more people should know about."

"Such as?"

Her eyes sparkle. "I found a first edition Charlotte Franklin poetry book here earlier this year. I'm kicking myself for not buying it."

I don't know who Charlotte Franklin is but from the way Kristen has lit up, I'm guessing she loves her writing. "Why didn't you?"

She looks like she might roll her eyes again, but she doesn't. Instead, she just appears unhappy. "Jeremy rushed me out of here before I had the chance. I think the fact I let him annoys me the most."

"He doesn't appreciate your love of poetry?"

She sighs like I've just asked her a hard question. "He thinks poetry is a waste of time."

"And you? What do you love about it?"

She doesn't rush her answer, taking the time to contemplate it before looking at me with soft eyes and saying, "Poetry unravels the complexities of the human heart and reminds me I'm not alone in my struggles. It's a whispered conversation between souls and I find solace in the shared experience."

Her words spark a memory of mine, one I'd long forgotten. "My mother used to read poetry when I was younger. She told me once that it invites us to truly see each other."

"Yes! That's exactly how I feel." She turns her body fully to mine, inching a little closer. Her eyes are wide open and sparkle like stars. The enthusiasm in them mirrors the infectious smile stretching across her face. "Do you know who her favorite poet is?"

Keeping my thoughts in a straight line is difficult as I watch and listen to her. She's so damn beautiful but when she's alive like this, I couldn't even begin to describe her allure.

"I don't. I'm not as close to Mom as I am to Dad. She can be distant at times."

"Is that because she's busy with your family? Or do you mean she's emotionally distant?"

"Mom was raised to be the dutiful wife and mother, and that's exactly what she is. I think that's left her little time to build stronger bonds."

"Especially when she has five sons, right? Like, that's a lot of responsibility. I can't even imagine being responsible for five humans." She stops and thinks for a moment before asking, "Do you think she went into her marriage wanting five children?"

I lean in close to her, partly because I can't get enough of being near her, partly because her scent is like a drug, and partly because I'm spellbound by the depth of our conversation over the last four hours. "I like your version of getting to know someone."

She blinks. Then, she smooths her dress. Then, she gives me the kind of smile that settles itself low in my stomach. "It's not my usual style."

I wasn't lying to Kristen when I told her earlier that every guy in New York knows her name. They do. When she enters a room, she has all eyes on her. She glides through ballrooms like she was born to inhabit them, all sophisticated beauty and poise. Women watch her like they want to be her. Men are helpless but to follow her every move. I should know. The last time I saw her at a gala, my girlfriend spent the night glaring at me after I watched Kristen for a minute too long.

Up close, I see her differently. Kristen has far more to offer than flawless skin, full lips, beautiful blue eyes, long silky brunette hair, and curves for days. She's intelligent, thoughtful, and kind. But more than that, she's genuine and honest.

She's not as confident as she appears. I've seen moments of uncertainty and the kind of internal struggle that is real and raw and so fucking endearing. *That's* what I'm drawn to more than any beauty she radiates.

"You mean you don't ask every guy you meet about his mother?" I tease.

The corners of her mouth gently inch up at my banter. "I haven't met a guy who would have been willing to spend hours following me around a city answering every question I threw his way."

My gaze is firmly glued to hers as I say, "That's their loss."

Kristen blushes at that. It's the second time I've caused this reaction in her and I can't deny just how much I like what it tells me: that she's as attracted to me as I am to her. However, I can't do anything with that attraction. Or more to the point, *won't*. Not when we're both in relationships.

In an effort to shift my thoughts from this, I bring the conversation back to her last question. "So, if I tell you that my mother only wanted four children, will you tell me something you want in life?"

"Only if you also tell me something you want," she says and I'm almost sure she's trying to delay answering me. She's deflecting in the way she has a few times tonight when I've asked her something she didn't appear comfortable talking about.

"Deal."

She diverts her gaze from mine and does more of that dress smoothing I've worked out is a nervous habit.

"You can just tell me what you want to eat for breakfast tomorrow if that's all you want to share," I say.

She looks up at me and takes a deep breath before saying, "I want to help people. I don't know how yet, but I want to help women feel better about themselves." Her cheeks turn pink again. This time I know it's not because she's attracted to me, but because she's just shared something intimate and close to her heart that she possibly hasn't said out loud to many other people.

"In a mental health capacity?"

"Yes." She stops talking and I see the hesitation in her eyes when she continues. "I volunteered with a charity my mother works with a couple of years ago and met a woman who had been a successful accountant before losing her husband to cancer. Her life spiraled and she and her children ended up homeless. The charity helped her get back on her feet. Her boss wasn't supportive at all when her husband died. He looked out for the men who worked for him, but he told her that she must have gotten herself into this situation because she wasn't smart enough. Especially without her husband to help her." She skims her hands over her dress. "I understood her pain over that. Over being made to feel less than because I'm a woman." Her voice falls to a whisper when she adds, "I want to learn how to help women rise."

Fuck. Me.

I was not expecting her to bare herself in this way.

"You're not comfortable talking about this, are you?"

"The last person I talked to about this was my father. He listened for all of five minutes before telling me to stop with this nonsense. He made me feel silly for even thinking about it."

"This nonsense? What does he expect you to do with your education?"

"Another great question. I think my parents pay for college in the hopes I'll find a suitable candidate for marriage while there."

"How's that going for you?"

"My current candidate asked me to give him a blowjob at the ball and then got pissed at me when I said no. I'd say the quality of guys I'm finding in college isn't high."

"Classy guy."

Her nod says she concurs. Then, with a questioning expression, she says, "Can I ask you a guy question?"

"Go for it."

She brings one of her legs up to rest on the seat, really settling in. The gentle brush of her leg against mine as she does this sends desire racing through my body. I have to work hard not to take that desire and run with it.

"Do guys want sex anywhere and everywhere? My friend told me earlier that this is where I'm going wrong. That I should have sucked my boyfriend's dick when he asked me to, and that I should be prepared to give it to him in public places whenever he wants."

I want to tell her to ditch that friend but I gather my thoughts slowly instead of rushing in with that advice. "Guys want sex, period. The *right* guy wants you along with the sex and won't ever expect you to do something you don't want to do. And this *giving it to him*? You don't give your partner sex, Kristen. You share it with each other. And if you're with a guy who doesn't understand that, he doesn't deserve you."

"I agree, but I'm always surprised when girls think differently than me. I was beginning to wonder if I was wrong."

"You're not wrong. Don't ever doubt yourself on that."

"Thank you." She seems relieved to hear me say she's not wrong and I wonder how often she's told she *is* wrong. "Okay, it's your turn to tell me something you want in life."

I rest my back against the seat and exhale a long breath as I glance up at the sky and think about that. "I want conflicting things."

"What things?"

I look at her. "I grew up knowing my future holds politics, and while I want that, I don't want the bullshit that goes with it. I'm not interested in putting on a show to get what I want, but politics is all about the optics, so it seems that's my destiny if I decide to pursue this."

"I know all about putting on a show to get what I want."

"What are your thoughts on that?"

She smiles and I swear it's a smile that could light up the grayest of days. "Do you know, I can't recall a man besides one of my teachers ever asking my thoughts on something. Not even any of the men in my family."

"They have no idea what they're missing."

She takes that in, still smiling, and watches me silently for a beat before answering my original question. "I think so much of life is about putting on a show, even to ourselves sometimes. We're taught from such a young age to perform a certain way, and not just by our parents. We see it in movies, TV shows, social media, ads, magazines. Everywhere. I hate it, but I don't have an answer for how to solve it."

A few strands of hair fall across her eyes as she speaks and I reach out to sweep them off her face. She stops breathing as my fingers ghost over her skin leaving a trail of heat in their wake. The space between us crackles with anticipation.

My gaze drops to her lips and I fight like fuck not to take what I want.

Her mouth parts with a shaky breath.

It would be easy, *too easy*, to lean in and kiss her.

In the end, it's a loud siren cutting into the moment that pulls me back and reminds me nothing can happen tonight. I finish brushing her hair from her face and say, "I agree with everything you said."

She stares at me with astonishment, not saying a word for the longest time. Finally, she launches into a ramble. "No one ever just agrees with me or tells me they want to know my thoughts or asks me what I want in life. And there you are, doing all those things in one night. Seriously"—she narrows her eyes at me—"are you even real?"

I chuckle. "Absolutely real. And ready to hear more of your thoughts. Give me as many of them as you want."

"You should be careful what you wish for. I have a lot of thoughts on a lot of things. You might end up wishing you'd never asked to hear them."

"Try me, Kristen. I think you'll like the outcome."

She stares at me with more of that astonishment that is beginning to look more like bewilderment. Then, she stands, reaches for my hand, and pulls me up. "Okay, I'm going to begin boring you with my observations on things and you're going to take your turn while I do that."

As she drags me away from the bookstore and starts talking about an idea she has for a gala to raise money for a women's charity she supports, I ask, "My turn for what?"

She stops firing thoughts at me and turns her face to meet my gaze. "To show me your favorite parts of the city. Keep up, Bradford. We've only got a few more hours before my coach turns into a pumpkin and I want to see all your favorites."

I have never had a woman boss me around and fuck if I don't like it.

I'm almost certain Kristen Blaise could boss me into a thousand things.

It's a shame she might never get the chance.

3

ONE YEAR LATER

@thetea_gasp

JUST WHEN WE THOUGHT @bradfordblack might be changing his ways and making room in his life permanently for a woman, he ended his relationship with @shelbysmith. This breakup is on the back of his breakup eleven months ago with @catherinebranson, another woman we all thought he looked ready to make more long term. It seems Bradford is purely a situationship kinda guy. He has the rizz for it, and I'm putting my hand up to be next. I'm ready to move into my billionaire era, please and thank you.

4

BRADFORD

IF THERE'S anything that bores me more than a fucking gala, I don't know what it is. And the gala I've been forced to attend tonight may just be the worst one I've ever been subjected to.

All the primping and preening. The fake smiles. The shallow conversation. I want nothing to do with any of it. But the thing that will drive me to drink tonight is the question from everyone regarding the relationship I've just ended.

"I thought you two would last longer than five months," Jill says in between sips of champagne.

"Why?" Owen asks, looking anything but convinced.

"I don't know. I thought they had more between them than he's had with any of the other women he's dated."

I eye my best friend and his wife. "If I let you two continue debating this, is it likely we'll end up in another one of your arguments?" For a couple who've only been married for a few months, they've started arguing a hell of a lot.

"You make it sound like we argue all the time," Jill says.

I arch a brow. "Is that not true?"

She purses her lips. "God, you can be an asshole when you want to be."

I throw the rest of my whiskey down my throat. "If facing the truth makes me an asshole, so be it."

Owen steps in. He knows Jill's even more likely to pick a fight with me than with him. Looking at me, he asks, "What happened with Shelby?"

More of that infernal question. The same one my father grilled me on today. He was less than impressed with my choice to end things. Shelby was perfect "stock" as far as he was concerned. *She could have taken you all the way to the presidency*, he'd said before making it clear I had to find someone new for that task.

"She bored me," I say.

"You two couldn't keep your hands off each other," Jill says.

"There's a lot more to a relationship than sex, Jill. I need something more than that. Some fucking conversation for a start." Shelby loved sex as much as I do, but when it came to sharing ourselves in other ways, she struggled. Our conversations consisted of talking about the parties she wanted us to attend, the dresses she planned to wear and whether I liked them, her ideas for her next hairstyle, and gossip. I couldn't see myself enduring a lifetime of that.

Jill's only half listening. She's spied someone across the room that she's interested in. Looking at Owen, she says, "Ron Johansen just arrived."

Owen nods before glancing at me. "We're still on for golf tomorrow?"

"Yes. The helicopter will be ready to leave at six thirty in the morning."

Jill gives me one last glare before she and Owen make their way toward the man they're trying to win as a client for North Management, their hedge fund. Jill resents the time Owen spends golfing with me and has made that more than clear. As far as I'm concerned, she needs to get over that. I've known Owen since I was five; we'll be golfing into our old age.

I head to the bar, needing more whiskey to survive this night. My strides slow as I meet the gaze of the woman I haven't been able to get out of my head for the last year.

Kristen Blaise.

Those beautiful blue eyes of hers are etched into my memory. I'd be able to pick them out of a lineup of eyes only.

She smiles before turning and walking out of the ballroom. I don't waste a second before following her. I know exactly where she's going after having done this four times with her now. The rooftop. To escape the crowd.

"You look like you can't wait to get out of here," she says when I join her in the elevator. We're the only ones here, something I'm grateful for. I don't like sharing Kristen.

"What was the giveaway?"

Her eyes light up with mischief as she cocks her head. "Hmm, let me see...." She grins. "You do wear grumpy well."

"I'm not grumpy."

Still grinning, she says, "No? What would you call it then?"

"Not putting up with people's shit."

"I can see it now. *President Black, the president who didn't put up with anyone's shit.* I'm sure that will go down well."

"I think America's ready for a president like that."

"I think you're out of touch with the people if you think that."

I step out of the elevator when it reaches our destination and release a long breath as I look up at the night sky. "How do you do these things so well?" I'm convinced Kristen could excel at socializing in her sleep. Since that night we spent together a year ago, we've run into each other three times at galas. I've watched her move through each one effortlessly, like she was made to woo people.

"You do them just as well as I do."

I walk with her to the railing, doing my best not to glue my eyes to her body. Keeping my hands off Kristen is always my greatest achievement when I'm with her. "Outwardly, yes. On the inside, I hate almost every minute of them."

Kristen's eyes flare with understanding. She knows what I'm saying without saying it: I don't detest the moments I spend with her.

From the very first second we met, there was something between us. Hypnotic chemistry that made me helpless but to spend that entire night following her around the city. We talked until the sun came up and I carried her home on my back like she'd requested. I didn't want to let her go and that spell she weaved over me has drawn me back each time I've seen her since.

Kristen is unlike any woman I've met. She's strong and persistent; driven and resilient; kind and compassionate; and deeply vulnerable. In the conversations we've stolen over the last year, she's opened herself up and shared her dreams, the mistakes she's made with the people in her life, her fears of being rejected by her father, and some of the hurt she's experienced at his hands. She's also talked about her boyfriends with me and asked all kinds of questions about how guys think.

She's not afraid to search beneath the surface. It's this part of her that pulls me in the most.

"I heard you and Shelby broke up. Are you okay?"

Kristen and I have never exchanged numbers, we're not friends on social media, and we don't see each other outside of these minutes we steal. It's become an unspoken agreement; we keep these moments between us and we don't take them back into our lives.

Except, I do.

I suspected I wanted more with her from the moment she told me she was searching for her prince but wouldn't rely on him for things like returning her shoes. I *knew* I wanted more when she told me she wanted to help women rise.

I couldn't do anything with those feelings though because I was six months into a relationship that I thought was going somewhere. And Kristen was in a relationship too. I'm not the kind of guy to cheat on a woman or cut in on another man, so I went back to my life and let her go back to hers. When my relationship broke up a few weeks later, I took time off dating to figure some things out. A couple of months later, I looked Kristen up on social media and discovered she was dating another guy. She looked happy, so I let her be.

Our timing has been off all year. Each time we've run into the other, at least one of us has been dating someone. We've become one long missed connection.

"Shelby and I were never going to be long term," I say.

"How's your father taking the news?" She gives me a knowing look. I've spoken about my presidency ambitions with her, along with my father's expectations, so she knows his expectations of me marrying a woman who can contribute to our political aspirations.

"As well as you're assuming."

She places her hand on my arm. "I'm sorry. Even if someone wasn't going to be long term, it doesn't mean they didn't leave their mark on your heart."

Kristen's touch heats my veins like it always does. And just like every other time she's reached for me, I'm held hostage by her.

I feel closer and more connected to Kristen than to women I've spent far more time with. When she puts her hands on me, it's like she's touching parts of me that have never been touched. Parts I'm desperate for her to touch over and over.

I glance down at her hand. At her fingernails that are covered in bling. They seem out of character for her. She likes getting dressed up but never this much.

"Do you like my crystals?" she asks as I inspect them.

I meet her gaze. "Do you?"

Kristen's mouth curls up into a smile. "No, but you already know that, don't you?"

"Why are you wearing them, then?"

"Well"—she twirls, showing me the back of her dress—"they match the crystals all over my dress."

"*Fuck*." The curse falls roughly from my lips, slowing Kristen all the way down. Her movements, her gaze, her breaths.

The front of her floor-length dress already has my attention with the way it clings to her curves and leaves her shoulders bare. It's secured around her neck with a thin strap and reveals a hint of cleavage where some of the fabric is cut out. But the back of the dress is a whole other story. There's nothing covering her skin but a few glittery straps that help hold the dress up, and it scoops low, only just covering the top of her ass. An ass that she clearly works hard for, and one I would kill to get my hands on.

"So, you don't like my crystals but you like my dress," she says, her voice low and breathy.

I drag my eyes from her body. "It's not the dress I like, Kristen."

Neither of us have hidden our attraction, but besides the way we look at each other, we've never openly acknowledged it. I don't have it in me anymore to keep my thoughts to myself.

She's lost for words for a moment, and when she does find them she doesn't acknowledge what I said. "My sister convinced me to get the bling on my nails. She loves it, but I'm not so sure."

I want to move into her.

I want to put my hands on her.

I want to tell her I'm done with missed connections.

But I don't.

I can't.

I may not be her friend on social media, but that doesn't mean I don't look her up every now and then. And what I've seen over the last few months is that she appears happy with her current boyfriend. There's a light in her eyes that looks good on her. I refuse to disrupt that happiness for my own selfish desires. Because who knows, maybe this attraction is simply that: chemistry and interest that wouldn't work well in a relationship. I won't risk the happiness she's found for a possibility that might not turn into what I think it could.

"You look beautiful with or without the bling." I allow her avoidance of my admission even though it's the hardest thing I've had to do in a long time.

She smiles and all I can think is that she's fucking radiant. "Thank you."

"So, you graduated."

Her eyes light up with excitement. "Yes, and I've found a summer internship at one of Dad's magazines that I think would be perfect for me! I'm interviewing for it next week."

If I thought Kristen was beautiful before, that beauty had nothing on what I'm seeing now. Her passion for what she wants to do in life brings her features alive in a whole new way. It's heart-stopping.

"Does he know you've applied?" Her father owns Blaise Media, a publishing empire that distributes content through television, magazines, and digital media. He wouldn't have any idea who's applying for jobs in his businesses. I'm interested to know if Kristen has talked to him about this because he's never shown her any support or encouragement in her goals. From everything she's told me about their relationship, her father simply wants to marry her off. He's dismissive of her intelligence and tells her often that she can't do the things she wants to try.

"No. I want to get this on my own. It'll be an amazing opportunity if I do get it. I think working in media will be a great stepping stone to building a platform for what I eventually want to do."

"I agree."

"How about you? Have you done any more work on your app?"

She's referring to the time management app I've been slowly building for the last six months. I started working on it purely to help manage my own time, but a few months ago, Kristen encouraged me to consider publishing it, which I've put considerable thought into.

"No. I haven't had a lot of spare time. I've prioritized sleep over the app."

"Work or pleasure?"

"Not pleasure. Dad's got me working around the clock on some mergers." I've worked at my father's company since I graduated college, in the corporate venture capital arm. It's work I love, but it's comprised of long hours that leave little time for anything else in life.

Kristen's phone alerts her to a text that's just arrived. After she checks it, she says, "I have to go. Charlie's looking for me."

I hate his name on her lips.

As she slips her phone back in her clutch and readies herself to go back down to the ballroom, I curl my fingers around her wrist. When I have her eyes again, I ask, "Are you happy?"

She takes a moment searching my face. Kristen does

this a lot and I always wonder what she's thinking. She's the only woman I've ever wished for access to her thoughts. "Yes. Are you?"

I nod. "Yeah."

"I have to go. Hurry up and finish that app. I need it in my life." She smiles. "And don't give in to your father. Find a woman who makes *you* happy, Bradford, not him."

I watch her go. My eyes are on her body but I'm barely registering what they're looking at because the only thing I'm seeing is the woman I think could make me happy. The woman I have to fight myself over.

I am not a man who doesn't go after what he wants, but Kristen has been my exception to many things for a year now, and it seems she will continue being that exception.

5

KRISTEN - THREE WEEKS LATER

I STARE AT MY PHONE. At the unknown number that hasn't stopped trying to call me for the past hour. I never answer calls from people I don't know, but I'm beginning to think this person isn't going to stop. When the ringing ends, only to start again, I swipe the phone and put it to my ear.

"What?" That's not how I usually answer a call, but with the mood I'm in today, this is all they're getting from me.

"Kristen?"

My heart flutters at the deep voice on the other end. "Bradford?"

"Jesus, what have you been doing for the last hour?"

Bradford can be grumpy when he wants to be. Something he likes to refute whenever I mention it, but it's the truth. It's also something I find endearing. God knows why, because I don't find grumpiness endearing when it's coming from my brothers, but I can't deny how much I like it in Bradford.

"Ignoring you." I smile. "I don't answer numbers I don't know."

"Do me a favor and put my number in your phone for the next time I call you."

Another thing I can't deny is how much I like the idea of him calling me again. I have no idea how he got my number, but I'm glad he did.

"Are you planning on calling me again?"

"If I see you looking like you did last night again, yes. Are you okay?"

And just like that, the smile he brought out in me disappears.

We saw each other at a charity gala last night. From a distance. And instead of finding a way to meet him on the rooftop like I always do, I stayed with Charlie. Actually, I clung to my boyfriend because I couldn't face the emotions I knew Bradford would elicit from me if I spoke with him. Because that's what he does; he's the only man I've ever felt safe enough with to share my raw feelings with. Last night, I didn't want a thing to do with any of those feelings.

I want to tell him I'm okay, but I know he'll sense the truth, even over the phone, so I don't bother lying. "No." My voice wavers and tears threaten to wet my cheeks again. I've spent most of the past three days crying.

"Fuck, Kristen, what's happened? You looked dreadful last night."

"Thanks for that. It's just what every girl wants to hear."

"You know what I mean."

I do. He's always straight to the point and honest. It's

another thing I like about him. There's no pretense. It means I don't feel the need to put on a show either.

I take a long breath. "My father stopped me from getting that internship."

"Why?"

"He told me it was an absurd idea. Apparently, working is a pointless activity for me. He ordered the editor at the magazine to give the internship to someone else."

"He doesn't want you to work?"

"No. He told me a woman's place is behind her man. But then, I knew that. I was silly for thinking I could change his mind."

"You are as far from silly as you can get. He's wrong, not you."

"Well, that may be the case, but he won't ever change his mind."

"So, what's the plan now?"

The plan? I don't have one yet. Bradford thinks I'm this confident go-getter who will always achieve my goals. I've been that person many times in my life, but I don't feel at all like her this week.

Since my father shattered me three days ago, I've hardly left my bedroom. He said awful things to me that he's never said. Things about what a woman's place is in the world, things about my lack of ability, and many things about his expectations of me finding a husband and having a family. He hasn't spoken to me since. But this is what he does, so I shouldn't expect anything else. I'll be lucky if he speaks to me in the next two weeks. He tends to freeze people out for long lengths of time when they disappoint him.

"I don't have a new plan yet." I hate admitting that to him. Besides my siblings, Bradford's the only other person in the world who fully believes in me. I wish I had a new plan to share with him.

"You don't need his permission to do anything."

"I know, but—" My throat tightens as fear consumes me, and my words cut off. I try desperately to swallow that fear but I can't.

Losing my father's approval is the equivalent to losing his love in my messed-up brain. Since the very first time he withdrew his affection from me when I caused him embarrassment at his company's yearly dinner at the age of seven, I've done everything I can to please him. I'm distraught over what happened this week and have been unable to process it. All I know is I need to find a way to fix it.

"Kristen," Bradford says, his voice a mixture of tenderness and authority, "this is your life. Not his. Don't let him steal the future you want."

He's right.

I know he is.

But the vise around my chest makes it hard for me to acknowledge that.

"I won't. I just need a moment to get my head together." My words taste like a lie. One I hope he doesn't pick up on.

"I'm going to check in on you in a few days."

I like that he says this, that he wants to check in on me. It makes me think about how things could be different for us. I'm happy with Charlie, but I'd be lying if I said I never imagined being with Bradford.

He asked me if I was happy three weeks ago and I said

yes. I was happy because I was hopeful I'd get that internship. I'd graduated college and I felt like my life was all ahead of me. And yes, I like being with Charlie. We laugh and have a good time together. But it's not like the moments I spend with Bradford. That time is precious and I cherish every second of it. I want more of it like I want nothing else and I've found myself thinking about ending things with Charlie so I can explore my attraction to Bradford.

"Kristen," Bradford cuts into my thoughts. "Are you still there?"

"Yes, sorry. I was thinking about you checking in on me. I'd like that."

He's silent for a moment and when he speaks again, his voice is rough. "Don't keep me hanging for an hour when I call next."

I smile. I love that even when I'm drowning in sadness, he can make me do that. "Will it make you grumpy again if I do? Because I kinda like it when you're grumpy."

"I'm not grumpy."

My smile grows. "Goodbye, Bradford."

We end the call and I think about the second time we met up on a rooftop. I'd seen him first that night and when he finally laid eyes on me, I nodded my head indicating he should follow me. I wasn't sure if he would because he was at the gala with his girlfriend. It was exhilarating that he did follow me.

Bradford makes me feel good about myself. He helps me feel like the intelligent woman I know I am but struggle to believe in. I don't doubt myself when I'm with him. He also makes me feel special and desirable. When I add all of that to the attraction I have to him, I can't help but think that's what a partner should bring to the table.

We talked for nearly an hour that second night. I learned of his love for golf and that he and his best friend try to golf together every Saturday morning. I learned about the camping and fishing trips his father took him and his four brothers on throughout their childhood, and how much he loved that time with his family. I discovered that while politics is an expectation his father has for him, it's important to Bradford for many reasons too. One reason is that ever since he watched a school friend's family go through the injustice of asbestosis caused by poor regulations, resulting in the death of his friend's uncle, Bradford has wanted to make a difference in people's lives.

I've come to see that he's a determined, focused man with a compassionate and emotional side. I'm drawn to every part of him, but it might be his willingness to connect emotionally with me that I appreciate the most. Because if I know one thing about myself, it's that I struggle with my emotions, and if I want to be the woman Bradford sees in me, the woman *I* want to be, I need someone in my life who'll take the time and care with this side of me. Even if that person is only a friend and nothing more.

Oh, and that grumpiness of his? I like it more than I should. If we ever do take our friendship further, I want to experience a whole lot more of it.

6

KRISTEN - THREE DAYS LATER

IN THE MIDDLE of a week I can only describe as hell, Bradford calls and brings the sun with him. Until today, I'd not have thought that a five-minute phone call could be enough to lift a person, but it is.

"I see you've saved my number," he says when I answer his call.

I smile for the first time since he last helped me do that. "I was given strict instructions not to keep you hanging for an hour the next time you called, so I kinda had to save it."

"If only everyone was as compliant as you."

"I detect your signature grumpiness. Is there trouble somewhere in your paradise?"

He blows out a long breath. "Next question."

I settle back against the couch I'm sitting on. "No, you don't get to do that if I don't. Tell me who's ruffling your feathers."

"Ruffling my feathers?" Amusement has overtaken his grumpiness. I like that I caused it.

"Yes, I imagine you stalking around your office with those feathers all ruffled."

"Jesus, I need to give you better material to work with."

I squeeze my legs together.

I'd really like that material.

But since I still haven't done anything about breaking up with Charlie, because my entire life has centered around my father this week, I don't encourage this conversation. Instead, I prod him to open up. "Who made you grumpy today?"

"A work colleague who needs to learn to have some fucking respect for women."

Bradford rarely swears when he's with me. It tells me a lot that he just swore. "You sound stressed."

"Yeah. I need some time off. And for people to do what I say. But let's not get into that. I've only got a few minutes before my next meeting and I want to check in on you. How are you?"

"I'm sad. And hurt. And angry. But I'm okay."

"Have you come up with a plan?"

I really want to be able to tell him I have, but I haven't. "Can I say I'm still in the middle of figuring that out?"

His voice softens as he says, "Yes. You don't have to have everything figured out, Kristen. It's okay to not have a plan."

I frown. "I can't imagine you ever doing anything in life without a plan."

"You'd be surprised."

Those three words help clear the air clogging my lungs. I've always felt the need to have myself together, to have my life mapped out, to know where I'm going next.

It's tiring. And it's anxiety-causing. Knowing that a man like Bradford, who seems so put together and sure of himself, doesn't always have a map for his life helps me feel like it's okay for me not to.

I take a breath before saying the words that scare me. "I think I'm going to get a job."

"Good for you."

"I'm not sure what kind of job yet, but I'll figure that out."

"You will. You'll figure everything out that you need."

God, his belief in me is thrilling. It makes me think I can do anything I put my mind to.

"Shit," he says, "I have to go. I'm sorry."

"Thank you for calling," I say softly. I want to say so much more but I hold myself back. I might be okay sharing some of the things that scare me with Bradford, but my feelings for him are bigger than any I've known. I need to sort through them on my own for a little longer.

"I'm always here for you, Kristen."

And then he's gone.

And I know, surer than ever, that I have to end my relationship with Charlie.

7

KRISTEN - SIX MONTHS LATER

"Kris," Jenna, my sister says as I glance around the gala to see who's arrived. "I need you to fix my hair." When I don't respond straight away, because I'm madly searching for the man I haven't seen in four months, the man I'm desperate to see, she says, "Kristen. Are you listening to me?"

I bring my gaze to her. "Yes. I was just looking for someone."

"Who?"

I wave her off. "Just someone I need to speak with." I've never told anyone about my friendship with Bradford. I like having him just for myself.

She points at her hair. "Please tell me you can sort this mess out."

She's right, it is a mess. I noticed it as soon as I saw her, but besides my work here tonight, Bradford-spotting was my main focus so I quickly forgot her hair. I take hold of her arm. "Come with me."

She grins. "I love this new take-charge Kristen. I hope she sticks around forever."

As I drag her to the bathroom, I mentally sort through the things I need to make happen tonight. Jenna's correct; I have taken charge of my life. It took me a week after my father blew my internship plans apart to gather myself and make new plans. I've spent the time since then working with my mother doing charity work, helping her raise money through galas and other social events. It's unpaid work, but it's work that helps women, and that's what's important to me.

I spend almost ten minutes with Jenna. By the time we leave the bathroom, her hair is perfect. I also touch up her makeup. We run into our mother on the way out. Her *Oh, that's much better, Jenna* causes my sister to roll her eyes, but I take it as another job I've successfully ticked off my list. It's a never-ending list, but one that keeps me busy and focused. And if there's anything I like being these days, it's those two things.

"Oh, Charlie's here." Jenna grimaces. "Did you know he was coming?"

My breakup with Charlie was messy. And protracted. He didn't want to let me go and fought for me. It took him four long weeks to move on. In that time, I didn't feel right reaching out to Bradford, and then when I was ready to, he'd started seeing someone, and from what I could work out she was making him happy. He and I ran into each other just after that, and he was distracted. Not to mention, loved up. I've never seen him engage in PDAs like he did that night. I hated every second of it just as much as I hated that I missed my opportunity.

This is one reason why I've tried to stay busy. I don't

want to think about what could have been. Bradford is still with her, and they still seem just as happy. But since I saw his RSVP for this gala two weeks ago, I've had to fight to keep him out of my head. A futile exercise. He lives there rent free. The fact his girlfriend isn't attending tonight only helped all those thoughts about seeing him tonight. I'm hopeful he and I will find each other up on the rooftop at some point.

"Yes, I knew he'd be here," I say to Jenna as I zero in on my ex. "I don't think he'll be a problem. Not now he's got someone new keeping him happy."

I quickly get back to Bradford-spotting after satisfying myself that Charlie is happily occupied. Jenna leaves me to find her table just before I finally spy the man who has been featuring in my dreams.

I go weak in the knees while I watch him stride confidently into the ballroom. Bradford has a commanding presence, attracting attention everywhere he goes. He doesn't post on his Instagram account but he has his very own hashtag thanks to the gossip accounts on there. I spend time I'd rather not admit to scrolling his hashtag. There's no shortage of photos of him.

Tonight, he looks even more handsome than usual.

His dark hair is styled like he just ran his fingers through it and declared it done.

His three-day stubble beard is perfection.

And that tuxedo? He should live in it forever.

It's his presence, though, that demands I give up everything but watching him. Bradford owns a room when he's in it. I watch as every woman turns to look at him, and every man tries to catch his attention. He doesn't stop for any of them. Bradford has his own agenda and doesn't change it for anyone. I know that by following his business success.

A lot has been written about his family and their textile production company. The Blacks have a long history of wealth creation, and from what I've read, his grandfather left his sons and grandsons hundreds of millions each. Bradford's father is skilled at investing and has ensured all those millions have been turned into billions. His father has also brought Bradford into the family business and taught him everything he knows. Bradford has managed some highly successful mergers over the last year.

He's halfway to the table his company paid for when his eyes meet mine.

His strides slow before coming to a complete stop, and he holds my gaze for a long moment. He then skims his eyes down my body, taking almost as long with it as he did with my face.

I like the attention of men, but I especially like the attention of Bradford. Every inch of my body feels this man when he looks at me.

He lifts his chin to the side, indicating he wants us to slip out, and my skin blazes to life with anticipation. So does my core. God, how he affects me.

I collect my coat and a few minutes later, we arrive at the elevators. We're not alone, so he waits silently next to me, following me into the elevator when it arrives.

I endure ten levels of silence with Bradford standing next to me while we wait for the women in the elevator to reach their floor. His hand brushes mine, heating my skin more than he already has.

I want to scream at the unfairness of all our missed

opportunities. Why must he have a girlfriend? Why must Charlie have taken so long to let me go? Why must Bradford and I have met when neither of us were single?

He's right here, next to me, and all I want to do is turn and reach for him. Kiss him. Make him promise to end his relationship and choose me.

The elevator doors open.

The women exit, leaving us alone.

Finally.

I slow my erratic breaths and inhale a long, deep one.

Don't kiss him, don't kiss him, *don't kiss him*.

"How are you?"

God, I die for his voice.

I want to hear it every day for the rest of my life.

"I'm good." I look up at him, finding his eyes on me intently. "How are you?"

His eyes bore into me harder after I ask him that. He doesn't answer my question. Instead, he asks, "How are you really, Kristen?"

Only he would ask me this. Well, besides Jenna who likes to dig around in my feelings whenever she can. But he's the only guy I've ever known who wouldn't be satisfied with my first answer. "I'm okay. Truly."

"There's a difference between okay and good. Don't tell me you're good if you're not." And there's his signature grumpiness.

"I know there's a difference."

He arches his brows, waiting for me to give him more, but the elevator reaches the rooftop, saving me from his scrutiny.

I step out onto the rooftop and pull my coat in close while I walk through the mostly empty lounge and head for the railing. The winter chill is like a slap in the face, but it's a price I'm willing to pay to have this time alone with Bradford.

His hand comes to the small of my back as he moves next to me at the railing. His eyes hold concern. "We should go back in. It's colder than I thought it would be up here."

I quickly place my hand on his forearm and shake my head. "No. I don't want to."

His hand that's on my back slides slowly around the side of my waist, lingering there before he drops it. I have to fight not to beg for it back. "I've missed you," he says, using the voice I've only ever heard him use with me.

In the time I've known him, we've not only spent time alone; we've also joined conversations together that included other people. I've heard Bradford speak to businessmen, his brothers, friends, and his girlfriends. Not once have I heard him use this voice with anyone, not even the women he's dated.

His tone is laced with affection. It's deep, and warm, and filled with consideration and attention. I have never thought of anyone's voice in those ways, but Bradford's makes me *feel* those things. It makes me feel like he's been thinking about me, wondering about me, worrying about me. And underneath all those layers is raw desire that colors every conversation we have.

I move closer to him, putting almost no space between us. I'm unable not to take that step. Ever since I decided to act upon my feelings and break up with Charlie so I could pursue Bradford, the pull to him has become impossible to continue ignoring. It's only my respect for the sanctity of relationships that keeps me from acting on it. In moments like this one with him, guilt flares over the friendship we keep. I have to chase away thoughts that whatever this is between us, it doesn't feel like any friendship I've ever had. It's those thoughts and that guilt, I think, that make me limit my time with him. Bradford and I could never be friends who see each other all the time.

"I've missed you too," I say softly as I note the subtle changes in his face. I think his jaw is more defined if that's possible. And he looks tired. God, how I wish that knowing these things about him were part of my daily life. That I was the one who got to say *Come to bed, you're tired*.

"So, are you going to be honest with me and tell me how you've really been? I can see it in your eyes that something's off."

"You don't need to worry about me, Bradford. I'm busy working. I'm out having fun with my friends. My dad has been supporting me in my work. All is good in my world. Now, tell me how you are. What you've been up to. It's been so long since we've spoken."

He stares at me for a moment longer before raking his fingers through that beautiful hair of his and growling, "Fuck. Why do you feel so far away?"

"I'm not."

"You are."

Most of the time, I like Bradford being able to read me. I like him forcing me to tell him the truth. Now, not so much. The reason I feel far away is because I'm trying hard to distance my feelings for him. And I'm trying really hard to keep him away from the parts of my life I don't want to discuss with him. The parts I don't even discuss with myself.

Needing a reprieve from his determination to delve into me, I glance out at the sky.

Bradford only gives me a few seconds before bringing his hand to my chin and angling my face back to his. "You didn't get a job."

Straight to the point.

Damn him.

"I'm working." Even to my ears those words sound pathetic. I'm defending something we both know isn't worth defending.

"You're doing charity work with your mother that earns your father's approval, Kristen. That's not what you told me you wanted to do." He's gentle with the way he says this, but I know from the way he's looking at me with his trademark decisiveness that he's one step away from challenging me on my bullshit. Because he's right; the work I'm doing is not the work I wanted to do.

Without realizing I'm doing it, I place my hand to his abs. "Please don't push me on this. Not tonight."

His sharp intake of breath is his only acknowledgement of my touch. "Why not tonight? What's going on?"

"I've got a million things I have to ensure get done for this gala. And my mother is stressed, so I need to deal with that."

I grip his shirt while my heart and stomach and every other part of me do somersaults.

He saw my unhappiness in my eyes.

He's kept up with my work.

He remembers the things I've told him.

I want Bradford to notice all my details, every day, and

the fact he can't, that I'm not the one who holds that place in his life, tears me apart.

He curls his hand around my wrist before threading his fingers through mine. It's the closest we've ever come to physical intimacy. It affects me in a whole new way. A way that makes my heart try to force herself upon me and demand I stop denying what I want.

"I imagine you've got a million things to deal with every day," he says. "Are you going to make me keep putting this conversation off?" And there's that challenge.

I try to pull my hand from his but he doesn't allow that. He tightens his hold and says, "Talk to me. Tell me why you've chosen this path. I'm only interested in your happiness and if doing this work is making you happy, then I'll stop pushing you."

"It does make me happy."

"But?"

Of course he knows there's a but.

I exhale a breath, a long breath, before giving him a small smile and letting go of his hand. "Why must you be so good at this?"

"At wanting to know how you are?"

"No, at refusing to just take what I say as true. At being able to see the little things about me that no one else seems to see."

"The things they don't bother looking for. I will always look for those things, Kristen. They're important to me."

And there's that voice of his that wraps itself around me and helps me be brave.

"I like the work I'm doing, but yes, I want to do more. However, I think I need to take that slowly."

His brows pull together. "What does that mean?"

"I'm going to use this work to build my experience that will hopefully help me find a job that's more in line with what I want to do."

"How long do you think that will take?"

"Maybe a year."

"You could do this work on the side while you get a job. Double the experience."

"I could." There's no point arguing that. He'll just demolish any argument I present.

"But you won't."

Neither of us are calling out the elephant in the room, but we're both more than aware of it. I stare up at the sky while I arrange my thoughts. Bradford gives me the space to do that.

Finally, I look back at him. "I don't have it in me to go against him. Not yet." My confession falls between us with certainty. I might have a lot of uncertainty and doubt about myself, but this is the one thing I'm more than confident on.

My father's approval is more important to me than I wish it was. If I could change one thing about myself, it would be this. I would prefer to be like my sister who goes against him over almost everything. But as much as I try, I fail. I always, *always*, run back to him and do what he wants me to. As much as I hate being the good girl, that's what I am.

Bradford's hard edges soften as he looks at me with empathy. "Okay, so one year. I'm holding you to that."

"Deal. But you have to promise to be gentle with me. I don't do well with violence."

"I can promise not to be violent, but gentle may be a stretch."

I smile. "True. You have a way about you that's definitely not gentle."

He gives me a questioning look. "I have a way about me?"

"Yes." My hand seeks his body again but I only allow it to linger nearby. "I can only imagine what it would be like having you in my daily life. I think you would be bossy and demanding."

I'm cold but the heat that roars to life in Bradford's eyes is enough to up the temperature. "I would only be those things if you were denying me something like you have been tonight."

My mind explodes with images of Bradford wanting things from me. Things I desperately want to give him.

Don't kiss him, don't kiss him, *don't kiss him.*

"I'm not so sure. I think your determination and focus might make you bossy without you even realizing."

"Bossy gets things done, Kristen."

And now we've veered into dangerous territory. Not that he'd be aware of it, but for me, all I can think about is him bossing me into many, many things. This is territory I shouldn't be anywhere near with him.

I snatch my hand away from him. "I should get back to the gala. My mother is likely losing her mind without me there to help her."

The look in his eyes tells me he doesn't want to let me go, but he doesn't stop me. He does, however say, "I have something for you."

As I wonder what that could be, he pulls a small book from the inside of his coat and hands it to me. My heart slows when I realize what it is. A first edition Charlotte Franklin poetry book.

When I look up to meet his gaze again, I find him watching me closely. It feels like he's noting every inch of my face. Every curve, every shadow, every hollow. It feels like he's learning by heart how I respond to his gift.

I run my hand over the front of the book, the significance of the moment scattering goose bumps over my skin.

He gave me a Charlotte Franklin book.

He remembered my favorite poet.

He searched for this gift.

"Thank you." The two words fall from my lips so delicately that I wonder if he'll be able to hear them, but his thoughtfulness has affected me so greatly that this is all I have to offer him.

No man has ever given me such a meaningful gift or taken the time and care to learn what I would cherish.

"I read some of her poems. I see why she speaks to you."

The rhythmic fluttering of my heart echoes the intensity of my emotions. When it's obvious I'm lost for words, Bradford takes charge and tells me to go, that he's going to take another few minutes up here.

As I'm walking away from him, clutching my gift like it's the most precious thing in the world, I turn back and say, "You didn't tell me what you've been up to. Are you happy?"

He nods. "Yes."

My second to last thought before stepping into the elevator and forcing all thoughts but the gala from my mind is that Bradford didn't smile tonight. Not even a hint of a smile touched his lips.

My last thought as the elevator doors slide closed is that I wish I was the last person he saw as he put his head on his pillow each night. The person who gets to put their head on his chest and wrap their arms around him, knowing why he didn't smile that day.

8

KRISTEN - ONE YEAR LATER

MY TWENTY-THIRD BIRTHDAY came and went with little excitement two weeks ago. Not even my boyfriend made a fuss of me. Much like he's doing tonight. We've been together for eleven months and while I love spending time with him, there are some red flags. They haven't waved too frantically at me yet, though, so I'm waiting to see if they're perhaps linked to the stress he feels over his work. Mostly, I find him a little impatient with me too often and dismissive of my ideas at times. Nothing too big, but still, sometimes he doesn't make me feel good about myself.

I met him a few weeks after I had the conversation with Bradford about my work. *A few weeks after he gave me the Charlotte Franklin book.* A year ago now. Lyle pursued me with determination. He did make me feel good in those early months together. He helped distract me from watching Bradford with his girlfriend. The one who liked all those dramatic displays of possessiveness in public. He broke up with her about three months after I started dating Lyle and has had a succession of women on his arm since then. Lyle has distracted me enough that I actually haven't kept up with all those women. What I have kept up with is his success in his work. I've loved hearing about that. But it has kept us from seeing each other a lot this past year. Bradford has only been at two social functions I've attended and because I've been with Lyle, our conversations have been short.

Maybe what could have been between us was never meant to be.

That thought makes my heart hurt so I instantly dismiss it but I know that I'll take friendship with Bradford if that is all that's ever on offer. Even if have to endure watching his girlfriends put their hands all over him.

"There you are," Lyle says, joining me in the ballroom as I take a glass of wine from the waiter. "You're late."

I sip some wine. "Hardly."

He scowls. "I needed you here at the time I specified, Kristen, and that was ten minutes ago. Your inability to be punctual may have ruined my chance of networking with someone who can do a lot for my career. I required you by my side for that conversation."

Lyle can be ridiculous at times with the way he catastrophizes situations. "I highly doubt that. Show me who you need me to talk with and I'll help you."

His lips press together. "Do not trivialize this. I had hoped that conversation would lead to a couple's golf day tomorrow, but since you weren't here, I've missed out on that. John wanted to meet you. He won't invite me to golf until that happens."

I really don't appreciate his tone. "I'm not trivializing

it. And let's find John. You know I'm good at wooing people. We'll make this happen."

"He's already left." He glances past me. "I have to go and talk with someone else now. I'll be about fifteen minutes."

"I'll come with you."

"No. You're not needed for this conversation."

I stare after him as he stalks away from me. Lyle has been short with me the last few days, but this was next level. He and I will be having a conversation about that later.

As I turn back to look around the gala for people I know or want to meet, I find Bradford coming my way. The look in his eyes as he runs them over me, and the way he meets my gaze with heat tells me that even though we haven't talked a lot this year, everything is still the same between us. *Everything.*

By the time he reaches me, my heart is acting like we're in the middle of a race. She's beating so fast that I'm sure Bradford will be able to hear her.

"Hi," I greet him. The smile on my face is the most genuine one I've experienced for months.

"You look beautiful." His intense search of my face, along with his velvety voice stir all my butterflies.

God, how I've missed him.

My hands go to my stomach to smooth their way down my dress. The dress I wasn't sure about earlier. It's more fitted than any dress I've worn, which is saying something because most of my outfits are quite fitted. "Thank you."

He narrows his eyes at me. "You don't feel beautiful?"

I feel like I ate too much today to be wearing this dress tonight. "Not really, but I appreciate you saying it."

"It only matters what you think, though, Kristen, not what I think."

I know he's right, yet I struggle with that. I always have. Not wanting to get into that, I say, "You look good too."

He really does, but then, when has he ever not? Besides being so damn handsome it hurts sometimes, he's wearing another one of his tuxedos that I would beg him to wear all the time if he were mine.

"I look tired, but that's nothing new."

"You've been working a lot from what I've heard."

"I have." He takes a moment before asking, "How about you? How's the search for a job going?"

And there it is. The question he promised to ask me. I wish his memory was awful. If I worked for Bradford and a meeting request popped up on my calendar, I would mark it *meeting denied* because I am more than sure nothing good would come from it.

I don't bother lying to him. This man can see straight through me. "I stopped searching."

"Why?"

"I decided to follow my original plan and use the charity work I'm doing as experience for a job later."

"You told me that a year ago. You said you'd only need a year's experience. That time is up."

Holy wow, the forceful energy vibrating from him right now is a lot. I want to stamp *meeting denied* all over me and run away.

I push my shoulders back like I'm going in hard to

defend a choice he actually has a say in. "I didn't know for sure how much time it would take to gain that experience, Bradford."

Still giving off those hardcore *I'm right* vibes, he says, "I can assure you that you've gained all the experience you need."

"You don't know that."

"I do."

"How?"

"I know what you studied. I know you were top of your class. I know the experience you have. And since I'm well-versed in human resource requirements for a company, I know you're ready."

"You might know all of that, but *I* know me, and I'm not ready."

"I know you too, Kristen. Don't think I don't."

"Oh my God, you're being overbearing tonight. I'm not a fan."

"You're not a fan because I'm calling you out on your bullshit."

My eyes widen. "No, I'm okay with you doing that. I am not okay with the arrogant way you're going about it."

He doesn't even bother to argue with me on that. He just keeps looking down at me with that intensity I wish would disappear. "You're trapped under your fear. I'm being the friend you need right now and telling you what I'm seeing."

"It doesn't feel like you're being the friend I need."

"That's because you prefer everything in its order and smooth. Underneath all that, there's a whole lot of truth you're not facing. I don't like watching you lessen yourself for your father. Or for Lyle, for that matter."

There's a whole lot I hate in what he just said, but the last bit stands out. "What does Lyle have to do with this?"

"I just watched the way he spoke to you. He doesn't treat you well."

I'm running on a lot of self-doubt from this conversation, and when my insecurities take over, I don't make good choices in the moment. Add in the anger he's causing, and we've got a recipe for disaster. "Right, so you're the supreme master of knowing what I should do for work, and how experienced I am, and how I should run my relationships, are you? Please feel free to continue enlightening me. I'll be sure to take all your suggestions and action them."

He works his jaw as frustration radiates from him. "I wish you would take all my suggestions and action them, but since that's not about to happen, promise me you'll think about this after you calm down."

When a man tells me to calm down, you can be sure I will do the complete opposite. Those two words being uttered by a man rank as high on my list of hatred as two other words I hear a lot: good girl.

"Don't ever tell me to calm down, Bradford. I will think about what you've said because I respect you enough to do that, but let the record show I don't want a repeat of this kind of conversation with you again. And by that, I mean a conversation that involves your arrogance." I take a deep breath. "Also, let the record show that I am far from calm because when a man says that to a woman, it's fucking condescending and not calm inducing. Just something for *you* to think about."

I leave him, stalking out of the ballroom with all that *not calmness* raging through me. I never imagined the day he would upset me but here it is. I think it may be a little while before I feel like speaking to him again.

9

KRISTEN - SIX MONTHS LATER

"DARLING," Mom says over lunch late in June, "Don't forget we've got the Hardwick Benefit Ball coming up. It's on that weekend you just mentioned and I've already found you three dress options."

I try to ignore the annoyance coming from my boyfriend who is sitting next to me as Mom says this. He wants us to go away with friends the weekend she's talking about. It was his mention of it that caused her to remind me of the ball. Without even looking at Lyle, I know the expression that is now on his face and the thoughts in his head. He hangs off every word my father says, but he's dismissive of my mother. *Does she have anything in her head besides who she can impress, Kristen?* We've had more than one argument about the time I spend doing charity work with her, and how often it drags me away from him.

We're having lunch with Mom and Dad at her new favorite Hamptons restaurant. It opened a month ago and she's made three trips here since then. I think it's for the food but it could be for the visibility. Anyone who is anyone frequents this restaurant. Thanks to that, right now is absolutely not the time to make a scene with Lyle.

Things are getting serious between us. He asked me to move in with him last weekend. I said yes. I would have preferred for us to find a new place together but I'm sure I'll be happy in his condo.

And the weekend away he wants us to take? Of course, I'll be going with him. I'm just going to need to find the right time to break that news to Mom.

I reach for my glass of wine and take a sip. "I remember," I say to her. "You'll have to show me those dresses tomorrow when I come over." We have plans to work on the gala we're currently in the planning stages of. This one will raise money for a women's foundation that invests in projects to empower New York communities in their long-term economic security. It's a gala that holds a special place in my heart because I've seen what the money it raises can do.

Lyle eyes me. "We've got plans tomorrow."

I frown. "No, we don't."

He releases an impatient breath. "We do, Kristen. You need to start using that calendar of yours better."

I bristle at his tone. "What plans do we have?" It's Monday tomorrow. Lyle has work, so I can't understand why he thinks we've got something else planned.

"We're collecting Andrew and Elise from the airport." His brother and sister-in-law.

"Oh, right, yes. But I wasn't aware you wanted me to come with you. I thought you were doing that and then spending time with them on your own." What I actually want to say is that during the conversation we had over this, he made it very clear he doesn't expect me to tag along. I was hurt by the things he said. There's no way I got this wrong.

"No. I want you with me." And just like that, with a firm, unyielding tone, he lets me know this is what he expects.

I don't push back against Lyle often, but I can't let this go. Not when I was so upset after our last conversation about this. "That wasn't what you said when we discussed this."

"It was."

I turn my body to his. "No, Lyle, it wasn't. You said we weren't at the stage in our relationship yet that justified my assumption you'd want me to be there when you collected Andrew." I was stunned when he said this. I can move in with him but I can't go with him to collect his brother from the airport?

Before he can respond to that, my father says, "I imagine you misunderstood, Kristen, but perhaps if you want to discuss this, you could wait until you get home." Dad's displeasure is evident in his voice. Usually, that would be enough to stop me, but not today. I'm in a mood already from the way Lyle rushed me out the door this morning, telling me I waste far too much of his time getting ready. He had the hide to suggest I wake an hour earlier on the days we have plans.

I push my chair back, and at Lyle's frown, I say, "We'll take this somewhere private. I'm not waiting until we get home to finish this conversation."

Without waiting for him to agree, I walk away from the table toward the terrace. I've taken two steps when I lock eyes with Bradford who is sitting at a table in the corner watching me. He's watching me so intently that there's no doubt in my mind he's been watching me for a while.

The butterflies that I still feel for this man come to life and I bring my hand to my body, trying to calm them. There's no calming to be had, though. Not where Bradford's concerned. Even that god-awful conversation we had six months ago didn't send these butterflies away.

I've only seen him once since then and my attraction to him was as strong as ever. It was at a party. I had Lyle with me. Bradford's date was a woman I've seen him with a few times over the years. The four of us had a five-minute conversation about nothing in particular. My level of jealousy was wild. I hated watching her put her hands on Bradford. Lyle picked up on the vibes between Bradford and me, and we ended the night with the biggest fight we've had to date. That wasn't what I hated about the night the most though. No, it was the fact Bradford and I didn't find our way to the rooftop.

"Hurry up and let's get this over with," Lyle says, coming up behind me.

He doesn't wait for me to continue walking. Instead, he pushes past me and stalks out to the terrace.

Bradford doesn't miss any of it.

I watch the slight narrowing of his eyes as he tracks Lyle's strides.

I watch the pressing together of his lips as he does that.

I watch as he brings his gaze back to me.

I don't miss the disapproval in his eyes.

He looks ready to leave his chair and come to me. I give him a quick shake of my head and walk out to the terrace, hoping he reads me as well as he always has. The last thing I need is him joining Lyle and me.

"Why are you being so antagonistic today?" Lyle's question is out before I've even come to a stop.

I stare at him. "Are you serious?"

"Deadly. You've fought with me since we got in the car to come here. Over insignificant things."

"Insignificant things?"

"Is this conversation going to consist of you asking me inane questions, Kristen? If so, we may as well end it now because I don't have the patience for that today."

My eyes widen so much I should be concerned about wrinkles forming. "Firstly, fuck you for saying that." His shock at my use of a curse word I rarely use only fuels me. Lyle could do with some shocking. I want to shock him right into being a better man. "That wasn't a stupid question. I was legitimately asking you if you really thought the things I've argued with you over today are insignificant, because if you do, we've got a problem. I don't argue with you as much as I should, so trust me when I tell you that the things I do choose to fight over are very significant to me."

"Go on." He takes a cold tone with me, the one I receive when I've angered him.

"I did not misunderstand you when you said you didn't want me with you tomorrow. Don't you dare gaslight me on that."

"You say that like it's a thing I do often."

"You've done it enough times for it to be a thing, and I need you to know I'm done with it. If we're going to move in together and take this relationship to the next level, you need to know I won't be the kind of woman who just stands behind you and lets you treat me as less than you."

"Christ, I don't do that. I've never done that."

"You have, Lyle."

His nostrils flare. "I fucking haven't." His cold tone has disappeared. He's now drawing attention with his angry, raised voice.

I'm about to argue that again when Bradford joins us, eyeing me with concern. "Is everything okay here?"

Lyle turns a dark and furious glare on him. "Everything is fine here."

Bradford doesn't remove his gaze from me. "Kristen?"

Before I can reply, Lyle snaps, "I've already told you we're okay. You can fuck off now."

Bradford finally looks at Lyle, treating him to a look that's just as dark and angry as his. "I wasn't asking you." He moves closer to me. "Do you need me, Kristen?"

"No," I start, but Lyle cuts me off.

Stepping between Bradford and me, he pushes his shoulders back and faces Bradford. "The last person she needs is you, and if I have to look at you for another fucking second, you'll regret not leaving."

"You've got a problem on your hands, then, Lyle," Bradford says. "I'm not going anywhere. Not until I know that Kristen is okay."

I move around Lyle so I'm standing next to him. Shooting him a glare, I say, "I'm quite capable of speaking for myself." I then look at Bradford, my expression softening. "I promise you I'm okay. We're just having a disagreement over something."

I'm torn because I desperately want time with Bradford, but I also don't want this situation to escalate. If the look on my boyfriend's face is anything to go by, that's exactly what's going to happen. Especially since Bradford doesn't appear ready to walk away yet.

When he spends time searching my face rather than leaving, Lyle loses his shit.

"You know what"—he looks between Bradford and me, an almost violent expression on his face as his gaze settles on mine—"you stay and talk with him. It's obvious that's what you want to do. When you've got what you need here, come and look for me. I might still be around."

My heart is beating hard as I watch him stalk away.

I should follow him. He's the guy I'm about to move in with. The guy I've started making plans for a future with.

But the man who stole my heart years ago is looking at me like I'm the only person in the world right now. He's looking at me like my very existence is the only thing that matters to him.

"He doesn't treat you well, Kristen."

"You just catch him in bad moments. Everyone has those. I'm sure you do."

He gives me a pointed look. "I have my moments, yes, but I would never treat you like he does."

"You don't know how well he treats me, Bradford." It's true. When Lyle is good, he's amazing.

"I'm not here to debate your relationship. I'm here to make sure you're okay, and from what I've seen each time I've watched you with him, I don't think you are."

"You've seen me with him twice. That's hardly enough to form a complete picture."

"I've seen you with him six times and not once have I

seen him treat you well. I'd say the picture I've formed is accurate."

I blink.

My mind swims.

Six times?

"It's only been two times," I blurt. "Not six."

His eyes refuse to let mine loose. "It's been six. Trust me. I wish it hadn't."

All my thoughts catch up with each other. "Why didn't I know you were there?"

"Because you were busy putting up with Lyle's bull-shit. You deserve so much more. When are you going to realize that?"

This conversation feels a lot like the one we had six months ago. The one in which he wasn't gentle like I'd asked. He never promised he would be, but I wasn't ready to hear what he had to say, particularly not when he laid his words down between us with more determination than I cared for.

We didn't get anywhere with that conversation. Not anywhere good. I know he left it feeling frustrated with me. I left it feeling like a mess of a person.

Bradford was right that I was trapped under my fear, but I couldn't see a way out of it. I pushed him away a little that night. I think that's why we didn't meet on the rooftop the last time we saw each other.

I'm probably about to push him away some more now. I don't want to. God, how I don't want that. But I'm not sure I'm ready to walk away from Lyle.

"I'm quite capable of knowing what I deserve, Brad-ford. I am not the stupid woman so many people think I am. Please don't treat me like that."

"Fuck." He rubs his hand down his face. "I never treat you like that. You're one of the most intelligent women I know. But you're not making a smart choice with Lyle. Or with your work. And I can't figure out for the life of me how to make you see that."

I hate this conversation. I hate it so much.

"Well, that's not your job. *I'm* not your job. You don't have to spend your time trying to help me. You're free to go back to your life and leave me to mine." The words are out of my mouth before I can control them. I instantly wish I could put them all back in.

I see it in his eyes that I've said the wrong thing. That I've hurt him. But it's too late now to do anything about it. My words lie tattered and torn between us. They feel as frayed as the threads between us. We've spent three years circling each other, learning the deepest parts of each other, but now here we are, hurting each other, slowly ripping those threads apart.

"Our lives might be separate," he says, his voice raw with emotion, "but I don't feel separate from you. And I sure as hell don't think of you as a job. You might be able to deny this thing between us, but there's something there, something *I* can't deny. I want the best for you. I want you to be happy. And I want you to choose those things for yourself." He pauses. "I'm sorry if my delivery was off, but I won't ever apologize for speaking the truth."

Oh God.

"Bradford—"

My father cuts me off, striding into the middle of our conversation without a care for any privacy we might have preferred. Anger covers his face. "Kristen, I don't know what you said to Lyle, but you need to get out to the car where he's waiting and sort this out with him. And perhaps the next time you think it a good idea to engage in a fight in public, you might think that through a little better. I don't appreciate the whispers circulating."

He doesn't give me an opportunity to respond. He leaves as fast as he arrived, taking my pride, my breaths, and all my smart thoughts with him.

I hate so much about this day.

Bradford stares after my father before turning back to me. "Jesus."

I put my hand up to stop him saying anything further. I know what he'll have to say and I can't listen to any of it. I need to fix this problem I've caused.

"I'm sorry, I have to go and deal with this."

He grasps my arm as I try to move past him. "Do you remember the things you told me when we met? What you wanted to do with your life?"

"Yes." I really don't want to do this with him. He needs to let me go. And yet, I make no move to pull out of his hold.

"Tell me you'll think about them."

I feel like a chastised little girl right now. Bradford has told me what he thinks of my choices, and so has my father. None of it feels good and I don't want to promise anyone anything. But putting on a show is one of my skills, so I nod. "I will."

When he finally lets me go, I don't look back. I hurry to where Lyle's waiting for me and begin putting us back together.

I have to.

My father wants me to marry this man.

10

___

ONE YEAR LATER

@thetea_gasp

@KRISTENBLAISE AND @lyleastor have called it quits. But, my friends, wait for it, let's sip the tea together because Kristen has been spotted with @johnathon-swindle #gasp Whatever will her mama say? The sheets at Lyle's are still warm. But then, there's been talk that this relationship was off the rails a long time ago, and we did spot Lyle looking a little cozy with a redhead three weeks ago, so we're all for Kristen's #savage move #thankyounext Stay tuned, friends. We'll report back when we know more about this #situationship . Kristen is a fave of ours on the NY social scene and we're cheering for her to find her man #goqueen

11

KRISTEN - SIX MONTHS LATER

"DAD'S IN A MOOD TONIGHT," Jenna says as she reaches for the cocktail on the table in front of her. "I wish I'd known he would be before agreeing to come to this ball. It's the absolute worst way to spend Christmas Eve."

"Your father's always in a mood," Johnathon, my boyfriend drawls.

Jenna rolls her eyes at him. "And yet you love him. Oh, that's right, because he never takes his mood out on you. You're the guy who can do no wrong in his eyes."

She's right. Dad loves Johnathon more than he loved Lyle, and that's saying something because Lyle was his golden boy from day one. He gave Lyle a job at Blaise Media and moved him up the ranks fast. The fact Lyle still works for the company, that Dad didn't find a way to fire him after he treated me so badly, is something that still hurts. My father didn't come out openly and say it to me, but what he did say implied he thinks I was to blame for the breakdown of my relationship.

I smile at Johnathon. "Give him time. Everyone does wrong in Dad's eyes at some point."

Johnathon returns my smile before leaning in and saying, "Dean just arrived. I'll be about half an hour."

"Okay."

I watch as he walks across the ballroom toward one of his clients. Johnathon works a lot more than any man I've dated, often disappearing when we attend social events. I'm okay with this; he's super attentive when we are together, and I know he's busy building his future.

"Are you guys actually going to skip dinner tomorrow?" Jenna asks.

I nod. "Yes. We're leaving for Paris tomorrow morning."

"Wow. I'm impressed. How's Mom taking it?"

"So, here's what I've learned in my twenty-five years. Mom and Dad are good with almost anything if they adore the guy you're sleeping with. I could write you a manual on how to keep our parents happy if you'd like." My tone is sarcastic with that offer, but it's true; I could write her a manual.

"Yeah, because that would be something I'd read."

I laugh. "Where's Declan? His appearance here would earn you a tick from them."

"He can't make it tonight. He's got something on with his family."

I arch my brows. "And you weren't invited?"

"Kris, we're two months into this relationship. I'm good with not being invited to his party tonight." She narrows her eyes at something across the room. "Oh, God. Declan's best friend is here. If I have to speak to him, there may be a knife involved. You have to save me. Do not let that man near me."

"Who, Beckett?" I gaze across the room at the tall, good-looking man she's talking about.

"Yes. He's so fucking arrogant. I seriously want to stab him every time he opens his mouth."

I've never met Beckett, but I know of him. I've seen him at quite a few galas and he reminds me of Bradford. They're the kind of men who are confident in their own skin, who dominate a room simply with their presence.

Thoughts of Bradford cause me sadness. Ever since the day he broke up a fight between me and Lyle, our friendship has been different. I've been less open with him; he's been less inclined to push me on my life choices. We've slowly drifted apart. There are so many unspoken things between us now.

We see each other every few months or so at parties or galas, but we never find ourselves alone. I miss him, but there's a part of me that breathes easier not having to explain myself to him.

A text alert sounds from my phone.

> **JOHNATHON**
> I need longer with Dean. I'm sorry, but I'll make it up to you later.

> I'm holding you to that.

> **JOHNATHON**
> You know I will, baby.

"I love that dreamy look you get when you receive texts from Johnathon," Jenna says.

I look at her with a huge smile on my face. "I'm in love with him."

She smiles. "I know. And I love that for you. But just so you know, if he hurts you, *I* will hurt him. After the shit Lyle put you through, I'm keeping a close eye on all the men you date."

Jenna is the only person who knows the extent of the hurt Lyle caused me. I don't have close friends like she does, and I don't share my feelings with the friends I do have. And I certainly don't talk to Mom about hard things. She's not interested in anything too deep, which honestly, works for me. I'm more like Mom than Jenna who I have no doubt would unload all her feelings onto a stranger if she needed to.

"You don't have to keep a close eye on Johnathon. He is nothing like Lyle."

"Still, I'm watching."

Her phone starts ringing and when she sees it's Declan, she says, "I'm gonna take this outside so I can hear him."

"Don't do anything like stabbing men while you're gone," I say as she stands to leave.

She grins. "I'm liking this sense of humor you've had lately. I need to see more of it."

I like that she thinks I have a sense of humor. I always feel so rigid and tight but have always wanted to be fun. Being with Johnathon has been easier than being with any boyfriend I've ever had. He's the life of any party he attends. He's charming and affectionate. Never demeaning. He makes me feel safe and loved, and he helps me loosen up a little.

Mom interrupts my thoughts when she takes the seat

next to me. She frowns as she inspects my face. "I think you might want to pop to the bathroom and fix your makeup."

My hand instantly goes to my face, horrified that there's something wrong with it. *Why didn't Jenna say something?* "What's wrong with it?"

"It just needs some touching up."

I'm on my feet straight away and hurrying toward the bathroom, hoping that no one stops me on my way.

Thankfully, no one does, and I find the restroom empty when I arrive. I quickly move to the mirror to see what my mother was talking about. It's my turn to frown now. There's nothing wrong with my makeup. It's perfection if ever I saw it. I paid good money to have my face done and should have known my mother was being dramatic.

I roll my eyes as I reach into my clutch for my lipstick. My lips don't really need touching up but I do it anyway.

I'm halfway back to the table when I run into Bradford. Literally run into him. He's turning to walk the way I'm coming from and collides with me.

His hands come straight to my arms, gripping me firmly to steady me. His eyes meet mine, holding them just as firmly as he says, "Kristen."

And just like that, my butterflies are set free.

Why must he be the man who owns those butterflies?

Not even Johnathon can unleash them like this.

They're wild and free with Bradford. Like they've been caged for too long and can exhale in their freedom.

"Hi." The word stutters out of me in bewilderment because I'm suddenly aware we're not alone. Bradford's girlfriend is right behind him.

Carla Byrd.

The woman he's been dating for seventeen months now. Not that I'm counting. The longest relationship he's ever had. Not that I'm keeping track.

She laughs as she moves next to him. It's a tinkling laugh. I hate it. "Darling"—she eyes him—"you need to watch where you're going. This body of yours is capable of causing serious damage."

I hate that she knows what his body is capable of. I hate that she's anywhere near his body.

Bradford doesn't seem to register that she's even spoken. He's watching me intently, his eyes searching mine.

The connection between us might be tattered but it's not broken.

When neither of us respond to her, she says, "Mom and Dad just arrived, Bradford. I need to speak to them before Lana does. I want us to be the ones to tell them."

The ones to tell them.

He finally lets go of my arms. Nodding at her, he says, "I'll be a minute."

My breaths slow.

"Okay," she says before smiling at me. "I'm sorry I can't stay and chat. Next time."

The ones to tell them.

She breezes away from us. I stare after her for a moment longer than I prefer. Carla is everything I wish I was. Intelligent, independent, confident. She's a lawyer who is gaining a lot of attention worldwide for her work on international criminal law.

I can barely feel my legs.

I look at Bradford and ask softly and with more difficulty than I've ever had with any question, "What are you telling her parents?" Even as the question leaves my lips, I know the answer. I feel the answer deeply in my soul as it twists and turns and slices.

"We're engaged."

Those two words slay me more than I ever thought possible.

It's in this moment that I finally acknowledge I thought that somehow we would end up together. I thought our timing would one day be right.

I've kept Bradford to myself and while I've not invited him into my daily life, I've lived with him in my soul. Men have come and gone in the time I've known him, but if I'm honest with myself, he's the one who sat on the throne in my heart.

I swallow hard.

I dig deep for strength.

And I paste a smile on my face, because if I've trained for anything in my life, it's this moment. *Maintain perfect composure at all times in public* is the mantra of my existence. "Congratulations."

The ballroom begins spinning.

I can't breathe.

He looks at me with an expression that seems to be a frown but looks a lot like torment. We're stuck in the middle of this moment when someone calls out to him.

Glancing toward the voice, he holds up a finger, indicating he needs a minute. When he gives me his eyes again, he says, "Happy birthday for tomorrow, Kristen. I hope it's a wonderful one for you."

I. Can't. Breathe.

My heart splinters into a thousand tiny pieces as I

watch him walk away from me. I briefly wonder how a person puts a heart back together. It's not lost on me that in all the breakups I've endured, I have never contemplated this.

I'm not sure it's possible to put my heart back together.

I'm not sure I want to.

This pain crushing me is what I have left of him, and if I know anything right now, it's that I never want to let him go. This pain may be the only connection to him I have left.

12

KRISTEN - THREE MONTHS LATER

"I HAVE NEVER SEEN you eat this much ice cream or listen to a playlist of sad songs on repeat like you are," Jenna says before her eyes widen. "Oh, shit, has something happened between you and Johnathon?" She sits next to me on my couch. "I swear I will do damage to him if he's done something."

I don't want to but I turn the music down. I've had "A Thousand Years" by Christina Perri on repeat for weeks and I still haven't had enough of it. I feel like I need a thousand more years of this song to even come close to erasing my sadness.

Bradford announced his engagement days after he told me and as much as I've tried to avoid reading anything more about it on social media, his relationship is everywhere. Since launching his time management app just over a year ago and turning it into the number one productivity app, the world is even more interested in him than it already was. And Carla is the current it-girl of New York. Not only is she super successful in her career, but she also comes from the kind of family Bradford's father would be wetting himself over. Her fashion sense is pure perfection. And she has all the right friends in her circle. Neither she nor Bradford post their lives on social media, but it seems like everyone else fucking does.

I've actually stopped scrolling Instagram this week. Something I never thought I'd do.

I can't look at another thing about them. I just can't.

All I want to do is listen to this song and eat ice cream.

I look at my sister who is staring at me, waiting eagerly for me to shed light on what's happening in my brain. "Nothing has happened. Johnathon and I are good."

We are. Because he's oblivious to half the stuff going on in my life. I love him, but I'd like it if he was as good at paying attention to my details as Bradford is.

Oh, God.

Was.

As Bradford was. Not is.

I stop the sob threatening at the back of my throat.

I've had three months to come to terms with this and I am nowhere near close to reconciling it.

Jenna frowns. "So, what is it? And don't tell me it's nothing, Kris. I know it's something."

Bradford is still my secret and I have no intention of telling Jenna about him now. But I know she won't let this conversation go without me giving her something. "It's Dad." That's not a lie. He's always doing something that's hurtful.

"What did he do?"

"He promoted Lyle."

Her eyes widen more than they did before. "You are fucking kidding me."

I give her a look that says I'm not while spooning more ice cream into my mouth. "Can we swap lives?"

She laughs. "Okay, so now I know things are really bad. You would hate my life."

I sigh. I probably would. Jenna's carefree and doesn't care what anyone thinks of her. I'd like to try that life out, but I don't think my personality is built for it.

"You should come out with me tonight," she says, getting excited at the thought. "Shona and I are checking out a new club that's just opened." Jenna and her best friend love to dance the night away in clubs I'd rather pretend don't exist.

I shudder. "I think I'll pass." I can't think of anything worse than drinking and dancing in a club filled with men who want to put their hands all over me. No, thank you.

She nudges me with her foot. "Come on, Kris. You might have some fun."

"I also might not. Besides, Johnathon and I are planning a quiet night in. He's worked late every night this week and wants some time alone tonight."

"Does that man ever not work?"

I don't miss the criticism in her tone and suddenly feel defensive of the man I've just moved in with. "He doesn't work all the time."

"It feels like he does."

I'm about to continue defending him when a text distracts her. After checking it, she groans. "I have to go. Declan and I were supposed to be meeting at eight tonight, but he gave me the wrong info and I have to be there in the next ten minutes. Honestly, how hard is it to get the details right?"

I think about that long after she leaves. It's not hard to get the details right, just like it's not hard to pay attention to them in your loved ones.

I may not be big on sharing my feelings with Jenna but I always know what's going on with her. I make it a point to find out. Just like I do with my mother, father, and brothers.

Jenna's currently frustrated with her boyfriend and a woman she works with.

My brothers are both doing well at the moment. Grayson wishes his new girlfriend wouldn't leave the mess in his condo that she always does. Oliver is training for a marathon and wishes the women he sleeps with wouldn't call him because he's not interested in a relationship.

Mom is frantic over the remodeling she and Dad are doing.

And Dad is busy making new plans to expand his company.

Those things don't come close to the details I've cataloged about them this month. I'm the one in our family who cares enough to check in on everyone regularly. And I'm the one to rally the family if one of us needs help.

I don't expect anyone to pay this much attention to me, but after knowing what it's like to have a man care enough to do it, I wish Johnathon tried just a little bit harder.

"A Thousand Years" begins from the beginning again and I turn the volume back up. If I make it loud enough, maybe I'll drown out the sound of my heartache.

That sound never ceases.

It sounds like *you should have told him how you felt.*

It sounds like *is he happy?*

It sounds like the question I ask myself every night as I rest my head against my pillow. *Did she make him smile today?*

13

ONE YEAR LATER

@thetea_gasp

GATHER ROUND, friends! We have some happy news for you today. @kristenblaise is getting married! #yaas We're jealous AF over that rock on her finger. @johnathonswindle is the lucky man our girl has decided to give up her single days for and we couldn't be happier for them. They've quickly become one of New York's popular couples, showing up at all the events that are reserved for the New York elite #thenewfourhundred. We're keeping a close eye on the wedding date announcement and all the dress news because if anyone will have a wedding dress worth drooling over, it will be Kristen. Our girl knows her fashion and has been on fire this past year, always wowing every crowd she's part of #allthegoals

14

KRISTEN - TEN MONTHS LATER

JOHNATHON

> Babe, I'm not going to make it to your ball tonight. Work is kicking my ass. I'll make it up to you tomorrow.

I STARE at the text from my fiancé and fight not to scream. He knows how important tonight is to me. But letting me down is fast becoming his reliable move.

Mom glances up from her clipboard that holds our to-do list for tonight. "What's wrong, darling?"

"Johnathon isn't able to make it tonight." I do my best to hide my anger and disappointment. Not a hard thing to do since that's now *my* reliable move.

She waves the news off. "He's busy with his work. It's understandable."

I don't share her sentiment.

I don't think it's understandable for the significant other in my life to blow off an important moment in my life.

However, dwelling in my feelings is not productive,

and it's something I try to avoid these days. I have things to do and spending time stuck in my emotions won't get those things done.

"Okay," I say to her, "I'm going to check on the volunteers and ensure they have everything they need. Can you go and see that the kitchen is running on time?"

Mom and I have spent over a year planning this charity ball that is on track to raise around ten million dollars. It's the first time we've held the ball and the support for it has blown my mind.

I called in every person in my network, knocked on the door of fashion designers and celebrities asking them to get involved, and asked for a million favors from so many people to make it a success. Never in my wildest dreams did I imagine it being the success it is. I'm not only proud of the work I've put into it, but I'm also proud of what we will be able to do with the money raised. When I think of the number of women we'll be able to help, I tear up.

This is the work of my life.

"Yes," Mom says, "And I'll also make sure things are running smoothly outside." She's referring to the red carpet that celebrities are currently walking to enter the ball.

"Great," I say, quickly moving onto my next thought, my next task, barely noticing Mom's departure.

It turns out I love this work. It may be unpaid, and it may not give the kind of recognition a job would, but what I'm doing feels important. It also turns out that what I really love is being in charge of a project like I am this time. Usually, I'm part of a planning committee, but this ball was my idea, my baby, and I'm head of the committee. It's fulfilling in a way I never imagined.

I make my way toward the volunteers. I'm stopped quite a few times by our team to answer questions and give directions, so it takes me longer than I prefer to reach my destination. I'm almost there when I hear a deep voice I would know anywhere. A voice that never fails to slow me down.

Bradford's eyes meet mine when I turn to look at him. He's talking with his best friend, and while he continues the conversation, he doesn't remove his gaze from me. When Owen says something to him after eyeing me, he nods and walks my way.

I'm suddenly nervous in a way I haven't been since the last time we spoke just over six months ago. That was a conversation I wished I wasn't a part of because it involved his fiancée who was holding the floor with three other couples besides Johnathon and me. Carla has a way of holding everyone's attention based solely on her intelligence that makes me wish I was as smart as her. I'd caught Bradford watching me during that conversation but I'd quickly glanced away. I couldn't look at him while he had his arm around her the way he did.

I've made it a point to avoid him at every turn since then. I don't need the reminder of what I can't have.

"Hey," he says when he reaches me.

God, this man knows how to wear a tux. I think about being the woman in his life who helps him with his bow tie. The woman who sits on the bathroom vanity talking to him while he shaves. The woman who slides her hands up over his pecs at the end of the night and shrugs that jacket off him.

I smile even though I don't feel in a smiling mood. "Hey."

Something flashes in his eyes. It's the look he used to get when he was about to ask me what was wrong. Tonight, he doesn't pursue that line of questioning. "I heard how much you've raised so far with the ball. You've done an incredible job, Kristen."

My hands go to my stomach. They're trying to get my butterflies under control. But just like every other time my hands try to settle the feelings that Bradford causes in me, they fail. There is never any settling to be had in his presence.

"Thank you." His praise feels good. Genuine. This time, my smile is authentic.

He turns silent and in my desperation to fill the gaping space between us, I blurt, "Congratulations on the success of your new app." Bradford launched another app a few months ago, a business management app that's also gone to number one in its category.

"Thank you."

God, we're in a wasteland of stilted conversation with too many things left hanging between us. And since I'm a woman who doesn't do well with awkwardness, I feel the need to fix this. Not that it can be fixed in the way I want, but at the least, I can make it so that when we run into each other we're not stuck where we are right now.

I turn my smile up. "You and Carla must be excited. Not long now until the wedding. Where are you honey-mooning?" I don't actually want to know the answer to that question. I don't even want to attend his wedding. Not because I don't want to see him happy, but because I don't think I can handle seeing him say *I do* to another

woman. But he invited me and I called upon deep
reserves of strength and said yes.

I may not want to see Bradford with another woman,
but I do want happiness for him.

"We're not taking a honeymoon straight away. We've
both got a lot going on at work at the moment."

I'm secretly glad to know this fact. I instantly push
that thought aside. I'm engaged to Johnathon, after all. I
love Johnathon. I'm going to be Johnathon's wife in eight
months. Bradford is in my past and I need to let him go.

I look around the ballroom, trying to find someone,
anyone, who needs me. When no one puts me out of my
misery, I meet Bradford's gaze again, smoothing my dress
over my stomach while smiling brightly at him. "Well, I'm
sure you two will find time soon." I glance past him, at
nothing in particular but trying desperately to make out
that I'm looking at something in particular. "I better get
back to work. There's still so much to do."

I try to step around him and almost succeed in my
mission, but his fingers curve around my wrist and he
stops me. "How are you, Kristen?"

Oh, God.

No.

I don't want to do this with him tonight.

I look up into those eyes of his, eyes that see too many
things. There's something extra in them. A questioning
look. Like he already knows how I am but needs to hear it
from me. That's not possible, though. Nobody knows how
I really am. Not Jenna, and certainly not Bradford. It's
been a long time since we've had the kind of conversation
that would give him that knowledge.

"I'm busy. And good."

Regret flashes in his eyes now, confusing me. "I know we haven't spoken for a long time. Really spoken. But you can call me anytime. I want you to know that."

I frown. "Bradford, I'm good. I promise." Even I buy my own lies these days. Most of the time, anyway.

He stares at me like he's taking in every line, every angle of my face. "Just remember what I said." With that, he lets his fingers slip from my wrist and steps aside to let me past.

I leave him, still confused, wondering what he left unspoken because I'm absolutely certain there was something on his mind that he wanted to discuss. For the life of me, though, I can't think what it would be.

Throughout the night, I return to our conversation many times. I'm still not able to figure out why he made such a point of letting me know I could call if I needed him. It leaves me feeling unsettled, like something bad is about to happen, and even in amongst the success of the night, that bad feeling doesn't leave me.

15

KRISTEN

I SLEEP BADLY after the ball, tossing and turning all night. Johnathon slides into bed just after three a.m. I'm awake but I don't let him know. My disappointment and anger with him over not making it to the ball for even a short time, along with his lack of awareness of what that meant to me, has only grown over the course of the night. If it doesn't lessen by the morning, I think we may end up having a fight over it because I won't be able to hold my tongue like I usually do every time he blows me off for work. I understand having to put in the hours, but not when he's missing something so important to me.

The last time I see on the bedside clock is five a.m. I must fall into a deep sleep after that because when I wake, it's almost ten a.m. and Johnathon has already left for work.

My morning is slower than usual. I'm not showered and ready for the day until lunchtime at which point my sister texts me.

JENNA

> Why haven't you replied to my texts? Are
> you still asleep or did Johnathon finally
> take a Saturday off and demand you
> have sex with him all day?

I scroll up and find two other texts from her congratulating me on the ball and telling me she hopes I'm giving myself time to rest today.

> Saturdays are the new Friday. Didn't you
> know?

JENNA

> Wow, Kris. The sarcasm. I'm impressed.

Jenna might have been a fan of Johnathon's in the beginning, but she isn't so much anymore. She's never said anything to that effect, but I know my sister. She's bored by him. He doesn't engage in thought-provoking conversations with her like she'd prefer. And she doesn't like that he cancels plans often so he can work.

> I'm awake, dressed, caffeinated. I'm
> thinking of booking in a Pilates class this
> afternoon. My body is sore and stiff
> today.

JENNA

> Great idea. Maybe take a bath too. And a
> long nap. You've worked hard and
> deserve some time to yourself.

Time to myself? No woman has time for that. My sister lives in dreamland if she thinks they do.

I'm about to reply to her text when my phone lights

up with a call from my father. Weird. He never calls me in the middle of the day.

"Hey, Dad," I answer.

"Kristen."

"What's up?"

"I want to invite you and Johnathon for dinner tonight. To celebrate the success of your ball. Your mother and I are very proud of what you achieved last night and she's asked Sarah to cook your favorite meal."

Every cell in my body floods with warmth and happiness. And pride like I've never known.

Your mother and I are very proud.

I've waited a lifetime to hear those words from my father.

"I'd love that." My voice cracks. *I'm going to cry.*

"And Johnathon? He can make it tonight too?"

"Yes, we had plans we can change." I will make sure he knows this is non-negotiable. But then, Johnathon never lets my father down, so I don't think he will tonight.

"Good. I also want to discuss the condo your mother and I will buy for you and Johnathon to live in after you're married. Have a think about where you'd like to live. We'll go over that tonight. And Kristen, that job we discussed for you at the magazine looks like it might open up sooner than I thought. We'll talk some more about that too."

I stare at my phone for a long time after we end the call. I then place it down and take some steadying breaths.

My father has overwhelmed me. Congratulating me on my success is one thing. A big, massive thing. But involving me in a decision like he's just indicated he will, is also a big thing.

I wasn't aware he planned to buy us a condo, and as far as I know, he hasn't spoken to Johnathon about it either. That surprises me because it isn't the way he usually goes about his business. I would have expected he'd talk with Johnathon before mentioning it to me. Not that I like that, but it's just how he's always done things.

And the job at his magazine—the job he instigated— is everything I've wanted for so long.

I feel like I may burst with happiness.

When my phone sounds with a text, I assume it's Jenna and quickly swipe it up to reply.

> BRADFORD
>
> Are you home at the moment?

I blink.

Bradford has never texted me. Not once in the seven years I've known him.

> Yes. Why?

> BRADFORD
>
> I'm coming over.

> Why?

> BRADFORD
>
> I'll be there in about twenty minutes. I'll tell you then.

By the time he arrives, I'm in a state of utter confusion over what's happening right now. Over what's happening *today*.

First, my father's phone call. Then, Bradford's texts and visit. I can't keep up.

"Hi," I greet him as he steps off the elevator into my condo. "This is a nice surprise." I'm lying. I don't find any surprise nice. I like to know plans in advance.

The regret his eyes held last night is still there now. Only, it's stronger, like he *really* regrets something.

I frown. "What's going on, Bradford?"

"Let's sit."

The unsettled feeling I had last night roars to life.

Bradford never texts.

He's never visited me in my home.

None of this is normal for us.

My hands go to my stomach. Not to calm butterflies, though. To calm the sense of foreboding swirling through me.

"I don't want to sit. I want you to tell me whatever it is that had you running here."

He remains silent for what is likely less than thirty seconds but feels like thirty hours. When he finally starts speaking, his voice is rough like every word is a hardship for him. "It's about Johnathon. He's cheating on you, Kristen."

Me entire body stills. I actually stop taking breaths. No woman wants to hear her partner is cheating on her, but hearing it from the man who still owns a key to her heart is brutal. Heartbreakingly, devastatingly fucking brutal.

I try to swallow the agony but it's too bitter. Too sharp. Too intense.

"No." It's a denial. It's also an accusation. *Why is he hurting me like this?*

Bradford's features twist. "I've heard gossip for a little while now, but I witnessed it for myself two weeks ago. I would have told you earlier but I didn't want to mess with your headspace while you were busy with the ball."

"You must have misunderstood what you saw. Johnathon would never cheat on me. Besides, he works so much that he wouldn't have the time."

"Are you sure he's working?" He uses the gentlest tone he's ever used with me. I don't pay attention though because his question is not gentle as far as I'm concerned. It's harsh and it *hurts*.

"Of course he's working."

"Kristen—"

I put my hand up to stop him.

I need him to stop.

Just stop, stop, *stop*.

"No, Bradford. I'm not defending my fiancé's work ethic to you. Johnathon is busy building for our future. He's a good man. He treats me well and loves me like no one has ever loved me. Please stop saying these things to me."

Bradford looks at me for a long moment. He appears to be weighing something up. I think he should stop weighing everything up and just leave. But he doesn't. Instead, he says, "I've always been honest with you, Kristen, and I'm not going to stop now, even if telling you this is the very last thing I want to tell you. I wouldn't bring gossip to you, but I saw him. He *is* cheating on you. He might treat you well when he's with you, but a man who doesn't respect the trust his partner gives him is not a man who treats you well."

I have a whole future mapped out with Johnathon.

One that will make me very happy. I'm not listening to this. I can't listen to this.

I shake my head as I take a step away from him. "No. You've got it wrong. I have no doubt that when I ask Johnathon about this, he'll clear the confusion up. We're very happy together." I smooth my hands down over my stomach while thinking that I might need to sit after all.

Bradford reaches for me, but I jerk my arm away. I do not want him touching me. Not ever again.

"Kristen," he says, his eyes full of an apology I also don't want anything to do with. "I know this is hurtful, but it's the truth. I would never lie to you."

"No!" I yell, losing all ability to keep my emotions tightly locked up. They explode all over the place. In between us. Above us. Around us. "I've had to listen to your thoughts on my work, on my father, and on my choice of partners for a long time now, and I'm done. Done! You should go back to your happy life and your perfect fiancée and stop worrying about me and my life. We were only ever friends, Bradford, and not good ones at that. I think there's a reason why we never joined each other's life in a meaningful way. We weren't supposed to. And now we know that, we can finally end whatever this is."

Everything I say is a blow to him. The way the lines of his face contort and the look of pain that fills his eyes tell me that. When he speaks, the crack in his voice leaves me with no doubt. "The definition of a good friend isn't one you see or hear from every day. Not in my estimation. It's one who is always honest, always thoughtful, always kind, always trustworthy. It's someone who does those things with good intentions. And sometimes it involves giving the hard truth. We were always good friends, and as far as I'm concerned, you have been in my life in a very meaningful way."

"That's utter bullshit, Bradford. If I was in your life in that way, I'd be *in* your life. I'd know what you're doing each week. I'd know what's making you happy, what's frustrating you, what you're looking forward to. Let's not pretend we were more than we actually were."

Frustration fills his face. "If you want to fight this out, if that's what you need for me to get you to see the truth of your life, I can do that."

My eyes widen. "The truth of my life? Can you be any more condescending?"

"Fuck, I'm not trying to be condescending. I'm—"

"Well, take it from me, you are being exactly that. And I don't like it."

"You don't like a lot of things, Kristen, and yet you stay with men who do things you shouldn't like, and you keep doing work that isn't what you actually want to do. How many more years are you going to keep all this up? Or are you planning on filling your entire life with these things?"

Anger chokes my heart, my body, my soul. The throne he has owned for so many years bursts into flames and I violently throw away the key he held to me. "Get out." My breaths are rushing through me, and my chest feels like the skin there might actually split apart. "Get out now!"

His nostrils flare. "I'm not done."

"Oh, you are. You really fucking are. I refuse to listen to another word you have to say."

"Kristen—"

"No!" I scream. I stalk to the elevator that delivered

him here and jab the call button before looking back at him. "I want you to leave and I never want you to come back. I never want to speak to you again. If you see me out, do not come anywhere near me. This is done. *We* are done."

Bradford has the good sense to stop fighting me. He doesn't look happy about any of this or about leaving, but he does. The last thing I see on his face as the elevator doors close is more of that regret in his eyes. I hate that look on him. I hate it so much it physically hurts.

After he leaves, I sit.

I take deep breaths for a long time and push the anger from my body.

And then I think.

I think about what I have to do today. Pilates, errands, home stuff, and letting Johnathon know about dinner with my parents tonight.

I think about the job Dad's giving me.

I think about the wedding dress I'm probably going to choose.

I think about the honeymoon we're planning to take in Greece.

I think about where Johnathon and I might like to live after we're married.

And I force all my unwanted feelings over Bradford back into the box they belong in. The box I intend on throwing away just as soon as I can shut the damn thing.

Johnathon is not cheating on me.

He just isn't.

Bradford needs to get his eyes checked.

And he needs to stop paying attention to any of my details.

When he texts me an hour later, I think about blocking his number.

BRADFORD

We're not done. We are far from done. Good friends don't walk away when things get hard, Kristen.

16

KRISTEN

MONDAY ARRIVES FASTER than I prefer, especially since Johnathon and I spent a whole day together yesterday, wrapped up in each other in our bed. He made love to me on and off all day. In between, we talked about our wedding, finalizing some plans. He was even more attentive than he usually is. It was bliss and I never wanted the day to end.

I didn't bother bringing up what Bradford told me. There was no point because I fully trust Johnathon. His actions aren't those of a man who doesn't love me. And he's not a man who needs to look for sex somewhere else. I give him sex whenever he wants. We have a fantastic sex life. I even give him blowjobs when we're out sometimes. I know he loves that, so I make it a point to do it for him.

He made love to me again this morning before leaving for work and he's texted me a few times during the day letting me know he's been thinking about me.

At around three p.m., he texts me.

JOHNATHON

A last minute work meeting has come up for the weekend, babe. It's in London. Friday to Sunday. I'm sorry I won't be able to attend Lesley's party with you on Saturday.

My heart sinks. I really don't want to attend Lesley's engagement party on my own. God, how I don't want to do that. Lately, she's taken to noting how often Johnathon misses a party or a social function. *You must hate attending everything on your own, Kristen.* I took great pains to have her note I don't attend everything on my own. We've been friends since school, but lately I've been feeling less inclined to spend time with her.

I could come with you. I don't need to attend Lesley's party.

JOHNATHON

No, babe. I'll be busy working all weekend. There's no point in you coming. You may as well go the party.

I don't really want to go to be honest. And I'm okay if you're working all weekend. I can occupy myself. It's London, after all!

JOHNATHON

No. I can't see it happening. How about you and I go away at the end of the month? I'll take a weekend off for it.

He can't see it happening? I have no idea what he means by that, but I know him well enough not to harass him with a question about it.

That sounds perfect. I'll start thinking
about where we can go.

If there's one thing I want to be, it's a wife who doesn't nag her husband. I shudder at the thought. No, my mother taught me by example that not clinging and not dwelling in the hard moments is one of the keys to a long marriage. From a young age, I watched her hold down the fort at home while Dad worked hard. I watched her spend her time raising four children without complaint. I learned that compromise is important.

I intend on enjoying a lifetime of marriage to Johnathon, and I know that will involve give-and-take.

The rest of my afternoon is spent going over the financials of the ball with Mom. It's a great afternoon because I'm so excited to see all the ways we'll be able to help women with this money.

Just after five p.m., Bradford calls me.

I stare at my phone, my heart beating wildly.

All the emotions that should be in that box in my heart, never to be felt again, burst free.

They invade me.

They're like an attack, a physical assault.

A violent invasion.

Damn Bradford for not giving me a reprieve.

For always forcing my emotions on me.

I don't answer his call.

I think again about blocking his number.

The fact I don't is just another tangled mess in my mind I push to the side.

When he texts, I think about deleting it without reading it, but I don't. God, I'm pathetic.

BRADFORD

I'm going to keep calling, Kristen.

He can keep calling all he wants.
I can keep ignoring him.

17

TWO WEEKS LATER

@thetea_gasp

Shock horror, girlfriend #gasp @bradfordblack has called off his engagement to @carlabyrd. Whispers have been circulating for months now that all wasn't well in paradise for Bradford and his bae but since their wedding was supposed to take place next weekend, we thought those whispers were just gossip. It seems though, that Bradford really is the CEO of not committing. Which, honestly, is a real mood for us. Daddy, we're DTF if you're looking. Just sayin' #goals

18

KRISTEN

I LOOK at the name flashing across my phone screen.

Bradford.

I've lost count of how many times he's called me over the last month. He tries almost daily to get me to talk to him.

I haven't answered a single call or text.

And yet, he still tries.

I don't make an exception today.

I ignore the call and slip my phone into my purse before giving my sister all my attention.

Except, I don't give it all to her because ever since the day I read the news about his broken engagement on Instagram a week ago, a tiny speck of my attention is fixated on Bradford.

He called off his wedding.

As much as I think about that, and as often, I don't know what to do with that information. So, I do nothing.

I'm getting married in seven months after all.

And Bradford and I are done as far as I'm concerned.

19

KRISTEN - TWO MONTHS LATER

APRIL IS CHILLIER in New York than usual. The weather is in line with my mood. As I glance around the restaurant Mom chose for lunch today and smile at all the people I know, which is most of them, I wonder why humans don't hibernate like animals in the colder months. Not that the weather this month is that cold, but still, hibernation feels like a solid plan these days. I'd like to shut myself away from life for a while.

"So, your father won't be arriving until late Saturday," Mom says, drawing me back into the conversation.

"Oh," I say, "Johnathon can't make it now, so it'll just be me."

Jenna frowns as she reaches for her drink. "Why not? This weekend has been planned for six months, Kris."

Honestly, if people keep hounding me for details on why Johnathon works so much, I may hurt them. *I don't know*, I want to scream at them. I'm not in charge of my fiancé's schedule. It would look a lot different if I was, but

I'm not, and I never will be. So, for the love of God, everyone needs to stop questioning me over it.

"I know it has, Jenna, but he can't control work commitments."

"Yes, but—" she starts.

"But nothing. Please stop pestering me about his work. I'm tired of it."

"I'm not pestering you. I'm honestly wondering what's keeping him from such an important family weekend. We never all spend time together like this. I'd have thought he'd want to be there for it. And I know Dad won't like him canceling."

Mom shakes her head. "No, your father will be okay with this." She pats my hand reassuringly. "Don't worry over that. He understands that work comes first."

"It'd be nice if he understood that when it comes to my work," Jenna mutters under her breath.

Mom purses her lips at Jenna. "Let's not ruin lunch, Jenna. Your father's thoughts on your work are complicated and best not gotten into when we're trying to enjoy time together."

"Right," Jenna says. "Avoidance is the Blaise specialty, after all."

"Jenna," Mom says, using the sharp tone that both my sister and I know means this topic of conversation is finished with.

We move onto discussing the social events we all have coming up. Mom and I meet regularly for lunch, but Jenna only joins us every now and then. Her personal styling business keeps her super busy. I love having her here today, but my thoughts are too distracted to fully enjoy her presence.

Things haven't been great between Johnathon and me the last few weeks and there was something off about him this morning. Something I can't quite put my finger on.

He came home later than usual last night. Like, really late. Around three a.m. And when I tried to initiate sex with him this morning before he left for work, because we haven't had it for two weeks, he wasn't interested. *I'm tired, babe*, he'd said as he pushed me away and left the bed to take a shower. His second shower in three hours because he took one when he arrived home.

Johnathon is never too tired for sex.

Dark thoughts that have been crowding my brain lately ran wild while he took that shower.

He's cheating on you, Kristen. I would never lie to you.

Bradford's words have been on repeat for a week now while things between Johnathon and me have spiraled. I try to drive them from my mind but I fail. They're stuck in a groove that my brain seems to like.

He's not cheating on me.

He's not.

He loves me.

Oh, God.

My stomach lurches and I'm almost certain I'm going to vomit.

I shove my chair back and rush to the bathroom as my face flushes with heat and my mouth suddenly becomes watery.

I make it just in time, vomiting violently and sweating just as furiously.

It leaves me feeling faint and once I'm sure I won't vomit again, I flush the toilet and sit on the toilet lid.

The minutes pass while I catch my breath and try to get myself in order. I'm not sure how much time passes before I hear Jenna's voice.

"Kris, are you okay?"

I am as far from okay as one can be, but there is no way I will tell her this. Whatever is happening between Johnathon and me needs to stay between us. I'll fix it and no one will ever need to know there was a problem.

"I think I ate something that didn't agree with me."

"You ate some bread. I've never known anyone to get food poisoning from bread. What's really going on? You've been off since we arrived."

"I know people who've had food poisoning from bread." I stand and exit the stall, coming face-to-face with her assessing eyes. My sister is always trying to get me to share my problems with her. It's exhausting. "I'm okay now."

"Right, but why are you off today?"

Oh my God.

Enough!

The scream that is perpetually trapped in my throat begs me to let it loose.

"I'm not off," I snap, forcing that scream into submission. "I'm tired. I'm allowed to be tired and quiet, aren't I?"

Her eyes continue narrowing at me. "Yes, but—"

"Stop it with the buts, Jenna! I've had enough. I've got a lot on my mind. I don't need you adding to any of it."

She gives me a frustrated look but finally lets her line of questioning go.

As we walk back to our table, I spot Carla Byrd entering the restaurant.

"Fuck me, can this day get *any* worse?" Seeing her is like seeing everything that's wrong with me, because she's everything I am not.

Jenna frowns at me. "What's wrong?"

I don't bother answering her. Instead, I say, "I have to go." I reach for my purse and look at Mom. "I'm not feeling well. I'm going to go home and lie down. I think I'll call Johnathon to come home and look after me." That last bit about Johnathon is a lie, but I know it'll smooth my exit for Mom.

She gives me a sympathetic look. "Of course, darling. Go home. Feel better. I'm sure Johnathon will look after you beautifully."

Jenna tries to come with me but I don't let her. We bicker over this for a few minutes. Minutes I would rather be anywhere than in this restaurant because I'm facing the table where Carla is sitting and she's so fucking amazing that I want to vomit again.

As I walk out of the restaurant, I think about the fact Mom didn't ask what was wrong with me. She didn't bother to ask after that detail.

I then chastise myself for thinking about that.

I do not need anyone noticing my details, asking after my details, or wanting anything to do with my details.

And goddamn the man who even made me aware of all of this.

20

KRISTEN - TWO MONTHS LATER

I STARE at the dress my stylist helped me choose for the party I'm holding this weekend. It's the annual party I throw each summer at my Hamptons home. It's one of *the* parties of the season to be seen at and almost everyone who is anyone always attends. This dress is all kinds of wrong. I'm sure of it.

I should have asked Jenna to style me. She always offers, but I never want to take up too much of her time since I know how busy she is with her work. Right now, though, I feel sick over not asking her. She would never have left me with this horrible dress.

Johnathon walks into our bedroom and past me into the bathroom. It's nine p.m. and he's just arrived home from work, and like he's done for the last few nights, he barely registers my presence.

"Oh, hello, Kristen," I say, unable to stop my bitter tone. "How was your day, darling? Good? Mine too."

He stops and turns back to me, his face a picture of irritation. "Is this how tonight's going to go?"

"I'd prefer it not to, but it's quite awful when your fiancé comes home from work and doesn't even say hi to you."

"I need to take a shower and eat some dinner before doing some more work. I don't exactly have the same kind of time you do, Kristen, to have a fucking conversation."

My eyes go wide.

My self-worth feels like it's been slapped.

"The same kind of time I do? What do you mean by that?"

"Fuck." He shoves his fingers through his hair. "Can we not get into this tonight? I'm days behind on this project and really need to get through a lot of work tonight."

"You've worked late every night for weeks, Johnathon. Why are you days behind?"

"You wouldn't understand."

Oh, no he doesn't. "What, because I don't have a paid job?"

He shakes his head. "No, I'm not doing this tonight." With that, he enters the bathroom, slamming the door behind him.

My dress is the furthest thing from my mind now.

Now, I'm angrier than I've ever been with him. I've had almost three months of this and I think I've reached the end of my patience. I think I'm finally done with being made to feel like *I'm* the problem. I seem to excel at finding men who are good at twisting everything around to that.

Deciding I need a stiff drink while I wait for him to finish his shower, I go in search of one. I'm on my way when I hear a succession of text messages come in on his phone. Somewhere in my messed-up mind and anger, I do something I have never done with any man. I locate his phone and read the messages sitting on his lock screen.

JULIE

That meeting was hectic at work today. But you made everything all better.

JULIE

I'm looking forward to seeing you tomorrow.

JULIE

I'm thinking about wearing this.

My hands shake as I take a guess at his pin to unlock his phone.

Who the fuck is Julie? And why is she texting my fiancé?

I guess his pin on my third attempt and suddenly my whole world lies in front of me. If I tap the Messages button, I'll have access to every conversation he's ever had. I'm not sure I'm ready for that.

A man who doesn't respect the trust his partner gives him is not a man who treats you well. I would never lie to you.

If I ever manage to get Bradford out of my head, it'll be the best goddamn day of my life. And if I read these messages and find he was right, I'm left with the biggest decision of my life. Stay or go. I never ever imagined being a woman who thought there *was* a choice, but here I am.

In spite of the nerves rushing me, and in spite of my

fear of what lies ahead, I tap the button and open Johnathon's messages.

I then tap the messages from Julie.

The last one sent was a photo of her in a sexy dress. A dress that is nowhere near appropriate for work.

I scroll their conversations for a long time. They've been talking for a long time. There's a lot of texts about work stuff, but in amongst that are very suggestive messages from Julie. On quite a few occasions, she's let him know she wanted to hook up. She promised him super explicit things. He hasn't ever replied back with anything sexual, but he hasn't exactly told her he's not interested.

He hasn't reminded her that he's fucking engaged.

"Kristen."

My head snaps up and I meet Johnathon's eyes. He does not look pleased to see me with his phone. I can't find it in me to care.

I hold the phone up. It feels far heavier in my hand than it is, but then, it's the thing between me and happiness right now. "Who the fuck is Julie?"

He scowls. "Don't use that kind of language. It doesn't suit you."

I grip the phone harder. "I don't give a fuck what suits me, Johnathon. I care that Julie told you she wants to get on her knees and suck your dick under your desk, and that you didn't bother to correct her thinking that you're available to have your dick sucked by anyone other than me." I throw the phone at him as anger crowds my veins. "Tell me who she is!"

He ducks to avoid the cell smashing into his face.

"Jesus Christ, Kristen. What the fuck has gotten into you?"

I jab my finger at him, seeing only red. "You! Months of you treating me like shit has gotten into me! And now, Julie! You need to explain that to me because if you don't, I think I may do something very fucking bad to you."

"Julie's a work colleague. Nothing more. I don't know why she texts me that stuff. I never respond to it. You would have seen that." He's talking in that voice I hate. The one that says *You're not intelligent enough to understand this.*

"Do not treat me like I'm dumb, Johnathon. I'm done with that."

"You're being a little hysterical now. How about we calm down and discuss this like adults."

The scream that has been trapped in my throat my entire life lets me know it's as done with me controlling it as I'm done with being treated like an idiot.

Hysterical?

I'll fucking show him hysterical.

I madly reach for the first thing I can find. Locating a vase, I throw it at him. While he ducks to avoid it smashing into him, my hands take on a life of their own. They're in a frenzy, reaching and throwing items at him. My whole body takes on a life of its own. It's like my limbs detach from my mind, desperate to escape the hold it's had on them for too long.

My body demands freedom.

My hands want to hit something.

My feet want to kick something.

My stomach wants a fucking end to the anxiety that's always had it in a tight hold.

My neck is frantic for a release from the tension that never stops hurting.

I throw item after item at Johnathon. I'm looking at him while I'm doing it, but I've disconnected, so I'm not processing everything that's happening. I'm only aware of his arms flying all over the place, his face turning red, and his mouth opening and closing. He's yelling at me, but I don't hear a word he's saying.

I want to break every item in our home.

Trash it all.

Hurt everything.

Make it all shatter like I am.

I continue my war on Johnathon and our home for what feels like a long time. I just keep going after him, forcing him here, there, and everywhere. He's not a small guy, but the anger that's flooded my body gives me the edge to drive this war.

It's not until I stumble around a coffee table that he manages to restrain me.

"Fucking hell." He wraps his arms tightly around me, yelling, "Stop!"

I let my scream loose.

I open my mouth and just let it all out.

Johnathon's arms go even tighter around me and he tries to cover my mouth with one of his hands. All the while, he's yelling words at me. Words I don't care to figure out. All I care about is letting all my feelings loose. Letting the scream that I think might never end out.

I have no idea how long this goes on.

When I finally reach the end of my scream, I'm breathless. My lungs cry out for air and I feel their pain just as keenly as I feel the pain in my heart.

"What in the actual fuck was that?" Johnathon demands as he lets me go.

"Do you still love me?" I find it odd that I'm looking at the man I've loved for years, yet it's as if I'm looking at someone I don't even know.

He clenches his jaw. "You didn't answer my question. What's going on?"

"My question is the more important one right now. Do you still love me?"

"Why?"

"Oh my God, Johnathon!" I yell. "Just answer my question."

He stares at me like I'm asking him to give me the world when that's the last thing he wants to give me. "I do still love you," he says too carefully for my liking.

"But?"

He blows out a long, harsh breath. "Fuck. But things have changed."

"What things?"

"I don't know about marriage. I'm not sure I'm ready for it."

The words no bride-to-be wants to hear three months out from their wedding.

My head spins.

My eyes swim with dots.

"You don't want to get married period? Or you don't want to get married to me?"

"I think I should move out for a while and get my head together."

Why can't men just fucking answer a question?

"Do you want to marry me? It's a yes or a no."

"I don't know."

I'm done.

I swear I'm done.

No, you're not, Kristen.

Think about this for a moment.

Think about everything you'll give up if you're done.

We don't want to be done.

I take a deep breath. "I will *not* be the bride who has to tell guests a week out from the wedding that it's off." I jab my finger at him and he has the good sense to look fearful of another war with me. "You move out. You take a break. And you figure this out fast."

He nods. "I do love you, Kristen."

"Just not enough to know for sure that you want to marry me."

While he packs his bag, I think about Julie and the fact we never did finish discussing her. I think about the fact I'm unsure I want to. It's the kind of conversation I desperately know I need to have while also desperately wanting to run from. Because if my gut is right, it means Bradford was right all along. It means my fiancé has cheated on me, lied to me, and not respected my trust.

It means my entire life will come crashing down.

It means I will have to make the kind of choice I've avoided my entire life.

My self-respect or my father's approval.

@thetea_gasp

OH, my poor heart, girlfriends. It's official: our girl @kristenblaise is single again. Rumors of splitsville circulated last week, but movers were spotted today at her condo. That's after the hot mess of her annual Hamptons party for the sparkling people over the weekend. The mess in which Kristen got drunk and let her hair down like we've never seen. Photos were shared anonymously with us showing her grinding all over three different men #hellyeah #getitqueen We want whatever she was drinking. But then @johnathonswindle's cheating #bodycount was the highest we've ever heard of, so we've no doubt that whatever she was drinking was needed #facts Sometimes, getting ghosted in the beginning of a relationship is the preferable option. Here's our advice, honey: say good riddance to trash, wipe your hands clean, and find yourself a new #zaddy. Goodness knows the line for your affections is long. We're staying tuned to see who you choose #zaddywatch

@thetea_gasp

HELL HATH no fury like a woman scorned. Especially if her name is @kristenblaise TBH we can't blame her, but holy wow, friends, have you seen her latest Insta post? #savageAF We bow down to you Kristen. We've never seen such bold moves. And we are here for all of them. In case you missed her post, girlfriend, she posted about burning @johnathonswindle's belongings. She also spent a huge chunk of his cash on clothes, shoes, jewelry, and a European vacation. Kristen is our new CEO of moving the F on. We can't wait to see her next move. And for those of you wondering what Johnathon is up to now... No one here cares, honey, and if you do, there's something wrong with you. Didn't you know? Girls run the world now.

23

BRADFORD

I THROW some whiskey down my throat and wonder what the hell I'm doing in this club at one a.m. in the middle of the week. Nightclubs aren't my scene but my brothers dragged me out tonight after telling me I've been working too hard lately.

The music that's louder than I'd prefer, the bodies packed together, the sticky alcohol on the floor, the sweat that's clinging to the air. None of this appeals to me and I make a mental note not to say yes to Callan or Gage again if a club like this is on their agenda.

Callan found himself two women to leave with forty minutes ago, and Gage's assistant called him half an hour ago with an urgent problem she needed his help with. I decided to end the night with one last drink before heading home. I should have just skipped the drink.

I finish my whiskey and stand from the couch where I've been sitting. I've been watching one particular woman dancing with two guys. She's sexy as hell but it wasn't her beauty that caught my eye. It was the way she's moving. Wild and free.

I continue watching her while I make my way out of the club. I've yet to see her face, and as I move closer, she turns in one of the guy's arms. Her head is thrown back and my eyes are glued to the wide diamond choker necklace that takes up half her slender neck. It's a bold statement piece that sparkles as much as the energy she's bathed in.

She brings her head forward and curls her hands around her dance partner's neck. I trace my gaze up her neck, to her mouth, to her eyes, and fuck me, my legs stop working.

It's Kristen.

She's cut her hair. It's short at the back and sides, and slightly longer on the top. It's an Audrey Hepburn-ish cut but longer and edgier. She's kept her same brunette color but has added hints of the sun in there. She's stunning and I can't take my eyes off her.

She's wearing a slinky, shimmering black dress that ends mid-thigh. The frill at the bottom has had a lot of my attention. Almost as much as the three tiny straps crisscrossing her back. Now, I take in the V of the dress between her breasts. I've never seen Kristen wear something that reveals as much skin as this outfit does. I've never seen her breasts but I'm staring at them now because that dress does a hell of a job of showing them off.

I watch her with the two men for a few minutes, both loving and hating what I'm seeing. Kristen's taste of freedom has been coming for too long, and while I've wanted it for her, I don't like seeing her sample it with these assholes.

They've got their hands where no one's hands should be on her. And their mouths that are all over her? I want to rip their lips from their faces.

I'm about to stalk over there and pull them both off her when she sees me. She doesn't stop dancing but she doesn't take her eyes off me once she finds me.

We watch each other for a few minutes. Every one of those minutes physically hurts me, in the same way every minute I've had to watch her with various men over the years has. When she kisses one of the guys, my body fills with an energy I've never known. It's intense, fierce, *feral*. When the other guy joins in, I'm unable to control my own actions.

My legs carry me faster to her than they've ever carried me to anyone or anything, and I've wrenched both the men from her before my brain can catch up. This has been coming for eight long years. I'm not thinking anymore; I'm only feeling.

"What the fuck, man?" One of the men glares at me while I force him away from Kristen.

The other guy is just as pissed off and shoves me.

"She's with me." I slam that statement down with force while readying myself to defend it.

"It sure doesn't seem like it." The first asshole throws out a challenge.

I direct my gaze to Kristen who's looking at me like she wants to both fuck me and kill me. I'm already hard for her; that look only gets me harder.

Glancing back at the two men, I say, in no uncertain terms, "Trust me, she is."

Kristen mutters something I can't hear because the music is too fucking loud and she's too fucking far away. She might only be one step from me, but even that is too far.

The guys look between Kristen and me. They seem to pick up on the vibes between us and give each other a look before walking away.

I close the distance between me and the woman I've wanted since the night I met her. She mutters something else I can't hear and turns her back to me as our bodies meet.

My arms slide around her waist, fitting there like they were made for it. Fuck, my body pressed to hers, my arms around her, and my dick against her ass are the best goddamn things I've ever known.

Kristen lifts her arms above her head and sways her hips to the beat. She might have turned her back to me, and she might have spent seven long months avoiding me, but she's not making any move to force my hands from her.

I've kept up with some of her moves since she broke her engagement to Johnathon a month ago. I've seen the actions of a woman who is hurting deeply but I've also seen the actions of a woman who has been trapped under the weight of her father's expectations her entire life. Her rebellion over the last month has been exhilarating to watch. Kristen told me years ago that she wanted to help women rise. She's finally letting *herself* rise. A beautiful phoenix I'm mesmerized by.

I bend my mouth to her ear while I dance with her. "I called you today."

She angles her head back slightly. "I didn't answer."

"I'm aware."

"You need to stop calling me. We're done."

"If we were done, you would have blocked my number."

"Trust me, I've thought about it." She presses her ass back against my erection, circling those hips, hypnotizing me even more.

We are so fucking far from done. There was a good reason I ended my engagement, and that reason had everything to do with Kristen.

I bring my hands to her hips and grip them while I grind my dick against her. Dropping my lips to her bare shoulder, I leave a kiss there before bringing my mouth back to her ear. "Why are you running from me?"

"I'm not running from you, Bradford. I've already done that. But it's no surprise that a man thinks any action I'm taking has to do with him. It's so fucking predictable."

Fuck, I love this fire she has. I've seen glimpses of it over the years, but now it's blazing and it looks good on her.

Owen has asked me why I've never gone to Kristen and told her I wanted her. Why I've let our shitty timing all these years get in the way. As much as I've wanted to go to her more times than I can count, Kristen has too much baggage surrounding her father for me to do that. A relationship would never have worked between us while her need for his approval was her driving force in life. She hasn't liked me challenging her over this; she'd be desperately unhappy with me doing that more often. And since the one thing I want more than to make her mine is her happiness, I've chosen not to pursue her.

"I like being called out by you," I say.

"Good, because if you keep harassing me, I'll do more of it."

I snake one hand around her waist and slowly glide it up her body to rest under her breast. "Do you want me to harass you, Kristen? Because I can assure you I've come nowhere near harassment levels yet. And I'm more than happy to up my game if that's your preference."

She pushes her ass back against me again. "Instead of you telling me what you think I want, how about I tell you what I do want?"

"I'd fucking love to hear what you want."

She turns in my embrace, killing me with the way she crushes her body to mine before curling her hands up my neck. When she pulls my face down to hers, my lungs almost stop working. Her eyes lock with mine for a beat and then she moves her mouth to my ear. "I want you to make me come. You scared away the men I'd lined up to do that, so now my orgasm is on you."

Now that she's facing me, I know she's been drinking. I don't think she's drunk, but the booze has loosened her up and I don't want to fuck her while she's in this state.

"No."

I expect her to argue with me but she doesn't. She keeps swaying her hips and says, "Well, that's a shame. I imagine you're good at giving a woman an orgasm. I would have liked to be treated to one from you."

She removes her hands from my neck and steps back.

I reach for her hand as she turns to walk away from me. "Where are you going?"

"I'm going to find someone to do what you won't."

Fuck.

This is her pain talking. I might support her uprising, but this isn't Kristen. This is her pushing her boundaries in an unsafe space.

"No, you're not."

She shoots me a scathing look that would cause a lesser man to wilt. "Why do men think it's okay to tell women what they can and can't do?"

"That's not my goal here. I want you to make your own choices, but I want them to be safe."

"That's still telling me what to do."

"You've been drinking. Put yourself in my shoes."

"I don't want to. I'm tired of putting myself in other people's shoes."

I've got two options here. Give her what she wants or let her go and find it with someone else. Just the thought of another man's hands on her is hellish. But besides that, allowing anyone to take advantage of her tonight isn't something I can do.

I blow out a frustrated breath. "Let me take you home, Kristen."

"You'll fuck me?"

Jesus, this is *not* her.

"If that's still what you want when we get there, yes. Although, I would have preferred our first time to be a whole lot different than this."

"Oh, don't fool yourself, Bradford. This won't ever happen again. There won't be a second time for us." She grips my shirt. "And I've just changed my mind. I want you to fuck me here."

"Fuck, no." Kristen spent a lot of time asking me questions about guys and sex when we were younger. We discussed her sex life enough for me to know she doesn't like having sex in public. And as much as she's pushing back against everything in her life, I can't see that having changed.

She gives me a look that can't be confused with anything but *Oh, yes, you are*. She grabs my hand and leads me off the dancefloor to a couch in one of the corners. The club is dark and the couches appear set up for this kind of thing. For maximum privacy. They've even lowered the music a little in this area.

I sit on a couch, expecting Kristen to join me. She doesn't. Instead, she dances in front of me, gyrating her hips while skimming one hand down over her body from her neck to her leg. She lifts her other arm above her head before bringing it down her body too. Her hand slows when it reaches her breast and she tweaks her nipple while biting her bottom lip. Keeping her fingers working that nipple, she slips her other hand under her dress and reaches for her pussy.

My hand is instantly on my dick and I stroke myself while watching her touch herself.

Kristen's hips move with the beat of the music and I have to work hard not to take hold of them and pull her down onto my lap so she can move them on me to the beat.

She dances for me for a few minutes before straddling me. She brings herself down slowly, rolling her hips all the way along my legs until her pussy is against my dick and her tits are against my chest.

Tracing one of the fingers she just had to her pussy over my lips, she says, "I've thought about your dick more often than I care to admit."

Hell.

Her scent fills me. I can't get enough of it and I can't recall the last time I was as hard as I am now.

I place one hand on her bare thigh while fighting with myself over putting my other hand where I want it. If this was happening between us in the way I'd have preferred, my hands and mouth would be *everywhere*. There would be no hesitation. "You have a filthy mouth."

She forces my lips apart wider and lets me taste her. "Are you complaining?"

"I'll never complain when you embrace yourself."

"It sounded like a complaint."

"Well, my delivery was off, then. It should have sounded like a statement of appreciation."

She grinds herself on me. "Touch me, Bradford."

I groan at how good she feels. How good she smells. How fucking good she tastes. "I am touching you."

"You have one hand on my leg. Very chaste of you." She brushes her lips against my ear. "I want you to do filthy things to me. Indecent, nasty things that you'll never forget. I want you to have trouble looking at me the next time you see me because you can't think about anything but the way I took your dick. The way I rode your fingers. And the way you ate me out."

My hands are on her face before she has time to take another breath, and my eyes have hers firmly in their grip. "Do you really want me to fuck you like that?"

Her breaths come faster. "Yes."

I search her eyes while my dick begs me to give her what she wants. I need to slow this down, though. I need to ensure she's aware of what she's asking for.

I tighten my hold on her. "I can give you all of that,

Kristen, but we're going to need a lot more space and privacy than we've got here."

She reaches for my hand and directs it under her dress. "Start here. Show me what you can do with your fingers. And then we'll move somewhere else so you can have all the space you need."

Before I can argue and try to get her to leave the club, she brings her mouth to mine and does the one thing I've thought about from the minute she stepped out of that elevator onto that rooftop all those years ago.

She kisses me.

She tastes like whiskey and longing.

Her hands thread through my hair while her lips explore mine. Slowly and then deeply. She moans into the kiss and it's like she's trying to get closer to me even though there's no physical way she can.

For a woman who's begged me to fuck her in ways that will create filthy memories between us, I would have expected a different kind of kiss. A *let's get down and dirty* kiss. Kristen surprises me with what she gives me instead.

I want hours of her like this but she doesn't give me that. She takes what she wants, ending the kiss to say, "I want your fingers inside me."

"I want your mouth back on mine."

"We can't all have what we want, Bradford." She guides my fingers closer to her pussy.

I finally begin giving her what she wants.

I rub her clit over the lacy fabric of her panties, not taking my eyes off her as the pleasure I'm giving works its way across her face. When she bites her lip again, I growl, "Kiss me and I'll touch you."

"You are touching me."

"No, I'm rubbing your clit. I'll fuck you with my fingers when you kiss me."

"I told you I want you to do nasty things to me. How about you start doing that? Take what you want yourself. Use me how you want."

Fuck.

I grip the back of her neck as I sit up straighter, every fiber in my being straining to take everything from her that she wants me to. I crash our mouths together, consuming every breath of hers, tangling our tongues, and showing her what she does to me. I reach inside her panties and find her more than ready for me.

She rocks with me as I push a finger inside her, moving in ways that I won't ever recover from.

With her kisses, her dirty talk, and the way her body fits with mine, Kristen is ruining me, one demand at a time.

She comes up from the kiss, panting for more. Her face is flushed so fucking beautifully. Her eyes are alive like I've never seen them.

I rub my thumb over her clit while fingering her.

"Fuck," she moans, circling her hips and arching her back while using my shoulder to hold herself up.

I slip my other hand into her dress, over her breast, and roll her nipple between my fingers. Dropping my lips to her collarbone, I kiss my way along it and up her neck to her mouth.

"Holy fuck, I'm going to come," she says, gripping my shoulders with both hands, her hips moving faster.

I kiss her, desperate to taste her again. She kisses me back, just as desperately.

We're reckless, frantic, wild.

This kiss, my fingers inside her; it's years of bad timing and missed connections taking control.

"Oh my God...fuck...Bradford..." Her fingers dig into my arms as she comes.

I drag my mouth from hers so I can see her experience an orgasm. She drops her head back as the pleasure moves through her and I commit every second of it to memory.

The curve of her throat.

The parting of her lips.

The pure ecstasy on her face.

Kristen is even more beautiful when she allows pleasure to control her. She's so fucking free.

When she finally looks at me again, she says, "Fuck you for being right."

I know what she's referring to without her elaborating.

Johnathon.

The ache I feel coming from her kills me. Fucking breaks my heart.

I want to pull her into my arms and tell her I'll fix this for her. That I'll make her happy. But I know that's a shortcut not worth a damn. We can't take away someone else's pain, can't fix the things that come from soul-deep baggage, can't make someone else happy. Those are the things in life that require a journey to hell and back to work through and can only be done by the person suffering.

"You're still angry with me," I say.

"I'm angry with everyone."

"I'm not the one you should be angry with."

She puts her hands to my chest, like she's trying to

push me away even though the look in her eyes says the complete opposite. "I know. I know it's irrational. I know it's unfair to you. I know it's fucked up. And yet, I can't, for the life of me, get rid of that anger. I'm angry with the whole fucking world. Including myself."

Now, *I'm* angry. I'm fucking angry that after all these years, after us working our way here to this moment, that *this* is where we are. That I'm taking the anger and hate that Johnathon earned. "So, what, everyone but me will get the Kristen that's moving on, finding herself, while I get the Kristen that wants to stay stuck in her anger?"

"I told you there is no us. You don't have to get any Kristen. Leave me with my anger and go live your life. God knows I don't want to inflict my hurt on you."

"Fuck, Kristen. When are you going to get it? I want you. I don't like that your anger is directed at me, but I don't want to leave you with it."

She tries to move off me but I quickly take hold of her hips and keep her where she is.

Still fighting against me, she demands, "When are *you* going to get it? I don't want to be with you."

"That's bullshit if ever I heard it."

Her eyes widen, but then, she's not used to me being so blunt. I've always been more careful with Kristen than with any woman. Even when she thought I wasn't being careful with my words, it was still more than I've given anyone. "It's not bullshit," she says. "Have I answered any of your calls this year? Have I sought you out? Did I come running to you after I broke up with Johnathon?"

"We both know the real reason why you haven't done any of those things. How about we address that? And how about you tell me when you're going to fucking do something about it?"

Her eyes widen even more. "I just got out of one bad relationship. I'm not about to start a new bad one."

"And the lies just keep coming." My anger is on a roll now. "Don't fool yourself that a relationship with me would be anything like the relationships you've had to date. You have a knack for selecting assholes. It perfectly complements your talent for keeping Daddy happy."

She slaps me before scrambling off my lap. Straightening her dress, she looks at me like she's wishing death upon me. "I believed you years ago when you told me you would be gentle. It seems I really do have a knack for choosing assholes."

I stand and look down at her as the sting from her hand still heats my cheek. I'm fucking drowning here. This is the first relationship in my life I feel powerless in. The fact it's the one relationship I want to work out is destroying me. "I never promised I'd be gentle. You're remembering that incorrectly. I only ever promised not to be violent."

"You need to look the meaning of that word up, then." She snatches her purse off the couch. "I'm going home and am going to forget tonight ever happened."

"We both know you won't ever forget what happened tonight."

With one last glare, she turns to stalk away, only getting two steps from me before I reach for her arm and turn her to face me again. This can't be how we leave this. Even with all the hurt we've hurled at each other, we can't fucking leave it like this.

"Tell me you want me," I demand.

"I don't," she throws back at me, her face twisting with the lie she's still clinging to.

I grip her arm harder and pull her to me. "Stop lying to me, Kristen. You were happy to tell me all the ways you wanted me to fuck you, tell me that you want me to love you."

Her breaths come hard and fast as she stares up at me. Those beautiful eyes of hers are filled with a storm of emotions. I want that storm. I want all of it. With her. I'll take her hate. I'll take her anger. I'll take everything if only she'll let me love her.

"I want you." Those three little words choke out of her and mean the fucking world to me. "But I can't give you what's left of me. I will ruin you and I refuse to do that."

Doesn't she see? She's already ruined me.

"I want all of you, Kristen. Every good part. Every beautiful part. And every dark, painful, shattered part. You won't ruin me. Not when you're the one thing I need to breathe."

Tears spill down her cheeks as she shakes her head madly at me. "All this time, I thought I had to fix myself so that everyone would love me, when what I had to do was *love myself*." She wipes her tears but they just keep falling. "I can't tell you I want you to love me because I can't promise you anything in return. I can't even promise myself a fucking thing." She moves into me and pulls my face down to hers so she can kiss me. It's a heartbreaking kiss. I feel the agony deeply in my soul.

And then she lets me go, destroying me completely when she whispers, "Goodbye, Bradford."

PART II

17 MONTHS LATER

24

KRISTEN

"TINDER CAN SUCK A BIG, hairy dick. I'm done with it." I gulp some wine. "And while we're at it, I'm also done with recharging my vibration. Oh, and flossing. I'm done with that too." I finish my glass of wine and look around the table at my sister and her friends who I'm having afternoon tea with. "I also think I should be done with men."

Holy heck, is it hot in here?

And where did all those words come from? I don't say things like that.

I pull at my blouse and undo the top button.

I'm really hot. Like, *overheated* hot.

Maybe the heating is set too high.

I glance around the elegant dining room. It's one of my favorites in Vegas with its soaring coffered ceiling, custom Bernadaud chandeliers, subtle touches of opulent gold throughout, large-scale landscape paintings, and floor-to-ceiling Las Vegas Boulevard backdrop. However, today the blended sound of laughter and conversation, along with the tinkle of glasses and soft music, is too much for me.

I'm usually good with busy. I generally live for it. But not today. Not when I feel like I can't possibly squeeze one more thing into my head.

"You should not give up flossing," Poppy says. "Quit Tinder. Quit recharging your vibration." She cocks her head and narrows her eyes at me. "What does that even mean?" Before I can answer, she carries on. "And yeah, maybe you should quit men for a while. But don't give up flossing."

"Do you floss?" I ask. I've always been a flosser, but I recently read that less than fifty percent of Americans floss. Quite honestly, I could do with those extra minutes in my life, so I've been contemplating giving this habit up.

She nods. "Fuck yes. I will never not floss. And I make sure Seth does too. No flossing, no blowjobs."

Adeline arches her brows. "That's a rule in your relationship?"

Poppy looks at her like she just asked a stupid question. "Is it not in yours?"

Charlize laughs as Adeline blinks. It's not often Adeline does the slow blink. Nothing usually surprises her.

"Jameson and I have never discussed our flossing habits," Adeline says.

Poppy looks positively stunned. She also appears lost for words, which is a rare occurrence. Poppy normally has a lot to say on most matters. She stares at Adeline for a few moments before bringing her gaze back to me. "Don't stop flossing. And when you find your husband, don't be like Adeline. Flossing must have boundaries surrounding it."

"I'd like to point out that we both floss," Adeline says. "We just don't talk about it or have rules about it."

My sister, Jenna, looks at me. "*I'd* like to point out that we've just dedicated time I never imagined dedicating to discussing flossing."

"It's an important discussion, Jenna," I say. "I'm trying to reclaim time in my life and I'm wondering if flossing is a pointless exercise."

"I agree," Jessica says. "Reclaiming time is important."

Lorelei looks at her. "Right, but flossing is important too. My dentist is fixated on it, always telling me to do it."

"Stop," Poppy says with a stern voice. "Just stop. This discussion is finished." She points at Adeline. "You're going to think about some new boundaries." She points at the rest of us. "You all are too." She then jabs her finger at me. "And you're going to never stop flossing, and you're also going to figure out where to find better men to date because quite honestly, I think those Tinder men are messing you up. If you had some good dick in your life, I am absolutely certain that giving up flossing wouldn't even be a thought in your head."

She's right.

Those Tinder men *are* messing me up.

In much the same way the heating in here is messing me up.

I undo another button on my blouse and fan my face with my hand.

"It's hot in here, right?" I say to everyone.

Jenna shakes her head. "No, Kris, it's not." She frowns as she looks me over. "Are you okay?"

I draw in a long breath and then release it while making eye contact with the waiter and pointing at my wine glass to indicate I'd like another. Then, looking at my sister as the girls move on to a conversation about what they want to do after dinner tonight, I say, "No, I don't think I am." I'm many things, but okay is not one of them. *And* I'm hot. It will be a miracle if I don't start stripping soon.

I didn't want to come this weekend. After a particularly awful date last night, in which the guy told me he was friends with Johnathon and that he'd heard about my "inability to provide adventure in the bedroom", all I wanted to do was stay home and lick my wounds.

Jenna forced me to come. She said it would do me good to be with people. This is her group of friends we're here with, not mine. They get together once a week, and I've tagged along a few times over the last couple of months. They also come on these couples' weekends every couple of months. I like these women, but the entire friendship group experience is foreign to me, so I find it awkward at times.

For instance, sharing that you won't give your husband a blowjob if he doesn't floss isn't something I'd discuss in a group setting. I'd talk about that with my sister privately, but I wouldn't broadcast it to the world.

Except, lately it feels like everything is changing.

It feels like *I'm* changing.

My thoughts. My feelings. My behavior.

All of it.

And it's got me flustered, bewildered, *unsure*.

I mean, telling these women that I think I should be

done with men? Those are not words I ever imagined coming out of my mouth.

I don't think I should trust myself at the moment.

My therapist thinks I should.

She's all for my confusion. She tells me it's exciting because it means transformation is happening. I think I maybe need a new therapist.

This doesn't feel anything like what I thought transformation would feel like. I imagined sunshine and smiles. Happiness like I've never felt. Skipping through a field of flowers. Well, maybe not that, but certainly not this state of *what the actual fuck is going on*. And yes, the part of me that likes her f-bombs roams a lot freer these days. The other parts of me have given up trying to control her. *Show compassion to all your parts, Kristen.* Yeah, I'm still figuring out how that even works but my therapist assures me I'm doing well. The people pleasing part of me likes that approval so we keep going back for more.

Jenna's face softens with compassion. "Is this because of that asshole last night?"

Charlize, who is sitting on the other side of me, over-hears Jenna's question and leans in. "What asshole?"

The waiter reappears with my drink, and I take a long sip before answering her. In that moment, I have all eyes back on me.

I meet their gazes while formulating an answer for Charlize. I'm okay with telling them who he was, but then they'll want to know *why* he was an asshole and I'm not interested in talking about that.

I throw out the name of the guy from last night and

follow it up with a wave of my hand and: "He was a jerk and I've moved on."

"He was more than a jerk," Jenna says.

"What did he do?" Lorelei asks.

I make eyes at my sister. She shouldn't have said that because now these girls aren't going to let this go. Then to everyone, I say, "What they all do. He wasn't interested in getting to know me."

"Kris," Jenna says softly. "Don't do that."

"Do what?" I take another long sip of my drink.

"Don't brush this off. You were really hurt last night. Talking about it might help," Jenna says.

I stare at her.

Actually, it's more like the beginning of a glare.

She knows that talking is not my thing.

Jenna's a talker. A digger. She likes to dig all over the damn place. Into her feelings. Into everyone else's feelings. Into places she has no business digging.

I am *not* a digger.

All the thoughts and feelings I've buried? Consider them laid to rest. I never want to revisit them. Not even with my therapist. But she's a pushy woman and forces me into digging. I really *should* find a new therapist. One who can't see, hear, or speak.

Jenna reaches for my hand and squeezes it as Adeline says, "Anything said here stays here, Kristen."

I'm about to find a way to change the conversation when the sound of plates crashing to the floor disturbs my concentration. It turns into a whole commotion a few tables away and it throws me off.

My brain rebels at the overstimulation of noise and

heat. That's the only reason I have for opening my mouth and allowing words out I am certain I'll regret. "He knows Johnathon and told me that he's heard I bring no spice to the bedroom."

"I hope you didn't listen to him," Jessica says.

"I ended the date soon after that."

"Good," Adeline says. "What an asshole."

He absolutely was, and yet I've had his words stuck on repeat. It seems it doesn't matter how much fucking therapy I do; people still have the power to cause my insecurities to blaze brightly.

"The thing is," I say slowly, surprising myself that I'm still talking about this, "it helped make sense of something another guy said to me a couple of months ago."

"What did he say?" Jenna asks. I didn't share this with her last night.

I run my fingers around the stem of my wine glass, staring at it before looking at her. "He said something during sex. Something about loving a good vanilla girl. Then, later after we were finished, he told me he was sorry that Johnathon had treated me so badly, and that he appreciated what Johnathon never did. It was all very weird and I never saw him again after that, but now I think he was referring to Johnathon wanting more than I gave him in the bedroom."

Holy hell, I don't care what Jenna says, it *is* hot in here.

Jenna reaches for my hand and squeezes it. "Whatever he meant isn't something you should even think about. Don't let these guys screw with you, Kris."

"I imagine he doesn't floss," Poppy says. "Fuck him.

You don't need a man like that in your life." She raises her glass to me. "*He* can suck a big, hairy dick." She takes a sip of her cocktail.

Charlize laughs, as does Jenna.

Adeline smiles at me before taking a sip of her cocktail and then says, "Whether you're into vanilla or kink doesn't say anything about the heart of you. It's just one preference of yours in a whole life of preferences."

Adeline is my sister's business partner and I liked her the minute I met her last year. She was one of the world's top fashion models before starting her own company. Fashion and beauty are her things. They're also mine, but that's not why I feel drawn to her. It's the way she sees my pain and says things like this to me.

She doesn't even need me to dig deep for her. She just gets me.

I can't deny that while navigating my way around this whole friendship group experience isn't something that comes naturally to me and causes me some anxiety, I like not feeling judged by these women. I like feeling accepted however I come.

I return Adeline's smile. "Thank you for saying that." I didn't even know I needed to hear it.

My phone sounds with a text and I check it while the conversation carries on about the New York dating scene.

PHILLIP

What are you doing tonight?

Phillip and I have been on-again, off-again for almost a year now. Our latest off period started two months ago and I'm not sure we'll have another on period.

Another message comes through.

PHILLIP

I miss you, Kristen.

I'm having dinner with friends tonight.

PHILLIP

Cancel and come over to my place instead.

Oh, Annabelle's not available tonight?

PHILLIP

That's not fair.

It's very fair.

PHILLIP

I told you it's not serious with her.

And I told you I'm not interested in sharing you, Phillip.

His reply doesn't come straight away. He takes a couple of minutes.

PHILLIP

I'll end it with her.

You do that.

PHILLIP

I'm serious.

I am too.

PHILLIP

I'll call you tomorrow after I speak with her.

I inhale a long breath and put my phone down again.

There's definitely something wrong with me.

The old me would have handled that conversation very differently.

The new me isn't even convinced she wants Phillip to end things with Annabelle.

Oh God, was my therapist wrong about my transformation? Is this an actual mid-life crisis?

Is that why I'm so hot too?

Early menopause?

Jesus.

I'm not even thinking like myself.

This is how I imagine Jenna's brain looks inside. A hot mess.

My brain is usually ordered. Arranged. Tidy.

I'm the sister who always has herself together. Well, except for that month after my breakup with Johnathon. But we don't ever talk about that time in my life.

Right now, I don't even know where the real Kristen is. She's certainly not sitting here having afternoon tea.

"You should come to the spa with us tomorrow," Charlize says, jolting my attention back to the group.

Good God, *no.*

Jenna's told me all about their spa days. Hours of all that emotional sharing they do with each other? No, thank you. My life is complete without all that. I may have tagged along for the weekend, but I made it clear to my sister I wasn't in for the Saturday spa day that's become their tradition. I'll find my own spa to go to, by myself.

I force a smile. "Thank you. I'll think about it."

Poppy gives me a knowing look. "That's code for *no fucking way.*"

Adeline nods. "It really is."

The good girl in me, the one I'm doing my best to ditch on the side of a road somewhere, dies a little on the inside at being called out like this. Clearly, my therapist still has her work cut out for her with that part of me. "No, I promise it's not. I don't want to intrude on your time together is all."

Charlize shakes her head. "You're not intruding on anything, Kristen. We'd love you to come."

Adeline's phone saves me from enduring more of this conversation. It rings, and when she checks who the caller is, she announces to everyone, "Oh, this should be good." Her tone implies that whatever it is, it likely *won't* be good.

Jenna exchanges glances with her, the kind that business partners share when they're on the same page. I'm guessing this has something to do with their work.

Adeline pushes her chair back and stands. "Let's take this outside," she says to Jenna who promptly stands and follows her out of the restaurant.

I use the opportunity to excuse myself and go to the bathroom. I'm forty minutes into this afternoon tea and need a moment to gather myself.

A text sounds from my phone as I enter the restroom.

MOM

> Darling, I just heard that Michael Randall is single again. He'll be at the gala next Saturday night. I think you should consider changing your dress choice. Perhaps to that gold dress we saw last week.

My chest tightens as I read her text.

Heat flushes my skin *again*.

And with the thoughts racing through my mind, I know I really *am* in the middle of a fucking mid-life crisis rather than a transformation.

Galas are my thing.

Socializing is my thing.

I may not have been built for friendship group dinners or spa days, but I excel at parties and galas.

Knowing the right people. Networking with the right people. Connecting the right people. I could do those things in my sleep.

Lately, though, things feel off.

I'm growing bored.

I want more in life. Different.

I don't want to attend this gala.

And Michael Randall?

I'm just not interested.

And that right there is perplexing because Michael is handsome, successful, and from what I know, a good man.

Another text comes in while I'm fighting with my brain.

MOM

Are you free tomorrow for lunch? We should strategize.

I reach to undo another button on my blouse, at which point I realize I can't undo any more. I'm already showing too much cleavage.

When my phone sounds with another text, I almost throw it across the bathroom.

I take a moment before reading the message.

If I was still recharging my vibration, I'd likely close my eyes and recite one of those ridiculous affirmations Jenna put me onto. *All I need is within me right now.* No, thank you. Not for me. And as far as I'm concerned, anyone who thinks reciting affirmations will fix anything in their life needs a good talking to. Not to mention a list of practical tasks they'd be better spending their time on.

I don't even know what a vibration is, let alone how to recharge it. Jenna tried explaining it, but I swear she was talking in another language.

Another godforsaken text lights up my phone and I finally, *finally*, lose my last thread of sanity.

"No, I don't want to wear that gold fucking dress!" I screech at my phone while stabbing at it to open the messages. "And I don't want to bat my fucking lashes at Michael Randall, or make small talk with him, or sell my soul for a fucking date with him!"

By the time I get all those words out of me, I'm breathing hard and fast.

My head may explode any minute.

And I'm sweating.

My blouse is sticking to me, which is just another perplexing thing because I don't perspire. Even when I exercise, I barely break a sweat.

I glance down at my phone and note the second text wasn't from my mother. It was from Lila James, a girl I went to school with. I read her message first.

LILA

> Hi Kristen, just a quick heads up that our annual reunion will be in January now rather than April. An invitation will go out, but I wanted to give you extra notice. The new date is January 14. Looking forward to seeing you there.

I thought her text would be far less of an assault to my mind than Mom's.

I was wrong.

I now have six weeks to find someone to escort me to that class reunion. Which usually would be fine, but when one is in the middle of a mid-life crisis and apparently contemplating asexuality (if one's extreme disinterest in Michael Randall is anything to go by) the last thing one wants to do is search for a date to a reunion. I have a mind to challenge her on the regularity of these reunions. Most classes hold them every five or ten years, but no, not our class. We're overachievers. Lila insists on seeing everyone every year.

My early menopause kicks in harder and I contemplate removing every scrap of material from my body. I'm halfway through that thought when a woman enters the bathroom. She doesn't notice me before locking herself into a cubicle, which is a good thing. I'm in no state to be seen by anyone right now.

I switch to my mother's message.

MOM

> I just heard that Andrew Barry is also attending the gala. He's just back from London after expanding his company. I'm going to ask Candy to change the seating plan so you're at a table with both Andrew and Michael.

This is too much. And suddenly, I'm aware of where today's fresh round of hell is coming from. I've finally reached the end of my lifelong patience with my mother and her matchmaking.

I can't do it anymore. Not for a second longer.

Yes, I want to find love, but these days I no longer think about dating in the way I used to.

I let go of many things in my life after I broke up with Johnathon, including all the emphasis I put on getting married. I date now to find a man who will love me how I should be loved and I don't hesitate to let them know when they don't. Never again will I end up with another man who cheats on me, lies to me, or disrespects me in any way.

I took the job I got at my father's magazine and ran with that. I put all my efforts into building a career in publishing, working my way up from the entry-level job he gave me to become the Assistant Content Product Manager. My promotion had nothing to do with my father and everything to do with my dedication to my work. It turns out being able to say *I'm proud of you* to yourself feels even better than hearing it from someone else.

I've fought Dad every step of the way to keep that job.

He only offered it to me because he thought I was marrying Johnathon. He thought I'd completed my "mission" in life and whatever I did after that didn't matter. And while he didn't want to give it to me after my broken engagement, I forced him to and my mother supported me in that.

I had to let go of my involvement with gala planning, but that was a trade-off I was willing to make. However, I still socialize almost as much as before I began working because I'm focused on building a strong network that I hope will be invaluable when I find a way to pursue my dream of helping women.

As another text from Mom lands on my phone, I decide the nun life seems more appealing every day. I'd miss my job but I wouldn't have to scroll dating apps, go on date after date, engage in boring fucking conversations with men I honestly couldn't care less about, or pretend to enjoy mediocre sex. And God, I could stop worrying about my hair, my face, my body, my everything.

With all these thoughts scrambling my mind, I exit the bathroom in search of more wine. I don't usually drink this much, but if an early mid-life crisis doesn't demand liquor, I don't know what does.

I take it as a sign from the universe that I'm meant to have another drink when the first person I see is a waiter holding a tray of the complimentary wine.

"Thank you," I say as I accept a glass, which I have to my lips within a second.

I'd like to say I sip my drink, but guzzle may be the more appropriate word for what I do. I'm halfway toward emptying the glass when a new wave of heat does its best to melt me and I decide I need to get out of here. If even for just a few minutes, I need to escape in search of cooler air.

I turn to leave and run smack bang into a hard chest. What's left of my wine spills all over my white blouse as strong hands grip my biceps to steady me. It all happens so fast, and since my mind is in a hot mess, it has trouble keeping up with what's happening.

When a deep voice I know intimately says, "Kristen," my head jerks up to see if I'm hallucinating. To see if I've just imagined Bradford Black into existence.

Arresting blue eyes meet mine.

Bradford's eyes.

Eyes that are imprinted on my soul.

No, no, *no*.

He can't be here. I know he's part of my sister's group, but Jenna never told me he was coming this weekend. I would *never* have come if I knew.

He frowns, the lines on his forehead etching their way into his tanned skin.

Bradford has a face I could stare at forever.

His bone structure is chiseled to perfection with high cheekbones I swoon over.

And then there's his full lips.

I don't want to think about them.

I can't think about them and what they're capable of because I will lose the remaining pieces of my sanity if I do.

But, *oh God*, my body remembers and if I thought I was hot before, I had no idea what hot really is.

His grip on me tightens. "Are you okay?"

"Do I look like I'm okay? Thanks to you, I've ruined my new Chanel blouse."

The concern I saw in his eyes a moment ago disappears completely and in its place is the cold glare I've been treated to every time I've seen him over the last nine months. "Thanks to me?"

I pull out of his hold. "*Yes*. You ran into me and now" —I look down at my wine-soaked top—"I'm covered in wine."

My brother-in-law, Beckett, gains my attention when he interrupts us. *How did I not even see him there?* He eyes Bradford. "Jameson just texted. He's with Seth and Owen. They're about ten minutes away. And Ashton, and Jack aren't far behind."

Bradford nods, not removing his eyes from mine. "I'll be a minute."

After Beckett leaves us, Bradford says, "Let the record show, I did not run into you. It was the other way around."

This man is infuriating in his ability to argue with me. I refuse to engage in an argument with him over this. Instead, I snap, "Why are you here?"

"My guess is the same reason you are. I was invited."

"Don't be smart with me, Bradford. I'm not in the mood."

"Neither am I. I was simply stating the obvious."

Oh my God, if there is one man in the world who has the ability to ruffle me, it's Bradford. Consider me ruffled.

"Will you be at dinner tonight?" I demand.

"Yes."

"Breakfast tomorrow?"

"Yes."

"Dinner tomorrow night?" Jenna told me all the guys will be out golfing tomorrow, so I know he won't be at lunch.

"Kristen, I'll be at every meal."

I mentally start planning a flight home. One that leaves in the next hour. I knew I should have licked my wounds at home.

"I'll stay out of your way just like I'm sure you'll stay out of mine," he says. I don't miss the subtext relating to my *talent for avoidance* that he's brought up as often as possible over the years, and I sure as hell don't miss the arctic air filling the space between us.

"There are only fourteen of us here. You will be in my way even if you try not to be."

He looks at me like he's assessing the greatest problem of his day. Of his month. Of his life. "I remember a time when you would have begged for me to be in your way."

"That time has long passed. You made sure of that."

The slight arch of his brow drives me insane. It's so fucking superior. "I see you're still as good at lying to yourself as you always were."

"And I see you've been sharpening your asshole skills." How we ended up here I will never know, but Bradford is now the master when it comes to hostility and I'm always caught unawares.

He works his jaw as the chill vibrating from him turns positively freezing. "If you ask for something, Kristen, don't be surprised when you get it."

Ask for something?

I'm left wondering what the hell I asked for as he walks away from me. I watch his sure strides, taking in the hard set of his shoulders while I rack my brain for the answer to my question.

Everything began changing for us ten months ago. I hadn't heard from Bradford since the night I begged him to fuck me. Then, he showed up at my condo asking me if I was ready yet. I knew instantly what he meant and I didn't have the answer for him that he wanted. I'd done a lot of work on myself but I was nowhere near ready for him. I wasn't even sure I'd ever be ready because Bradford deserved so much more than I might ever have to give.

We fought.

You're happy to fuck other men but you're not happy to be with me?

I felt his hurt. God, how I felt that. But if my therapist has helped me understand one thing, it's that we can't give fully to others when we haven't given to ourselves first. I've spent a lifetime giving, giving, *giving*. That had to stop before I could even begin to heal.

I couldn't ease his hurt because I was still hurting too much myself.

Six weeks later, I read about his engagement to Cecelia Aniston and I knew our last chance to be together was gone because the name of his fiancée signaled that this wasn't a marriage based on love. This was a political move, and that was the clear sign to me that we would never be together.

Bradford has moved on for good. He's now chasing

his lifetime ambition of becoming the president of the United States one day.

I'm not sure I'll ever recover from losing him. But if anything can help me with that, it's this new asshole side he wears so well.

If I could go back to that night we met nine years ago and change everything, I would.

25

BRADFORD

I WALK AWAY from Kristen and just like every other time I do that, my legs don't want to work.

Fuck.

If I'd known she'd be here this weekend, I would have stayed home. I've got too much I need to focus on and the only thing in the world that has ever been able to distract me is Kristen Blaise. Regardless of anything I've said to her, I don't want to walk away from her. And I don't want her to walk away from me. But if the years have taught me anything, it's that Kristen doesn't want to run to me, only from me.

Kristen isn't the one who got away. She's the one I never got.

My father drags me from my thoughts when I receive a text from him.

DAD

Sources tell me Senator Adler will be indicted for fraud soon.

> How soon?

DAD

> Likely within the next month. Possibly as soon as two weeks.

> Good. Keep me updated.

Adler looks like he'll be my ticket into the Senate. If he is indicted, his New York Senate seat will become vacant. Governor Wakefield has indicated that he'll select me to fill it.

I slip my phone back into my pocket and make my way to the table where everyone's sitting. As I take a seat, Jenna finds my gaze. "Where's Kristen?"

"She left."

Jenna frowns at that before turning to Beckett and saying something while pushing her chair back. Watching her walk away from the table, I wonder how much she knows about me and her sister. I suspect not much since I'm the guy Kristen kept to herself, and Jenna has never given me any indication that she's aware of what happened between us.

My phone sounds with a message from my assistant and I deal with that while the girls discuss their spa day plans for tomorrow. It's a work problem that takes five minutes of my time. I've just finished with that when my brother texts me.

HAYDEN

> I thought we were done with the marriage contract?

I frown. I thought so too.

> We are.

HAYDEN

> You might want to talk with your fiancée.
> I've just received an email from her.

Christ.
Cecelia will be the fucking death of me.

> Forward it to me.

HAYDEN

> Done. I won't do anything until I hear
> back from you.

My attention circles back to the girls when laughter erupts around the table.

Adeline catches my eye. "It's good to see you, Bradford. You've been working too much lately. We've missed you."

I was dragged into this group six months ago when my best friend, Owen, met the love of his life, Charlize. I never had a chance in hell of not joining with Charlize in control. She has a magnetic way about her that I'm convinced would encourage people to follow her into outer space if that's where she decided she wanted to go. The first time I met her, she dropped into Owen's place while we were in the middle of a dinner party. She stayed for dinner and by the end of the night she had the women eating out of her hand without even trying. She had me eating out of it from the second time we met, something his ex-wife never managed to achieve.

Over the last six months, I've enjoyed dinner with the couples every few weeks, caught up with them at various galas, and have now joined them on two of these Vegas weekends. I'd never experienced a couples' weekend away before they invited me and didn't think I'd enjoy it. However, here I am again, and not because Charlize twisted my arm.

I look at Adeline. "I agree, I have been working too much."

She smiles. "Congratulations on For Me. I can't wait to see what you guys do with that app."

She's referring to my latest investment in a start-up tech company that's developing a mental health app called For Me. My work on this deal is part of what's kept me from the group over the last month. Mostly though, it's been the fundraising and PR work I've been doing for my political campaign that's kept me busy.

"Thank you. I believe we'll do important work through the app."

"I do too," she says as her husband, Jameson, arrives with Owen and Seth, Poppy's husband.

"Dinner has been pushed back half an hour due to a mix up with reservations," Jameson says to the group. It's his hotel we're staying in and he doesn't look pleased about this mix up.

While the group discusses dinner, Charlize, who is sitting next to me, leans in and nudges shoulders. "I'm so glad you came."

I turn and catch her warm smile. "I suspect you would have found a way to kidnap me if I hadn't."

Her smile morphs into a full grin. "Now we're getting somewhere. Seriously, though, Owen was so excited when you said yes."

I arrow my brows. "So excited?"

"That's girl speak. Translated to bro speak, he casually told me you said yes and then said something in golf speak about 'only birdies' for him during your game tomorrow. I still have no idea what that means, but I know it will make sense to you. What I took from the whole conversation was that he was so excited to have his best friend along for the weekend."

"He won't be so excited when he's hitting out of the rough tomorrow. Your boy has been off his game lately."

"I love it when you guys talk to me in a different language."

"If you played a game with us every now and then, it wouldn't be a different language."

"That's a no from me."

One of the things I appreciate about Charlize is her determination to give Owen space to maintain his friendships. I know her choice not to play golf with us is for two reasons: that determination, and because she doesn't really enjoy the game.

"Perhaps one day you'll find the same taste for golfing that you have for hiking."

Poppy, Charlize's cousin, hears this and looks at me. "No woman in the history of women ever preferred golfing to hiking, Bradford. It disturbs me that you would even consider that a possibility. I think you need to find new hiking buddies because it sounds like yours aren't doing it right."

The entire table is now in on our conversation and laughter breaks out at the hiking reference, which is a sex reference. That second night we spent time together, Charlize and I had a conversation while she was drunk; a conversation in which she began referencing sex as hiking. It's now a common topic with this group.

Adeline raises her wine glass. "To men who hike well."

Poppy lifts her glass and gives Adeline a pointed look. "And to men who floss."

Adeline rolls her eyes but laughs and nods. "To women who like to boss other women into better boundaries."

Owen eyes me. *You got any idea what they're talking about?* I give him a look back. *Not a fucking clue.* He nods. *Sounds about right.*

Time spent with these women can be enlightening as to what women think about many topics but generally, I wade my way through most of it without any notion of what they're talking about.

Charlize leans in again and asks quietly, "How's Cecelia?"

"Next question."

"Okay, I'll rephrase it. How are you?"

"I'm good, Charlize. You don't have to worry about me."

"It's my job as your second best friend to worry about you."

"My second best friend?"

"Yes, surely being your best friend's fiancée makes me your second best friend by default."

If there's one person who never fails to draw me from a mood, it's Charlize. The things she comes out with always make me smile.

My phone sounds with a text as I think about this.

CECELIA

I take it Hayden has contacted you regarding my email to him today.

Fuck.

I look at Charlize. "You woke the dragon from her slumber and now I have to make a call."

"Should I order you a whiskey?"

I stand. "You should order two." I'm going to need both in quick succession after this call.

My phone is to my ear by the time I exit the restaurant. "What's going on, Cecelia? I thought we'd finalized everything."

"Yes, as usual you think that what you say goes, Bradford. It doesn't."

I rake my fingers through my hair as frustration courses through my veins. "Care to explain what that means because I haven't a fucking clue."

"There are a lot of things you don't have a fucking clue about. This particular one involves our social calendar. Perhaps if you'd bothered to read the email that I'm sure Hayden forwarded you, you'd know this."

"Jesus. I'm away with friends, which you know. I haven't had a chance yet. Perhaps if you'd bothered talking with me first, we could have avoided this conversation."

"That would have been possible if you actually talked to me. Since you prefer to avoid me, having conversations proves difficult. Going through your lawyer works wonders at getting your attention."

I should have said no when my father presented Cecelia Aniston as the perfect candidate for a wife. I knew it at the time, but I allowed my ambitions to get in the way, particularly when he pointed out the benefits to our family if we joined the Blacks with the Anistons. *The power couple of this generation*, he'd said. I've no interest in being part of a power couple, but I am interested in political power. I was blinded by that and now I'm paying the price. I can only hope it's a price worth paying.

"Okay, so talk to me now. What do you want?"

"I want a guarantee that you'll commit to a social calendar that includes multiple functions every weekend."

"Marrying for convenience is all about being seen socially, Cecelia. That's a given as far as I'm concerned."

"I don't think it is. You certainly haven't committed in the way I would have preferred during our engagement."

"That's bullshit."

"It's not, and please don't use that kind of language with me. You know I don't care for it."

I inhale a long breath.

Dealing with Cecelia requires every ounce of patience I possess. She's spent the last nine months doing her best to steal every last speck of it with her demands for us to socialize, to give interviews together, and to act in ways that are acceptable to her.

Finally, I say, "I've set down what I see as a reasonable social schedule for us going forward. I've agreed to certain conditions for interviews, and I've committed to an annual joint vacation. Anything beyond those things is not required to reach our goal."

"You're underestimating what's required then, Bradford. Becoming president of the United States is going to take everything you have to give and then some. We need to revisit the contract. I want it stipulated that you agree to every weekend, both days, because as it stands, you haven't. You've been very vague as to what you intend. Oh, and we need to have two children, not one."

I should have had Charlize order me three whiskeys. Or better yet, a never-ending fucking supply.

At this point, the only thing going for me is the fact Cecelia isn't into men. Otherwise, I'm convinced our marriage contract would also make demands for me to fuck her on a schedule.

"I'll read over the email from Hayden and spend the weekend considering your requests. You'll hear back from us on Monday."

"Make it first thing Monday. I want this resolved by close of business that day. And don't forget we have dinner with my parents on Monday. Do not be late."

Whoever said power tends to corrupt, and absolute power corrupts absolutely was dead on the money. Cecelia knows the power she holds over me with this marriage and I have no doubt that power will corrupt her over time.

She wants me to consider her new requests this weekend. I realize now that what I'll actually be considering is whether I'm willing to hand any of that power over to her after all.

26

KRISTEN

WHY I still scroll Instagram is a mystery to me. Using the app for platform building is one thing, but casually scrolling it is a whole other beast. Early Saturday morning, I'm busy minding my own business in my suite after taking a shower when a friend sends me the link to a beauty product she knows I love that has been sold out for weeks. I click the link and it takes me to Insta, and right after that, I tap something I didn't intend to tap and end up on Annabelle's page. *The* Annabelle that Jenna had to endure when she first started dating Beckett, and the one I'm now enduring in my off period with Phillip.

I am not a fan of this woman but (shoot me now), I'm intrigued by the earrings she's wearing in the photo I'm looking at, so I tap the post. For what, I have no earthly idea. After that, I'm one scroll away from being sucked into the vortex.

Minutes later, I land on her story (I know, I can't even with myself either) that features a video of her with

Phillip at dinner last night. They're laughing and kissing, and her hands are all over him.

I wasn't convinced I wanted anything more to do with Phillip, and now I know for sure I don't because now I know he really is full of shit rather than just thinking he is.

Regardless of not wanting him anymore, it's not nice to see this video. This is what I get for scrolling Instagram. I should delete the damn app from my phone. Marie Kondo the hell out of it since it's not sparking any joy for me.

I'm this close to texting Phillip exactly what I think of his bullshit when someone knocks on the door of my suite.

Placing my cell down, I tighten the towel around me and pad to the door. A woman with a smile that is far too big for 6:30 a.m. delivers the coffee I ordered before my shower. I've almost closed the door behind me when I realize she's forgotten the sugar I requested, and as much as I shouldn't have the sugar, I desperately need it this morning. Just a teaspoon. It's my one guilty pleasure I allow myself every morning. And since I always ask the hotels I stay in to remove all sugar from my suite, I don't have any here.

"Excuse me," I call out to her as she walks back toward the elevators. "I asked for sugar too."

When she doesn't stop, I notice her adjusting the AirPods in her ears.

Damn it.

The towel I'm wearing barely covers my ass. Running after the woman while wearing it isn't appealing, but neither is coffee without sugar.

I blame Instagram for the bad choice I make to go after her. If it wasn't for that fucking app distracting me with stories I really don't want to see, I wouldn't step out into the hallway and accidentally lock myself out of my suite.

"Shit!" I stare at the locked door, my sugar quickly forgotten. "Shit, shit, *shit!*"

"Problem?"

I jump at the sound of Bradford's husky voice behind me. Spinning, I come face-to-face with his frosty gaze. "Why are you here?" God, does he have some special power that allows him to materialize all over the place?

Bradford has perfected the look that says *You're really asking me that?* He gives me that look now. "My suite is next door to yours." His gaze drops to my body. "The question is why are you out here in a towel?"

My arm immediately comes up and around my towel to hold it in place. The very last thing I need is for it to drop. "I've locked myself out of my room. Do you think you could go downstairs and ask for a replacement key card?" I hate asking him for help but I'm kind of out of options here. If I'd had a say in who got the suite next to me, I would have gone as low as choosing Hannibal Lecter in preference to Bradford.

He gives me more of that look. "How do you think that will go down? I'm quite sure they'll just hand over a room key for you if I ask them politely enough."

I will kill him once I get this sorted.

"It's no wonder you're marrying Cecelia Aniston." The ice queen who we all know is only marrying him for the power it will give her. "I can't imagine any other woman wanting to marry an arrogant ass like you."

"That wasn't me being arrogant, Kristen, but I can be if that's your preference."

He's right about that. I've seen arrogance on him more than once and this is far from it.

Also, he's right that I won't get a replacement key by sending him in my place.

Shit, shit, *shit*.

While my brain tries to kick into gear, Bradford instructs, "Come with me." Then, without waiting for my response, he turns and strides toward the suite next to mine. This is classic Bradford Black behavior: making a decision and expecting others to fall into line. And since Hannibal Lecter is nowhere to be seen, I follow him.

He unlocks his door and opens it. Standing with his back to it, he motions for me to enter. "You can call downstairs and ask them to bring a key up to you."

Oh, how I wish I didn't have to rely on him. Or be inside his suite. Or walk so close to him that I can smell that woodsy scent of his that brings back too many memories.

I take in the state of his suite, begrudgingly admiring the tidiness. It's almost as if no one is staying here. He's packed most of his belongings away. The only personal item I can see is a book on the couch.

I want to sigh at the beauty of it. If only all men were as ordered as this.

I go to the phone, place my coffee down, and call reception. After a quick conversation in which I agree to produce identification once I'm let into my room, the man I speak with promises to send someone straight up.

After ending the call, I turn to thank Bradford and immediately wish I didn't already have my contact lenses in. There are benefits to short-sightedness, namely not being treated to the good looks of men you'd rather think of as ugly.

I've never seen Bradford in golf attire before. It turns out I'm experiencing the desire for many wishes this morning, because I also wish I didn't have to look at him wearing those clothes.

Dark navy pants that fit exceptionally well over his legs. A lighter shade of navy polo shirt with long sleeves and three buttons that aren't all done up, drawing my attention to the collar that sits wide and reveals that fucking perfect Adam's apple and neck of his. Hell, I even like his white golf shoes.

I could stare all day. Especially at the way his thighs wear those pants so well. A little *too* well. It's frankly all too much to handle. Bradford can take his golf balls away from me, thank you very much.

I pick up my coffee. "Thank you." I hold my breath while I walk past him. It's no use, though. I can't escape that purely masculine scent of his that does things to me I wish it didn't. Oh, so many wishes and it's not even seven a.m. yet.

"Kristen," he says as I open the door to leave. "I'll be finished with breakfast in half an hour."

I glanced back at him when he called my name. I could have just made my call and slipped straight out. I could have ignored him. I could have done so many things. But no, I looked at him. And damn him for still owning my butterflies.

I already know my next Google search: *the fastest way to kill butterflies. And men.*

I'll be finished with breakfast in half an hour. What an asshole, telling me when I can arrive for *my* breakfast.

I gave him an hour because I really don't want to chance running into him again. Thankfully, he was nowhere to be seen and I was able to eat in peace.

The girls are booked in for the spa at nine a.m. I am too. They talked me into it over dinner last night. It was the wine I drank that did it, I think. Not to mention Poppy's ability to convince anyone to do whatever she wants them to. She's strategic in her methods and I'm sure she waited until I'd had just the right amount of alcohol before pouncing on me.

My mother texts me right after breakfast. After all the texts I received from her yesterday with the plans she has for me, I'm surprised she didn't start up with her messages earlier this morning.

MOM

> Kristen, what time are you arriving home tomorrow? I was thinking we could get together tomorrow night to take another look at your wardrobe rather than waiting until Monday night. We don't want to leave ourselves short on time if we need to find a new dress for the gala.

This is the reason I didn't book a flight home last night. I was torn between wanting to escape Bradford and wanting to escape my mother. The desire not to see her was greater, so here I am, still in Vegas. I'm currently contemplating moving here permanently.

I can't count on two hands the number of texts like

this one I received yesterday while my mother got herself into a giddy state about my chances of meeting my future husband at the gala next weekend.

I reply to her text.

> It will be too late for that.

MOM

> How late?

Oh. My. God.

She's relentless.

I look at Jenna whose suite I'm in while she finishes dealing with some work stuff that came up overnight. "I've lost my phone, okay?"

She glances up from her laptop with a frown. "Huh?"

I hold up my phone. "I lost it if Mom asks you why I'm not responding to her texts or calls."

"She's still bugging you about the gala?" My sister is well versed in our mother and her desire to marry us off. Jenna no longer suffers this, although she's now suffering through *When will you give me a grandchild*? This means I now have most of our mother's attention.

"Yes," I answer Jenna. "She won't stop, and I'm done. In fact, I'm so done that I want you to take my phone and not give it back to me until we get home."

I force her to take my cell.

"Right, so while I fully support you being done with Mom over this, I don't know that it's a great idea to go without your phone in Vegas."

I shrug. "I'll be with you. And if not you, I'll be with someone from our group. I don't need my phone." When she still looks unconvinced, I add, "I'm not taking it back.

I also had to sit through an Insta story this morning of Phillip and Annabelle. I'm tired of seeing all that stuff. I need you to help me stop."

Her frown deepens. "Wait. I thought you were done with Phillip?"

"He's been texting me. Feeding me bullshit about wanting me back. And before you say anything, I didn't believe him."

"Okay, I'll lock your phone up. Actually, I'll give it to Beckett in case you harass me for it."

That makes me laugh. We both know I will absolutely harass her for it, just like we both know she'll cave and give it to me. Beckett, on the other hand, won't.

"There's only one problem with that. He's golfing until late this afternoon. Who will save us today?"

She grins as we both have what I assume is the same thought. "Poppy."

On our way down to meet the girls at the spa, I say to Jenna, "I'm pretty sure that if I promise Poppy to always floss, she'll give me my phone."

"No way. That girl has strong boundaries."

So true.

I need to learn how she sticks to her boundaries so fiercely. I feel like that would be one thousand percent more useful to me than learning about vibrations.

Poppy takes my phone and locks it away in her room for the day. She also gives me a lecture on curating my social media after Jenna drops the info about me scrolling through Annabelle's posts and seeing that story this morning. Jenna and I engage in a glaring match for a good minute after she shares this news with everyone. Honestly, sisters! There is such a thing as the Sister Vault of Secrets, and I need to make her aware that everything I ever tell her is firmly in that vault.

By the time I've endured hours, and hours, and *hours* of the spa and everyone sharing far too much personal information (I am quite positive I do not need to know all the ways everyone here deals with sex during their period) and emotions (God, shoot me now, please), I need some space and time to myself. After excusing myself and promising not to wander off on my own without my phone, I head up to my room.

The hotel is super busy this afternoon and I step into a packed elevator, not paying too much attention to anything or anyone because my thoughts have moved back to the mess of my life and the fact I'm in the middle of *maybe my first mid-life crisis but could just be the transformation from hell.*

I squeeze into the elevator with a million other people. I'm jostled backward and almost lose my balance. My back collides with the chest of the person behind me and as I smell the woodsy scent that I'd know anywhere, hands grip my waist to steady me.

Bradford's mouth brushes my ear. "It's a shame you ditched the towel."

I hate that his voice goes straight to my veins in a way no other man's voice ever goes there. "Just like it's a shame you're bad at reading women and whether we care what you think."

Keeping one hand on my waist, he brings the other one up to slowly sweep my hair across my shoulders. His touch is light across my back. I feel it everywhere and squeeze my eyes closed while letting the pleasure work its way through me. I should tell him to stop, to keep his hands to himself, but I don't. I'm unable to because my mind and body have gone to war, and there's no way my body is giving up control here.

With his mouth still to my ear, he murmurs, "You still use the same shampoo you did last year."

I suck in a breath, and still no words come to tell him to stop.

His fingers curl into my waist as his other hand trails a line down my back, leaving a shiver in its wake. And then he removes his hands from me and turns silent, leaving me in a state of *I really hope Google has a good answer for me about the best way to murder a man.*

What even was all that? And why does he think he can touch me?

I check how many floors away from mine we are. It's in this moment I remember his suite is next to mine. In precisely ten floors we'll be alone.

Why must he come back into my life at the exact time I'm having a mid-life crisis? I could manage him much better if I was running at full capacity.

The elevator arrives at our floor, and I don't hesitate to exit. I walk as quickly as I can down the hallway toward my suite, doing my best to ignore the fact Bradford is right behind me.

He lets me get to my room without another word.

I fumble in my purse for my room key, my heart beating like it thinks we're being chased by a tiger.

Shit. I drop the keycard.

Bradford doesn't stop when I bend to pick it up. He keeps on walking to his room.

I should let him go without a word, but I prove how bad I am at making good life choices when I straighten and say, "Why are you such an asshole to me these days?"

His strides slow but he takes a few moments to come to a complete stop. Turning back to me, he says, "There's a difference between an asshole and a man who doesn't want to get into a conversation. I'm not an asshole."

"Trust me when I tell you that you've pulled some real asshole moves on me this year. Just because you didn't get what you wanted doesn't give you free reign to treat me badly."

"That's fucking rich coming from you."

I hate that he has a point and immediately feel guilty over that. "I'm sorry I used you that night. I shouldn't have done that. But I haven't treated you badly since then, Bradford."

"I'm not referring to that night."

"What are you referring to, then?"

He clenches his jaw while looking at me like he can't believe he's even talking to me. "I'm not doing this with you. I should have listened to you that night when you told me we were done because we really fucking were."

My eyes go wide at the same time my words fail me. I'm left staring after Bradford in silence as he walks away from me.

The soft click of his door as it closes behind him leaves me alone with my thoughts. Well, actually, it leaves me with only one thought: what the fuck is he talking about?

And as I continue standing there staring at the empty

hallway, wondering what the hell is going on, I latch onto another thought that is far more useful: wine was surely made for this sort of thing.

I need some.

No, I need a *lot*.

And if Vegas is not the place to consume as much wine as possible, I don't know what is.

27

BRADFORD

I LOOK at Kristen who's sitting across from me at dinner. She's doing her best to avoid eye contact while drinking wine like it's going out of fashion. The success she's having with the wine outweighs the success she's having at pretending I don't exist.

Getting her out of my head has proved difficult this weekend, particularly so after we argued this afternoon. That was right after I put my hands on her and initiated a conversation I never should have started.

Fuck.

I'm still as attracted to her as I ever was. I still fucking want her. And not even going out of my way to avoid her has helped any of those feelings disappear. I'm convinced they'll never go away.

"So," Charlize says looking at me, "I heard you ended up in the rough today. What happened?"

"Have you figured out what the rough is yet?"

"No, and honestly, I'm really not that interested in knowing. But I did pick up from what you were putting down yesterday that it's not ideal. Were you off your game today?"

"I think the fact I won the game speaks for itself."

Charlize smiles. "Well, there is that, but"—she narrows her eyes at me—"you know I'm always trying to figure you out. I wondered what thoughts were going through your mind for you to end up in the rough."

"The only thought ever going through Bradford's mind is how to get what he wants," Kristen says from across the table, her eyes firmly on mine.

I hold her gaze, unable for the life of me to look away and not engage. "Isn't that part of what life's about? Finding ways to get what we want."

"Sometimes it is," she says as everyone stops the conversation they're having so they can listen to ours.

"And at other times? What's life about then?"

"Oh, I don't know, letting people come to breakfast at whatever time they prefer."

She's referring to this morning when I told her what time I'd be finished breakfast. I don't bother correcting her that my intention was for her to know when I'd be done so that she didn't have to run into me if she didn't want to.

I throw back some whiskey before commenting, "No good deed goes unpunished."

"It seems you still don't know what some words mean. You need to add a dictionary to your wish list for Christmas. I highly recommend you look the word *good* up. And while you're there, take another look at *violent*."

"I'm good on that one. You taught me the meaning nine months ago."

Jenna takes this moment to trudge into the conversation. Her expression tells me she's concerned that Kristen and I will just keep going until we spill blood. "Kris, let's get some air."

Kristen's eyes can't be swayed from mine just as mine can't be coaxed from hers. Not even as others join the conversation.

"I, for one, would like to get what I want more often," Poppy says.

"I think you do just fine," Adeline says.

"There could always be more sex," Poppy says.

Kristen finally looks away and glances at Jenna as some of the group discuss getting more sex in their lives. Kristen says something to her sister before standing and leaving the table.

I watch her walk to the bathroom.

The look on her face as she got up to leave was pure anger, which confuses me. I'm the one who received that text from her nine months ago. Not the other way around. She acts like it was nothing. It wasn't nothing to me. That was a conversation that should have been had in person. It surprised me that she didn't show me the respect I thought I deserved by coming to me with it.

It fucking killed me that the woman I loved had it in her to do that to me. And then to see me three hours later at a gala with Phillip on her arm and ignore me the way she did. There's no way I will ever forget her actions.

I stay out of Kristen's way for the rest of the night. I play some Blackjack with the guys in between answering texts from Alan, my political consultant. We've been working together for six months and he's competent as hell. The guy doesn't sleep as far as I can tell. There's nothing he can't sell, including my marriage to Cecelia. He's spent the six months with me working on selling that, and the pollsters have just come back with information that tells me he's been successful. Cecelia was always going to be a hard sell due to the fact she's a successful lawyer with a highly public profile and has openly stated in the past that she wasn't interested in dating men. Alan told me he could fix that and it seems he didn't lie. We've still got work to do, but we've come a long way in a short time.

After all the couples head up to their rooms, I stay at the tables and play for longer. I leave about half an hour later after my winning streak disappears. I receive a text from Beckett on the way to the elevator.

BECKETT

Bradford, this is Jenna. Are you in your room?

> I will be soon. Why?

BECKETT

Can you please do me a favor and check on Kristen. She's in the room next to yours, right?

> Yes. Is she okay?

BECKETT

She doesn't have her phone on her and she's not answering the phone in her room. I'm sure she's okay but I just want to check.

> I'll check on her and let you know.

BECKETT

Thank you!

The elevator arrives and I step inside, trying to deny the concern I'm feeling over Kristen. It doesn't seem to matter how much I think I've moved on; I can't help worrying about her.

She doesn't answer my knock, and after spending a couple of minutes trying to gain her attention, I decide she isn't in there and make my way back downstairs to look for her.

It takes me five minutes to locate her in one of the casino bars. She's sitting on a stool, talking with the bartender. I slow my approach and watch her for a minute, taking in how animated she is, how expressive her face and hands are. Whatever they're discussing is something she's highly passionate about.

This is the Kristen I haven't seen in years. Her energy reminds me of the night we met. The night she lit New York up for me.

She laughs, sweeping her long brown hair off her shoulder, revealing cleavage that the sexy, glittery gold dress she's wearing does nothing to hide. The neckline is a deep V that slices almost all the way to her waist, and since the tiny dress is held up by two thin straps, there's not a lot to it on the top half. Christ, there's not a lot to the dress on the bottom half either. It's designed to slay any man treated to it.

She catches sight of me and her sparkle dims. When I move next to her at the bar, she says, "For a man who doesn't want to have a conversation with me, you're failing epically this weekend."

"Jenna asked me to check on you."

She lifts her cocktail to her lips and takes a sip. As she places it back down, she says, "Consider me checked on. Your job here is done."

"How much have you had to drink?"

"I highly doubt that question was part of your assignment."

"Fuck. Can we act like adults? You don't have your phone and I don't want to leave you alone without it if you intend on getting drunk."

"Okay, I won't get drunk," she says with a casual shrug that says she has no intention of putting any effort into following through on that.

"I'm not leaving you here alone, Kristen."

"So, you're staying? We're going to have a drink together?" She widens her eyes and gasps while covering her mouth briefly. "You're going to talk to me?"

I scrub my hand down my face. I'm too fucking tired for this. "I meant it when I asked if we could be adults."

She leans closer to me like she's about to tell me a secret. "A hot tip for you is that when a man says things like that to me, it only makes me want to do the opposite." She straightens on her stool. "It's pretty much the equivalent to *calm down* and you know my feelings on those two words."

"Since I intend for this to be our last conversation like this, you won't ever hear any of those words from me again."

"The burn, Bradford. It's so harsh. I hope it makes you feel good." She drinks some more of her cocktail and with the flick of her wrist lets the bartender know she wants another.

Since I know I can't sit through this with her tonight, and since I don't want to leave her without a phone, I pull my cell out. I send a message to Beckett letting him know Kristen is safe, and then place the phone down on the bar. At her questioning look, I say, "The passcode is 0606. You can return it to me in the morning."

The shock in her eyes is strong. She shakes her head and pushes the phone back to me. "I'm not taking your phone."

I pick it up and place it in front of her with determination. "You are, and you aren't going to continue arguing with me about it. I'm tired and I'm in no mood for you." I exhale a long breath. "I'll see you in the morning."

I don't wait to hear her thoughts on that or to see the annoyance disappear from her eyes. I'm in the elevator a couple of minutes later. The whiskey I pour myself a minute after I reach my suite is the strongest fucking drink I've ever made myself.

I'm two drinks in when there's a knock on my door. I don't want to answer it because I'm not in the right frame of mind to see anyone, so I'm slow to make a move towards it.

The knocking grows louder and more insistent as I draw closer, and then I hear the sultry voice I can never ignore. And if I'm not mistaken, she sounds pissed off. "Bradford! I have your phone and I have a whole lot of things to say to you! Let me in!"

28

KRISTEN

FIRST THINGS FIRST. Bradford receives a lot of texts. A *lot*. I've had his phone for twenty minutes and nineteen messages have come in for him. Mostly from a man called Alan, but also one from Hayden, one from Cecelia, and two from his father. Let the record show that I did not use the passcode he gave me to go through his phone and spy on his life.

That took a lot out of me.

Nowhere near as much, though, as it took to bring his phone to him so he doesn't have to wait until the morning to read those texts. I figured they might be important. The ones I read on his lockscreen from Alan certainly seemed important.

Yes, I did read those messages. I'm no angel. Plus, I'm having a mid-life crisis; I needed *something* to distract me.

I didn't even finish my cocktail. I think that says a lot about the work my therapist needs to do on the part of me that is in denial over Bradford being an asshole. I need to ditch her on the side of a road with my good girl if I can ever figure out how to do that.

Bradford's taking his sweet time answering his door. Surely he hasn't fallen asleep already. After I call out to him, I knock a little louder.

The door swings open and those blue eyes of his meet mine. Holding out his hand for his cell, he says, "I'm about to go to bed. Can we skip whatever it is you want to say? There's nothing I want to hear."

I shove past him, ignoring everything he says, and walk through the marble foyer into the living room that has a stunning backdrop of the night lights of Vegas through the large windows. Holding his phone up, I say, "Cecelia sounds like a lot of fun. Based on the text she just sent you, I predict you'll be a silver fox before forty." I spin to face him, trying hard not to look at the top few buttons of his dress shirt. They're casually undone and reveal tanned skin that, damn it, I want to touch. "And Hayden seems exasperated with her." I cock my head as I watch him walk my way. "And Alan. He's lying to you. There is *no way* everyone will buy Cecelia being into dick. Her appreciation for pussy is legendary. Alan is clearly polling the wrong people. If you need help, I can put him in touch with the right people. I really don't want you to screw your run for president up before you even get started."

He looks down at me with a thunderous expression as he reaches for his cell. "Are you finished?"

"Actually, no. I'm just getting started."

He snatches his phone from me and slips it into his pocket. "No, you're not. You're leaving." Still with that dark expression.

"How do you cope with all those texts? There was one pretty much every minute, and that was late on a Saturday night. I shudder to think how many you receive on a workday."

"Kristen." Now, his tone is dark, matching his face, a deadly storm on the horizon.

I think it's hearing him say my name that does it. Or it could be the fact his passcode is the date we met. Or maybe it's just being so close to him and having him feel so fucking far away. One of those things, or all of them, or a million other little things between us cause me to snap.

The tattered threads of us that I've been clinging to completely come apart.

I'm so fucking angry.

At what has become of us.

At his refusal to let me reach him.

At him for giving up on us.

I jab his chest as my anger spills from me. "She won't make you happy. You know that, right? She might get you to the White House, but she won't fucking make you happy!"

His nostrils flare as he crushes his fingers around mine. "I gave up on happiness. You saw to that."

"I didn't! I told you I wasn't ready."

That deadly storm rages to life in his eyes. "Yes, while the guy you were fucking at the time had free fucking roam of your home you told me you weren't ready. I gave you space to heal. I gave you time. I gave you everything you asked for, and then, when you were ready to date again, you didn't choose me."

His hurt screams at me and I understand it. But as much as I wish I could have made different choices, I chose him even though he doesn't realize it. "I couldn't choose you, Bradford."

He lets go of my hand and jerks away from me. "That's utter bullshit, Kristen, and I'm not fucking buying it."

I try to close the distance between us, but he takes another step back like he can't bear to have me close. Reaching for his shirt, I grab a handful of it and pull him toward me. "I'll tell you what would have happened if I chose you then. I would have destroyed everything we had. I was angry. I was hurting. I was toxic. And I would have taken all of that out on you. I hated men during those months that I didn't date. I wanted to retaliate with my own awful behavior, and I knew that, so I stayed away from dating. When I was ready to go back out into the world, I chose anyone but you. I needed to figure out how to date with my new boundaries so that I didn't screw things up with you when we started dating." I grip his shirt harder. "I chose you by not choosing you."

The look in his eyes tells me he wants to believe me, but he doesn't. "I'm still not buying it. Not with that text you sent me and not with what you did afterwards."

"Oh my God, Bradford, I don't fucking know what you're talking about!" I'm clutching his shirt like my life depends on it, yelling in his face, and I can't stop any of my pain from crashing out of me. "You keep talking in riddles, saying things that make no sense, acting like *I* did this to us. I didn't do this to us! This is not on me! I did the work on myself that we needed if we were ever going to have a chance together. You didn't wait. You told me I was the one thing you needed to breathe, and you told me years ago that good friends don't walk away when things get hard. And then you did exactly that." I let go of his shirt so I can smack my hands to his chest. "You did this, not me!"

His hands seize mine. Gripping my wrists tightly, he yanks my body to his. "I was the best friend you ever had, Kristen, and I did *not* do the walking away. Even after you told me you weren't ready, I waited. But that text...*fuck*"— heavy breath forces its way out of him as those dark rolling clouds in his eyes look ready to unleash danger— "when you send a man a text like that, it fucking destroys him and he's left with no choice *but* to walk away." More of that ominous heavy breath finds its way from him to settle between us. "You did do this."

My heart is violent in my chest. "I didn't send you a text! Show me!"

He doesn't let me go, doesn't move. He just keeps his hands tightly around my wrists and my body hard against his while he watches me like he's furiously trying to contain the storm that's raging inside him.

I attempt to wrench my hands free but my strength is no match for Bradford's. But still, I struggle against him, yelling, "Show me!"

The hurricane of emotions he's kept to himself finally thunder out of him.

Instead of doing what I say, he brings one hand up to wrap around my throat while keeping a firm hold of me with his other. Forcing me back against the wall, he brings his face down to mine. "It wasn't enough for you to torture me for the last year and a half? You want to keep going?"

Savage dark energy twists its way around us as Bradford presses himself into me. He wears fury, he exudes fury, he breathes fury. And I don't understand any of it.

I try to remove his hand from my throat but he doesn't allow that. "You're the one doing the torturing. You're—"

"No!" He yells, his face so close to mine that his voice is a weapon. "I loved you and you took that love and destroyed me with it."

The violence in my chest stops.

He loved me.

He loved me.

He loved me.

I grasp his face with one hand while my other one grips his shirt. I'm trying to get closer. I need to get closer. "You loved me."

His breaths come faster as his eyes demand mine never leave his. "Yes."

My fingers dig hard into his face. I want to own this face. I never want to let it go. "You still love me."

His jaw clamps down under my hand while he goes to war with himself over that statement. No air finds its way into my lungs while I wait for him.

Time stands still.

Seconds tick by.

Excruciatingly slowly.

A flood of memories fills my mind.

All the little ways Bradford showed me his love.

All the little things I didn't pay enough attention to because if I had, I would never have wasted a second being with anyone but him.

"Bradford," I beg, gripping his face harder. I'm

desperate for time to stop standing still. I'm desperate for him to tell me yes.

"Fuck." His fingers bind tighter around my throat as he breathes that *fuck* over me like a dragon breathes fire. "*Fuck*." And then his lips are crashing down on mine, and he's breathing life into me.

He kisses me with all the torture he's feeling. Like he needs me to take it from him and never give it back. Like he won't survive if I don't keep it from touching him again.

His hands are in my hair.

They're angry.

They're vicious.

They're *possessive*.

I'll take the pain they cause every second for the rest of my life just to feel that urgent desire and dominance.

Bradford has always been the king of my heart. I want him to own it forever.

He tears his mouth from mine and kisses his way down my neck to my throat and collarbone. Every press of his lips to my skin is fire to my soul. I thread my fingers through his hair and arch my body into his. I never want him to stop.

Moving down my body, he shoves the straps of my dress off my shoulders and groans as he kisses my breasts. His hands are rough as he takes hold of them and sucks a nipple into his mouth.

"Oh God," I moan, wrapping a leg around him, searching for friction as I grind my pussy against his erection. I need him inside me.

Bradford isn't delicate with my body. His hands are

crude, his mouth is indecent. He strips my dress from me inconsiderately.

When he drops to his knees and takes hold of my waist with both hands, I roll my hips his way. His feral growl right before he presses his face to my panties slams into me. Into all of me. I squeeze my fingers into his hair, craving more. So. Much. More.

He tears my panties off. I watch him while he slows himself down to look at my pussy. His shoulders are rigid like he's working hard to control himself. I don't want him to control himself. I want him to take me. All of me. I want him to wreck me.

I squeeze his hair. "Bradford." It's a beg that draws his eyes to mine. "I need you."

That brutal look in his eyes flares and then he snaps. Loses all control. And finally, *finally*, gives me everything.

He brings his hands to my pussy and licks the entire center of me. He does this so fucking slowly, and so deeply, and with that guttural growl of his. It's the filthiest thing a man has ever done to me. It's intimate in a way that's new to me.

When he gets to my clit, he circles his tongue over it and then sucks.

My back presses into the wall because my legs suddenly feel weak.

Bradford takes his time with my clit. Then, he kisses his way down to my opening, kissing and sucking me there before slowly pushing his tongue inside me.

I hook one leg over his shoulder and he makes a rough sound of approval while fucking me with his tongue and rubbing my clit.

As I grow wetter, he opens me up further and presses his face harder against me, his tongue reaching deeper.

I grind myself into him, wanting, needing him deeper.

I want Bradford so far inside me.

It feels unlike anything I've ever known.

It feels reckless, carnal, *primal*.

My orgasm edges closer and I rock and grind, seeking what I need.

Bradford swaps his tongue for his fingers, first pushing one inside me and then two.

I squeeze myself around those fingers. They feel so fucking good there. Bradford's eyes find mine as I clench. He holds my gaze while he sucks my clit into his mouth and fucks his fingers harder and faster into me.

My orgasm consumes me while he watches.

I close my eyes and come so hard I see color.

It's gold. Indigo. Red.

Everything is wiped from my mind but this orgasm, this pleasure, this man.

"Fuck, you're beautiful." Bradford's voice is rough and he sounds pissed off about thinking I'm beautiful.

I open my eyes as he stands. I'm barely finished with my orgasm when he lifts me over his shoulder and strides into the bedroom, dropping me on the bed. His hands are on his shirt the second I land on the mattress, and he's ripping buttons and looking at me like he can't do any of this fast enough.

My skin blazes with the fire he causes in me, and I scramble up the bed, ready for every single thing he's planning to do to me.

He tears his shirt off, belt off, trousers off.

He strips out of his boxer briefs and I suck in a breath

at the size of him. I can't even imagine him fitting inside me, but that thought is erased while I watch him put a condom on.

Then, he's on top of me and roughly pulling my leg up over his shoulder as he looks down at my pussy. Lining his cock up, he finds my eyes again. "I hope you're good with it hard because I don't have it in me to give you anything else." The way he says this lets me know he feels like I've caused this. It lets me know he's wild and desperate in a way that I've brought out in him.

Without waiting for my response, he thrusts inside me exactly how he promised he would.

My world explodes.

I grip his neck and move with him.

He pulls out and slams inside again.

His eyes are glued to mine.

That wild storm still rages in them.

I see anger.

I see hurt.

I see the kind of love that is given against his consent.

Bradford loves me but he doesn't want to.

"I love you." The words tumble out of my mouth without me knowing they were coming. I don't think when I'm with this man; I only feel. I feel in a way no one else ever makes me feel. I have no power over how I express my emotions with him, and that's both scary and the best thing in the world.

His eyes flash with torment.

He thrusts harder.

And he growls, "Don't say that to me."

I grasp his neck and fuck him as madly as he's fucking me. "Don't tell me what to do."

He drives his dick harder into me.

I claw his skin with my nails, loving the hiss that escapes his lips even more than I love the pleasure he's giving me. "I did not send you a text."

"You fucking did."

I crush my fingers around his neck harder. "Why did you choose Cecelia?"

"She can get the job done."

"I hate her for you."

The approval that flares in his eyes can't be missed.

His hips move faster and determination fills his features.

"*Fuck*," he rasps as everything gets faster, as his arm and shoulder muscles flex tighter.

I come while he keeps pumping into me.

I see all that color again and it only grows more intense, more overwhelming when Bradford thrusts one last time and comes. When he drops his head to my shoulder, the color bursts into brighter shades of red.

I want his head on my shoulder every day.

I want him inside me every day.

I want to know if he smiled every day.

He pulls out and moves off the bed without a second glance, stalking into the bathroom. The slam of the door behind him moves through me with the kind of chill that is bone deep. Soul deep.

I don't think; I feel.

I move off the bed and go in search of his phone in the pocket of his trousers. I key in his passcode and pull up his messages. Scrolling back so far that it hurts, I finally locate my name and tap it.

My heart beats so goddamn fast it feels like it could

burst while I read the last two messages that were sent nine months ago.

BRADFORD

I'm waiting for you, Kristen, but it's fucking killing me.

KRISTEN

Stop waiting. I've changed my mind. I'm done. I was wrong to think you could ever give me what I need. I'm going to marry Phillip.

I stare at the messages, reading them over and over. And over.

I did not send that message.

I would never send Bradford a message like that.

"Did you get what you need?"

My head snaps up and I find Bradford standing over me, looking down with more of that darkness.

I scramble to stand. "I promise you I did not send that text to you. If I had my phone here, I would show you."

"Show me what? That you deleted it from your phone?"

This man.

He's hurting so much.

"Bradford, think about everything we've been through. God, so many years of wanting each other. Think about what I said to you that night in the club. Really think about it. And think about what we just did. About everything I've said to you this weekend." I step closer to him and gently place his phone in his hand. "Do you really think I could send you something so hurtful?"

I put my hand to his cheek, taking in the lines on his

face that are new to me. He's so handsome. So devastatingly good looking but, in this moment, so fierce in his brokenness. "I hate the things we've said to each other. I hate that I can feel our connection so strongly, yet we're letting so much bullshit get in the way of that. I've been through too much to let this go without fighting for you. I need you to hear me. I want you. I never stopped wanting you. I'm sorry I hurt you by choosing other men to work my shit out with, but I want to choose you now. And I know you're engaged to that ice queen, and I know she's the smart choice for you, and I know it would cause a shitstorm of epic proportions if you ended that engagement, but I want you. And I want you to choose me."

He takes a long time with that.

So long that I begin to wonder if I've failed to reach him.

Then, he exhales, the tension easing from his shoulders.

I slow down.

I call on every ounce of patience I have.

And I wait for him because he waited so long for me.

Finally, he says, "Your timing is fucking woeful."

I stay slow. Like a hesitant deer. In case I'm misreading him. "I know. But in my defense, I would have timed it sooner if that text hadn't come between us."

His chest rises and falls as he works through his breaths. "Jesus, Kristen."

I smile. I can't help it. Bradford looks a little bewildered. I've never seen him with this expression on his face.

His grumpy look flares. "This isn't a smiling matter."

I keep smiling. "I'm aware, but still."

"Still what?"

"You look so cute when you're bewildered."

"Cute?"

Oh, how I live for his grumpiness.

I move into him, my arms going around his waist. "Yes, cute. It makes me want to kiss you."

One of his arms comes around me while he runs a hand through my hair. The tenderness that's now in his eyes is everything. *Everything.*

He bends his face to mine and kisses me. He takes his time, not rushing even a second. Deepening the kiss with every swipe of his tongue over mine.

Bradford's lips are where I want to live. They're my safe place. I never want to know a day without them again.

When he drags them from mine, I have to fight not to argue with him. But he quickly removes that idea from my mind when he says, "Perhaps the next time you keep me waiting for something, you don't take so long."

The next time.

The air I was holding onto tightly while waiting for him exhales out of me. "I won't keep you waiting for anything ever again."

His phone sounds with a text that he ignores. "I won't allow you to."

Another text comes in for him.

"I hope you don't." Oh, God, how I hope he doesn't. When his phone sounds with another text, I say, "Maybe you should check your messages. They might be important."

He doesn't move. "Nothing is as important as this conversation."

I want to spend time in those words. And I want to stay in Bradford's arms, but when his phone rings, I don't want to come between him and the things that are important to him.

I move out of his hold. "Take the call. I'm going to get dressed."

After locating my clothes, I spend longer in the bathroom than I thought I would. I need the time to catch my breath over everything that's happened tonight.

My thoughts run wild with homicidal ideas about what I will do to Phillip. He must have intercepted that text from Bradford and sent the reply.

Nine months ago, Phillip and I were in one of our on-periods. As far as he was concerned, we were *really* on. I knew Phillip had plans for marriage early in our relationship even though I made it clear I wasn't looking for a long-term relationship with him. It was this agenda that always led to our off-periods because I had no intention of marrying him. Not when the only man I wanted to marry was Bradford.

I remember the night Bradford thinks I ignored him. It was the only time we saw each other at that time.

I'd had an argument with Phillip and was in a foul mood all night. When I saw Bradford, I avoided him because of that mood. I was also wary of a conversation because we'd fought weeks earlier when I told him I wasn't ready for him yet. He was angry and hurt over my relationship with Phillip. I wasn't ignoring Bradford at the gala that night; I didn't want to inflict my boyfriend on him.

Phillip had overheard our fight when Bradford came to my condo to see me. He discovered our history and was jealous. He exerted an over-the-top display of posses-siveness the night I avoided Bradford.

None of that night was good. And I can see how Brad-ford interpreted it in context with that text. God, how I wish he'd come to me over that, but I understand why he didn't. Every time he'd shared his hurt and tried to get me to move forward with him, I'd pushed him away. I'm not sure I would have gone back for another round of pain either.

Phillip will incur all my wrath over this bullshit. And then some. It's a real fucking shame for him that I'm good at getting in touch with my feelings these days.

I finish in the bathroom and go back into the bedroom. Bradford has left and I can hear him talking out in the living room.

He's sitting in one of the armchairs, dressed only in his trousers. He continues talking while I walk toward him but by the way he watches me, I think I've got most of his attention. When I try to sit on the sofa next to him, he reaches forward and hooks his arm around me so he can pull me onto his lap.

The energy vibrating from him is all power and domi-nance. I've seen these qualities in him throughout the years. They're his signature style but experiencing them as a woman he desires is a whole other thing. A thing I am all here for.

"Yeah," he says into his phone while dropping his gaze to my chest. "You take care of that and I'll do my research. Let's get together tomorrow when I'm home. I'll be back in New York by four."

I watch Bradford check me out. When he glides a

finger over my collarbone, I wonder how I'll survive the minutes before he strips me again.

He ends the call as his eyes find mine. "How many dresses do you own like this one?"

I smile. "Totally not what I imagined you saying next."

He arches a brow waiting for my answer.

Oh, hello Mr. Demanding.

"A lot."

"Jesus. We need to get you some new dresses."

I cock my head. "You don't like this style?"

"I fucking love this style. That's the problem."

I brush my lips over his. "I'm getting more just like this one."

His hand grips the back of my neck. Possessively. "They won't last long on you."

"I hope not."

His grip tightens and he takes a moment before he says, "This is going to be messy, Kristen."

I turn into him more and curve my hand over his chest and around his body. "*This* being us?"

"No, we've made it through our mess. Although, when I get hold of the person who sent me that text, *that* will get fucking messy. But I mean extricating myself from Cecelia. The party won't like it and she won't take it well."

"I know. And I know I'm being selfish here, wanting you to put your career at risk." I bite my lip, desperately not wanting to say the words on the tip of my tongue, but helpless to stop them. "If marrying Cecelia is what your career needs, you shouldn't choose me."

His reaction is immediate and it leaves me in no

doubt as to what he wants the most in the world. "There's no way I'm letting you go now that I have you. You let me worry about my career."

"Okay, but what's the plan?"

A tug of his lips is the first taste of a smile he's given me this weekend. "I like this impatience you have for me."

"It's not new, just FYI."

"You've done a hell of a job hiding it."

Another text comes in for him.

I glance at his phone that he placed on the table next to him. "Is it normal for you to get a text a minute?"

"Highly normal."

"Good God. When will we ever get time for sex?"

A look of desire that I want to always inspire comes to life in his eyes. "That's not the question I'll be asking myself."

Being Bradford's friend was always the best thing in my life. I think being his partner will far surpass that.

His phone lights up again and I eye it. "I'm going to order some food while you deal with that. Do you want anything?"

He tightens his hold on me when I attempt to move off his lap. "How hungry are you?"

"Starving."

"Fix your hair. We'll go out and get food."

"I don't want to leave this suite."

"You're leaving it. I know a place you'll love."

"I knew you'd be bossy."

He jerks his chin. "Up. Sort your hair."

I touch my hair. "What's wrong with it?"

He leans forward and kisses me. "Fucking nothing, but I know you would never go out with just-fucked hair."

He's right about that.

Just like I was right about him being bossy.

The thing about that? I want Bradford to boss me around for the rest of my life. I just hope we can figure out a way to be together that doesn't cause him too much hell.

29

BRADFORD

Kristen is lighter than I've ever seen her. Freer. Happy. Even though she thinks she's in the middle of an early mid-life crisis, I can see the difference in her.

I brought her to the restaurant I've been eating at since the time my father introduced me to it at the age of twenty-one. It was my first time in Vegas. A father-son trip that is stored in the section of my memories labeled *Meaningful*. He and I have made many trips back here since then and we always eat at Don's restaurant.

Kristen's eyes light up when Don brings another dish in for her to try. I requested a private dining room and a selection of dishes. This one features Shrimp Toasts, a favorite of mine.

He places it on the table and eyes me. "I'll bring the hummus next."

"Oh my gosh" Kristen puts her hand over her stomach. "I don't think I can eat anything else. I'm almost bursting."

The shrimp is the fourth dish we've sampled. Kristen

tried to talk me out of ordering more than one dish. *It's almost midnight*, she'd said, *Far too late for a second dinner.* I'd pointed out that she hardly ate at dinner, choosing instead to drink wine and threaten me with war. She'd only continued arguing with me for another minute after that, quickly realizing I had every intention of ensuring she eats. If I had my way, we'd try every meal on the menu so I can begin learning her favorites.

Don gives me a questioning look at Kristen's insistence that she's full.

"We'll skip the hummus tonight," I say. "We'll have it next time."

With a nod, he leaves us.

Kristen tastes the shrimp and briefly closes her eyes while enjoying the food. "I can see why you love it here. Don is an amazing chef." She glances around the private room, taking in the luxurious Art Deco style. Gold, black, and deep purple fill the room, along with mirrors, large vases of white calla lilies, and a chandelier that drew her attention when we first stepped inside. "And the restaurant is gorgeous."

We've spent the time here talking about easy things. My golf game earlier today, Kristen's spa experience with the girls, a conversation she had with Jack about a movie he's working on, her love of his movies, and the mid-life crisis she's going through. That topic intrigued me the most and I quizzed her on it. She waved her hand in the air, telling me her therapist says her confusion is good but that she's not so sure. When I asked her what confusion, she gave me wide eyes and told me that she'd just contemplated becoming a nun yesterday and that she hated the idea of going to one more gala. *Can you believe any of that?* she'd questioned me like there was no way anyone would believe those things. She went on to tell me she also decided yesterday that she was done with Tinder. *A great fucking decision*, I'd told her. She'd smiled at me in the way that is my downfall before saying she hoped all these odd thoughts passed soon because she's tired of being in crisis mode.

While we eat the shrimp, she moves away from easy topics. "How are we going to do this, Bradford?"

It's an understatement to say I like her asking me this. Our attraction to each other has never been a secret between us, but I've always wondered if mine was greater. Kristen seemed content to leave me in the friend zone for years. And while I waited for her after the night in the club, I still wondered if she would ever want me. She's not hiding how much she wants me now and that is something I needed.

"I'll meet with my team tomorrow and hash out a plan."

"Yes, but what are you thinking that plan will entail? Your wedding is supposed to take place next month."

"I don't want you to worry about this, Kristen. I'll handle it."

She shakes her head. "No. That's not how I do relationships anymore. We're equals or we're nothing. I want to be involved, even if all that means is you talk to me about things and share your next step and your current concerns." Her voice softens. "I want to know your heart and all the ways it's breathing."

Every second I waited for this woman was worth it. *Every second.*

"Cecelia isn't going to take this lightly. She had her

own ambitions she was using this marriage for. She'll likely go out of her way to make our life hell. I'll have Hayden do his best to stop that, but I may not be able to protect you from it all."

She gives me a look of pure confidence. "You forget where I grew up and the girls I grew up with. Trust me when I tell you I've dealt with some bitches and have come out on top. I'm not afraid of the ice queen."

Her jealousy feels good and that's not something I ever expected of myself. Possessiveness isn't something I've easily tolerated in women, but every time Kristen refers to Cecelia as the ice queen or shares her hatred of the marriage I'd locked myself into, I feel it deeply in my gut.

I'm not convinced she understands just how ruthless Cecelia is, but since I plan for Hayden to take care of her, I don't worry Kristen needlessly by reiterating my concern. "I'll talk with Cecelia tomorrow. Hayden and I will draft an NDA for her to sign. I'll also meet with Alan so we can figure out how to handle the PR of this."

"I don't think we should make our relationship public straight away."

That was not in my plan. I want everyone to know Kristen's mine. "I don't see the need to hide it."

"Bradford. Think about this like a politician. It won't look good for you to end an engagement and immediately be seen with another woman."

I know she's right. Fuck, do I know that. And yet, I don't want to think like a politician when it comes to her. "Okay, we'll wait a few weeks."

She gives me an amused look. "Yeah, no. More like a few months."

My response is immediate because my entire body feels it. There's no fucking way I'm waiting months to live my life with Kristen by my side. "We'll wait a few weeks only, Kristen."

"Bradford—"

"I told you I wouldn't allow you to keep me waiting for anything ever again and I meant it. That starts now."

Her eyes flare at my tone. And before I know what's happening, she's moved from her chair and is sitting on my lap with her arms around my neck, her breasts pressed to my chest, and her beautiful face so close to mine it hurts. "Let the record show that I *really* like this grumpy, bossy side of you." She kisses me, not giving me her mouth for anywhere long enough. "I'm sure I'll argue with you over it, but still, I like it." Her voice turns soft and so fucking sweet when she adds, "It makes me feel cherished."

My arms are around her and I claim her mouth, demanding more than the kiss she just gave me. I'm consumed by this woman. Her thoughts, her heart, her soul. I want to make her feel cherished every day for the rest of my life.

When she tries to end the kiss, I refuse to let her go. By the time I finally end it, she's breathless in the exact way I want her to be.

She slides her hands down from my neck to my chest. "Promise me you'll kiss me like that every day."

I grip the back of her neck and pull her lips back to mine. This kiss is quicker but no less intense. "I would kiss you like that every minute of every day if I could."

"We wasted so many years."

"I agree."

"Although"—she brings her hand to my face, touching me gently like she's sorting my features into a list in her mind—"my therapist would tell us that we needed all those years."

"You say that like you don't believe her."

She rolls her eyes. "I don't trust anything that woman says."

I chuckle. "And yet you keep going back."

"Let's just say that she and I have a love/hate relationship. As in, I hate every minute I have to sit on her couch vomiting my feelings all the place."

"And the love? Where does that come in?"

"The love is all on her end. It's a toxic relationship if you ask me. She loves breaking me down."

I lightly rub my thumb over her neck. "You might feel broken, but all I see is the strongest woman I've ever known. I hope you continue working with her."

She takes a moment with that, like she's just heard something she needed to hear. She appears a little overwhelmed by it. Then, like she's filed it away for later, she moves on. "Oh, don't worry about me ending our relationship. She's a pushy bitch and would hound me to show up for another appointment. Currently, we're working on me finding fun. If she's not careful, she's going to have to begin hounding me soon." Her eyes widen. "I mean, who has time for fun in their life?"

I could spend hours with Kristen discussing this. She's telling me she's struggling, and I can see that, but mostly what I see is her finding herself. It's so fucking beautiful to watch. "What kind of fun are you chasing?"

More of that eye widening. "If I knew that, I think I really could break up with her."

"What initiated her telling you to go in search of fun?"

She glances down at my chest. One of her tells I've picked up on over the years is that she breaks eye contact when she's feeling especially vulnerable. It's been in these moments that I've had to decide how hard to push her to crack herself open for me. I've learned that Kristen sometimes needs a far gentler approach than comes naturally to me. After not having her in my life for a year and a half, and after what's happened between us tonight, I'm unable not to push her now. I need everything from her.

I lift her face back up to mine. "Talk to me. I want to know all of you."

Her eyes search mine for the longest moment. "I told her I feel like I missed out on fun while dedicating all my efforts in life to pleasing my father. Which is silly, I know, because I've had amazing experiences that many will never have. But, still, I didn't do all the dumb, fun things that my friends were doing in school and college. I was too serious, too focused on the future to live in the now. I want to live in the now more."

I want to give her all of that.

"We'll start tonight."

She frowns. "What?"

"We're going in search of fun."

"Bradford. It's midnight. It's time for sleep."

"Contrary to popular belief, the party can start at midnight. Your coach won't turn into a pumpkin and I'm more than happy to carry your glass slippers when your feet get sore." I brush my lips across hers one last time. "Let's go have some fun."

@thetea_gasp

OMG GIRLFRIENDS, do we have some juicy tea for you tonight?! Gather round. @bradfordblack our favorite sexy future Presidential candidate (we hope!) just got married and NOT to his fiancée #gasp We can confirm he married @kristenblaise tonight in Vegas. No official statement from either party has been released but look at the happy couple in that photo #swoon. We all knew Bradford and @thececeliaaniston lacked something, and now that we've seen this photo of him with his new wife, we can see what that was - #passion. Stay tuned for more soon because you just know there's going to be so.much.more from this couple.

31

KRISTEN

BRADFORD'S PHONE WAKES ME. It's vibrating with text after text, missed call after missed call. And it's doing all of that from underneath me.

What even is going on?

All this vibrating is too much.

I'm trying to wake up enough to pull it out from under me, but I'm struggling with that mission. It doesn't help that Bradford's arm is around me so tightly and my body is pressed so hard to his that I never want to move again. I like fitting with him like this.

More messages vibrate under me.

I crack my eyes open and look at Bradford. He's sleeping like the dead. He has no awareness of the work that awaits him on his phone.

Wait.

Why is his phone underneath me?

I scrunch my eyes as I rack my brain for that information. That hurts enough for me to stop immediately.

Whoa, I have a headache. It's not raging, but it's enough for me not to engage in too much thinking just yet.

I run my gaze over the man lying next to me, holding me like he maybe won't ever let me go again. I hope he never does.

I take in his stubble. It cannot be emphasized enough how much I like that stubble. If he wasn't sleeping so peacefully, I would reach out and touch his cheek. I'm a little concerned that my hands are going to have stalker vibes when it comes to Bradford and I'm wondering how good he's going to be with that. He's never really been the kind of man to engage in shows of affection in public. Well, except for that one girlfriend he had that we never speak of. *We* being me, me, and me.

His phone vibrates again and I decide it's time to retrieve it. These messages might be important.

As I move to find the cell, a massive, sparkling rock on my left ring finger smacks into my sight. It's the most gorgeous diamond I have ever seen in my life, and I've seen a lot. A *lot*. And HOLY SHIT, what is it doing on my finger and why do I suddenly have images of Elvis in my head? Elvis, Bradford and me.

"Ohmigod! Holy fuck! Shit!" My hand is on Bradford's chest before I can stop it and I'm shaking him. "Bradford, wake up!"

I locate his phone as he stirs. "What?"

"Why am I thinking we did something very bad last night?"

He looks at me. "Huh?"

I stare at his phone. At the messages that fill his lockscreen. And since he doesn't seem to understand the urgency here, I take matters into my own hands.

"I'm making an executive decision and using your passcode to open your phone so I can confirm what I'm thinking is right. You have two seconds to tell me not to use your passcode. After that, I'm going in."

"Go for it." He throws the bedcovers off and leaves the bed to walk into the bathroom.

I tap in the passcode and start reading.

BECKETT

Bradford, this is Jenna. Can you please get Kristen to call me?

ALAN

Jesus Christ, I just woke up to your news.

ALAN

You're making fucking headlines everywhere and not for the right reasons.

ALAN

What were you thinking?

ALAN

Fuck, the next time you want some sex, don't marry the woman while you're at it.

Oh. Fuck.

I was right.

Elvis didn't just sing a song for us.

Also, Alan is already one of my least favorite people.

ALAN

This shitshow is going to be hell on earth, Bradford. I hope you know that.

ALAN

Call me as soon as you wake up. We
need to put a fucking plan into action
ASAP.

HAYDEN

I'm billing you double for the work I
endured on your marriage contract to
Cecelia and triple for what we'll have to
do about the prenup you chose to get
married without.

GAGE

Jesus, you're so fucking competitive.
Even when you're out there fucking up,
you're making sure you rank #1 at it.

CALLAN

Holy fuck, big brother, I'm always
impressed with your choice in women.
Well, except for the last one. Congrats.

CHARLIZE

Your second best friend approves. I think
this means you're out of the rough now.
Right?

CHARLIZE

Also, I'm so excited that we will be celebrating our wedding anniversaries on the same day every.single.year! Owen took me to Elvis last night too. He may have actually been the REAL Elvis, Bradford! He was so old! I need to know what package you guys got. Your bestie was stingy and only paid for one song. He refused to get the package with extra songs and Elvis sunglasses. If you got the sunglasses, what can I do to encourage you to give them to me? I mean, if Kristen wants them, then obvs they're hers because she's your wife (YOUR WIFE!!), but if she doesn't want them, please make them my wedding present. Kisses x

ETHAN

Dad's losing his shit, just FYI. But I am so fucking glad you didn't marry that dragon woman.

DAD

Call me.

CECELIA

This is going to cost you your reputation. I will make sure of that if it's the last thing I do.

OWEN

Never saw that coming. Congrats. Is golf still on Tuesday morning or are you taking a honeymoon?

MOM

> I tried to call because I wanted to say this to you rather than text it. I imagine you're busy, so I'll text it. I love you, Bradford and I hope Kristen makes you happy. It makes my heart so happy to know you chose to marry for love rather than for your career (I'm hoping that's what this is. I can't imagine you doing what you did for any other reason). Call me when you get a chance xx

I scroll through a stack of texts that are business related until I get to a text thread from a woman called Jane. These were sent during the night in the early hours and they've already been read. I read from where last night's texts started.

JANE

> Calling me at this time of night to get me to arrange a last-minute wedding is not in my job description, Bradford. The next time you do it, I would prefer more than one minute's notice. Just so we're clear on this.

BRADFORD

> Consider us on the same page.

JANE

> I'll text you as soon as I've sorted everything for you.

JANE

Okay, the marriage license guy is awake and heading into the office now to arrange the license for you. And the jeweler will be at his work in half an hour, so by the time you get the marriage license, he'll be ready for you.

BRADFORD

Thank you. I appreciate this.

JANE

You better. I was sleeping like a baby.

JANE

Oh, and PS I quit.

Oh, shit.

I glance up as Bradford comes back into the bedroom. I really want to take a long moment with his naked body and all those muscles of his, but there's no time for that. "We got married last night."

"Yes."

I blink. "And?"

"And what?"

I blink again. Twice. "Why are you being so calm about this?"

"Why are you not being calm?"

My eyes widen. "Umm, maybe because you're engaged and the whole world now knows you cheated on your fiancée so you could get Elvis to marry us on a whim in Vegas."

He frowns. "How does the whole world know?"

"I don't know, but Alan says you're making headlines and none of it is good." I go back to his phone and google him. "Oh. God. This isn't good."

He comes to me and takes his phone from my hands. "Don't read that stuff."

I stare up at him. "Why would you let us get married?"

He gives me one of his trademark brow arches. "This is on me? I seem to recall having a partner in crime."

I stand as my memories of last night come to me. "I know I suggested it, but that was the alcohol talking. For future reference, I don't make good life choices when I've been drinking."

More of that brow arch. "So, marrying me was a bad life choice?" I know from his tone that he doesn't believe that. I know he's just making a point.

I take a deep breath and smile. Moving into him, I slip my arms around his waist. *My husband.* "It was the best life choice I have ever made. But seriously, you've now got a PR nightmare to deal with and I hate that for you."

He looks at me with so much love and tenderness I think I could die right now and feel like I achieved everything in life I wanted to. "Any nightmare I have to deal with is worth this."

The romantic in me loves what he just said. *Loves.* She wants to shut the world out and enjoy our first day of being married. The rest of me knows we don't have that luxury. Well, Bradford doesn't have that luxury. Not if he wants a political career.

I let us have another minute of ignoring what we have to sort through and then I press his phone to his hand and say, "You need to get to work. Oh, and your assistant quit."

He reaches for his trousers. "She didn't quit."

"She did. I don't think she was happy you woke her in

the middle of the night and forced her to pay off people so you could get what you wanted." I grimace as my headache increases a little. "Also, why did you make me drink so many cocktails last night?"

He finishes dressing and comes to me with a hand to my neck and a kiss to my forehead. "Again, I seem to recall a partner in crime for all that fun we had last night. A partner who found her *new favorite cocktail*...three times. And Jane didn't quit. She's always displeased with me. She quits at least twice a week." He looks at me with concern. "I've got Advil in the bathroom if you need some."

"I do." I assess him and the headache he doesn't appear to have. "How do you not have a headache? You drank a lot too."

"I have a slight headache. I drank more water than you did last night." A look of heat passes between us. "It seems I found something I can't boss you into."

Memories of him trying to force water into me when we got back to the suite flood my mind. I was more intent on sucking his dick than drinking that water.

I pat his chest. "I'm making a mental note: water before dick."

With that, I walk into the bathroom to find Advil and take a shower while he goes through his messages.

I kind of need this time alone because while I'm loving this new space Bradford and I are in, I'm also in the space of *holy shit, I got married*. Yesterday we were warring with each other. Last night at dinner I wanted to hit him over the head with a hardcover dictionary. A very large one. Today, I'm Mrs. Black. While marrying Bradford was absolutely my best life choice, he's right that my timing is fucking woeful.

We were supposed to take weeks before showing up in public together. I mean, I wanted to fight him over that and make him wait months. But no, the part of me that really needs to be taken out into the middle of nowhere and left there, took charge and was all *bitch, we're getting this done now*. She wasn't waiting even a day.

Some people get divorced when they're in the middle of a mid-life crisis. Not me. I go all out and get married.

I'm chasing this thought spiral when Bradford comes into the bathroom and holds out his phone for me. "It's Jenna." As he turns to leave me to take the call alone, I curl my fingers around his wrist, letting him know I want him to stay.

"This is the last time I ever let you wander Vegas without a phone," Jenna says as I watch Bradford rest his ass against the vanity. I'm turned on by the purely masculine way he settles into place, crossing his arms and legs. I'm also turned on by the way he looks at my body while he does this.

"Kristen, are you there?" Jenna pulls me back to our conversation.

"Yes, and surprise, I got married."

"You two are all over social media. Does Bradford know that?"

I look at my husband who is still enjoying time with my body. God, his attention is intoxicating. "Yes."

"Okay, good. I imagine he's doing massive damage control. The photos of you two that people posted to Instagram last night are not what I imagine his party would approve of."

I smile as I watch what Bradford considers damage control. "Well, if you call looking at me and thinking about all the ways he wants to have sex with me *massive damage control*, then yes that's exactly what he's doing."

Bradford's gaze settles on my left hand by my side.

"I'm impressed," Jenna says. "You found a man with great priorities."

"Wait. How bad were those photos?"

"Let's just say they were one step away from you releasing your very own sex tape. And can I also just say, you let me down. We could have been known as the sisters who brought shame onto their family rather than that just being me who did that."

"Oh, I'm pretty sure this marriage will do that." My father is *not* going to like this.

"Yeah, speaking of that, I'll bring your phone to you. It's blowing up with calls and messages. And Kris?"

I already know what she's about to say. "Dad?"

"I've had him on the phone this morning asking me why you're not answering your calls and whether I know what possessed you. He's not happy."

The fact I didn't think about my father once before I married Bradford is all the proof I need to know that while I'd like to send my therapist to outer space with some of my parts, every second I've sat on her couch and ripped myself wide open for her has been worth it.

I gave up on gaining my father's approval the day I ended my engagement to Johnathon, and although it's been a hard road to where I am today, I haven't looked back. Once I tasted that freedom, I never wanted to give it up again, and I haven't.

"I can imagine."

"Seriously, how the hell did you two end up married? After what went down between you two at dinner last night, I'm guessing there's history there?"

"I'll tell you all about it later, but mostly I'm married because Bradford is the bossiest man I know." This catches his attention and he gives me a look of *that's how we're playing this*? I smile at him before saying to Jenna, "Let's just say that I randomly, in the spirit of having fun, suggested that getting married in Vegas could be fun, and he ran with it. And because he has more money than anyone should, he could make it happen."

I'd be lying, though, if I said I didn't die for the way he took charge and made it happen. There's something about a man with that kind of power that gets me hot.

"I need this story soon." She pauses and I hear Beckett say something to her. Then, she comes back to me. "Beckett's going to bring your phone to you. Unless you need me." She adds that last offer softly and I hear all her heart in her words. In amongst all the pain of my broken engagement was some gold, my relationship with my sister being gold I treasure. We're now close in a way we never were.

"No, I'm good."

Bradford pushes off the vanity after I end the call. He takes his phone when I hand it back. He then lifts my left hand, looking at the rings he put there last night. "These look good here."

There's something new in his tone. Something that's not been there before. "As in you like them or as in you like what they tell people?"

The intense way he looks at me can't be confused with anything but what it is. "I've lived through too many years of you not being mine. We're never doing that again. And every asshole out there will now know that too."

I would never have thought Bradford was the possessive type. I've witnessed him with a lot of women and not once has he displayed any kind of possessiveness.

I look at the ring on his finger, feeling the same kind of intense emotion about it. "I like every woman knowing you're mine too."

He drops his lips to mine and steals a kiss that leaves me a little breathless before striding out of the bathroom. I place my hand to my stomach as my butterflies let me know they're as desperate for more of his kisses as I am.

And then I have the strangest thought: if I could go back nine years and change everything, I don't think I would. I think Bradford and I are exactly where we're meant to be.

Beckett delivers my phone and gets into a conversation with Bradford. I go to my suite to pack while they talk. I'm flying home with Bradford in his jet and we're leaving soon. Before I start packing, I check all the messages and missed calls on my phone. I don't have as many as Bradford had, but there are a lot.

Jenna's friends surprise me with messages. They forced me into swapping numbers over the weekend.

ADELINE

How did we not know you and Bradford
had a thing? Huge congratulations.
Drinks to celebrate as soon as you
can xx

CHARLIZE

I adore Bradford for you! I think this
makes us third best friends. And thank
you for saving all of us from Cecelia
shudders Can't wait to catch up soon! x

I have no idea what she means by third best friends,
and I think maybe *I* should shudder at that but for some
reason, I don't. This mid-life crisis is causing all kinds of
strange reactions to things.

POPPY

When I said to quit Tinder, this wasn't
quite what I had in mind. And when you
two were playing your very own version
of Fuck, Marry, Kill at dinner last night, I
honestly thought kill might be in the
cards. Congrats, babe. And for the love
of God, I hope you two agreed on
flossing as part of the prenup.

JESSICA

That's how it's done! Make a decision
and execute it straight away. No messing
about. I like your style. Congrats!

LORELEI

Congratulations, Kristen! Australia is a
great honeymoon destination. Just
saying. Ashton and I would love to see
you guys out here one day! Xx

There are messages from my brothers.

OLIVER

Bradford Black, huh? If anyone in our family knows how to cause a scandal, it isn't Jenna. I want to say congrats, but I need to see this marriage in person before I commit to that.

GRAYSON

Let me know when you're home.

Grayson's message is actually code for *If he breaks your heart, I will destroy him.* Oliver's text is only one step down from that. I may never have had my father's love in the way I wanted it, but my siblings have always gone above and beyond loving and protecting me.

And then there's a nasty message from Phillip.

PHILLIP

I knew you were a slut for him. You could have had me, Kristen. I would have given you everything.

I can't believe I gave any of my time to that man. But then, he did help me work out some of my boundaries when it comes to men, and that will help me in my marriage. Maybe I'll send him a bottle of his favorite scotch and thank him for being a real dick.

Noticeably missing is a text from my mother. There are a lot of unread texts from her yesterday when I didn't have my phone, but she hasn't called or texted about my marriage.

I move on from thinking about what that means to the voicemail my father left. The one demanding I call him straight away.

I don't call him straight away.

I put makeup on.

I style my hair.

I choose a dress to wear on the plane. One that is sure to drive Bradford wild.

I pack.

And then I call him.

"Kristen," he answers and I know that when Jenna said he wasn't happy, what she really should have said was that he was furious in the kind of way that means he'll withdraw his love for longer than the standard couple of weeks he usually does when I've angered him.

"You heard my news."

"I've called our lawyer to draw up divorce papers. He'll be here at eight tonight. I expect you then too."

"I'm not getting a divorce, Dad."

"You are. I forbid you to stay married to that man. The Black name is not one I will ever tolerate anywhere near the Blaise name." His steely tone causes me to pay closer attention to what he's saying. Not to mention the fact he disapproves of Bradford. I didn't see that coming. I knew he'd hate the way I got married, but I thought he'd eventually be happy with the marriage. After all, Bradford ticks all the boxes my father has for worthy husband material.

"Why?"

"The history between our families is not one I care to revisit."

"What history?"

"Just end it, Kristen. You won't like the consequences if you don't."

32

KRISTEN

JENNA

Whatever you do, don't go on social media.

> Bradford's been telling me that all day.

JENNA

Let me guess, you ignored him just like you're going to ignore me.

> Did you avoid social media when your sex tape went viral?

JENNA

You know I didn't. And that's why I'm qualified to give you this advice.

> Honestly, I can't look away. This is getting out of control and I'm worried for Bradford.

JENNA

How is he?

He spent most of the flight home working through the damage control plan his political consultant put together this morning. He isn't anywhere near as stressed as I would be if I was him.

JENNA

How are you?

Let's just say that this doesn't feel like a great start to a marriage. Like maybe I've really messed things up for Bradford.

JENNA

Just don't do what I did when I was worried I'd screwed things up for Beckett. Don't run. Keep talking and figuring things out together.

I'm not going to run.

JENNA

Good.

Question: do you know what the history is between our family and Bradford's?

JENNA

What history?

Dad said he won't tolerate my marriage because the history between our families is one he doesn't want to revisit.

JENNA

Wow. I know nothing about this history. Does Bradford know?

He's been busy all day. I haven't asked him yet. I'm going to call Mom later and ask her.

JENNA

Are you okay? Do you need me when you get home?

> No, I'm okay. You know Dad, he'll freeze me out for a while and then we'll just move on.

JENNA

I know, but still. I know how upsetting it is when he does this. I'm here if you need me.

> I love you.

JENNA

Okay, keep me updated on what Mom tells you. And we need dinner or lunch or breakfast or anything ASAP because I need to know everything there is to know about this wedding! OH, and where will you be living now? At Bradford's?

> We're on our way to his place now but we actually haven't discussed this yet.

AFTER A GREAT START to the day in which I felt like I could handle this marriage, I'm now feeling a little out of my depth as the reality of our situation settles in. I mean, who gets married on a whim to a man they weren't dating? A man they've never lived with or spent an extended amount of time with? No one. That's who. And yet here I am, married with no clue as to how we'll blend our lives or whether we'll even be a good match once we're living together.

Another text comes in from Jenna, but Bradford reaches for my hand from across the car and says, "What are you thinking?"

I put my phone down and look at him, noting the concern in his eyes. "That I don't even know if you snore. Or if you put your socks in the laundry basket when you take them off. Or if you use too many plates and glasses when you could use less. Or if you steal all the blankets in bed. Oh, and I have absolutely no idea how you eat bananas." My eyes widen a fraction. "A girl should never marry a man without knowing these things about him."

Bradford's brows pull together. "Surely there's only one way to eat a banana."

I like that he's humoring me. That he's not mentioning the meltdown I'm beginning to feel in my bones. "There's not. I dated a guy once who divided them into quarters lengthwise before eating them. If you tell me that's how you eat them, I'm going to need to re-evaluate this marriage right now. I can't be in the middle of a mid-life crisis *and* a marriage crisis at the same time."

He considers me for a long moment before finally saying, "What's really worrying you?"

"All of those things are worrying me."

"We can go through all those things tonight, and anything else you want to know about me. But I need to know how your heart is breathing right now, Kristen. What's actually worrying it. That's how we're doing this marriage."

Not one man I have ever dated has listened to me the way this man does. I've always known Bradford listens intently to everything I say, but I love (more than can actually be expressed) that he's actioning what I told him I needed from him in this relationship.

I squeeze his hand as I take a breath. "Something you need to know about me is that I overthink everything.

And I worry about every tiny detail of every tiny thing. So, there's a lot I'm thinking about and worrying about right now."

He gives me a tender smile. One that's filled with care. "I already know this about you."

I breathe in more air to try and calm my nerves. I take the longest minute with this breath before saying, "You have to admit we've acted very recklessly."

"I would say wildly, not recklessly."

Bradford and I haven't had a great deal of time to talk at length about our marriage yet. After the initial shock of it this morning, his political consultant was on the phone to him and consumed most of his time today. Bradford was regretful and apologetic about that but I insisted he not feel that way. His career is important to him and I don't want our marriage to come between him and his goals.

The thing about getting married recklessly like we have is that I'm second-guessing everything now. Worst of all, I'm second-guessing myself. I've worked hard in therapy to erase the self-doubts I have about myself, and while I've done a good job, this situation is causing them to flare.

Will I drive him crazy with the way I talk in my sleep?

Will he grow frustrated with my inability to ever be on time?

Will I be smart enough to keep up with him?

Will he regret marrying me instead of Cecelia?

"Kristen." Bradford's insistent tone brings me back to the conversation. "Talk to me."

"I can't stand cracked heels or dry skin," I blurt as all my feelings clog my lungs.

He keeps a straight face and I know he's working overtime to figure out where I'm going with this. "Okay."

"That means I have a weird habit of checking my partner's feet and insisting they moisturize often. It will drive you insane."

Understanding washes over him and his shoulders relax. "You're worried we don't know all these small things about each other. And that they will come between us."

"Yes! It's the small things that add up over time that allow the big things to break a couple. What if you can't stand my small things?"

"What if I can?"

I blink. "No one has ever been able to stand my small things."

He frowns. "You were engaged."

I know what he's asking without asking it. How was I engaged if my partner couldn't tolerate my quirks? "Yes, because I changed for him. I took painstaking care not to do the things he didn't like. It was exhausting and I won't ever do that again. I'm not sure I'm marriage material anymore."

"You're only questioning that because of the men you've chosen in the past. Now, you've chosen me and I'll show you how wrong you are about that." There's a fierceness in his eyes when he continues. "I'm completely captivated by you, Kristen, and I have been since the night we met. You have a heart unlike any other I've ever met. If the only way to have you in my life is to moisturize my feet or eat bananas in a particular way, I'll willingly do it."

I skip a breath.

Actually, it's stolen from me.

By my husband.

And I instantly know that it doesn't matter what Bradford's small things are either; I'll willingly put up with them to have him and his heart in my life.

If we weren't separated by the center console in Bradford's Bentley, I'd climb onto his lap and show him exactly what I think of what he just said. Damn him for having a luxury car. Instead, I say, "The next wild thing you need to do is buy a new car. One that doesn't have this divider keeping me from your lap."

Heat immediately blazes in his eyes and I swear I see the switch in his thoughts to pure filth. "Consider it done."

Oh, my.

The gravel and growl in his voice is enough to stir all my butterflies. "I was joking. You should not waste your money on a car."

He gives me more of his signature intensity that I think could resuscitate me if I needed resuscitating. "Anything that gets you on my lap is not a waste of money. You have no idea just what I'd part with for that."

A text comes in for him as he says this, which stops me from saying to hell with the console and scrambling over it to get closer to him. Not that that would be a bad thing, but tonight, it would be. We're on our way to Bradford's home to meet with his political consultant, father, and brother to go over the damage control plan they've assembled. Arriving in a just-fucked state for that is *not* how I want my first meeting with these people to go.

I watch as Bradford reads the text. If I had to guess at the feeling it's stirring in him, I'd say anger.

"Is everything okay?" I ask.

He glances at me. "It will be."

He doesn't elaborate and I don't prod for more information. I'm actually not sure I want to know what it is because I can only assume it's more backlash to our marriage. However, it's a reminder of everything we're up against. "I promise this will be the last time I ask you this," I say softly. "Are you absolutely sure about this marriage? About what you might be giving up by choosing me? Maybe you should take a night by yourself to think about it again."

Bradford doesn't hesitate with his answer. "I'm not taking a night by myself, Kristen. I'm never taking a night by myself again unless it's unavoidable." His decisive tone goes straight to my stomach, settling low there. It reassures any remaining hesitation I have over hurting his career and I decide that this really will be the last time I ask him that question.

Bradford's driver pulls the car into the garage of the tower he lives in and five minutes later, we're in the private elevator on our way up to the penthouse. We stop at the 129th floor and exit into a gallery that leads to a grand salon that is one of the most luxurious rooms I have ever been in. I don't have near enough time to take in the sumptuous creams and grays that fill the room because I'm immediately presented with three men staring at me like I've created the worst problem of their lives.

I recognize his father and brother, Hayden, and am guessing the third man is Alan, his political consultant. Alan reminds me of that actor, Jon Hamm in looks. Dark hair, strong jaw, tanned. Good looking. Just not as tall.

And definitely not as friendly looking. He's watching me with an assessing look. No smile in sight.

"Gentlemen," Bradford says, extending his arm to pull me next to him. "This is Kristen." He then goes around the group and introduces me to everyone.

"I wish we were meeting under different circumstances," Edmund, Bradford's father says, his eyes and voice filled with displeasure. "However, here we are and my son seems adamant that this marriage is here to stay, so welcome." Edmund might be welcoming me, but it's obvious he wishes he wasn't.

I call on my manners and smile at him. "It's lovely to meet you." Looking at Edmund is like looking at an older version of Bradford. I read once that fathers have the upper hand when it comes to gene expression in their children and that is more than true with the Black family. Edmund's five sons all have their father's dark hair, height, and good looks.

We move to the dining room and sit at the large table that can seat twenty.

"Let's get straight down to business," Hayden says, his tone clinical.

Bradford cuts in. "Let's come back to that." He looks at Alan. "Your plan is good, but there's no way Kristen is attending all those social events."

I frown. We haven't talked about this. "Which events?"

"The ones we need you to attend if we've got any shot at salvaging your husband's political career," Alan says. The way he utters the word "husband" leaves me in no doubt that he wants me to disappear.

"Alan," Bradford says, his voice holding a warning.

I touch his arm to stop him. "No, it's okay." I look at Alan, feeling more than confident I can handle this man. A year and a half of standing up to my father has given me skills I never had before. "Go on."

Alan details weeks of daily functions that include breakfasts, lunches, dinners, and galas. He's also scheduled some media interviews in a few weeks. The hope is that by then the scandal will have died down enough to begin a media campaign to win support. When he gets to the media outlets owned by my father's company, I shake my head. "You can take the last five off your list. My father's company owns them, and based on the phone call I had with him today, he won't allow interviews with Bradford and me to appear in any of his publications."

"Jesus," Alan mutters. "The day just gets fucking better."

"Enough," Bradford snaps, his tone sharp enough to gain everyone's full attention. The severe expression on his face is one I would shrink from if it was directed at me.

Alan has the sense to take heed. He doesn't dwell on the Blaise Media issue. He moves on, giving me a full rundown of other social appearances that he's proposed for Bradford and me over the next few weeks.

"Okay," I say, "I can do a lot of those, but some will clash with my work and a couple of things I already have planned that I know I can't get out of. How about I email you that information so you can rearrange what you can?"

He appears okay with that and nods his agreement.

"You've packed too much into the weekends," Bradford says. "Remove everything from the Sundays. Kristen needs a day off."

"No." I look at him. "It's only for a few weeks, right?"

"Yes, but I don't want you run ragged for weeks." Bradford appears anything but convinced.

"Trust me, I've worked harder before." I eye Alan. "The Sundays are fine."

Bradford and I engage in a war of looks. His say *stop arguing with me on this*. Mine say *stop being so overprotective*.

Alan cuts into our war. "The Sundays stay. We don't have time to fuck around with this, Bradford. You made your choice, and just so I'm leaving you with no doubt about this, it was a choice that may end your political career before it even starts. The sooner we rectify it, the better."

I try to keep my breaths calm. "What do you think the likelihood of this ruining Bradford politically is?" When I asked Bradford about Alan on the plane, about his political experience, he told me Alan is the best at his job. I might not like the man so far, but I trust Bradford's appraisal of him and that means I have to trust his assessment of this situation.

Alan's eyes bore into me in a way that makes it clear he wants me to really listen to him. "The party won't like what he's done and this will lose their favor. It may end his bid for this Senate seat. Sure, he can come back later and try again, but I know your husband and I know he's hungry for this now, not later. As far as the likelihood of this happening? It's fucking high. Don't kid yourself that it isn't." He says "husband" again like he wishes Bradford was anything but that. I like him even less than I like his assessment of the damage he says we've done.

"I agree," Edmund says, joining the conversation. "This isn't good, son."

Bradford nods, the gravity of the situation settling into his features. But still, he appears firm on his decision. "It will blow over. I'll make sure of it."

Alan doesn't argue with him but it's obvious he doesn't agree. He moves on from this into a conversation regarding the rest of their plan to win the party over.

Half an hour later, Alan leaves and I exhale a breath of relief. His energy is too aggressive for me. I feel the change in the air the minute he steps out of the room.

"Okay," Hayden says, "Can we go over Cecelia now? And then discuss the postnup."

Bradford shakes his head. "No, we'll just go over Cecelia tonight. I received a text from her earlier that tells me she's going to be a problem, so the sooner we move on that, the better."

"I'd prefer to begin working out the postnup tonight. I don't have a lot of spare time this week," Hayden says.

"We'll leave it until you've got more time." Bradford looks anything but worried over this.

Hayden, on the other hand, appears disturbed by that idea. "I don't advise that."

"There's no rush," Bradford says.

"There is." Hayden is emphatic.

Bradford seems annoyed with his brother. I can't tell if he wants to wait so he can discuss this with me first or if he really isn't concerned.

"We should do it now," I say.

Hayden looks at me. "Thank fuck one of you is using

your brain." I've met Hayden a few times over the years at various parties and have always liked him. What I like right now is his attention to boundaries. Everything about my marriage to Bradford feels like a whirlwind my brain needs to catch up with; I like Hayden taking charge of this one thing.

Before Bradford can respond to that, his father stands. "I'm going to leave you three to this. I have some work I still need to get through tonight." He glances between me and Bradford. "We need dinner this week. Let your mother know which night works best for you two. We'll make it happen."

Bradford stands and moves to his father. "I'll let you know tomorrow." I watch as they embrace and say good-bye. This isn't something my father has ever done with any of his children. I've definitely gotten the impression tonight that his father is just as ruthless as I've always thought, but I can see warmth in this moment.

Edmund and Hayden share a similar embrace and then Edmund leaves, at which point Hayden gives us both a look of anticipation. The postnup.

"Okay." I take the lead. "Let's do this."

Bradford eyes me with that protective look in his eye again. "Kristen—"

"Not that I ever plan on divorcing you or letting you divorce me," I cut him off, "but if that should happen, we'll walk away with what we came into this marriage with. I absolutely refuse to lose my home in the Hamptons." I turn to Hayden. "Please note that. A girl needs to ensure she's protected. I'm also keeping my Manhattan condo. He can't have my homes if he leaves me."

Hayden's lips twitch. "Smart."

I glance between them. "Right, so does that take care of it?"

Bradford is looking at me with the same amusement his brother is. I mean, the man has billions. *Billions.* And homes scattered around the world. There's never any fear of him coming after my two homes. "We'll make sure that's noted in the agreement but we'll divide my assets."

"I don't want your money, Bradford."

"I know. And trust me, I won't allow our marriage to come to it, but if I fuck it up, I want you provided for."

"What if I fuck it up?"

"There's not one thing you could do that would make me walk away." He looks at Hayden. "Split my assets down the middle."

I refrain from telling him what I really think of that. "You'll just keep arguing with me if I keep arguing with you, won't you?"

Hayden laughs. "You know my brother well, I see."

I roll my eyes. "You have no idea."

He smiles and it feels like a *welcome to the family* smile. "I think I might. I'm already seeing the difference in him."

I eye Bradford. "I might cheat on you. Are you saying you'd tolerate that? Or still want to give me half of your belongings?"

He gives me a look. "We both know neither of us are cheaters."

I'm suddenly feeling flushed as memories of the times I wanted to cross that line fill my mind.

He's right. Neither of us are cheaters. And since that's really the only reason I could see our marriage ending, I know this postnup won't even matter. Bradford will never have to part with his money for me, so I let the argument go.

My phone buzzes with a text and when I see Lila's name flash across the screen, I look at Bradford. "Tell me you're free on the fourteenth of January. And if you can't tell me that, tell me you'll find a way to be free that night."

Alan steps back into the room as I say this. "I just scheduled you both to attend a charity breakfast tomorrow morning." It's not a question but he waits with an impatient expression for our confirmation.

Bradford shoots me a questioning look.

"I can do that." I mentally rearrange my morning tomorrow to make this happen.

Alan taps out a message on his phone before meeting Bradford's gaze again. "You'll be taking part in a business panel. They need you there by six a.m. to get you prepped for it."

At my wide eyes, Hayden laughs and says, "I imagine that whatever you need my brother for on the fourteenth won't even come close to making up for all these early mornings you've got ahead of you."

Alan narrows his eyes at me. "What's on the fourteenth? We'll need to check the schedule."

"No," I say. "The fourteenth of January, not December." I look at Bradford. "It's my school reunion."

"I'm free," Bradford says without hesitation and I can see it in his eyes that even if he has something planned for that night already, he has every intention of canceling it.

Alan pulls up Bradford's schedule. "You've got a party on that night. At the Hale's."

"Not anymore," Bradford says, squishing my heart all the way together.

This only earns me a sharper look of disapproval from Alan. "It's an important party. You don't want to piss Senator Hale off."

Before I can cut in and tell Bradford that he should go to the party, he says, "I'll chance it."

"Fuck," Alan mutters.

Bradford simply gives him a brow arch in return and even I understand this form of communication they seem to have nailed. *Don't argue with me.* Perhaps I should learn how to give that brow arch.

Alan takes a deep breath before glancing at me. "Send me the details of your reunion. I'll add it to the schedule and maybe we'll see if we can capitalize on it. Fuck knows that people like to see the human side of a candidate. Attending a wife's reunion fits that bill."

As he slips back out of the room, I stand and follow him. "Alan," I call to slow him down.

He turns back to me. The annoyance written all over his face would have stopped the old me from saying what I came to say. The new me still occasionally struggles with wanting approval, but far less these days. When it comes to Alan, I don't care if he never approves of me.

"I understand this situation isn't ideal, and that it makes your job more difficult, but I'm not going anywhere, so you and I need to find a way to work together."

"*Not ideal* doesn't even come close to describing what this situation is, Kristen. Whatever you think you might know about politics, you don't. You have no clue what Bradford is up against here. My job was difficult before you came along. Now, it's a goddamn fucking headache. I *will* fix this because that's what I do, but don't confuse what you and I are doing here as working together. You are simply a pawn in my game that I will move where I need."

If my father prepared me for anything in life, it was Alan. I might dislike him but I understand his job.

I step closer to him, holding my body perfectly straight and tall. "I might not know all the intricacies of politics, but I know all about power and the world of men that Bradford moves in. I've been dealing with these men and the women in their lives my entire life. I know how they think and I might even know more about the web of secrets and lies between them than you do. I'll be your pawn, for Bradford, but you'd be a fool not to align with me and work with me."

All he gives me is a press of his lips and a long moment of scrutiny. Then, he simply carries on with his imperious ways. "Don't be late tomorrow morning. It won't be a good start for us if you are."

Some fucking men can go fuck themselves. I'm not even determined to win this one over. I'm just determined to help Bradford as much as I can and if a by-product of that is making Alan happy, so be it.

When I rejoin Bradford and Hayden, Bradford looks at me like he's assessing me for damage. "Everything good?"

I take the seat next to him again and nod. "I think Alan and I understand each other."

"Right," Hayden says, interrupting us when he stands. "I'm going home. I'll draft this agreement and get it to you tomorrow. I'll also draft the NDA for Cecelia with the points you just mentioned. And if you need me to ask Olivia to help with your PR, let me know." He smiles at me and it's such a warm and genuine gesture that I feel it deeply. "Congratulations on your marriage. I, for one, am glad to see my brother happy. Don't let Alan get to you. He'll come around when he realizes he has no other choice." His smile turns into a grin. "Just don't be late to any of the events he's lined up. I've seen that guy in action and it isn't pretty when someone's late."

"Oh, I can imagine. He just made it perfectly clear how detrimental to our relationship it will be if I'm late tomorrow."

"Fuck," Bradford curses and I turn in time to see his brows furrowing.

"It's okay," I reassure him. "My skin is thick. He doesn't worry me."

He still doesn't appear convinced, even after Hayden leaves. "I'll talk with Alan tomorrow. I won't allow him to treat you like this."

I place my hand on his arm. "Please don't. I have to stand on my own two feet if I'm going to have any chance of gaining his respect."

"He should respect you, period, Kristen."

"I agree but let's be honest here, men like Alan don't respect women like they should. It's bullshit but it's all I have to work with. Let me do this my way."

The look in his eyes tells me he's not a fan of this approach but I also see that he'll give me what I've asked for. This might be one of my favorite things a man has ever given me.

When Bradford takes my hand and says, "Let's get you settled in," I think about Alan again. *You have no clue what*

Bradford is up against here. He's right; I don't. Not the full extent of it. I trust that Alan isn't catastrophizing this. He is the best at what he does after all. He did say he'd fix it, and he did seem quite sure of that, but still, the unease sitting low in my stomach isn't going away.

I can only hope that the best thing that has ever happened in my life doesn't turn out to be something Bradford regrets.

33

KRISTEN

BRADFORD'S HOME IS JAW-DROPPING. Occupying the top three floors of the tower, it has seven bedroom suites, eight bathrooms, a private ballroom, an observatory, a library, a gaming room, a media room, a professional-grade catering kitchen for the ballroom as well as a kitchen for daily use, a gym, and a magnificent terrace. Private elevators connect each floor, as does a grand spiral staircase that is a work of art.

The extravagant furnishings and decorating throughout have nothing on the view of Manhattan from all the rooms. After I follow Bradford into the primary suite that has a bedroom, two dressing rooms, two bathrooms, and a sitting room, I walk to the floor-to-ceiling windows. I take in the stunning city backdrop and can imagine how airy and bright it will be in here in the morning.

I turn and find him watching me intently. "This view. My God. I think I could live in this room and be happy."

"Do you want to live here?"

I glance at the beauty surrounding me. My condo is gorgeous but it's smaller than his. It also doesn't have the same kind of view. However, those aren't the things that make a home and I'm well aware of that. "I haven't thought about it. Do you?"

"There's a lot we'll have to figure out but we don't have to do it all straight away."

He's right. Most couples slowly bring their lives together. They get to know each other first. They build their boundaries before they get married. I imagine that marriage brings a new pulse to a relationship, but that pulse doesn't usually involve the kind of figuring out that Bradford and I have ahead of us.

"I don't do well with not knowing, Bradford." I inhale a long breath. "Oh God, why did we drink so much and think it was a good idea to ask Elvis to put rings on our fingers?"

"Elvis didn't put that ring on your finger. I did. And I'd do it again in a heartbeat, sober."

He's right, and I like that he's reminded me of this fact.

"Okay, it's time for you to start learning my small things. I take a long time to get ready every day. And when I say long, I mean *long*. I'm rarely on time. And I don't like being called out on that. In fact, I may do physical harm to you if you mention it. I've tried to change this about myself and I'm just not built that way, so it'll be up to you to recalibrate your schedule to make allowances for it. And I'm at the point in my therapy where I now make no apologies for that." I take a breath before continuing. "I really, *really* love strawberry jam. Clean sheets are important to me. As is having time every night to read. And if you ever make fun of the spicy romances I read, you will regret that. I love watching the same movies over and over. I love Valentine's Day and you should spoil me on that day just as much as I will spoil you. Sunday mornings should be reserved for sleeping in, breakfast in bed, and reading. Oh, and anything you have in the kitchen that has sugar in it will have to go. That's a non-negotiable for me. I can't be trusted around sugar."

His lips twitch. "But strawberry jam stays?"

My eyes widen. "God, no. Strawberry jam can never make its way into our home. Ever. If you do bring it here, your life will be hell for at least twenty-four hours and I really don't think you'll be sleeping in our bed with me that night."

"If your non-negotiable is a ban on sugar, mine is that I won't ever allow either of us to sleep in a different bed. I don't care if you bring knives to bed with you, you're sleeping with me." The way he says this so fiercely, combined with the matching look in his eyes reaches low in my stomach.

"Also," he adds, coming to me, his hands sliding around my waist to rest on my ass, "I'm good with your plan for Sundays but we need to add sex into the mix."

Yes, yes we do.

His grip tightens on my ass and I fight to stay on track with this conversation. "Those are only some of my things, FYI. You need to prepare yourself for a lot," I say.

"Consider me prepared."

There are a lot of things I love about this man but one of the very top things is the way he makes me feel safe. Protected. Like he'll always ensure nothing bad will come my way under his watch. Right now, I have zero doubt he's prepared for whatever I throw at him.

"Tell me some of your things," I say as his eyes drop to my breasts.

"I don't like strawberry jam, which is good since it's not allowed here now." The mirth in his eyes when they find mine again is everything and causes flutters in my stomach. "I run every morning, usually at five. And I hit the gym Mondays, Wednesdays, and Fridays." He brings one hand to my neck and sweeps my hair from it before kissing my skin there. "I don't read romance, but I support anyone who does." He slides my dress off my shoulder. "My preference is biographies and thrillers." He gently pushes my bra strap to the side and bends to kiss his way down from my shoulder to my breast, pretty much ensuring I'm only taking in half of what he's saying now. "I've never spoiled a woman on Valentine's Day but I look forward to doing that next year. And"—he lifts me into his arms and moves us to the wall, holding me against it—"my preference for Sundays has just changed to spending them fucking you. If I'm going to recalibrate my schedule to allow for you running late, you're going to adjust your plan to include only one hour of reading on a Sunday morning."

I suddenly want to remove reading from my Sundays.

I also want him to always watch me with the kind of heat he now is.

And anything I can do to hear him promise to fuck me is my highest priority from here on out.

Bradford's phone has been vibrating with text after text that he's been ignoring to have this conversation. I love that he makes no move to check any of those messages. However, I also war with myself over suggesting they might be important.

I'm about to mention the texts when his mouth seals over mine and he kisses me so thoroughly that I struggle to even recall what I was thinking.

My legs are around him, my arms are around him, my heart is around him. And he's drawing me into a place I never knew existed. Into the kind of bliss and need I had no idea could be felt.

I have never wanted a man as much as I want Bradford.

"I can't fucking get enough of you," he rasps when he finally comes up for air. That's right before he roughly pushes the top of my dress and bra down so he can take hold of my breast and suck my nipple into his mouth.

My back arches and I moan as the pleasure fills every inch of my body.

"Oh, God." I grip his hair and when he groans his approval of that, I squeeze it tighter between my fingers.

Before I know what's happening, he's taking me from the wall to the bed, laying me across it. He then falls to his knees between my legs, roughly yanking me to the edge.

His smoldering eyes meet mine when his hands go to the bottom of my long sweater dress. "Do you own any dresses that don't make it hard for a man to breathe?"

Intense lust sparks along my skin at the raw hunger radiating from him.

I'd hoped the simple red midi sweater dress I chose for today would steal Bradford's attention with the way it clings to my curves, but I'm not sure I'd expected it to turn him on to this degree.

"I'm getting rid of the ones that don't," I breathe, barely able to form a coherent reply.

His deep growl of support for that statement only gets me hotter.

He shoves my dress up, pulls my panties off, and spreads my legs. His gaze locks onto my pussy like nothing else exists in this world.

That damn phone of his, though. It hasn't stopped vibrating in his pocket.

"Maybe you should check those messages." I hardly know what I'm saying. I just know that my brain is scrambled by those texts and I'm concerned he's missing something important. What I really want to say, though, is *throw the fucking thing away*.

He doesn't shift his focus. If anything, he fixates even harder. "I have better things to do right now." The rasp in his voice vibrates through my body, intensifying my desire for him to white hot levels.

He runs his hand up the backs of my thighs to take hold of my ass while sinking lower on his knees. Then, he pulls me to him and buries his face in my pussy.

Oh, holy God.

My back lifts up off the bed as he flattens his tongue to me and slowly licks from my entrance up to my clit. He spends time with my clit, circling it over and over before sucking it into his mouth and using his tongue on it in ways that threaten to make me come straight away.

I grind myself against his mouth and grasp his hair, trying desperately to find more, more, more.

He gives me what I want, licking and sucking for what feels like forever but still isn't, *could never be*, long enough. When he lifts his mouth, I want to force it back down. I want to beg him *to keep going and never stop*. I can't find the words, though because I'm a lust-filled mess of need. Instead, I hook my legs over his shoulders and beg him that way.

He reaches up to pull my legs from around his neck and presses them wide to the bed, keeping a firm hold when he has them where he wants them. In the deepest, most gravelly voice I've ever heard, he says, "Do you remember that night you begged me to do filthy things to you? To make it so I would have trouble looking at you the next time I saw you because all I could remember were those indecent things we'd done?"

"Do you seriously think I could ever forget that night?"

"Tell me you've replayed it over and over in your mind like I have."

"I have. God, you've no idea how often I've done that. Even when I was with other men, all I thought about was you and that night."

His eyes flash with something dark and his penetrating gaze is uncompromising when he commands, "I don't ever want to have to imagine you with another man again, Kristen."

Don't ever mention other men to me again. That's what he's saying and I hear him loud and clear. I also hear and *feel* his possessiveness, and it unleashes a whole new level of craving within me. It causes me to sit up, fling my arms around his neck, and crush my mouth to his.

Our kiss is an all-consuming flame. An inferno of passion, sweeping us up, shutting out the world, making us lose all sense of anything but each other.

My hands are on his chest, his shoulders, his neck, in

his hair. They're greedy. Rough. Demanding. They can't get enough fast enough.

His are the same. They're all. Over. Me.

He yanks my dress over my head in one swift movement and then he's got his mouth on my breast and I might just burn alive if he doesn't hurry up and get inside me.

I grip his face and drag it back to mine. "I need you to fuck me. Right now."

"Fuck," he rasps as I begin madly undoing his belt.

Before I get it fully undone, he's up and has me in his arms. He throws me on the bed and just when I expect him to join me, he goes in the other direction toward his dresser.

"Where are you going?" It's a lusty, crazed demand, but really, *where is he going*?

He doesn't stop. "I'm getting a condom."

That statement is an assault on my brain. I don't want to think about the fact he has condoms here because *that* makes me think about the fact he's brought other women here.

"I'm on birth control," I throw out. "And you need to throw all those condoms away."

That last bit comes out harshly enough to stop Bradford mid-stride. The unmasked rawness in his eyes when he turns back to me shows that he understood exactly what I meant by that statement.

Before I know it, he's on top of me, his eyes blazing with want and possession and so many emotions I can't even begin to pick apart right now. "Don't ever stop feeling possessive of me." It's an order. A forceful, wild demand that comes from his heart, his bones, his soul. I feel it everywhere.

I kept this man waiting so long.

Too long.

And now we need only each other. Need everyone to know we're taken.

I clutch his face. "Don't *you* ever stop feeling possessive of *me*."

His nostrils flare. His eyes darken again. "If another man even breathes in your direction, I will make it so they regret that."

Then, his mouth is on mine and he's showing me just how much he wants me, loves me, *is ruined by me.*

This man owns me.

Forever.

And I will never allow anyone to come between us again.

By the time he finally thrusts inside of me, I'm so turned on and ready for him that I almost come straight away. I don't, but it doesn't take long. I lose myself in the orgasm and when Bradford comes, I'm so overwhelmed by him that I tumble even further into the ecstasy.

I imagined him like this for so many years, but the reality is a million times better than I ever thought it could be.

His scent surrounding me.

His body on mine.

His voice scattered over my skin.

His powerful muscles working for our pleasure.

His hunger for me.

His devotion.

His love.

I'm so affected by him and will never stop wanting him.

After, as he gathers me in his arms, I slide a leg over his and look up at him. "I hate that I took so long to find my way to you."

He tightens his hold on me. "You kept me in that friend zone for a long time." It's a statement, but I hear the question in it too.

"I know," I say softly. "You were the only person in my life who really pushed me to face the choices I was making with Dad. Deep down, I knew I wasn't ready to be done with those choices. We would never have worked back then." I smile as I tangle our legs and trace my finger over his chest. "I actually did break up with a guy once so I could tell you how I felt, but by the time I could do that, you already had a new girlfriend."

"Our timing was always off."

"Always. But I think it was meant to be."

He curls his hand around my wrist and strokes it lightly with his thumb while contemplating that. His touch instantly speeds my pulse.

Finally, he says, "It was a hell of a road to get here and you should know I won't ever let go of you now."

The forceful energy vibrating from every word he says only quickens my pulse more. "I'm not ever letting go of you either."

His phone sounds with another text. He ignores it, keeping his sole focus on me. I wonder what he's thinking while he looks at me, but I really don't need to because his eyes whisper every loving and besotted thought.

We share this moment for a long while before he

brushes his lips over mine and asks, "Do you want to eat?"

"Yes, but you should probably check your phone first. I imagine there are four thousand, five hundred, and seventy-two messages for you to check."

Amusement fills his face. "I like this side of you."

"Good because I'm thinking of letting her out for a while."

"Letting her out?"

"Yes." At his continued frown, I add, "Welcome to parts therapy. You'll now be doing it with me. Well, not *with* me, but since I have conversations with my parts, you'll probably hear me talking to myself."

"I presume that when you say 'parts', you're referring to all the different sides of yourself?"

"Yes." I reach across to the nightstand and locate his cell where it got dumped in our frenzy to get undressed. "Please make sure nothing urgent is waiting for you."

He takes his phone as the frown on his face gives way to more amusement. "I like this bossy part, too."

"She has nothing on your bossy part."

He pulls my mouth to his. After he kisses me thoroughly, he says, "You have no idea what she's capable of bossing me into." The growly tone he uses is enough to jumble all my thoughts, let alone what he says.

He finally checks his phone before saying, "I have to call Alan. It could take a while."

I know what he's asking without asking it. "Go and make your call. I'm okay."

He gives me one last kiss before letting me go. As he does this, I reach for his arm and stop him. When he looks at me questioningly, I say, "I know Cecelia was your choice because of what she could do for your career, but why didn't you find someone else? Someone you could have found happiness with too?" I've wondered this for nine long months. I found it hard to believe he'd given up on love, no matter how strong his goal of the presidency was. Bradford has too much soul to spend a lifetime in a loveless marriage.

He doesn't have to think about his answer for even a second. "If I couldn't have you, I didn't want anyone."

Twenty minutes later, Bradford is still on the phone with Alan. I've taken a shower in one of the bathrooms attached to Bradford's bedroom. I chose the largest bathroom on offer because it has a bath as well as a shower in it. The bath overlooks Central Park and as far as I'm concerned, this is now my bathroom. I love it that much I will go to battle with him for it.

I'm dressed and am unpacking my suitcase when my phone rings. It's my mother.

"Mom." I answer the call.

"Kristen, where are you?" She sounds a little panicked, which is odd for my mother. She's been known to spiral into panic when something goes wrong with one of her galas, but when it comes to everything else, she always remains calm.

"I'm at Bradford's. Why?"

"The lawyer is here. We're waiting for you."

"I told Dad I'm not getting a divorce and I meant it."

"Oh, Kristen, you don't know what you're saying. You

don't know that man. How can you possibly think a marriage with him will work out?"

"Why do you sound so panicked?"

"Because my daughter just got married to a man she doesn't know. A man who was engaged to another woman. I'm worried that you aren't in your right mind because this is very impulsive and you are far from an impulsive person. I know that getting married is everything you've ever wanted, but darling, this was not the right way to do it."

"I do know Bradford, and my mind is in the best shape it's ever been in. Oh, and I gave up on pursuing marriage when I left Johnathon. I just want love now. You and Dad need to accept that I'm not divorcing Bradford."

When she turns silent, I ask, "Did you hear what I said, Mom?"

"I did." There's a lot more alarm in her tone now. "Will you come over and discuss this with your father and me? Please?"

"There's nothing to discuss. Except the history between our families that Dad mentioned. What did he mean by that?"

"It's nothing for you to worry about. He shouldn't have brought it up."

"Well, he did, so clearly he wants me to know about it."

"No, he doesn't. He wasn't thinking straight when he said that."

"Oh my God, Mom, just tell me."

"I'm not discussing this with you, Kristen. Please just come over so we can sort this nonsense out." She ends the call abruptly in a way she never ends a call.

I'm staring at my cell in shock when Bradford enters the bedroom.

"What's wrong?" he asks, frowning at the expression on my face.

"Did you know there's history between our families?"

"No. What kind of history?"

"I don't know. And Mom's refusing to discuss it with me. Whatever it is, though, has my parents on edge and my father ready to disown me for longer than he usually does when he's angry with me."

My phone rings again and when I see it's my father, I answer it immediately. "Dad."

"Kristen, this is the last time I will say this. Come home and sign these divorce papers." The ice in his voice settles over me but I don't let it affect me how it once would have.

"And this is the last time I will say *this*. I'm not divorcing Bradford."

"I will disinherit you if you don't divorce him. I will give your job to someone else. And you won't be welcome in my home ever again."

My heart slows all the way down as his words bleed into me.

I feel dizzy, like I might pass out.

"You won't do all that." Even as the words breathe out of me, I know I'm wrong. He will do all those things in the blink of an eye. My father is an expert at withholding love; I have no doubt he'll be an expert in denying my existence and taking as many things from me as he can.

"I will. If you're not here within the next hour, I will do all of those things."

I don't even have to think about my choice, but that

doesn't make it hurt any less. This decision might be the easiest one I've ever made, but it destroys me in so many ways. Ways I'm not sure I'll ever recover from.

"You can take all those things from me, Dad, but I'm not divorcing Bradford."

The silence that greets me as he ends the call feels like a sharp blade through my heart. I have no idea what it feels like to bleed out, but I imagine it might feel how I do right now.

I'm weak.

Numb.

Dizzy like I've never been.

I think I might be sick.

"Oh, God." When Bradford's strong arms come around me, I madly shake my head, trying to push out of his hold. "I'm going to vomit."

He gets me to the bathroom just in time, holding my hair while I'm violently sick.

All my feelings of not being lovable, not being good enough, not being *enough* have flared up and it feels like this is my body's way of forcing them all out of me.

I am lovable.

I am good enough.

I am enough.

One thing I've learned in therapy is that while my mind can be good at denying the truth, my body knows it deeply and experiences it as anxiety. I've done a lot of work on easing my anxiety and I'm not going backward now. I refuse to allow my father to undo all my hard work, even if it involves me chanting fucking affirmations about being enough,

I clean myself up and lift my face to look at Bradford.

"Dad's disinheriting me and he made it clear I'm never welcome in his home again. And I've lost my job."

"Fuck." He gives me only one word but I hear and see it in him that that word covers everything. It's filled with anger, compassion, concern. He cradles the back of my head with one hand while the other one curves around my body so he can pull me close. He doesn't say anything while he holds me, but he doesn't need to. Bradford's actions always speak for him.

I cling to him for a long time. My mind doesn't race with wild thoughts about what my father is doing. Instead, I surrender to it because that's all I *can* do. There is not one thing I can do to appease my father except the one thing I refuse to do.

Bradford gives me all the time I need, and when I finally lift my tear-stained face to his, he looks at me with the kind of tenderness and care no man has ever looked at me with. "Is this what you want, Kristen? You've asked me if I'm happy with my choice, but I haven't asked you."

"Yes."

"It's a lot to walk away from. I understand if you need time to think about it."

"I don't need time, Bradford. I chose you a long time ago, you just didn't know it. I'm never walking away from you again." I wipe my tears from my face. "A parent shouldn't intentionally inflict pain so they can get what they want. And now that I've learned about setting boundaries, I see that he's always done this to me. I'm not walking away from him so much as I'm walking away from *that*. I need to put myself first." I smile sadly at him. "I never really had my father. Not in the way I needed.

You can't walk away from something you never had to begin with."

His eyes hold a thousand emotions and I watch as he wars with himself over this. "I agree with all of that, but—"

I press a finger to his lips. "No buts. I want you. I choose you. And I choose me too."

34

BRADFORD

"Kristen looks tired," Alan says as he narrows his eyes at her early Monday morning while she's talking with a woman. We've made it through most of the breakfast Alan added to our schedule last night and have about fifteen minutes until I have to leave for work.

I give him a pointed look. "You would too if you were dealing with what she is."

Kristen's father made good on his threats last night. Precisely one hour after issuing them, he emailed to inform her she no longer had a job, that she's not welcome in his home, and that he's updating his will to remove her from it. Neither of us got much sleep. Kristen's not only tired, she's also putting on a brave face while processing her emotions and enduring the nasty whispers about our marriage.

He watches her for another few moments before eyeing me. "She made her own bed, Bradford."

"Ease up on her, Alan. I won't tolerate this for much longer." What I want to say to him is *back the fuck off my wife*, but since Kristen asked me not to intervene, I don't. If he keeps this up, though, I won't be able to give her what she wants.

"Easing up isn't what you pay me for. If you want to run this country one day, you'll start thinking with your brain rather than with your dick. And I can assure you, you'll thank me for not easing up in a month when your approval rating is back where it should be."

He stalks away from me to have a conversation with our campaign finance aid who has just arrived. Kristen catches my gaze as I watch him. She's now alone. When she makes wide eyes at me, I walk over to her.

"That woman—" She doesn't finish that statement, but rather communicates her bewilderment with more of those wide eyes. "She wouldn't stop asking me about our wedding. She was all about the gossip and scandal. Apparently, the story circulating is that we've been having an affair for months. And apparently, Cecelia's response is helping that story gain credibility."

Alan has already briefed me on this. Cecelia is being highly strategic, remaining almost tight-lipped but giving just enough of a hint of the scorned woman that people are reading into it that I cheated on her. He's concerned about this but I have faith his PR plan will work to change the narrative. As will the NDA Hayden presents Cecelia with when we meet today.

"The story will change after Cecelia signs the NDA."

"Have you considered that she may not sign the NDA?"

"She'll sign it."

"She may not."

The contract Hayden's drafted includes a mutual

agreement to never disclose any information about our engagement and the marriage we were going to enter into, as well as a considerable cash payment for Cecelia to remain tight-lipped about the end of the relationship. If there's one thing I know about Cecelia, it's that she likes money. And a lot of it.

"I'll make it worth her while to sign it."

"Sometimes women do things that make no sense to men, Bradford. And sometimes, not even money can make up for the hurt or anger they're feeling."

We're interrupted by Alan's assistant who handles all media requests. She's one of the most competent people I've worked with and this morning she's all efficiency with the questions she's been firing at us. To Kristen, she says, "Johnathon Swindle has just been interviewed and spoke about the time you burned his clothes after you broke up." She glances at her notes. "He says you spent all his money on clothes and vacations after the split. We're going to have to draft a response to this."

"No," Kristen says sharply. "I didn't spend *all* his money."

"But you spent a lot, right?"

"I spent *some*. If he's saying something different, he's lying." Kristen's done a good job of hiding her anxiety this morning, however I see it and I fucking wish I could remove all the social events we've got lined up from her schedule. I *would*, in a heartbeat, but she won't allow me to. She made that more than clear when I brought it up with her this morning.

"Do we have to respond?" I ask.

The woman looks at me like I just asked the dumbest question she's ever heard. "We do. I'll draft it now and send it to you to fact check before I issue it." She leaves us, heading back to Alan who looks like he's about to explode.

"Fuck," I mutter, wondering what the hell has happened now.

Kristen follows my gaze. "You should go and deal with whatever that is."

I should, but I don't want to leave her to handle the malicious gossipers on her own. Watching her sit with them while I took part in the business panel earlier was the hardest thing I've had to do in a long time.

I settle my hand on her lower back and lean in close. "You don't have to do any of this. I can find other ways to fix this."

She gives me her fierce look, the one that says *don't argue with me*. "I'm doing this, Bradford. Stop worrying about me. I'm made of tough stuff."

If there's one thing Kristen's made of, it's absolutely that. But that doesn't mean I'll ever stop worrying about her and wanting to protect her.

I bend my mouth to hers to steal a kiss. "I'll take care of this and then we'll leave. I'll drop you at your place on the way to work." She told me she's going to spend today packing her belongings to move in with me. That was after we had a discussion over me taking the day off work to stay with her. Another conversation in which she refused to back down. *This isn't the first time my father has hurt me*, she'd said. *I'll be okay.*

She places a hand to my abs, her touch flaring my desire to lock us both away from the world for the rest of our lives. "No, you just go to work. I'll find my own way."

I pull my phone from my pocket. It's been vibrating for the last few minutes. "I'm taking you."

As I glance down at my phone, she grips my shirt and says, "You are maddeningly bossy at times."

I find her eyes again, enjoying the shot of heat I see in them. "Bossy gets things done the way I want them done."

I stride away from her, sensing her attention every step of the way. I fucking like it and will do anything to ensure she can't ever take her eyes off me.

When I reach Alan, he launches straight into the reason he looks like he could kill an entire army single-handedly. "Hale isn't impressed with your marriage."

He doesn't need to spell out what that could mean for my senate bid. Governor Wakefield might have the responsibility of filling the seat should it become available, but we both know that senior New York Senator Hale has his ear.

"We will ensure he has a change of heart."

"Says the guy who is happy to decline an invitation to his party." Alan's expression is savage when he adds, "You need to go to that party. A fucking high school reunion is a waste of your time."

My response is just as vehement. "I'm attending Kristen's reunion. You will find other ways for me to win over Hale."

Alan clenches his jaw. "I can find you numerous ways to win him over, but not attending his party will be all he hears. If you want me to do my fucking job, let me."

"I don't pay you to argue over my decisions, Alan. I pay you to get creative and figure out how to achieve my goals in spite of them."

His phone rings and with a shake of his head, he stalks away from me to take the call.

Alan and I have often gone head-to-head over my choices, but he hasn't ever taken a stand against me quite like he is now. He will learn that where my wife is concerned, he has no say. That is between me and her only.

After dropping Kristen at her condo, I spend the day in meetings and going over budget issues. Alan is on the phone to me throughout the day with new headaches to be solved. I knew my marriage would hit the headlines but not to the extent it is. I have my suspicions that someone is pulling strings in the background to ensure this becomes a full-blown scandal and when I meet with Cecelia just after lunch, those suspicions only grow.

She refused to take my call yesterday and communicated through her attorney that she will not speak with me without him present. When Hayden and I arrive at her office, she greets me with a chill that could freeze the entire city. "Greet" is an exaggeration of the reception I receive, but that was to be expected. Especially since our relationship was already strained, and especially since she had big goals that relied on our union.

We don't exchange a word for the better part of the meeting. Our lawyers negotiate the terms of our NDA while Cecelia glares at me from across the table. She lets the proceedings carry on until we've almost come to an agreement, at which point she looks at me with smug satisfaction and says, "This isn't going to work for me. I'm not signing anything."

The room turns silent until Hayden says, "What doesn't work for you, Cecelia? Everything is negotiable." His tone is impersonal, purely business, like he expects to simply carry on with the negotiations. I know better though, based on the glint in her eye and the conversation I had with Kristen this morning.

"Everything is not negotiable." She's speaking to Hayden but her attention is firmly on me. "You should have used your brain when you went to Vegas, Bradford, not your dick."

If only she knew the organ I'd really used. But then, if she did, she'd know I'd do anything, pay anything, to fix this for Kristen. Because while everyone in this room thinks I'm here for my own interests, I'm really here to do whatever it takes to stop this scandal from hurting the woman I love more than it already has. My ambition can wait. It'll survive this, one way or the other. I'm more concerned about how this marriage is affecting Kristen.

"What would you like—" Hayden starts but I place my hand to his arm to stop him.

When he eyes me, I say, "She's not signing it." I stand and button my suit jacket. "We're wasting our time here."

Cecelia pushes her chair back and rises, her hard expression consuming the room. "If anyone wasted their time, it was me. I gave up almost an entire year for you." She releases a furious breath. "That will not be forgotten. Not ever. And by the time I'm finished with you, you will wish you never wasted even a second of my life." She looks at her attorney. "Please ensure they leave immediately." With that, she exits the boardroom without a backward glance, leaving me without a shadow of a doubt that she intends on doing her best to destroy me.

I have to agree that I would feel the same if I were in her shoes. But still, I'm frustrated that we couldn't come to an agreement. I'm also angry at myself for ever getting involved with her.

"If only your previous fiancée was as willing to negotiate as your current wife is," Hayden mutters as we step into the elevator. "Fuck knows where this will end up now."

"It will end up with her doing her best to fuck with me. We both know that."

We go our separate ways when the elevator reaches the lobby and fifteen minutes later, I'm back in my office and looking at the back of my father who is standing at the floor-to-ceiling window that fills one entire wall and looks out over the city.

"I wasn't aware we were meeting today," I say as I move to where he stands.

He turns and I see the same displeasure in his eyes that I saw last night when he met Kristen. "I hope you know what you're doing, Bradford." His voice is filled with the same disapproval. "Because from what I'm hearing, this marriage is causing more harm than good."

"I know exactly what I'm doing."

He lifts a brow. "Are you sure about that?"

"I'm more certain of Kristen than anything, Dad. You need to trust me. You also need to trust that Alan's strategy will ensure my marriage doesn't become a defining factor in my career."

He considers me for a long moment before finally asking, "How long have you known Kristen?"

I know my father, so I know what he's really saying is *Fucking tell me you didn't just marry a woman you barely know.* "Almost a decade." I pause as his eyes flare with surprise, giving him a moment with this information. "I would have married her years ago if I'd had the chance."

He doesn't bother with any further questions about our relationship because that's not his style. My father only concerns himself with facts that he considers relevant to whatever outcome he's pursuing. He loves his family but at times he can come across as cold-blooded. Instead of pursuing that line of enquiry, he says, "I trust you, son, but I can't help worrying that your heart is getting in the way now. You've wanted this career your entire life. I'd hate to watch you throw it away because you got swept up in this woman."

My parents have never been swept up in each other as far as I'm aware, which means I've found something Dad can't guide me in. He has no experience of a marriage that was entered into because of love, so I have no example to follow here. The person I'm closest to who has shown me what love can add to a life is Owen. He was willing to give up everything for Charlize and I've watched him change since she came into his life. Watched his happiness grow.

I want that kind of love. That kind of life.

"I understand your concern." I do, even if I believe it's unwarranted. "But let me get swept up, Dad. Let me choose happiness. My career will recover from the hit."

His shoulders don't relax, but he says, "I hope so."

We're interrupted by a phone call he receives. He speaks with his assistant for a couple of minutes, and when he comes back to me, I ask, "What's the history between our family and Kristen's? Her father has done everything he can to force her to divorce me because of that history."

Dad scowls. It's such an unusual expression for him that it surprises me. "William and I were friends in college but his competitive streak ended that friendship. He didn't like the fact I was more successful than him."

"That's it?" That hardly seems enough of a history to cause the actions he's taken to remove his daughter from his life.

The rigid set of Dad's jaw tells me there's more, but his expression relays reluctance to divulge it.

"Kristen is in the dark, Dad. Her parents refuse to tell her the reason for her father disinheriting her. Tell me what happened so I can help her make sense of what William is doing."

I watch as he fights himself over this. Finally, he says, "This is between us, Bradford. You can share it with Kristen, but I would appreciate it if you ask her to keep it private."

"Okay."

"Kristen's mother and I were also close in college. I thought it would go further than friendship but William cut in and pursued her with relentless determination. She and I drifted apart once my friendship with him ended, however I spent a night with her a year after Callan was born. I'm not proud of that fact and I never saw her again after that night. It seems that she told William."

Fuck.

"Does Mom know?" I mentally calculate the timeline of our family, working out that he cheated on Mom in between them having Callan and Ethan who is the youngest.

He nods. "Yes. I told her a few weeks after it happened. She and I were having problems and she suspected another woman. Learning I cheated almost destroyed her and I will always regret that."

My brain is still putting together the timeline. "Is that why Mom was so low after Ethan was born?" She had post-natal depression that resulted in her withdrawing from us. I was six at the time and recall how everything changed in our life. It took her more than a year to recover. Her relationship with Ethan has always been difficult and distant, and I now wonder if this is the reason.

"Yes."

I have never seen my father look the way he does right now. He's clothed in remorse. For a man who can be merciless when he wants to be, and hard-nosed about many things in his life, this is a very different side to him.

"Just how stubborn is William Blaise?"

"He's the kind of stubborn that doesn't ever forgive, Bradford. I wish Kristen luck with changing his mind."

35

KRISTEN

ON A DAY that has been one of the worst days of my life, Bradford comes home from work wearing an expression that makes me think I may need strong liquor to survive the night. He appears troubled by something when he finds me in the kitchen just before seven p.m. and I'm pretty sure it's only the disaster he walks in on that stops him from telling me what that trouble is.

He comes to a halt when he sees the mess of cooking utensils, dishes, and burned food, but before he can say anything, I hold up my hand, indicating he should not, under *any* circumstance, make a comment on the state of the kitchen. He has the good sense to take heed of my warning and simply says, "I thought I'd take you out for dinner tonight."

"You are a smart man. But today, I'm connecting pretty fucking deeply with my desire to never go out again, so I'm going to say no to that." I throw my arms wide. "Welcome home, honey. I made you dinner."

He curses under his breath and comes my way. "Today was pretty rough, huh?"

"Rough doesn't come close to accurately describing today. I think I'll come up with a new word for the dictionary that defines today's feelings." I cock my head. "How do you think one goes about submitting new words for consideration? Maybe I'll steal some of your money and bribe the dictionary people."

"Do you think a million will cover it?" He snakes his arm around my waist and pulls me close, looking down at me with an expression that says so many things. He's worried about me. He's ready to kill whoever upset me. He's desperate to take all my hurt and suffer his way through it for me. "Or maybe a billion?"

I grip his shirt with both hands and inhale his scent. God, I love how he smells. I want to wear his cologne just so I always have him with me. "You'd be that crazy, wouldn't you?"

"Whatever you need, Kristen. It's yours."

I glide a hand up his body so I can curve my fingers around his neck and pull his mouth down to mine. "You are reckless," I breathe before kissing him.

His body responds immediately, like he's been starved of me. His mouth parts and his tongue slides over mine while his hands take possession of me. They demand I press myself hard against him. Mold myself to him. Explore him.

It's been the longest day, *the worst day*, and I've felt like I couldn't breathe through most of it, but this moment with Bradford clears all that stress away. It unravels the knots in my stomach. Releases the thick air strangling my lungs. Moments like this aren't something that have ever existed for me before, and knowing I have them now with my husband is one of the best things I've ever known.

He drowns in this kiss with me and when we finally drag our mouths from each other, I cling to him, grasping his jacket like my life depends on it. "I forbid you from ever going to work again," I say breathlessly as I stare up into eyes I want to lose myself in for eternity.

"I knew I should have stayed with you today," he says at the same time that texts begin lighting up my phone. Six arrive quickly, one after the other. Bradford reaches for my cell that's sitting on the kitchen island and hands it to me.

I don't check who they're from because I'm certain they're from Jenna and the girls who have been bombarding me with messages all day. A group chat might just be the bane of my existence if it involves as many daily texts as I received today.

"You don't want to check those?" Bradford asks when I silence my phone.

"God no."

That look of *I'm going to fucking kill someone* returns to his face. "Is it your father? What's he done now?"

I smile as I place my hand to his chest. To his heart. "I love you wanting to protect me, but you don't need to kill anyone right now. Those texts are from the girls and I refuse to read them."

"Why?"

"Because I've already read ten million texts from them today. Group chats should be banned. Today alone, I've learned exactly which vibrators and dildos are Poppy's favorites; that Adeline's planning to check out a new sex club; that Lorelei has had sex with Ashton in public places all over the world; that Jessica is up for almost anything sexually; and that Charlize gets off on praise kink." My eyes widen as amusement fills Bradford's. "These are things I do not need to know about people."

"And now I also know more about those women than I ever needed to know."

"You're welcome. And you should prepare yourself to learn more because if I have to suffer through thousands of texts, you'll have to as well. Especially since it's your fault I'm now in that group text."

He chuckles. "It's my fault because I talked Elvis into putting that ring on your finger?"

"I told you you're a smart man."

"And that was absolutely the smartest thing I've ever done." He pulls me in close for another kiss before searching my eyes. "What was the worst thing about today?"

"You know, most people want to know the good things that happened when they check in at the end of the day, not the worst."

"We'll get to those things, but first I need to know what I can fix."

"Not everything can be fixed, Bradford. And trust me, that was a hard lesson to learn in therapy, but it's the truth."

"Well, it's not a lesson I've learned, so humor me. Tell me how your heart is breathing and why."

"I think you just need to take a look around the kitchen to know how my heart is breathing." I glance at the chaos strewn from one end of the kitchen to the other, hating the fact I not only failed at cooking dinner, but also hating that I now have to clean it up. Bradford's housekeeper buzzed around me earlier, wanting to take over, but I refused her help and told her I would clean up as well. "I really wanted to have dinner ready for you when you got home, but it turns out I probably won't ever be a domestic goddess." I've been trying for years now and I think I'm finally giving up on that goal.

"What were you cooking?"

I sigh. "Seared scallops and mushroom risotto with chocolate molten cakes for dessert. I'm pretty sure I'm the only person who could ruin those dishes and make such a mess doing it."

"I appreciate the gesture but I wasn't looking for a domestic goddess when I married you." He slides some strands of hair from my face, securing them behind my ear. "Was this the worst thing about your day?"

"No." I swallow the rising emotion threatening to make me cry. As far as I'm concerned, I'm all cried out and want nothing to do with any more tears. "I actually don't know if I can decide what was the worst. It's a competition between not having a job to go to this morning, receiving a box containing all the items from my work desk that were just dumped in there like they don't even know me or care about me, being called awful names on social media for being a homewrecker, being stared at and whispered about, and being ignored by my father when I called him." My voice catches in my throat when I mention my father, telling both of us that this was in fact the worst thing about my day.

Bradford's arms circle me and he pulls me close as he

curses softly. He cradles my head and I rest my cheek against his chest.

I wrap my arms around his body and feel instantly safe. "Having everyone know that my own father has disowned me...it's awful. And I know I shouldn't worry what other people think, but it was how I was raised and it's fucking hard to unwire that thought pattern."

"Who knows about it? I don't imagine he's broadcast the news."

"Some people at work. I received emails today advising me that I won't be able to access the building anymore due to my father's instructions. It won't take long for word to spread. And then everyone will have even more to gossip about."

"I've got my team working on the social media slander. Hopefully that will die down soon. Did you speak with your mom today?"

I lift my face to look at him. "No. She called a couple of times but I couldn't bring myself to answer her calls. I'm too hurt and still making sense of everything. But then there's this part of me that wants her to force her way in, to explain it all to me. The fact she didn't even try to force herself on me...that hurts almost as much, you know?"

He nods before saying, "I found out what the history is between our families."

"What is it?"

A look of misgiving flashes in his eyes and I know that *this* was why he came home wearing the expression that warned me to search for hard liquor. "This isn't going to be easy to hear."

"Nothing about today has been easy. Just tell me."

He stalls for another moment before giving me a nod. "Our fathers knew each other in college. They were friends, but rivals. My father said your dad was the competitive one, but I don't doubt for a second that Dad was also so inclined. And then there was your mother who they also knew." He pauses, searching my face like he's looking for reassurance that I'm ready to hear the next part of what he has to say. "Fuck, Kristen, this is going to change so many things for you."

Apprehension skates down my spine, and my breath quickens. "What did she do?" A million scenarios clamber for space in my brain and if Bradford doesn't *hurry up and just tell me already*, my head may explode.

"She was close with my father and he thought a relationship might develop, but your father pursued her. Dad used the word *relentless* to describe his style. Again, that was his version of events. The three of them drifted apart after your parents began dating and I got the impression Dad didn't have anything to do with your mom again until years later." He stops for a moment. "They slept together twenty-eight years ago, and based on your father's reaction to our marriage, Dad suspects your mom told him about it."

I stare at him as the words *they slept together* splinter into random letters and float around my brain individually. It's like I can't catch them and put them back into words that make sense.

What did he say?

I blink. "What?" My mother. His father. "They had an affair?"

"Not according to Dad. He said it was a one-time thing."

"Twenty-eight years ago?" My mind whirls. My heart fractures. "That would have been just after I was born. Mom had sex with another man just after having me?" *Mom cheated on Dad.* Four words I never imagined saying.

"Yes." He only says one word, but Bradford's devastation can be felt in every letter he utters.

"Does your mom know about this?"

"Yes. Dad told her not long after it happened."

"God." I release a long breath. "You know, if someone had told me that one of my parents cheated on the other, I would have guessed it was Dad. And maybe he did too. Maybe they both had affairs. Maybe—"

Bradford puts his finger to my lips, quieting me. "Don't let your mind run in any direction yet. Wait until you talk with your parents about this."

He's right, but if he thinks I'll be able to stop my mind from doing all that wild running, he has a lot to learn about me. I mean, a twenty-eight-year-old woman doesn't end up in the middle of a midlife crisis without doing a lot of wild mind running. It's my special talent. And on top of that, *my mother cheated on my father.* And *I'm* the one who has to suffer now because of that. There's no way my mind won't be running in all the directions tonight.

I take a long look at him, at the strain on his face. "How are you?"

"This came as a shock today. I don't know what to make of it yet."

"How about everything else that's happening. Are you okay?"

"You don't need to worry about me, Kristen. Everything else is under control."

I've always known Bradford to be strong and steady, practical and pragmatic. He was always there for me, making sure I was okay. Even when I wouldn't allow him close, when I pushed him away, he was trying to look out for me. Now, it's time for me to do that for him.

"I know you're a strong man and are good at managing all the things in your life that require managing. I'm not asking about whether you have things under control. I'm asking how your heart is in this moment. And I'm not asking so I can worry about you. I'll do that anyway because I love you. I'm asking so I can be here for you. So that you know you're not alone in the world."

He listens intently to what I say and then he gives me his heart like he always has when I've asked for it. "I'm feeling the same kind of confusion you are over what our parents did. It slants things about my family in a whole new way and I don't know whether to open that door and ask more questions or whether to let it stay shut like my father wants me to. I can't help but feel that asking the hard questions might bring me closer to my mother, though."

I see and hear his inner conflict. His shoulders carry the same tension his face does.

"Whatever you decide to do, I'll be right by your side."

He takes that in for the longest moment before pulling me close and brushing his lips over mine. "I know today was hard, and I know life is going to be hard for a while, but I will make the rest of our lives so fucking worth it, Kristen, because you are the absolute best thing that has ever happened to me."

I clutch his shirt and pull him close so I can kiss him again, showing him what I think of that declaration.

When I'm finished showing him that, I ask, "How skilled are you at cleaning a kitchen?"

He glances around the room. "We have a housekeeper for things like this."

"It wouldn't be fair to expect her to clean this kind of mess up." I glide my hands down to his pecs and out to his shoulders to shrug him out of his suit jacket. He watches as I clear space on the island for it and then proceed to roll his shirt sleeves up.

"Have you ever washed dishes?" I ask as I make my way up his arm, doing my best not to just strip him and beg him to fuck me rather than bother with the dishes.

He gives me his amused look. "You don't think I'm capable of washing dishes?"

"I think you're capable of anything you put your mind to, Mr. Black, but I'm just wondering if this will be a first for you."

He lets me finish with his sleeves before gripping my wrists and stopping my next move. "I'm very capable, Mrs. Black. I've also been told I'm very bossy, so I'm going to take charge of this job to ensure we get it done as efficiently and quickly as we can. And then"—his hands tighten around my wrists and his eyes heat—"I'm going to lay you out on this island and bury my tongue in your pussy so that if you ever again think I want a domestic goddess, you can come in here and remember I'd prefer to eat you rather than any meal you might cook me."

Bradford makes good on all his promises.

He bosses me around while we clean the kitchen. Mostly, he does all the work while I drool over the way he owns the kitchen. I mean, is there a room or a job in life that this man can't take ownership of? It's hot as hell watching all those muscles of his get the job done.

Then, he lifts me onto the island, slowly removes all my clothes, and gives me two orgasms I will never forget. He's right; whenever I think I need to be a domestic goddess and cook my husband dinner, I'll just recall the time he ate me for dinner in this kitchen.

After he gives me those two orgasms, he bends me over the island and gives me a third.

Then, he whispers against my ear, "What were the good things that happened to you today?"

I turn in his arms. "My first morning waking up with you here. Filling my new closet in our bedroom with my clothes. And cleaning this kitchen with you."

He arches a brow. "Cleaning beats sex, which didn't even make it onto your list?"

I grin. "Well, I'm pretty sure I can get sex from you every day, which means it will just be a given on my daily list. I'm going to reserve my nightly list for the special things that are firsts for me or that I don't get to experience every day. Oh, and the other good thing that happened today was having our new bed delivered. When I told you to throw away all your condoms, I didn't expect you to also get rid of your bed. However, I tested it out and it's even more comfortable than your previous bed. And just so you know, if you ever leave me, I'm taking the bed. I already texted Hayden to have him add that to the postnup."

"You did, did you?"

"Yes. He said he'd add it in."

"Without speaking with me first?"

"Well, he and I both know that when it comes to this

marriage, you're being quite reckless, so I think he just assumed you'd give me what I want."

"That bed was expensive. I'm going to need to get my money's worth out of it before I ever agree to part with it."

I lean into him. "How expensive?"

He kisses the side of my neck, adding just the right amount of teeth. "The kind that means both you and that bed are with me for life." The decisive way he says this lets me know, in no uncertain terms, that he never intends on letting me go.

"Thank you," I whisper as he trails kisses down to my throat.

His eyes meet mine again. "For the bed?"

"No. For cherishing me."

"There won't be a day in our lives that I don't cherish you."

He scoops me into his arms and as he carries me out of the kitchen, I ask, "Where are we going?"

"To christen our new bed."

36

KRISTEN

I ALWAYS IMAGINED what it would feel like to be the woman who got to sleep next to Bradford every night. To be the last person he saw before he closed his eyes. I never spent any time imagining what it would be like to be the woman who woke up with him every day. I've now had that privilege three mornings in a row and it has to be said that I love it even more than going to sleep with him each night.

Just after five-thirty Tuesday morning, he spoons me, cups my breast, nuzzles my neck, and murmurs, "How did you sleep?"

I sink into his embrace. "Not great, but better than Sunday night. How about you?"

"About the same." He kisses a slow trail along my shoulder. "I should have cleared my entire week to spend with you."

I smile, beginning to wake up fully thanks to the way he's touching me. "A honeymoon in bed?"

"We haven't discussed a honeymoon. Where do you want to go?"

"You don't have time for a honeymoon right now."

"I don't think you have any idea of just what I would make time for, Kristen."

This is officially my favorite way to wake up.

"Let's get through this scandal and then talk about a honeymoon."

His teeth graze my skin. "What are your plans for today?"

"I thought I'd visit my husband at his work and make him fuck me on his desk."

"Fuck," he rasps, taking hold of my cheek so he can angle my face to his and kiss me. He unleashes thousands of my butterflies when he says, "If Jane refuses to let you ruin my schedule, tell her she's fired. You come before everyone on my calendar."

"My only plans for today are to pack some more of my belongings and go and see my mother," I say as Bradford starts kissing his way down my neck.

He stops what he's doing. "Do you want me to go with you?"

I smile. Always my protector. "No, but I love you for offering. I do think, though, that I really may need to call you and take up some of your time after I see her."

I went to bed last night feeling confused about everything. Hurt and disappointed. This morning, I'm angry and I need to get that anger out of me. I have no idea what my mother is thinking, but if I know her as well as I think I do, she's busy doing all that smoothing she does. My mother is an expert at polishing the facade of her life, making it as shiny as she can for the world. It's a skill that has been passed down from generation to generation, one I learned, but one I've chosen to unlearn. I'm breaking the cycle and that starts today. It's time for me and Mom to have the realest conversation we've ever had.

"Call me or come and see me," Bradford says. "I'm in and out of the office today for meetings so just check with me first to see where I am."

I curl my fingers tightly around his arm. "Thank you."

He slides a leg over mine and goes back to teasing me with his lips. "I had a filthy dream about you last night."

Holy God, I change my mind. My favorite way to wake up is *not* Bradford telling me he'd give up many things to make time for me; it's him telling me, in the sexiest voice, that he had a filthy dream about me.

I bite my lip as smutty words fill my mind. Words I've never said to another man. "Was I sitting on your face?"

He tweaks my nipple and grinds his erection against my ass. "That dirty mouth of yours will be my downfall." His hand glides down my body to spread my legs before making its way to my pussy. He rubs my clit, groaning when I arch my back and press myself against his dick. "You were on your knees with your wrists in restraints while you gave me a handjob. It was so fucking hot watching you stroke my dick while your wrists were bound. After that, you demanded I blindfold you and fuck you for hours." He pushes a finger inside me. "You begged for it to be rough."

Holy God, right now I want to beg him to just fuck me already.

"What else?" I urge him to keep talking dirty to me while rolling onto my back and opening my legs for him.

He grips my thigh and pulls my leg wider before

skimming his hand up my thigh, back to my pussy. Taking his time, he rubs my clit. Circle after circle of pleasure relaxes every muscle in my body, pushes every thought from my mind but what Bradford is doing to me.

"How rough do you like it?" He pushes two fingers inside me. They slide in easily because I'm so damn wet. "Harder than I've already fucked you?"

I roll my hips, moving with him as he finger fucks me. "I don't know."

His gaze is focused intently on mine. He knows what I'm saying. I've never been fucked as hard as he has fucked me. "Do you want to find out?"

God. Yes.

"Yes." I close my eyes as his fingers move inside me with skill. "I also want you to tell me more about your dream."

He increases his tempo as he bosses, "Look at me."

It's an order that thrums in my veins. I almost want to not look at him. Defy him. Just to make him even bossier. My body lives for this side of him.

I do as he says, meeting his searing gaze for only a second before his lips collide with mine in the kind of desperate kiss that arouses every inch of me and awakens parts that I didn't know existed.

I grab his neck, my fingers carving their print into his skin while I kiss him with the same level of need. I always want him to wake me up like this. *Always.*

He ends our kiss but keeps his face close to mine while continuing to finger fuck me. "You begged me to fill your mouth with my cock." He licks my neck and kisses it. "You told me to come down your throat."

I squeeze my pussy around his fingers. "I need you to fuck me. *Now*."

He thrusts his fingers deeper, curling them to stroke my G-spot, and it's so.damn.good.I.may.just.die. I sink my fingers even harder into his skin and squeeze my eyes closed as pleasure consumes me.

"Give me your eyes, Kristen."

I almost forget to breathe thanks to the growl in his demand.

I open my eyes. "Give me your dick."

He fucks me faster with his fingers. "I will, baby, but first I want to watch you come."

Baby.

He's never called me that.

It does things to me.

Makes me feel things I never knew could be felt.

My back arches.

My toes curl.

My pussy clenches.

Ecstasy pulses in my veins. Lights up my skin. Pulls me under.

The pressure builds and I feel everything at once and nothing at all.

I lose myself.

And then I'm coming.

Letting myself go.

Falling off the cliff.

It's not until Bradford kisses me that I find myself again.

"You are so fucking beautiful," he says.

I roll onto my side and reach for his dick, loving the way his face reveals his pleasure as I stroke him. I could spend hours watching him like this. "I can't decide if I want to ride your face before I ride your dick." I barely recognize myself. These are not words I use during sex, but hot damn if this man doesn't bring them out in me.

"*Fuck*." His hands are on me before I realize, and he's pulling me on top of him. "I haven't got it in me to wait even another second to fuck you. You can sit on my face tonight. Right now, you're taking my dick."

He grasps my hips and positions me where he wants me, his strength making it so that he looks like he's lifting a feather rather than my body. When I take his hard length as deeply as it will go, his groan is guttural and the most masculine sound I have ever heard.

His eyes are on my body, glued to my tits while I swirl on him slowly. He reaches up and grabs one of my breasts, squeezing it roughly in a completely impolite way. A way I really fucking like.

It's that coarse move that unleashes my inner bad girl. A girl I've not yet met. But holy hell, she's been woken up this morning.

I take hold of Bradford's wrists and press them to the bed. "Keep these here."

Surprise flares in his eyes, right alongside burning desire. That heat intensifies when I shift, placing my feet either side of his body and bringing my knees up in squatting cowgirl position. I rest my hands behind me on his thighs, roll my hips, and move my ass back and forth while I fuck him.

Bradford's gaze locks onto my pussy that's on full display to him. My gaze is fixed to his face. To the expressions that tell me he can't get enough of me.

"Fuck, Kristen." His hands snap around my ankles. "I'm going to jerk off to this later."

I clench him inside me, which causes his fingers to squeeze tightly around my ankles. It also earns me another one of those groans of his I love. "Promise you'll text me before you do, so I can get off at the same time." Who even am I right now?

His eyes come to mine, intense and so damn turned on. "Such a filthy girl."

"Only for you."

His dick is so hard inside me. *Throbbing.*

He's let me take charge, but when I tell him I'm only a filthy girl for him, he lets go of my ankles and reaches one hand around my hip and the other for my breast. He pulls me forward so my position changes and his hips jerk up and he goes balls deep into me. And then he comes.

"Oh, God," I cry out as another orgasm shatters through me.

Bradford tenses and jerks again, filling me for the longest time as he comes.

Then, he's sitting up, taking hold of me, and crashing his lips to mine. His tongue forces its way into my mouth, taking ownership of me. I grab his hair, pulling it between my fingers as I kiss him back as wildly as he's kissing me.

His stubble scratches my cheeks.

His scent overwhelms me.

His everything ruins me.

"That's one way to wake a woman up," I say after he ends the kiss.

His hands move to my ass. "Even though you're not

adding sex to your nightly list of good things, *that* needs to go on today's list."

I grin. "We'll see. Maybe you'll do better tonight."

"You're going to keep me on my toes, aren't you?" His entertained expression is something I now live for.

"I think that might be one of a wife's jobs. I'll track that information down today and let you know if it is."

His phone vibrates with a string of texts.

"And there's Alan," I say. "He must have woken late this morning. Do you think that means he'll be grumpier than he was yesterday?"

Bradford reaches for his phone to check the messages. "That wasn't Alan." He hands the phone to me. "It was Charlize."

CHARLIZE

> Bradford! Can you please pass a message onto my third best friend who is ignoring our group texts. We're trying to plan lunch with her today.

CHARLIZE

> Sorry, hit send too early. If Kristen is free today, we're having lunch at twelve. We promise not to bombard her with more sex talk. We really just want to make sure she's okay.

CHARLIZE

> Oops, I forgot to tell you where we're going. Clementine's.

CHARLIZE

> Also, Bradford, I have to thank you for canceling golf on Owen this morning. He spent the morning hiking with me instead.

I frown and glance up at Bradford. "Have you eaten at Clementine's? I've never been there."

"No."

"Ugh, lunch with the girls and all their emotions at a restaurant I don't know…it sounds like a recipe for a bad time." At his look that says he's not convinced, I say, "You think I should go to lunch, don't you?"

"I think you should do whatever you want. I also think you might have fun with the girls."

"I think your idea of fun and mine might be different."

"I highly doubt that after what we just did." He leaves the bed. "I'm going to shower. Feel free to join me after you finish with your third best friend."

I roll my eyes at his grin.

I then watch him walk into his bathroom, struggling to remove my eyes from his impressive body. When I can no longer see him, I go back to his phone and reply to Charlize.

> Hey, Charlize, it's Kristen. I'm free for lunch. I'll see you there.

Right as I hit send, Bradford receives his first text from Alan for the day. I place the phone on his night-stand without reading it and then head into my bathroom. As much as Bradford told me to join him, I know he's got a busy day ahead and I don't want to make him late, which I know I would if we went for round two.

I shower and take my time styling my hair into long, loose waves before applying my makeup. I dress in a pair of black skinny leather pants, a white silk blouse, and black stiletto ankle boots. I then go in search of my husband and breakfast.

I find him downstairs on the bottom floor of the condo, talking with my brother in the grand salon.

"This is a surprise," I say, greeting Grayson.

My oldest brother has always been overprotective of me and I see in the hard set of his shoulders that this is the reason he's here.

"I wanted to meet your husband," he says, all business and determination.

My brows pull together. "You two have never met?"

"We have," Bradford says. "But only briefly."

"And not as family," Grayson says.

"Right," I say, rolling my eyes on the inside. "This is the obligatory *I'll make you hurt if you hurt her* meeting. Have you almost finished or did I interrupt before you got there?"

Grayson doesn't crack a smile, but then, I don't expect him to. He takes his older brother duties very seriously. When the full extent of Johnathon's cheating was revealed, he let him know exactly what he thought of the way he devastated me, and let's just say that my ex was lucky to limp away from that encounter. "Jenna tells me you two have known each other for a long time. That this wasn't just some accidental drunk marriage while blowing off steam in Vegas."

I caught my sister up on my history with Bradford yesterday and am thankful she's given Grayson the rundown. "Well," I say, smiling at Bradford, "we *were* drunk and it *was* accidental, but that doesn't mean it isn't real. This marriage is very real and you can skip the interrogation, okay?"

"No," Bradford says, "ask whatever you want, Grayson. I'd do the same if I had a sister."

Grayson assesses him, and if I'm not mistaken, he respects what Bradford just said. "Are you free for lunch today?"

I know Bradford isn't, so I'm surprised when he nods and says, "Yes."

"I'll have my assistant arrange it. She'll send you the details."

"I'm taking it that I'm not invited," I say.

Bradford's mouth quirks as Grayson says emphatically, "No."

"You're no fun," I grumble, but I'm actually not certain I want to attend that lunch. Grayson would likely annoy me. And since I know Bradford is more than capable of handling anything my brother throws his way, it's best to just let men be men and get this behind them.

"Mom told me you're not taking her calls," Grayson says to me.

"I wasn't but I'm going to see her today."

"Good. She's beside herself over everything that's happened."

That anger I woke with rises inside me. "I guarantee you she'll be even more beside herself after I speak with her."

"Because?"

Bradford told me last night that his father asked for me to keep the information he shared about Mom to myself. He then told me he had no intention of telling me what I should do with that information. He made it clear he'll support me in any choice I make. I think he knows I won't broadcast anything to the world in general. I think he also knows I'm no longer the girl who shoves dirty secrets away from the light.

"Did they tell you the reason Dad's disowned me?"

"No. Just that bullshit about some history between our families, but neither of them would elaborate."

"Right." I cross my arms, almost like I'm putting up a shield even though I'm not the one who needs to defend anything here. "So, the family history is that Dad knew Bradford's father in college. They were friends but super competitive with each other. Mom was close to Edmund but Dad pursued her and the rest is history. Except it's not, because Mom slept with Edmund just after I was born. And now I'm paying the price for that."

Grayson is suitably stunned. "Fuck me."

"Yeah," I agree. "I'm done with being the good girl who does what she's told, Grayson. Dad can take whatever he wants from me but I refuse to hand over any more pieces of myself. If he's waiting for me to divorce Bradford and beg to be a part of the family again, he'll be waiting a long time. And I'd really like my mother to support me in my choice."

My eyes meet Bradford's and I see the respect shining brightly in them. I always thought I just wanted a man to love me. It turns out I want his respect as much as I want his love.

"Dad's working from home this morning," Grayson says. "Do you want me to go with you in case he refuses to let you in?"

I drop my arms, feeling stronger than I ever have. Or maybe that's just the anger taking charge. "Trust me, there's no way he'll keep me out. Not today."

Grayson leaves shortly after I finish telling him I don't

need him with me today. Bradford and I eat breakfast together, and once he's assured I'm okay to see my parents by myself, he leaves for work.

I touch up my lipstick, put on my winter coat, and make what may be my last visit to the home I grew up in.

37

KRISTEN

"KRISTEN." Mom smooths her dress when she greets me in her great room. Her body is as rigid as her speech and she appears frazzled, anxious about seeing me.

I didn't have to force my way inside even though I was more than ready to do so. Clearly, my father didn't pass the memo on to his staff that I'm no longer welcome here. He's yet to show his face, but I'll be demanding that soon.

"Mom." I feel uncharacteristically confident. I think that's because I've had my come-to-Jesus moment and have no expectations for how this conversation will end. I've got nothing left to lose with my family and I never knew how freeing it could be not to be governed by fear. "Can you please get Dad? We all need to have a conversation."

She swallows hard. "He won't speak with you, darling, but I want to have that conversation."

I love my mother. Deeply. However, I'm too angry with her to tread carefully here. "The one in which we discuss the real reason why Dad has disowned me."

Alarm spikes across her face. "Your father hasn't disowned you, Kristen."

My brows arch. "Really? What would you call it then? Discarded? Rejected? Abandoned? I mean, take your pick. They all apply."

"No," she rushes to explain, "he simply wants you to know how strong his feelings are over your marriage. You have to admit that you rushed into it and—"

"No." I shake my head almost violently. "I might have rushed into marriage, but that's not the real reason Dad's doing what he is and you know it." She recoils like she's been slapped but I just keep going. "Dad's doing what he does best. He's withholding love to get what he wants. He's doing that because it's a tactic that's always worked with him where I'm concerned, but it won't work in this situation. It will never work again. I'm not the scared little girl desperate for her father's approval any longer, Mom. I see him for exactly what he is, a bully who has no idea how to be a father."

"Careful what you say, Kristen," Dad says, joining us with a thunderous expression on his face. "You won't be able to take it back."

I stare at him, wondering how I was ever scared of him. Why I ever needed his approval to believe I was a worthy human being. "I don't want to take anything back, Dad. I mean every word I'm saying."

His jaw hardens and his nostrils flare. "That man isn't who you think he is. He will break your heart, and when he does, I won't be there to pick the pieces up like I always have."

My eyes almost bulge out of my head. "Are you serious? When have you ever picked the pieces up for me?"

"I've had to do it every single time you've made a mess of a relationship."

Mom inhales sharply. "William. That's enough."

I hold up my hand at her. "No, Mom, let him say what he wants to say. I'm interested to see just how little he thinks of me."

She looks positively desolate. If I wasn't in the frame of mind I'm in, I'd feel for her position here. I'd admit she's caught between her husband and her child. But I'm in no mind to care about that. Today, I'm putting myself, and only myself, first. In fact, I'm pretending like no other person in the world matters right now.

"Kristen," Mom pleads. "Please don't do this."

"No!" I scream. "Fuck me, Mom. If I have to hear you say those words ever again, I will literally scream at you." I can't even count the number of times my mother has told me to *please don't do this*. It's a fucking wonder I even know how to take care of myself after having her helicopter around me my entire life.

Dad shakes his head and eyes me with contempt. "He's already changing you, turning you into a disgrace. That language does not become you, Kristen."

"Bradford *has* changed me, but do you know what? It's taken him almost a decade because all that time, you were there beating me back down, keeping me in the box you wanted me in, the one that worked best for *you*." I suddenly feel *very* intent on Dad knowing it is not okay to say a bad word against my husband. Stabbing my finger at him, I say, "Don't you ever speak against Bradford again. I won't stand for it. He's the best man I know and has only helped me, not harmed me like you have."

"It seems my time here is wasted," Dad says dismissively. He looks at Mom. "I suggest you don't also waste your time."

As he turns to leave, I say, "I know what happened between Mom and Edmund Black."

His back stiffens and his shoulders turn to stone before he slowly turns back to me. His face twists cruelly as he spits, "You know nothing."

"Kristen," Mom says. She wisely doesn't utter her standard request. Instead, she just stands there begging me with her eyes to *please don't do this*.

This is the moment I can't come back from. Once I speak my next words, there will be no hope for me and my father.

My entire life flashes through my mind.

Like a movie.

Mom smoothing me.

Ensuring I was polished for the world.

Dad pressing his lips in disapproval at me.

Denying me his love.

"You're cutting your child out of your life because your wife and another man made you feel deficient. Inadequate. Lacking. Well, welcome to my life, Dad. That's exactly how you've made me feel since I was born. The difference between us is that I took that pain and healed myself. I'll succeed in spite of you. You've had nearly three decades to heal, but instead of doing that, you spent all that time inflicting your pain on your family." I step closer to him, my shoulders pushed back, my head held high. "The world might think you're a success, but the world is fickle and doesn't remember much past each news cycle. You know who remembers? Your family. And, sadly for you, you've only given us awful things to remember. You're a bully and I hate that I took so long to see that. I wasted so much time."

I don't need to come back from this moment.

I need to set myself on fire and rise from it.

Those fucking affirmations were right all along.

I am loved.

I am worthy.

I fucking *am* enough.

Dad doesn't agree. He's looking at me like he doesn't even know me. Like he wishes I didn't even exist. Like I no longer exist to him. "Don't ever come back here. I never want to see you again." His words are bitter, filled with venom, and he stalks out of the room without another word said between us.

I know we will never have another conversation.

I will never celebrate my birthday with him again.

There will be no more Thanksgivings or Christmases with him.

And while it will take me a long time to come to terms with this, I'm okay to never have those moments with him again. I want to save my precious moments for people who treat me like *I'm* precious.

I glance at Mom after Dad leaves us. She's distressed and my anger has eased enough to put myself in her shoes. I don't know why she did what she did all those years ago, and while I sure as hell don't understand her marriage, I do know that no one besides the two people in a relationship know the intricacies of it. I won't tolerate cheating in my relationship, but it's not my place to judge her choices. And while I came here wanting to under-stand why her decision has changed my life irrevocably, I'm no longer interested to know anything about it. I don't need to grasp why Dad's done what he has because I've finally grasped that I'm so much better off without him in my life.

"Darling, your father is just—"

"No, don't justify his behavior, Mom. You've spent my entire life doing that and I have to wonder if you've ever thought about all the justifications you've felt the need to keep making. I'm not a parent, but I don't think children should have to put up with bad behavior being defended. When I do have children, I want them to know, without even having to think about it, that their father is a good man who does not need his actions explained away. A parent should strive to be an example of a good human being. Sure, some days will be a failure, but when the majority of days are like that, a parent should do better. Or just don't fucking have children."

"Do we really need that language, Kristen?"

No, no we don't, but you know what? I'm so done with being told how to *be* in this world, that I'm not giving her this today. "I'm making no apologies today, Mom."

She detests swearing but I think she's realized I'm in no mood to hear about that, so she lets it go and moves back to defending her husband. "Your father is a very complex man. He's tried to heal from what I did to him, but it's been difficult. I hurt him, and you of all people should be able to understand that."

"I should understand him because I was cheated on?"

"Yes."

"I understand that he was hurt by your betrayal. I also understand how hard it is to move through those emotions. But do you know what I'm taking away from all of this?"

"What?"

"That there are just some things in life we will never understand. And there are things we just don't need to know. I don't need to know or understand Dad. And that's the last I ever want to speak about this. I'm getting on with my life now and I hope you'll be a part of it."

She blinks and I think if I was to put my hand over her heart, it would be racing. Her life has been changed irrevocably too. "Of course I'll be a part of your life."

I know by the startled expression on her face and her high-pitched tone that she hasn't fully comprehended how everything has now changed for our family. For the family *she* built.

I crave to know my mother more deeply. I would love to know who she was before the world told her who she had to be. I think I'd like that girl. I've seen glimpses of her fire over the years, but it never seems to last. I recall the time last year that she shared with me and Jenna about how Dad's mom walked all over her for years. She'd told us she wouldn't stand for anyone making us feel the way Grandma made her feel. And yet, here we are. She's still making excuses for Dad walking all over us.

I collect my purse. "I'm living at Bradford's now. You're welcome to visit any time you want."

Thank God Bradford told me he'd make time for me today. I need the kind of moment only he can provide to ease all the turbulent emotions this conversation has flared. I never imagined the day where my mother wasn't fully in my life, and while I've struggled with her crowding my space, *this* wasn't what I wanted.

"Okay, darling," she says, looking as bewildered as I feel. "I'll come visit."

When I step outside a few minutes later, the winter chill settles over me like a too-heavy blanket in much the same way Mom's response to my devastation today is settling over me. I don't know what I was looking for from her, but if my feelings are anything to go by, it wasn't what she gave me.

I breathe fresh air in, pulling it all the way into my lungs so I can force out the toxic air my father put there. I wish my mother could give me more, but I'm not sure she ever will. That knowledge shreds its way through me, feeling like a thousand tiny paper cuts, reopening wounds that have never fully healed.

I remove my phone from my purse and send Bradford a text.

> Where are you?

I stand on the sidewalk outside my parent's condo and stare at my phone waiting for his reply as those cuts keep on slicing. Tears gather behind my eyes and I blink madly, willing them not to fall.

My mother let me down.

When I needed her arms around me, needed her warmth, she left me out in the cold.

My hands shake and my eyes swim as I continue staring at my phone.

I'm about to call Bradford when I see him coming toward me. His strides are purposeful, his expression intent. And those arms of his? They open and pull me in close when he reaches me. They tighten around me.

They give me the warmth I've been searching for my entire life.

I let my tears fall and bury my face in my husband's chest while he strokes my back and kisses my hair. While he loves me.

He gives me all the time in the world, simply holding me while I allow my emotions free rein. When I finally lift my face to his, I ask, "What are you doing here? You had meetings this morning."

He cups the back of my head. "The thing about meetings is they can be held anywhere."

I glance down the street at his parked car. "You worked here?"

"I did. And you're right about needing a new car without a center console. It's quite restrictive."

I clutch his arms. "You are *reckless*."

He wipes my tears. "Only for you."

This man.

"Thank you," I breathe before pulling his mouth down to mine and kissing him. When I let him go, I flash him a sexy smile. "I think it really might be time for you to get a new car, especially if you're going to stalk me around New York during your work hours."

"I told you to consider it done. Your new car will be here in a month." His hand curves around my neck and his mouth brushes my ear. "And it was more expensive than your bed, so I hope you know what that means."

I am never letting this man go.

Not ever, ever, *ever*.

38

KRISTEN

BRADFORD WAKES me early Wednesday morning. Way too early. He's very persuasive, though, and has my legs spread faster than I can tell him that four thirty is too early for sex.

He fucks me rougher than he has to date and talks dirtier to me than he did yesterday. I learn that my bad girl really likes a man being impolite to her.

After we're finished, he pulls me into his arms and asks, "What do you have planned for today?"

I roll in his arms so I'm on my side, looking up at him. Tangling my leg over his, I rest my arm on his stomach and trace my finger over his chest. "I'm going to start searching for a new job, and then, this afternoon, I'm going to buy a new dress and get a blowout for our date tonight."

"Our date?" He appears confused, which makes sense since we technically don't have a date penciled in for tonight.

"Yes. I told the girls at lunch yesterday that I've

decided our social engagements for Alan shall now be dates as far as I'm concerned."

"It's not a date if I have to share you, Kristen."

"So"—I reach up to run my fingers lightly over his lips —"we'll find a rooftop and have fifteen minutes of non-sharing time."

I see his brain putting this all together. I also see how much he likes this idea.

I snuggle closer to him. "I also want you to take me on a date with no sharing on Sunday afternoon after the lunch we have to go to. Can you make time for that?"

"You want two dates in one day?"

I grin up at him. "I'm demanding, I know. That was on the list of wife jobs when I checked the other day. I'm just doing my job."

"I haven't seen the proof that this list exists."

"It really does. And I have the husband list too."

"Am I performing well?"

"Well, that remains to be seen after you didn't agree to two dates in one day."

He surges up onto his side and pins his body over mine, entwining our fingers as he presses my hands to the mattress and gazes down at me with fierce resolve. "My Sunday is blocked off for you. I'm starting the day with your pussy where I intend on staying for hours before you get your hour of reading. Then, we've got our first date. After that, I'm going to need more time fucking you, and then I'll take you on our second date. I have ideas for where I'll take you but feel free to give me your choice and I'll make that happen." He lowers his face to mine and kisses me so slowly and passionately that I forget what day it even is for a moment. "When I get you home from that date, I'm going to take you upstairs and fuck you in the ballroom, under the stars. And I'm going to take my time, so you need to prepare for that because when I'm finished with you on Sunday, you're not going to be able to walk."

With that, he leaves the bed and walks into his bathroom. He gives me no backward glance but he doesn't need to in order to know how much he's affected me with that promise. I'm a hot mess of need now. Why is it not Sunday already?

I take a shower, dress for the day, and then eat breakfast with Bradford. He asks me about my search for a job while we eat, and I tell him I'm not sure what I'm looking for. We're in the middle of this conversation when the girls begin bombarding me with texts. I know it's them simply by the fact the text notification sound keeps alerting me to another text.

My phone is in my purse and I have to rummage for it, pulling half the contents of my purse out onto the table while I do so.

"Jesus," I mutter as the texts just keep coming. I give Bradford a stern look when I hear him chuckle. "I will hurt you."

I open the group chat as he tries, and fails, to wipe the smile off his face.

ADELINE

Jameson is taking up running marathons because I need a break from hiking.

POPPY

Said no girl ever.

JENNA

Are we talking four-thirty in the morning hikes? Because if so, I need a break from that kind of hiking too.

CHARLIZE

I thought you banned hiking between 2 and 6 in the morning?

JENNA

I did, but do we think my husband pays any attention to that ban?

LORELEI

So, is this marathon running really happening, Addy, or is that wishful thinking?

ADELINE

I signed him up for his first one and broke the news to him last night.

POPPY

And?

ADELINE

And the next time you all see him, you should ask him how that goal is going. He does well with public goals.

JESSICA

I'm reading that as: he hasn't started training yet.

I meet Bradford's gaze. "It seems I like to copy my sister."

"How?"

"By finding a man who likes hiking at four thirty in the morning."

"I like hiking at all hours, Kristen."

I squeeze my legs together, liking that statement a little too much. "Well, it's now banned between two and six a.m. And come to think of it, I recall you telling me you run every morning and hit the gym on Mondays, Wednesdays, and Fridays. Where's all that exercise this week?"

"I've found better ways of getting it in."

My legs press together again. "Okay, stop it. You already got me bothered when you told me your plans for Sunday, and now you're doing it again, and since you don't have time to fuck me again before you go to work, you need to stop saying things like that."

He checks the time on his phone as he stands and I know he's mentally calculating whether he could fit more sex in.

Before he finishes all that math, I stand and begin gathering my belongings back into my purse. Bradford looks up from his phone as I reach for the poetry book on the table. When he sees what's in my hands, he stops me and takes hold of the book.

"This is the book I gave you," he says as he flips through it, paying particular attention to the pages I've tabbed and some of the passages I've highlighted and annotated.

He's reading my innermost thoughts and I don't stop him, not even when he looks up and asks me if I want him to stop. He's the first person I've ever shared any of my annotated books with. Not even Jenna knows I annotate books.

I want Bradford to know me in this way and I adore that he's interested. That he's not belittling me.

He takes a few minutes, reading and flipping through

the pages before he stops at one poem and reads out loud. "You bare your soul and hand them the map...love is a dance, a sway, between the comfort of knowing, and the terror of becoming...it's the silent words in the middle of the night, it's the wounds that leave their mark...yet, it's in the jagged edges that the most beautiful love is seen... it's the ending and the starting...." He meets my gaze. "She captures it so well."

He didn't read every line of that poem, but the ones that spoke to him make me sigh every time I read them. "She puts words together that just belong together."

"Do you have any of her other books?"

"No, just that one. I only want that one." I move into him, the book between us. "I carry this book almost everywhere I go and I have since the day you gave it to me. I never told you how much your gift meant to me."

"Yes, you did." He places the book in my hands. "You just didn't use words." He brushes his lips over mine. "I have a meeting."

I grasp his suit jacket and pull him in close, inhaling his scent before he leaves. "I'll see you tonight."

He goes to work and I begin looking for a new job.

∼

POPPY

Kristen, how was the Grant party last night? Seth and I were supposed to attend but he got food poisoning so we had to stay home. I saw so many fit checks on Insta that were a slay.

ADELINE

I saw some too that I loved.

JENNA

I heard the Blacks were an hour late.

That was NOT my fault! I've been so careful all week not to run late for any of these events.

JENNA

Did Bradford blame you, though? Beckett always finds a way to say it was my fault when we're late because he couldn't resist fucking me while I got ready.

No, and if he did, I'd correct him very quickly. I refuse to take the blame when I was actually on time.

POPPY

Was your hair a mess by the time you arrived? Your makeup ruined? Honestly, men need to choose better times to stick their dick in us than when we've just done our hair and makeup.

JESSICA

IDK Poppy, I'm okay with Jack sticking his dick in me when I'm glammed up. What I'm not here for is when he wants to stick it there after not doing the laundry he promised me he'd do.

LORELEI

Ashton uttering the words "calm down" means he can keep that dick of his away from me for a very long time.

JENNA

Right? How do men not know that calm down means "you're out of control and an emotional mess right now and you should stop being hysterical"?

ADELINE

How did Alan cope with you guys being an hour late, Kristen?

He glared at me all night. I should have told him to calm down. I had to bite my tongue a lot so I didn't tell him I'd rather sit on Bradford's dick more than attend a party.

POPPY

Attagirl.

JENNA

I have never heard you say "sit on his dick". I am here for this.

Trust me, I'm saying all kinds of things this week. My bad girl part is just over here throwing herself a party. I truly hope she takes a long nap on Friday.

JESSICA

Why Friday?

I'm meeting Bradford's mother when she and Edmund come for drinks before the Swift Ball.

CHARLIZE

You're nervous about that?

Yes! Edmund hasn't been awful to me but I know he wishes Bradford hadn't married me. I have no clue what to expect with his mother. And Bradford's invited his brothers too, but so far, I only know that Hayden is coming. I don't cope well with not knowing things!

JENNA

You'll be okay, Kris. Bradford will make sure of it.

I know, but still, I don't want to cause more stress for him.

LORELEI

Where's your date tonight?

We've got a dinner at the Bing's and then tomorrow we've got a lunch, but I can't remember where right now.

ADELINE

Tell me you're staying off social media.

I haven't looked at any of it since Monday. I took your advice. But Alan sure lets me know things aren't good.

CHARLIZE

We're here for you, Kristen. Anytime.

Thank you.

I manage to stay off social media all week until Friday morning.

After waking alone because Bradford had a super

early meeting at his office he had to leave for before six a.m., I begin going about my morning, getting ready for the busy day ahead, and doing my best not to think about the fact his parents and some of his brothers are coming over tonight. It's been a long week and I haven't heard from my mother since I saw her on Tuesday, which has kept my thoughts in a spiral. I've also had to deal with Alan every day. Not what I'd choose as a life preference. And on top of these things, I've spent each day trying to keep my head held high while people whisper about me and Bradford everywhere I go. Time alone with Bradford on Sunday can't come soon enough.

I'm dressed and almost out the door when I receive a text from Lila James, the woman who plans the yearly class reunions.

LILA

> I'm so looking forward to meeting Bradford next month! I hope you're both okay after all the nasty things that have been posted on social media overnight. I'm thinking of you XO

I stare at my phone and am quite certain that after all these years of denying myself, I need to bring sugar into my home. I think if I didn't have to leave the condo to source my daily allowance of one coffee with sugar, I could drink it right now and avoid social media.

I take a deep breath and force the idea of checking social media from my mind. However, when I receive a text from Jenna asking me if I'm okay, that's it. I need to know what lies have been published about us now.

I check one of the most trusted Instagram gossip accounts first. They don't post lies, just facts and have always been kind to me even while sharing gossip about me.

@thetea_gasp

Holy wow, girlfriends, vibe check on the whole @kristenblaise x @bradfordblack situation? The scandal they caused when they decided it would be fun to forget he was engaged and run off to Vegas to get married is cray right now. We've never eaten so much popcorn in one week. It's been six days since they had that special moment with Elvis and while Kristen's fashion has never been so on point (I mean, look at her drippin'!), she's never looked as exhausted. Not even when @johnathonswindle's body count was revealed. While we're torn over wanting to have an excuse to eat more popcorn, we also just want our girl to be happy. We hope the storm finishes blowing through her life soon because this is not the #goals we wanted for her. Girl deserves to be able to enjoy that #zaddy in peace and welcome in her #sliving era.

Right. So maybe I shouldn't have checked there first. Exhausted? Of course I look exhausted. I'm fucking drained by the disinformation that's been spread about me. And since I've been offline most of the week, I don't even know the half of it yet.

I rectify that, and half an hour later, I wish I hadn't.

The new lies are that 1) Cecelia was pregnant with Bradford's child and miscarried this week because of the stress Bradford's cheating caused her. Bradford couldn't care less and has been spotted out socializing every night with the woman who caused this scandal. Spoiler alert: that woman is me. And 2) Some old photos from various galas over the year have surfaced that feature me and Bradford. They're group photos that have us standing with not only our partners at the time, but with other couples too. However, the gossip is that we were cheating on our partners back then. The other part of this lie is that I coerced Bradford into marrying me, that he wasn't thinking straight because I lured him with sex. Please, have these people met the man? No one forces Bradford Black into anything. If I could, I wouldn't waste that power on forcing him into marriage; I'd force him to entertain my bad girl all day long.

There are many other random pieces online about my colorful dating history, my loose ways (their words, not mine), that I'm only out for Bradford's money (if only they knew how he forced half his cash on me in the postnup and is refusing to give me the bed anytime soon), that I'm already cheating on Bradford with someone else (these people clearly have no idea that when Bradford fucks a woman, he gets the job done so well she has no energy left for pretty much anything else, let alone sex with another man), that Bradford is also cheating on me (see the previous point; I mean, I love his dick, but it doesn't have superpowers that I'm aware of), that his family refuse to welcome me, and that even my father has disowned me because I'm a disgrace.

That last point hurt, and it causes me to stop scrolling and shove my phone in my purse. I have a job interview this morning with a publishing company that I need to stay focused for; thinking about this gossip won't help me with that.

It turns out that I should not have gotten out of bed today. In the history of Fridays, this one soon becomes my absolute least favorite one of life.

39

KRISTEN

My job interview goes badly. And when I say badly, I mean it's one of the most hideous experiences of my life.

The woman interviewing me is more interested in discussing the scandals of my life. She brings up my marriage first, congratulating me but then subtly casting aspersions on it. Then, she mentions my failed engagement to Johnathon and fishes for more information on that time of my life. Right after I manage to dissuade her from that interrogation, she asks me why I no longer work for my father. The glint in her eye tells me she knows the answer to this already and I soon decide that she only called me in for an interview as a form of entertainment.

I feel frayed by the time I leave the interview. Bradford told me to call him once I was done and let him know how it went, but when I call, he's in a meeting. Jane tells me she'll have him return my call when he's free even though I let her know he doesn't need to. I get the impression she's been given strict instructions by my husband that she should never keep me from him.

After the interview, I go to my condo and pack some more of my belongings. I've only managed to sort through clothes, shoes, purses, and books so far, which means I've still got a lot to pack. Bradford dropped by quickly yesterday and suggested we hire movers to do it all for me, but I told him I want to go through everything myself. It's a big life change and I need to take a minute with it.

I spend a few hours packing and when I leave just after lunchtime, I run into one of my neighbors who makes some offensive comments about sluts who steal other women's men. I'm so stunned that I forget how to speak for a second. This only encourages her to keep going. However, I recover quickly and let her know what I think of her sharing her opinion with me and also exactly what I think of her using that derogatory term.

I'm wild by the time I finish with her. Furious that there are still women who exist who think using words like *slut* to put another woman down is okay. When I pay the dictionary people off with Bradford's money to add my new word, which I have yet to devise, I will take another billion from him and begin a campaign to teach people to do better.

My afternoon does not improve.

It's a rapid slide into my hair appointment running late because it was scheduled in their diary for next Friday instead of today. My hairdresser fits me in but it puts me an hour and a half behind in my day. On top of that, I have to endure the whispers and stares of the salon clients. I really want to scream at them to *just fuck off*, but I hold my tongue for Bradford.

I will not ruin his career.

I will not ruin his career.

I will not ruin his career.

I spend a great deal of time sitting in the salon wondering if it's too late for that, though.

Jenna calls when I'm on my way home from the hair-dresser to let me know the dress she pulled for me for tonight has been misplaced. She advises she's sourcing more options and will absolutely have a dress for me in time for drinks with Bradford's family.

I stare at the time on my phone as she tells me this. "They're arriving in an hour, Jenna." Panic begins building in the pit of my stomach. "I'll just go home and find another dress to wear."

"No." Her voice is calm but I hear the edges of it stretching with her own worry. "I'm going to find you a dress, Kris. I promise."

I agree for her to keep searching but I'm already mentally filing through my closet. I at least need to have another option planned in case she can't find me a suit-able dress.

She promises to keep me updated before ending the call. I haven't heard any news by the time I arrive home, so I proceed to go through my closet. It takes me half an hour to narrow my selections down to three dresses. A ridiculous amount of time. I wouldn't usually take that long but my brain is filled with so much clutter today that I'm finding it difficult to think straight.

A text from Jenna finally comes forty-five minutes after our phone call.

JENNA

> I'm on my way to your place with a dress!
> It's stunning and I think you're going to
> love it.

She sends a photo and she's right. I do love it. I just hope it fits.

> I love you. Thank you!

JENNA

> Also, I meant to tell you that I saw
> Grayson yesterday. He told me he had
> lunch with Bradford the other day.

> Did he tell you they're going to be golfing
> buddies?

JENNA

> Yeah. The Black charm was obviously in
> full effect during that lunch.

> The Black charm is always in full effect.

JENNA

> LOL. Okay, I'll be there in about half an
> hour. Hopefully.

Bradford's parents and brothers are due to arrive at six p.m. In fifteen minutes time. Bradford strides into our bedroom at 5:50 p.m. with a look of apology on his face. "I'm sorry I'm late."

He told me he'd be home by five p.m., but I'd already assumed from the fact I never heard back from him this morning that he must have been busy all day, so I wasn't expecting him on time.

"We're in a bit of a crisis here," I throw out, suddenly feeling frantic. "And I'm really sorry about it, but honestly, I don't think any of it was my fault. I mean, maybe I confused the hairdresser with my Fridays for her diary, but I don't think I did. The dress issue is definitely not my fault. And my makeup not being finished yet is not my fault. And—"

Bradford comes to me and silences me. "What's happened?"

My anxiety crashes around in my stomach and chest as I take a deep breath, but I don't even think breathing will help ease my turmoil. I don't think anything will do that. I make wide eyes at him. "My neighbor called me a slut."

He appears confused by that but rolls with it. "Because?"

"Because I married you and stole you from another woman."

"This triggered the crisis?"

"No. Lila James triggered the crisis."

"Who is Lila James?" A text sounds from his phone in his pocket but he ignores it.

"She's the class reunion planner."

"How did she cause the crisis?"

I make more wide eyes. "She texted me this morning to say she hoped we're okay after the gossip posted about us overnight. Let it be known that she does *not* care if we are okay. She just cares to know more of the details, of which I gave her none, because before her text I didn't know any of them."

"She told you about the gossip?"

"No. I looked online for it."

A look of apology flashes across his face. "I'm sorry I haven't been able to stop all the lies."

"They're not your fault, Bradford." He shared with me earlier in the week that he suspects people in the party who no longer want him to replace Senator Adler if he is indicted are behind the smear campaign. "And I should have stayed offline, but ugh, Lila always pushes my buttons. I have no idea why I still bother with her reunions."

"Why do you?" He ignores the second text that buzzes in his pocket.

"I'm going to have to put some thought into that. Also, I don't think I can go on without sugar in our home. I am certain that if I'd been able to have my coffee with sugar here this morning rather than having to go out for it, I could have avoided some of this crisis."

Now, he looks even more confused. "I didn't think you consumed sugar."

"I don't consume it at home, and I only consume a teaspoon of it a day."

"In coffee that you drink somewhere other than at home."

"Yes."

"Right. Got it. So we can have sugar here now?" He ignores a third text.

"You're getting off track here." Even I can hear the hysteria creeping into my voice. I'm not sure how Bradford appears unaffected by it. "I'm running late! And out of all the times that I could have run late this week, it's for your parents. And your brothers. And I may not have a dress! And I—" I cut myself off when another text reaches his phone. "Oh my God, *this phone*"—I pull it from his pocket and look at it, noting four messages from Alan before thrusting it at him—"I swear, if he harasses me tonight, I cannot be held accountable for my actions."

Bradford doesn't even look at the texts. "Alan's been harassing you?"

I stare up at him, taking in all the love and concern he's looking at me with, and my chest and stomach instantly quieten. They're not completely at peace, but the turbulence is gone and now it's a hum I can cope with.

"I shouldn't have used that word."

"But it's how you feel? Like you're being harassed?"

I sway into him and rest my hand on his stomach. "No. I was being dramatic. I'm stressed because I'm running late and I feel like the time it will take me to finish getting ready won't be anywhere near enough time for me to feel ready for tonight."

"How long do you need?"

"Well, I'm just waiting on Jenna to arrive with my dress, and I have to finish my makeup. Maybe another half hour or so."

"No, Kristen, how much time do you need after that to feel ready for tonight?"

My heart flutters. "I don't know why I feel so nervous to meet your family," I say softly. "But I've never been more nervous in my life."

"I understand that. You should take as long as you need. They'll wait."

"No, Bradford. We have the gala to get to as well." Mostly, though, I don't want to keep his family waiting.

"We have an entire lifetime of galas ahead of us. They'll all wait. My main priority is our marriage, and if you need a minute to feel ready for anything, you take it."

I'm lost for words.

I never expected to find a man who would stop time for me. It means more than Bradford will ever know that he's giving me this gift.

"I love you," I say, "and I would kiss you right now, but we both know that you have a little bit of trouble leaving things at just a kiss, so I'm not going to. But you should know that you're doing a lot of hiking later tonight."

Before I know what's happening, he's got one arm around me, my body hard against his, and his mouth on mine so he can take the kiss he wants. He is anything but polite with where he puts his other hand, and completely indecent with the way he kisses me.

"I'm canceling our breakfast tomorrow morning," he growls when he's done with me. "You won't have gotten enough sleep to even think about getting up for breakfast." He lets me go. "I'll have a quick shower and then I'll let Mom and Dad know there's been a crisis. You take your time, and if I even sense you're not ready when you join us, I'll put you over my shoulder and bring you back in here to finish getting ready." A dark look passes over his face. "And if I ever meet that neighbor of yours, she'll wish I hadn't."

After he leaves me, I spend precious minutes I don't have thinking about what our relationship would have been like if we'd found our way to each other sooner. I wonder if we would have been as right for each other when we were younger as we are now. I'll never know but I think maybe our timing wasn't always off; I think maybe it was perfect.

Jenna takes longer than she predicted to get here, flying into the bedroom with the dress ten minutes after

Bradford finished showering and dressing. "I'm so sorry I took so long! Traffic was horrendous."

She makes quick work of unzipping the garment bag and helping me into the dress. It's a strapless red dress with a fitted bodice that's adorned with floral lace applique. The long A-line skirt is made from layers of glitter tulle that float around me and make me feel like a princess.

"You look beautiful," Jenna says from behind me as she finishes fitting the dress. "I'm actually glad the other dress was misplaced. This one is just perfect for you."

I agree and I think about how she helped me today, and about how she always helps me. "Thank you, Jenna."

She stops what she's doing and smiles. "You don't need to thank me, Kris. I just want—"

"No." I place my hand on her arm. "Thank you for everything you've ever done for me. I couldn't have asked for a better sister. And I know we weren't always close because I held myself back, but I'm so grateful that we found our way here. I would not get through life without you, and I want you to know that."

Tears shimmer in her eyes by the time I finish speaking, which causes my own tears to threaten. At my wide eyes, because makeup!, she flutters her hands in front of her eyes to stop herself from crying. "Sorry! No crying!"

I fan my face too. "No crying. I cannot keep Bradford's parents waiting all night."

Once we've got ourselves under control, she says, "I hate how you got here, but I love that we're here too." We spend another few moments just silently watching each other with our hearts wide open before she says, "Okay, I'm gonna go and let you wow Bradford's family." She gives me a huge smile. "I am so happy for you, Kris. And I expect updates throughout the night."

I'm not sure why Jenna thinks I will even come close to wowing Bradford's family but I adore her belief in me.

By the time I join Bradford and his family in the grand salon, I've kept them waiting for almost an hour. You wouldn't know it, though, because they all greet me like I've arrived exactly when I should have.

Bradford's mother is elegant and so beautiful with her high cheekbones, long shiny brunette hair, wide green eyes, and porcelain skin that makes her look barely a day over fifty even though I know she's fifty-eight.

She smiles the minute she sees me and comes my way. "Kristen," she says when she reaches me. "I'm so happy to meet you. I'm Ingrid." She glances around at her sons who are talking with their father. "And these are my boys, but I suspect we'll have a few minutes to chat before they finish discussing the skiing trip they're planning for next month." She smiles again. "I don't know if you've spent much time talking about skiing with Bradford, but all my boys could talk for days straight about anything that involves the outdoors. Their father took them on camping trips a few times a year while they were growing up and they all take after him with his love of being out in nature."

I suddenly realize why I've been so nervous about tonight. I was worried that all Ingrid would see when she looked at me is my mother. The woman her husband cheated on her with. But I don't think that's the case. The sparkle in her eyes and the genuine interest radiating from her make me think she truly wants to welcome me into her family.

Her warmth puts me at ease and I return her smile. "Bradford's told me about some of those trips but we haven't really talked about his love of skiing yet. I have so much still to learn about him."

"You've got forever to learn it all," she says softly before admiring my dress. "This dress is gorgeous. Where did you get it?"

I look down at the dress at the same time Bradford appears by my side. "My sister is a stylist. She borrowed it for me, so I'm not sure where it's from." When I look up again, I find Bradford's gaze on my dress and I decide that I need to buy it. My husband likes it a *lot*.

"She's good at her job," Ingrid says. "It's like that dress was made for you."

The heat Bradford's eyes meet mine with say he agrees.

I'm flummoxed by the desire he's looking at me with while trying to navigate this meeting with his mother. My bad girl is fighting to be let loose and he really needs to stop looking at me like that.

"Yes," I say to Ingrid, while making eyes at her son that say *stop it*. "She's amazing at her job."

Bradford slides his arm around me, resting his hand on my hip. His scent engulfs me and I make a mental note to tell him never to wear it when I need to stay focused. I also make a note to tell him not to stroke my hip like he is when I'm standing in front of his mother.

"You look beautiful," he says.

"Thank you." I lean into him and kiss his cheek but what I'm really doing is whispering against his ear, "If you don't stop, there will be no hiking tonight."

"So," Ingrid says, glancing between us as Bradford's

mouth quirks, "Bradford told me he met you nearly a decade ago at a rooftop party you both gatecrashed."

"Yes," I say as he lets me go and finally stops scrambling my brain. "Did he tell you he carried me home that night on his back because my glass slippers were killing my feet?"

She laughs. "He did not. Do you still own those glass slippers?"

"No."

"She owns hundreds more like them, though," Bradford says to his mother. "Kristen's shoe collection rivals yours."

Before I can stop myself, I say, "You love shoes?" I'm only a little horrified that I gushed this question with way more excitement than is really warranted, but I can talk shoes like Bradford and his brothers can talk the outdoors.

Ingrid's eyes light up. "They're my favorite part of an outfit."

"Jesus," Gage, one of Bradford's younger brothers mutters as he joins us. Eyeing Bradford, he says, "Did you have to mention her shoes? There goes our night."

"Hush, Gage," Ingrid says but it's clear she enjoys her son's grumbling.

"He's right," Callan says, coming to stand next to his brother, a cheeky grin on his face as he looks at me. "Our mother will talk your ear off all night about shoes."

I've met Gage and Callan at galas years ago, but only very briefly. And I never saw their senses of humor, which I really like so far. They're both making me feel at ease.

"Well," Ingrid says as Edmund and Hayden join our circle. "I imagine Kristen will welcome the conversation, just like Luna does." She looks at Gage. "She's going to be excited to meet her new aunt who shares her love of shoes. Goodness knows her uncles let her down when it comes to dress-ups." She smiles at me. "It'll be nice having another girl in the family after all these years of only testosterone."

I know Luna to be Gage's five-year-old daughter and laugh at the thought of these men trying to play dress-up with her.

Bradford bends his face to mine as the guys ask Gage about his daughter's Christmas present wish list. "Would you like a drink?"

"No, I don't think so."

He takes a moment searching my face. "Are you ready for tonight?"

I smile. "More than you can imagine."

"Bradford," Gage interrupts us. "What are your plans for Christmas?"

"It's Kristen's birthday on Christmas Day," Bradford says. "We haven't discussed our plans yet."

"Oh," Ingrid says, "You must spend some of the day with us." She's looking at me. "We'd love to spoil you. It must be awful celebrating your birthday on Christmas Day."

"We'll discuss it and get back to you," Bradford says, his tone communicating to his mother that she should not attempt to force a decision now.

"I'd love you to spoil me," I say to Ingrid and I mean every word I say. "You're right that it sucks to share my birthday with Christmas."

"Great," Ingrid says. "How does lunch at our place sound?"

Bradford's giving me a *let's slow this down* look. I send back an *I'm okay with this* look. His mother appears to know exactly what's going on between us. I imagine she does. She's been married for decades and has a large family with her husband. I suspect she and Edmund have shared thousands of these silent conversations.

Bradford is still making *let's hold on* eyes at me, so in an effort to shush him, I say to his mom, "Lunch is perfect. It'll give us time to hike in the morning."

Callan's brows pull together, as do pretty much everyone's. "Hiking? On Christmas Day?"

I work hard to keep a straight face as I look at my husband who's now giving me an amused look. "Your brother does love his hiking."

Callan still looks confused. "Yeah, he does, but I would have thought he'd be more up for skiing than hiking."

"Let's save skiing for the 26th," Gage says.

"You're heading to Aspen?" Hayden asks.

Gage nods. "Yeah. I've got Luna this year while Shayla heads to Europe with her new partner, so I thought we'd spend a week there after Christmas."

Before I can commit us to anything, Bradford says, "We'll let you know."

"I'm in," Callan says. "Fuck knows, I need some down time. I'm wrecked after the last six months."

Hayden scrolls his phone before saying, "Yeah, I'm in too. But probably only for a few days."

"Anyone know what Ethan's plans are?" Gage asks.

"When does anyone in this family know what Ethan's

plans are?" Callan says and I get the impression from the brothers' responses that there's some distance between them and their youngest brother. The fact that Bradford hasn't spoken as much about Ethan as all his other family members over the years also lends itself to this thought.

"He's not coming home for Christmas this year," Ingrid says quietly, the sparkle disappearing from her eyes.

Edmund slips his arm around her waist and they share a moment before he looks around at the group. "Ethan is busy with work." He says this in such a way that lets his sons know this is the end of that discussion.

Callan, however, mutters, "Ethan is busy doing what he does best. Avoiding his shit."

Edmund eyes his son with disapproval and after that, the conversation soon shifts away from Ethan. Hayden takes charge and I sense he's the manager of the brothers. The one with his finger on the pulse of everyone's personality and needs. The supervisor making sure peace prevails as best it can. He's commanding without being bossy, which I really like. It feels as if he'd keep everyone safe and looked after in a dire situation. Much like Bradford would. Watching them now, I think they maybe work in tandem to look out for their younger brothers.

They spend the next half hour entertaining me with stories of some of the dumb things Bradford's done in his life, their words not mine. Callan mostly drives this conversation. He appears to love a fun time and seems to be the one who drags his brothers into trouble whenever he can.

I learn about the time Bradford broke his ankle while trying to impress a girl with his skateboarding skills when he was fourteen...having never been on a skate-board before. About the time he tried to impress another girl who loved art by painting a graffiti mural on an old warehouse...without first checking to ensure there were no security cameras. He spent weeks cleaning graffiti around New York after that. And about the Infamous Treehouse Incident in which he decided to build his brothers a treehouse at their grandparent's estate when he was thirteen. It turns out I've found a job Bradford isn't good at: building things with his hands. Everyone is in a fit of laughter by the time Callan finishes telling the story of the failed treehouse that was more like a park bench than a treehouse. And finally, I learn just how far my husband has come in the flirting department. He was known as the King of bad pickup lines when he was a teen. Callan's pick for the worst was "Do you have a map? Because I just got lost in your eyes." Gage chooses "Are you a magician? Whenever I look at you, everyone else disappears." And Hayden pitches in with "Are you a parking ticket? Because you've got 'FINE' written all over you."

"Oh my God." I grin at Bradford as everyone laughs. "I can't even put that boy and you together in my head as the same person. Were you really that bad at knowing what to say to girls?"

He gives me the equivalent of an eye roll. "They're messing with you. I never used those lines."

I look to his mom for the truth. "Did he?"

She laughs before shaking her head. "No, those lines were all Callan's. It's a wonder he had as many girlfriends as he did."

"Yeah," Hayden agrees. "Bradford never had to work

hard to woo anyone. But everything else Callan just told you is true."

Our conversation is interrupted when Alan arrives and pulls Bradford and Edmund away from us. I watch as Ingrid's easy mood disappears, replaced with tense energy. It's much the same as how my state of mind shifts, particularly when Alan's unfriendly stare settles on me.

I've worked hard this week to do everything he's expected of me at the social events Bradford and I have attended, yet nothing satisfies him. He's criticized my choice of outfits ("too fashionable, Kristen, be more conservative"), my hair ("not subtle enough"), my shoes ("too high"), my smile ("you need to look remorseful, not happy"), my nails ("cut them"), and even my fucking voice ("too sexy").

Criticizing my voice was a step too far. I told him in the sweetest tone I could muster that I was just using the voice that God gave me and surely he couldn't find fault with *that*. Needless to say, Alan and I are in a war. I think he knows I'd win the war if it really came down to it, simply because my husband is reckless, and that's why he truly despises me. What he doesn't know is that I would never allow Bradford to be *that* reckless. The fact Bradford knows nothing of Alan's war on every single thing about me is proof of that. My father's constant disapproval has trained me well. I can deal with Alan for as long as it takes.

After Bradford and Edmund leave us, and her other sons drift away to talk among themselves, Ingrid draws her attention from Alan who she hasn't taken her eyes off since he arrived. "I don't know if you're aware, Kristen,

but my father and his father before him were both
senators."

"Yes, Bradford has told me." He's also shared with me
that his parents' marriage was one of convenience that
their families wanted.

"My family and Edmund's have political blood
running through them. Every son knew what was
expected of him. Every daughter knew she had to
contribute too. Both Edmund and I did our part, and
while he's still working toward that goal, I quietly stopped
years ago. I don't go against him, but I don't encourage my
sons in that way anymore. I want different for them. I
want them to be able to choose their own path in life.
And to choose their own happiness." She places her hand
over mine. "Please keep letting Bradford choose you."

I was not expecting that. Not in any way, shape or
form, and it stuns me into silence.

We're in the middle of this moment when Gage
comes back to us. "It's time to go."

Ingrid gives him a nod before looking back at me.
Squeezing my hand, she says softly, "Remember what I
said. And keep your eye on Cecelia. That woman is the
most vindictive woman I have ever met."

40

KRISTEN

"WHICH OF THESE women do you want to kill?" Adeline asks when she comes to stand with me at the gala about an hour into the night.

I glare at the woman who is talking with Bradford and another man across the ballroom. "The blonde who hasn't shut up for the last five minutes and who keeps touching Bradford's arm like it's hers to touch. Oh, and about twenty other women who've already flirted with him."

I've spent most of the night by my husband's side as he networked and charmed his way around the gala. For a girl who has always loved the extravagance of this annual event with its exquisite glitter and grandeur, I've hardly noticed any of that tonight because the only things I've paid attention to are the women who want my man.

I turn to Adeline in time to see her studying her husband who is on the other side of the room also being ambushed by a woman. "The hazards of being married to a hot-ass man," she muses.

"I'm being ridiculous, I know, but I can't stop this jealousy and possessiveness even when I try."

"You're not being ridiculous. I completely understand." She shifts her gaze from Jameson to me. "Alan's at stabby levels of prickness tonight. How are you coping with him?"

The girls all know of my dislike of Alan. I may have started the week wishing our group chat would go poof and disappear, but I dedicated a good amount of time today texting them. And I didn't even hate it. They kept me sane during a day I could have lost all my sanity, and while Bradford had to reply to some texts on the way here, I tapped out a rant about how I'm going to start plotting Alan's death.

"Let's just say his death is imminent."

"I'll help you bury the body."

I smile. "Jenna's lucky to have you."

"We're all lucky to have each other."

"My midlife crisis obviously never ended because I'm beginning to think you might be right."

"I wouldn't blame you if you were having a midlife crisis. I know I would be if I had to endure Alan." She glances in Bradford's direction for a moment before coming back to me. "It's all well and good to be networking like you guys are, and winning people over, but are you going to tell your side of the story?"

I arch my brows. "Do you really think Alan would allow that?"

She doesn't answer that question; she just waits for me to answer hers.

"We've got some interviews lined up soon, but I doubt Alan will sanction our real story being told. I think they'll be more fluff than anything."

It's Adeline's turn to lift her brows. "I think you're wrong. Bradford has a massive profile and the entire country's attention is on him right now. People can't get enough of you. Have you seen the posts and comments from the public about their extreme interest in your marriage or are you just seeing the political smear campaign?"

"You girls told me to stay off social media, remember?"

"Right. But you looked today."

"Okay, so yes, but I didn't look too far. I mostly just saw the lies that are designed to hurt him politically."

"Trust me when I tell you the general public want to know more about why he would spontaneously marry you in Vegas when he was engaged to another woman. Yes, it's scandalous but people love a good scandal, and even more than that, they love a good romance. And I think that even the women sitting back judging your marriage secretly wish they had a man who looks at them the way Bradford looks at you." She gives me a pointed look. "These interviews aren't going to be just fluff, Kristen. I think they'll want to dig deep into your relationship. My advice is to take charge of the narrative and be honest with the world. People are tired of slick spin. They want real, even if it's messy."

"I agree with you, but I think Alan is the best at what he does, so we have to put our trust in him on this."

"I've checked him out. He is the best. But you know what? Sometimes people get it wrong, even when they're at the top of their profession." Her voice softens as she continues. "What is your gut telling you to do?"

"I'm a thinker, Adeline, not a feeler. I have *no idea* what my gut is saying."

"Yeah, you do. Just feel into it. No thinking. Does it feel heavy in there? Icky? Like you maybe want to be sick? If so, run the other way. But if it feels light, or excited, or a little like butterfly nerves, that's what you want to run to." Jameson catches her eye. "Okay, that's my cue. My husband has had enough for the night."

I frown. "It's only been an hour."

"Which is precisely one hour more than he wanted to give. And since I've already seen the people I came here to see, I'm going to let him take me home and do whatever he wants with me."

I watch her walk toward Jameson and think about what my gut is saying. I spend a few minutes on that, trying to decide if it feels heavy about Alan's plan or light, and decide that Adeline has no idea how my gut works. It doesn't. It's mute and always has been.

I'm in the middle of this when I see Alan pull Bradford away from that flirty woman to speak with him about something. It's the most useful thing Alan has ever done in my opinion. After they finish their conversation, I gain Bradford's attention. He stops what he's doing and watches me. Actually, he undresses me with his eyes and if that's not my signal that it's time for our date, I don't know what is. I nod my head at the door and he doesn't hesitate.

Five minutes later, we head for the elevator after collecting our coats. "Do you think you'll still eye fuck me in public when you're eighty?" I ask.

He settles his hand on my hip as we reach the elevator, pulling me close while we wait. "Do you think you'll still have this filthy mouth when I'm eighty?"

I turn into him and pull his face down to mine so I can whisper against his ear, "Yes, unless you've worn it out with your dick."

"Fuck, Kristen." He sounds like he's in actual pain.

The elevator arrives and the doors open. It's empty and no one else is waiting with us to enter. Bradford's hand remains on my hip as we step inside. I select the rooftop and the doors slide closed.

My husband wastes no time forcing me into the corner and pressing me up against the wall while moving into me. Reaching for my leg, he roughly pulls it up and around his body as his mouth crashes down onto mine. He takes hold of my face with both hands while kissing me with the same level of need I have for him.

We're wild and frantic. Careless with the way our hands are all over each other, touching, reaching, groping like sex-crazed teenagers.

When I tighten my leg around Bradford and grind myself into his erection, he thrusts against me and groans so loudly it causes me to forget where we are and lose myself completely in him.

By the time we reach the rooftop, I've climbed into his arms and have undone his top few buttons. I think he's just as lost in me because he hasn't stopped me.

The elevator doors open, at which point Bradford comes to his senses and drags his mouth from mine while I work hard to regain *my* senses. Thankfully, no one is waiting for the elevator and we're able to fix our clothes and hair before anyone sees us.

Bradford's hand finds mine and he leads me through the tables and chairs to a quiet spot away from everyone up here.

I stare up at the night sky as I put my hands on the railing, which is the safest place for them. The not-safe option is to do nasty things to his body and I really don't think Alan would approve of that.

Breathing the winter air in, I look at Bradford who is watching me intently, waiting for my opening question. I smile as I think about how well he entertains my silly routine of asking him a random question each night. "You really do love me, don't you?" It's a redundant question because I know he does, but it's my way of saying *I love how you love me in the tiny moments.*

"More than you'll ever know."

I lean in and kiss him. "When we can move on to full-length dates, I want you to take me dancing. Like, filthy, dirty dancing. We'll fly to the other side of the world where no one knows you and you'll take me to a packed club where no one's even watching anyone else because they're all too busy with their partner." I grip his coat. "You'll pull me in front of you and I'll rub my hips and ass all over your dick. Your fingers will dig into my skin so hard and so good that I'll bend over and stick my ass in the air, making it so you can't take your eyes off me and will be helpless but to get your hands all over me." I tease his lips with mine, loving how much I'm affecting him. "We'll dance for hours. You'll want to fuck me on the dance floor. Maybe I'll let you finger me. And when we finally get back to our hotel room, you'll strip me and fuck me before we're barely through the door, and then you'll fuck me on every surface of that room until the sun comes up." I glide my hands up his chest and slide them around his neck while pushing myself against him. Against his ear, I promise, "I will let you restrain me and blindfold me, and then beg you to fill my mouth with your cock. And then I will suck it until you come down my throat."

He grabs a handful of my ass, very disrespectfully, while curling his other hand around my neck. Tracing the hollow of my throat with his nose, he rasps, "If you think I have it in me to wait until I get you to the other side of the world for all that, you have no idea what you do to me."

"Maybe I'll let you restrain me on your jet and—"

He uncurls his fingers from around my neck and presses one to my mouth. "Maybe you'll show me some mercy and stop describing all the ways you want to suck my dick while I can't do anything about how fucking hard you're getting me."

I keep my body crushed to his and my hands right where they are around his neck while I take a minute with his face. He's so damn handsome and I will always think I'm the luckiest girl in the world to be the one who gets to stare at this face at the beginning and end of every day. "If you could have one superpower, what would you choose?"

"Where do you find these questions?" He's amused. Last night, I asked him what meal he would choose if he had to eat only it for the rest of his life. He selected steak but he took a long time deciding and tried to talk his way into being allowed to choose a backup meal. *Just in case the world runs out of beef*, he'd said. I'd rolled my eyes at him and refused his suggestion of a backup meal.

I shrug. "It's my special talent."

"No, your special talent is turning me the hell on."

"And it seems your special talent is delaying and avoiding. You will make an excellent politician."

"My superpower would be to have all the superpowers at my disposal."

"That's not an option."

"It's always an option."

"Says who?"

"Says me."

"Right, but you're not in charge here. I am, and I say you have to choose one."

"Baby, if you think I'm the kind of man who wouldn't find a way to have all the superpowers, we need to fix your perception of me. There's no way I'm ever accepting just one superpower."

And just like that, he wins, but only because he muddles my ability to think straight with that *baby*.

Also, he's right. There's no way Bradford wouldn't figure out how to have as many superpowers as he wants.

"What would your superpower be?" he asks.

"It would depend on the day."

"So, you'd only have one power at a time, but you'd choose which one you want based on the day you're having?"

"Yes, because I understand there can only be one superpower per person."

He grins. "But you wouldn't lock yourself into only one option."

"Well, I *am* a woman and as such I would reserve the right to change my mind at any time."

"What would you choose for tonight?"

"It would be a toss-up between being able to see through your clothes or being able to make the women who insist on flirting with you disappear."

That gets me his lips on mine and a kiss that makes my legs weak right before he says, "I would lend you my powers so you could have both at once. And while we're at it, we'd make all the assholes who looked at you tonight disappear too."

I bring one of my hands to his face, needing to touch it. "I wish we had more time like this."

His eyes offer me an apology but they don't need to. We both got us into this mess and now we both have to get us out of it.

Before he can verbalize the apology, I say, "I would marry you in Vegas again in a heartbeat, Bradford."

He turns silent for a moment. "Senator Adler was indicted today."

Oh.

I know what this means and now I know why I didn't hear from Bradford today. The countdown to Governor Wakefield appointing someone to succeed Senator Adler is on. Bradford is under pressure now. *We're* under pressure now.

"Tell me what you need from me," I say.

"Nothing that you're not already doing."

I narrow my eyes at him. "You didn't really cancel our breakfast tomorrow, did you?"

"I did."

"Jesus, Bradford. You're on a countdown now. You should not be canceling things that might help you."

"I've a mind to cancel everything Alan has on your schedule."

My eyes go wide. "Why?"

"Because you're dealing with enough other things at the moment. You don't need all these breakfasts, lunches and dinners getting in your way."

"What things?"

"You're trying to find a job. And packing your life up to move in with me. And finding your way with your mom."

"You worry too much about me."

Determination steals across his face. "That's my job now. Finally. Let me worry about you."

The way he says *finally* is everything. It *tells* me everything.

Bradford has wanted to be the one who gets to worry about me in the same way I wanted to be the one who knows if he smiled each day, and if not, why.

Please keep letting Bradford choose you.

His mom's request comes back to me.

"I'll let you worry about me if you'll let me worry about you," I say. "And also, is there such a thing as a voice that's too sexy when it comes to politics?"

He frowns. "Who told you that?"

"No one. It was just something I was wondering."

"Bullshit." He looks pissed off now. "Alan and I will be having words, and if he ever says anything like that to you again, I want you to tell me."

I really shouldn't have brought that up, but it has to be said that I really like the way my husband supports me. I'll be going out of my way to exhaust him completely during his hike tonight.

～

We spend two more long hours schmoozing our way through the gala. I stay with Bradford for most of that time but Bradford's mother rescues me from him and Alan towards the end of the night when she sees me beginning to melt down on the inside.

"Thank you," I say as she guides me away. "I think I was maybe a little too close to stabbing Alan with my stiletto."

Ingrid laughs. "I could see that in your eyes."

The pre-midlife-crisis Kristen would have been horrified that she could read me like that. Now, I don't care.

Ingrid and I haven't spent much time together since we arrived at the gala. She's been busy working the room with Edmund. She may not be encouraging her sons into the political sphere but from what I know of her and have seen tonight, she's very much the dutiful wife. I like that she left her husband to come over to me. Just like I loved how she embraced me into her family tonight.

I stop and turn to her. "Thank you for making me feel so at ease tonight. I'm not sure if Bradford told you, but I was super nervous about meeting you."

The lines around her eyes crinkle with kindness. "Do you know what I like the most about you so far, Kristen?"

I was not expecting that question. If anything, I imagined we'd have a slightly awkward conversation about my nerves (which I actually had *no* intention of mentioning, but hello, my new life, where I just blurt random truths) and then move on to chat about what we thought of the gala.

"I'm not sure," I admit.

"I like that you don't hide from the world."

I stare at her, stunned. And before I can stop myself, I

say, "I've spent my entire life hiding from the world, Ingrid, and I'm not sure I've changed that."

"Well, the Kristen who is married to my son sure seems done with hiding. You could have told him no to all these social events. You could have shut yourself away at home. But you've stood tall all week and shown your face in the middle of a scandal, and you've done that with grace." She stops talking but when she sees I'm lost for words, she continues. "I suspect my husband hasn't gone out of his way to welcome you to our family, but I want you to know that isn't because he doesn't support your marriage. He does, but he just needed some time to get his head around what that meant for Bradford's political ambition."

I swallow the thousand emotions I'm feeling, pushing them down to be sorted through later. "Thank you for saying that. I think I needed to hear it."

"It's daunting marrying into a large family. Especially one filled with so much testosterone. I know because that was my experience too. The boys were all more than glad to hear that Bradford married you, and so was I. And now that we've met you, we're even happier, and not just because we've seen just how happy Bradford is to be with you, but also because we like you and are looking forward to getting to know you better."

My eyes water and I blink a few times to try to stop the tears falling but I fail. "Oh, God." I wipe the tears. "I'm sorry. I'm not usually a crier. It's just been a big week."

Ingrid closes her hand over mine. "Never apologize for feeling things, Kristen."

I decide, in this very minute, that Bradford inherited

some of his best qualities from his mother. She might just end up being the best mother-in-law there ever was.

Gage joins us as I keep trying to wipe my tears. He glances between his mother and me before settling his gaze on me. "If anyone was going to make you cry tonight, I would have bet good money on it being Alan."

A laugh barks out of me and soon I'm both laughing and crying. I can't help myself; Bradford's family is being so beautiful to me and I'm not used to this kind of niceness.

Ingrid and Gage give me a minute to get myself under control. Gage waits patiently, not looking even a little perplexed at my outburst. Once I've recovered, I look at him. "I give you full credit for coping well with a woman who didn't know whether she wanted to laugh or cry."

"Sweetheart, I've got a five-year-old daughter and an ex who taught me that I knew not a fucking thing about women before I got one pregnant. Give me all you've got; I'll handle it."

I think I'm really going to like Gage.

"Okay, I'm going to the bathroom to clean my face," I say.

"Bradford's ready to leave," Gage says. "Are you?"

I nod as I look at Bradford who appears to be on his way to me. As a couple stop him, his eyes meet mine and he communicates how much he wishes they hadn't. "Yes, I'll just be a minute."

After Gage tells me the family will wait for me near the front door, I leave him and Ingrid and make my way to the bathroom. It takes me far longer to clean my face than I thought it would because there are a lot of women in here and some want to chat with me. Some also just want to stare and whisper among themselves about me. I have to bite my tongue not to tell them to *just fuck off*, which seems to be the anthem of my life these days.

Tonight has been exhausting with all the hushed murmurs and long stares I've been treated to. Thank God for Bradford who reads any room he's in perfectly and knew to keep his arm around me at times, making me feel safe and protected. Unfortunately, I don't have him by my side when I exit the bathroom. It's unfortunate because as I wind my way along the hallway that leads back into the ballroom, a woman crosses my path and stops me.

Her red hair catches all my attention first. Or maybe it's those green eyes of hers that are blazing with hatred. Or it could actually be her mouth that's pulled into the kind of vicious line that screams *you are everything that is wrong with this world*.

Holy God, how Bradford was ever going to marry this woman is beyond me.

Cecelia Aniston up close in the flesh is fucking scary.

"We finally meet," she says.

Alan would never have told her that *her* voice was too sexy. Terrifyingly violent perhaps, but definitely not sexy.

"Cecelia." I armor up, pushing my shoulders back and pulling oxygen in because I'm surely going to need it to survive this.

She rakes her eyes over me like I'm worthless. "I've been trying to figure out what he sees in you, but for the life of me I can't figure it out. I mean, sure, you've obviously got a pussy he wants, but we all know that never keeps a man interested for very long. At some point, Bradford is going to come to his senses and realize he's made the greatest mistake of his life." She leans in close, her cruel eyes communicating just how much she despises me. "He could have had you on the side, but no, he listened to his dick more than his brain. And that is something I am going to make him regret because no one makes a fool of me and gets away with it. *No one*."

I stand tall. "Are you finished? Or do you perhaps have more hot air in there that you feel the need to get out?"

Her lips press together so hard that her mouth turns white. "You really are as dumb as everyone says, aren't you?"

It's a good thing I've trudged my way through a broken engagement, a mid-life crisis, the loss of my job, and being disowned by my father because all of that has prepared me well for this showdown.

"No one says I'm dumb, Cecelia. They may say many things about me, but never that."

"You'd be surprised to learn what they say."

"You'd be surprised to learn that I don't care what they say."

"I know all about your kind, Kristen. You're shallow, stupid, and vapid."

My mouth opens to tell her what I think of that when Gage's dark voice cuts through the air as he comes up behind Cecelia. "Careful, Cecelia, or you'll have me to deal with. And we both know that between me and Bradford, you're better off dealing with him."

My mouth snaps closed as I take in the way she shrinks as Gage threatens her.

She recovers by the time he comes to stand with me but she's lost some of her fire when she says, "We both know that he keeps you on a tight leash, Gage. Your threats are baseless."

"Run with that assumption and see how far it gets you," he says, his voice deadly calm.

Her mouth flattens again and she glares at him for the longest time before finally snarling at me, "By the time I'm finished with you, you'll wish you didn't know Bradford."

I lean in close. "You think I can't take whatever you've got for me? Keep underestimating me. I dare you."

Cecelia looks like she's ready to do physical damage to me, and quite honestly, with the way I'm feeling, I'm ready to go a round with her. Gage must sense this because he hooks his arm around my waist and holds me to him while murmuring against my ear, "Eyes on the prize, Kristen. She's not worth it."

With one last barbed glare, Cecelia spins and stalks away from us.

"Jesus!" I step out of Gage's hold, wildly furious over that encounter. "She's a piece of work."

He nods while watching me like he's waiting for me to run after her and punch her. "Yeah, she is, and you should stay away from her."

"I don't plan on seeking her out, Gage."

"Good." He lifts his chin at the hallway. "Let's go."

As he leads us out of the hallway into the ballroom towards where Bradford is talking with yet another couple, I say, "What's the deal with you and Cecelia?"

"No deal. She just knows that I'm the one in our family who knows where all the bodies are buried and if Bradford wants ammunition for anything, he can come to me for it."

"Has he come to you for it?"

He looks at me. "You married the upstanding brother, Kristen. He won't ever come to me for the kinds of things I know. Alan, though, he's another story and Cecelia knows that."

41

KRISTEN

> Where is the best place to buy sex toys?

POPPY

Our work here is complete.

> I'm being serious, Poppy. I want to buy some and I have no idea where to go.

POPPY

I was being serious too. Look how far you've come, my darling. Back in the day, you used to ignore us and now you're coming to us. I'm a proud mother hen rn.

> *insert eye roll* But seriously, just tell me. I'm already feeling weird about not knowing where to buy them. Don't make me feel weirder.

ADELINE

Don't feel weird. We've been there, not knowing this stuff.

Right. But that was when you were like fifteen, not nearly thirty.

CHARLIZE

OMG bestie, we should go shopping on Saturday while Owen and Bradford golf. Eeep!! I am so here for this! I've got you covered.

POPPY

I'm coming too. I need to keep an eye on my baby chicklets.

JENNA

I'm in too.

I thought you and Beckett were spending Saturday together?

JENNA

We are. I'll break the news to him tonight that our Saturday will now begin after lunch. There's no way I'm missing girl time.

LORELEI

Jessica and I will need updates on all the things you buy!

I'm almost certain Jessica already owns all the things.

JESSICA

I'm always looking for new things. Jack's been getting a little frisky with his dick in public lately, which tells me he needs some new fun at home. Let me know what you find in case I don't have it.

Okay, gotta go. Alan is sending me death vibes for being on my phone. He also still hasn't let it go that Bradford had words with him about telling me my voice was too sexy last week.

ADELINE

My offer stands. I will bury that body for you.

JENNA

This is the longest Friday of all Fridays. Tomorrow can't come soon enough. What time are we meeting?

CHARLIZE

I'm free from 9:00 a.m.

ADELINE

Same.

Sorry guys, I have to cancel on you. Things have gotten hectic here after that fresh round of scandal hell yesterday and Alan has added a breakfast and a lunch to our day tomorrow.

CHARLIZE

You already had a dinner scheduled, right?

Right.

ADELINE

You must be exhausted. Didn't he add a lunch and dinner to today as well?

Yes. As well as a morning tea. I think he's trying a new tactic: death to Kristen by exhaustion or frustration, whichever comes first. He knows I'm trying to find a job, and I'm almost convinced he's adding in random events for me to attend so it inhibits my ability to attend job interviews.

LORELEI

Does Bradford expect you to attend all these things?

No, but I want to for him. It's crucial he wins the support of Senator Hale and the governor, and I do think we're getting somewhere with that. Senator Hale had a long conversation with me yesterday about what kind of work I'd like to do. He told me he'd keep his eye out for me.

JESSICA

Wait. What was the fresh round of hell yesterday?

Just more lies spread across social media about Bradford marrying a cheater. People are trying to insinuate I've cheated on all my boyfriends. There was also some stuff posted about me being an alcoholic. They used photos of me drinking at my party after I found out Johnathon cheated on me and are making out that I drink like that all the time.

JENNA

They're doctoring photos to tell whatever story they want about her.

> Yeah, Bradford's team is having to waste a lot of time trying to stop this, but the assholes just put more social media accounts up and new photos. It's a nightmare.

JESSICA

Jack has dealt with that kind of thing too. I'm sorry you're going through this.

CHARLIZE

Okay, so no shopping tomorrow. I'll send you links to my fave places. Maybe you can just order online until we can plan another girls' day.

> Thank you!

ADELINE

Hang in there, Kristen.

MY BIRTHDAY and Christmas week arrives faster than I can keep up with and feels all kinds of wrong. Well, except for the fact I have Bradford by my side, that is. But even though I have him, I don't have any other kind of normalcy in my life to anchor me.

My mother hasn't visited me in my new home yet and I've only heard from her twice since that awful day at her home with my father. That was sixteen days ago. Yes, I've been counting. And yes, I'm feeling all sorts of conflicting emotions about this. Feelings I haven't been sharing with my husband because he has better things to worry about.

Except, he doesn't. Not as far as he's concerned. And I

should know that even when he's distracted with work, he's still noticing all my little details.

"I think we should cancel going to Aspen with the family after Christmas," he says as he walks into our bedroom on Christmas Eve. I've been sitting in bed watching *Holidate* and annotating a book while he's been in his office finishing up some work.

I frown at him while he works his way down the buttons of his shirt, undoing them. "Why?"

"I want time alone with you."

"You're having time alone with me now."

He stops mid-unbuttoning. "This is nowhere near enough quality time. Hell, we've just spent Christmas Eve in separate rooms of our home because I had to work. Just like we've been doing for weeks now if we haven't had to attend a function. I've got three days off and I want to spend them with you."

If there's something better in life than the man you love telling you he wants alone time with you, I don't know what it is.

I beckon him with my hand. "Come here."

He finishes undoing his buttons and shrugs his shirt off before joining me on the bed. My hands are on his chest as he moves on top of me, and then they're around his neck so I can pull his mouth to mine for the kiss I've been thinking about for hours.

He gives me the kiss, but even though I feel his desire for me, I can tell he wants something other than a kiss right now.

I pull my lips from his. "What's on your mind?"

He drops down and settles on the bed next to me.

Pulling me close and dragging my leg over his, he rests his hand on my hip. "You."

I smile. "You're going to have to be more specific. I've yet to figure out how to read your mind."

"That's a pity. You'd like what you'd find in my mind."

I roll my hips into him. "Feel free to describe it for me."

He glides his hand up to my waist and squeezes it. "I'll save that for later. Right now, I want you to tell me about your week."

"I've spent my week with you. You know about my week."

"No, we've spent time in the same location during the week, and we've managed minutes together, but not enough for lengthy conversations. All I know is that you've been silently planning Alan's murder. I have no idea how your job hunting is going or what's going on with you and your mother. And I haven't seen too many more of your belongings here, so I'm not sure how you're going with packing. These are things I want to know, and I'm sorry I've had to work such long hours these last few weeks, but hopefully these hours won't last much longer."

I grin. "Can you read *my* mind? Like, how do you know about my murder plans?"

"I see it in your eyes."

He looks deeply regretful over this, and I don't want to dwell on it with him, so I move on to answering his questions. "My job hunting isn't going great. There's not much out there, but also, I'm not really finding what I'm looking for."

"What are you looking for?"

The last time he asked me this, I couldn't nail down an answer, but today I can. "I think it's time to finally do what I've always wanted to do. I'm considering starting a business."

"Helping women?"

"Yes."

"How? What are you thinking?"

I love how attentive he is. "Well, I was thinking about the mental health app you're helping develop and am wondering if I could use something like that to build a network to connect women to the services that could help them. And I'd have a fundraising arm of the business, utilizing all the connections I have. It's still an idea taking form, but I feel excited about it."

He asks me a million more questions and brainstorms ideas with me for an hour. The thing I love the most is that he doesn't try to take over. He doesn't try to tell me what he thinks I should do even though he's more knowledgeable about business than I am.

"And your mother?" he asks once we finish talking about my business ideas. "Did you end up having lunch with her today?"

"No, she had to cancel."

His brows furrow. "Why?"

"Something about Dad." I try to ignore the way my heart chokes, but it's impossible and Bradford doesn't miss it.

He curses softly and pulls me into his arms.

I rest my head on his chest and lie quietly with him. He gives me all the time in the world to gather my thoughts, and when I give them to him, he doesn't let me down.

"I invited her for dinner tomorrow night like we discussed, but she told me that she and Dad are planning to have dinner together. She seemed torn, and I know this is hard for her, being in the middle of me and Dad, but I'm sad that this is our life now."

"It's your birthday tomorrow, Kristen. The day she brought you into the world. I'm not a parent yet, but when I am, I will want to spend the day we brought our children into the world with them, celebrating them. I can't wrap my head around her not making time for you tomorrow."

My mother may have fractured my heart this week, but my husband knows exactly how to patch it back together.

I roll so I can look up into his eyes. "How many children do you want?"

Bradford understands that this is my way of saying *thank you for loving me and asking me about my mom, but now I need a minute*, and doesn't hesitate to roll with me. "Ten." At my brow arch, his lips quirk. "Wrong answer? Eleven?"

"If you put eleven babies in me, you will die a very unhappy man."

"I imagine I would die before I even got to put the fifth one in there."

"More like the fourth."

"So, what you're saying is that you want three children."

"I'm saying I want two. Three would be acceptable, but that's my limit."

"How soon do you want these children?"

"Not soon. I need time alone with you first."

"Right, because you have plans to make me fly you around the world and do filthy things to you before babies cut in on that time."

I lean up on my elbows and kiss him, leaving my lips to linger near his as I say, "I like that you have a good memory for the things I tell you."

His hand moves to my ass, squeezing it exactly how I like. "I need to get you naked."

"Yes, you do. I'm ready for my birthday week to begin."

Bradford wakes me early on my birthday. He takes his time with my body, giving me two orgasms with his mouth and fingers before I fuck him reverse cowgirl style. He then lets me lie in bed reading while he makes me breakfast and brings it to me. After that, he makes me sit on his face while he blows my mind with one of the best orgasms I've ever had.

"This is the best birthday of my life," I declare when I meet him in the bedroom after showering and dressing.

"We've barely gotten started," he says, sitting on the bed and pulling me to sit on his lap. He hands me a gift and spends a long minute kissing me. "Happy birthday, beautiful."

I undo the gold bow and carefully unwrap the gift. It feels like it might be a book and when I finish removing the paper, I find a gorgeous first-edition poetry book from a poet I've not heard of before.

"Have you read her?" Bradford asks as I flip through the pages.

"No." I read some of a poem, sighing over the beauty of the words. "But I think I'm going to like her poetry."

"I did a little research and people seem to think she's as good as Charlotte Franklin."

I look into his eyes and place my hand to his cheek, savoring this moment. I wish we could stay in it for the entire day. "You have a special way of loving a person."

"Of loving you. Only you."

"I'm so glad I found you on that rooftop all those years ago."

"I almost kissed you that night."

I slip my arm around him, threading my fingers up into the hair at the nape of his neck. "Really? Why didn't you?"

"A siren cut into the moment, but mostly because we were both in relationships. It took everything, though, not to take what I wanted."

"I know. I felt the same. I desperately wanted you to kiss me. And not just that night."

He curves his fingers around my throat and teases my lips with his. "How often did you think about me?"

This conversation has my butterflies dancing wildly. Or maybe that's his touch that's causing that. Whatever it is, I want so much more of it. "All the time. Every day. And ten years later, I want you even more than I did back then." I slide my hand down his neck and rest it on his shoulder. "I have a Christmas present for you that I was going to give you tonight, so that you didn't have to think about it all day. But I want to give it to you now."

His mouth smiles against mine right before he kisses me. "You got me something filthy."

"I did."

"You should not wait to give it to me."

I move off his lap and retrieve the gift. His eyes don't let mine go as he begins unwrapping it. They're filled with heat and a promise that is doing delicious things to me.

When he finally tears his gaze away and looks at his present, he rasps, "Fuck."

I watch as he takes hold of the leather wrist restraints and red satin blindfold. "Merry Christmas," I whisper against his ear as I crawl back onto his lap. "I'll do whatever you want with those tonight."

"Tonight?" His strong arms come around me and he lifts me with him as he stands. Before I know what's happening, he's got me on my back on the bed, and is forcing my legs apart with his knee as he moves on top of me. "I'm not waiting all day for this."

I don't stop him. I mean, there's a reason why I told him he could do whatever he wanted tonight, and it wasn't because I wanted him to wait until then.

I give Bradford his Christmas present. A few times over. And I don't even care that I make us very late for Christmas with his family.

"And thank you very much for pointing out to everyone that I was missing an earring when we arrived," I say to Callan about three hours into our Christmas lunch with the family. I've had a few drinks and have been chatting with him for the past twenty minutes, finding out more about him and his life.

He grins after drinking some of the hot buttered rum

his mom just brought over for us. "You guys were nearly two hours late. I couldn't let that pass."

"Well, you didn't have to mention the reason."

He chuckles. "I didn't. I simply mentioned your missing earring. Besides, everyone here knows Bradford inside out. He's never late for anything. I think we all knew why you guys were late."

"So," I say as I take a sip of my rum, "you're home for a while now?" Callan's company, Black Asset Management, has almost $300 billion in assets under management, including hotel, residential, office, and retail space across the States and Canada. He's also recently begun investing in renewable energy and infrastructure. The last six months have kept him away from home while work has kept him busy.

"I fucking hope so. I need a break."

I'm about to ask him what he plans to do on his break when his gaze is drawn to a woman who has just arrived. She's absolutely stunning with her curves, olive skin, and long brunette hair, and I can't take my eyes off her in much the same way he can't. Ingrid and Edmund fuss over her for a few minutes before Hayden steals her away to a corner in the great room where they chat for a little while.

"Who's that?" I ask Callan.

He brings his gaze back to me but I think he struggles a little doing that. "Olivia. She works with Hayden."

"And she's Callan's best friend," Gage says, coming to sit with us. "Her family lives in this tower and we all grew up together."

"She's the girl my sons tried to turn into a boy," Ingrid says, sitting on the sofa across from me.

"How so?" I ask.

"She's an only child, so they took her under their wing when she and Callan were eight. Whatever they were into, so was she because they taught her everything they knew. Olivia often went on the camping trips with Edmund and the boys. She was like the sister they never had."

"And now Hayden's my boss," Olivia says as she, Hayden, Edmund and Bradford join us. "Hi, I'm Olivia, but it sounds like you already know that." Her smile is so big and warm that I can't help but feel drawn to her.

"Hi, I'm Kristen." I return her smile as I take in the gorgeous red suit she's wearing. It has flared sleeves that steal the show, although it could be her cleavage that does that. The suit jacket is buttoned up with one gold button at her waist, and if she's wearing anything under the jacket, I can't see it. All I can see is cleavage I would kill for.

"Congratulations on your marriage," she says.

"Thank you." Then, glancing between Hayden and her, I ask, "You're a lawyer?"

"Yes, but I don't really do much in the way of the law at the moment."

At my questioning look, Hayden clarifies, "Olivia's specialty is crisis management."

"Which is just another way for saying I clean up messes. And I make sure that gets done in a way that the law will be okay with," Olivia says.

"It's also another way of saying she sometimes has to babysit assholes," Callan says.

Olivia rolls her eyes. "It's hardly babysitting, Callan."

"What would you call it then?"

"Managing their crisis."

"Those are fancy words for babysitting, Ace."

She shakes her head at him while smiling and saying to me, "Just ignore him. He's grumpy because he made a bet with the last guy I had to manage and it cost him some coin when he lost the bet."

Gage whistles low. "How come we never heard about this?"

"Because you guys don't need to know every fucking thing," Callan mutters.

Olivia laughs. "Yeah, he's still pissed off about that bet."

I'm intrigued. "What was the bet?"

Olivia's eyes sparkle with mischief and as she opens her mouth to answer me, Callan gives her a look and says, "That's between us, Liv."

She watches him with a wide smile and the kind of affection that comes from years of knowing a person before finally looking at me. "It seems my lips are sealed."

"Who's your next victim?" Gage asks her.

"I don't have victims," Olivia says.

"Yeah, you do," Gage says. "The way you boss them into things like curfews and budgets and respectable behavior...they're your victims."

"She's working with Slade Sullivan," Hayden says.

"Oh," I say. "The hockey player?"

Callan eyes me. "If you're thinking of the asshole who likes to get himself into bar fights while drunk, and who recently abused a fan for taking his photo, that's the one."

"We're cleaning up his reputation," Olivia says. "And I really need to go now because"—she checks her watch—"shit, I was supposed to be at his place five minutes ago."

She says her goodbyes and leaves. Callan walks her out while Bradford and Hayden get pulled into a conversation with their parents in the kitchen, leaving me with Gage.

"Have you seen or heard from Cecelia?" he asks.

"No."

"Good. I take it you didn't tell Bradford about running into her."

"No, and I take it you didn't either." Bradford hasn't raised it with me, so I assume Gage didn't mention it.

"I didn't. He's got enough on his plate." He throws some of his scotch down his throat. "You let me know if you hear from her and I'll deal with it."

"Gage," Ingrid says, coming toward us. "Luna has woken up."

He nods and leaves us to go check on his daughter.

Ingrid smiles at me. "I hope you're having a lovely birthday, Kristen."

"Oh my God, I am! It's been maybe the best birthday I've ever had." I grin. "I mean, I got three new pairs of shoes! What girl wouldn't call that her best birthday ever?"

Ingrid laughs. "Those boys of mine can be smart at times."

Hayden, Gage, and Callan all gave me a pair of shoes for my birthday. None of them were aware the others were gifting me shoes, but they'd all paid attention the night we met and they discovered my love of shoes. The fact they'd all managed to get my shoe size over the last couple of weeks touched my heart in a way I don't think it's ever been touched. None would disclose their methods, and Bradford had no idea either, so that's still a mystery, but if there's one thing I know for sure now, it's that the Black men are resourceful. Well, I don't know about their brother Ethan, though, because he didn't come home for Christmas, but I imagine he's just as resourceful.

I walk with Ingrid to where the rest of the family are. We've almost reached them when my biggest gift turns up. Jenna and Beckett make a surprise entrance, their arms filled with gifts and their faces full of smiles and Christmas cheer.

Jenna throws her arms around me and whispers into my ear, "You didn't think your family would miss your birthday, did you? Oliver and Grayson are on their way too. I would have invited Mom, but I really didn't think Ingrid would appreciate that." She kisses my cheek. "Happy birthday, Kris."

And there go my tears.

I look at Ingrid who I just know planned this and I stand in front of her crying again, like I did a couple of weeks ago on the night I met her. I mouth, "Thank you," and then go back to my sister who is unloading gifts all around.

My brothers arrive and the party really gets started.

Grayson and Bradford really are on their way to becoming besties. They've golfed once since their lunch and spend a lot of the night drinking and talking all things skiing which Grayson loves just as much as Bradford.

Oliver and Bradford meet for the first time and my husband continues charming his way into my family.

Jenna meets Bradford's brothers and demands they

share more stories about Bradford from his younger years.

Ingrid is the perfect hostess and Edmund loosens up with me, asking questions in an effort to get to know me.

By the time Bradford gathers me into his arms just after 9:00 p.m., my heart is so full that it might burst.

He takes me home while I promise to do bad things to him as soon as I get him alone. I think, though, that we both know I've had a little too much to drink and am a little too tired to make good on those promises.

I take hold of his coat in the elevator on the way up to our condo and pull him close. "It's a good thing I didn't make you wait for your Christmas present until tonight, isn't it?"

This gains me a sexy smile. "We both know you had no intention of making me wait for that present."

I laugh and God it feels good to laugh.

I loop my arms around his neck. "I love you, Mr. Black. Thank you for making today the best day of this year. Well, except for the day you made Elvis put that ring on my finger. That was the other best day of this year."

He kisses me roughly before saying, "Stop giving Elvis the credit for putting that ring on your finger. I put it there."

I grin and smack another kiss to his lips. "It's always so much fun bantering with you over that ring. Please never stop doing that. Forever and ever."

The elevator doors open and we step out into the reception gallery where we're met by Bradford's house-keeper who has a serious expression on her face.

She looks at me. "Kristen, you have a visitor. Your mother is waiting for you in the grand salon."

My mother?

I frown.

"How long has she been waiting?" Bradford asks.

"An hour." She rushes to add, "She asked me not to interrupt your night by calling to advise you. I'm sorry if it was wrong of me not to call."

"No, that's okay," I say before making my way into the grand salon.

"Mom," I say when I find her.

She's sitting on the sofa reading a book and stands as soon as she hears my voice. "Kristen." Her voice wobbles and I get the impression she might cry. "Happy birthday, my darling."

I move to her, trying to force my brain into working faster. The booze I've drunk today is slowing it down. "It's late."

She wraps her arms around me and that's when I see it. Her suitcase. But still, my brain won't work faster.

"I know it's late, but I couldn't not come on your birthday." She keeps her arms around me tightly. "I'm so sorry I didn't spend the day with you. I was a fool and made foolish choices that I promise you I will never make again."

I stare at the navy suitcase. "Why do you have a suitcase with you, Mom?"

She gives me a squeeze before letting me go and taking a deep breath. Then, her features crack a little, just like her voice does when she says, "I've left your father."

42

KRISTEN

"I'M GOING to move Mom into my condo," I say to Bradford the morning after my birthday as I snuggle into his chest. He's just finished giving me my second orgasm for the day and I'm about to convince him to go in search of strawberry jam for me. I've decided life's too short not to have all the things you love in it.

"There's no rush. She can stay here as long as she wants to."

I look up at him. "You say that because you've never experienced a full day with my mother. Believe me, we'll all be a lot happier if she stays at my place."

My mother left my father last night. And not because he gave her an ultimatum like he gave me, but because she chose to leave him. We stayed up talking for hours after I got home and she told me why she cheated on Dad and how unhappy she's been in her marriage for decades. *Decades*.

At first, I was stunned to think a woman could stay in a marriage that didn't fulfill her for that long. But then I thought back over my entire life and how I spent years unfulfilled because my unhealed parts made choices trying to protect me from the hurt I'd experienced in life, choices that kept me in a cycle of shame and self-doubt and anxiety and deep unhappiness without me even realizing I was doing that to myself.

Mom told me she's ashamed that she spent years defending Dad's treatment of me and my brothers and sister. She wishes she was a better parent. I was honest with her and told her I wish things had been different, but then I told her that I imagine every parent has regrets because no one gets a manual in life for anything. We cried together and then we smiled together while we talked about all the things we want to do together. All the fun things mothers and daughters do when they're not busy trying to earn other people's approval.

I think we're going to be okay.

I also think my therapist should never be sent to outer space. She needs to stay in my life for *life*. We don't have a love/hate relationship after all. It's love/love.

"I thought I'd take you out for some fun today," Bradford says. "But if you'd prefer to spend time with your Mom, you should do that."

I roll so I'm half on him with my chin resting on my hands on his chest. "What kind of fun are we talking?"

"I thought we'd start with ice skating before we take the helicopter out to the Hamptons." He smirks. "I haven't been to our place out there yet and I'd like to see it."

I grin. He's referring to my place that I told him to make note of in our postnup. "You'll love our place there."

I inch my way up the bed to get closer to his face. "We can spend tonight stargazing."

He's about to say something when his phone lights up, and when I say *lights up*, I mean it goes fucking crazy with text after text and then a phone call that turns into two phone calls when Bradford doesn't answer the first.

"Fuck," he mutters when he checks the texts. Sitting up, he apologizes, "Sorry, I'm going to have to take this call."

"I'll go check on Mom while you do that." I give him a quick brush of my lips as he stabs at the phone to return the call. His hand comes to my arm as I turn to leave the bed, and he pulls me back in for a longer kiss before letting me go.

I take a quick shower and get dressed and am about to go in search of Mom when Bradford comes into my dressing room. I only have to take one look at him to know something has happened that hasn't pleased him.

"Cecelia has thrown her hat into the ring for the senate seat and seems to have been working Hale for weeks," he says.

His tense shoulders and grave voice cause worry to knot in my stomach. "And?"

He rakes his fingers through his hair. "And Hale likes her for the job."

A million thoughts cascade through my mind. "Do you think she's behind the smear campaign?"

His eyes flash with something lethal, something I've never seen in him before. If I was the reason for that look, I'd fear for myself right now. "Yes."

"What are you going to do?" Because that look in his eyes tells me he's going to do *something*.

He checks a text that comes in before meeting my gaze again. "I'm going into the office to take care of this. I'm sorry this ruins our plans for the day."

"No, don't apologize. I want you to do whatever you need to."

"I'll keep you updated." He checks another text. "Fuck, I have to go." He moves into me so he can kiss me goodbye. Then, his eyes lock with mine and he says with the kind of request that I know is more a command than a request, "Please don't go online today."

Holy God, how does he not know that saying something like that to me actually puts that idea in my head? Like, *plants* it there as a tiny little seed that will just grow and grow and grow today, begging me to water it and help it see light.

When I don't answer him, his eyes bore into me harder. "Kristen."

I swallow the guilt of what I know might be a lie. "Okay."

And then he's gone and I'm left flailing about, trying desperately to do as he asked.

I will not go online.

I will not go online.

I will not go online.

Right.

Mom.

I'll make her distract me.

Half an hour after Bradford leaves, I've managed to get my mother to drive me crazy enough to force most of the thoughts of going online from my head. I simply asked her for decorating advice.

I told her I've been thinking about redecorating my

Hampton's home because I knew she'd take the opportunity to say *finally, it's about time we fixed that disastrous attempt of your previous decorator.*

I'm in the middle of this conversation when Bradford's housekeeper joins me and Mom in the family room. She advises that Alan is here to see me and against all my good judgment, I tell her I'll see him.

Leaving Mom, I head into the grand salon where Alan's waiting. When I reach him, he's standing with his back to me while he looks out the windows. He's a tall, imposing figure and I instantly feel unsettled that he's here. *Why is he here?* I thought Bradford was meeting him at the office.

He turns when he hears me and I skip a breath when I see his face. When I see the tension emanating from him like a harsh winter chill. His jaw is set hard, and his eyes contain unnerving determination. Every inch of him is tightly coiled, like a spring wound up to its limit, ready to snap at any moment.

"Bradford's not here. He's gone into the office." I smooth my dress as my stomach churns violently.

His movements are precise and controlled when he moves in my direction. "I know." He comes to a stop in front of me and I feel like a small animal caught in the gaze of a prowling tiger. "I'm here to see you."

"I can't imagine why."

"You've obviously not been on social media today." His voice sends chills down my spine. Or maybe it's the fact I know something very bad has happened that sends those chills.

"Bradford told me not to go online. I'm simply doing as I've been told." That last statement is an arrow aimed at him and all his fucking instructions he's been issuing since the day we met.

"Your little fairytale ends here, Kristen. It's time you pack your bags and get the fuck out of Bradford's life. He'll be far better off without you, and I'll be able to get back to doing the job he's paying me to do rather than this bullshit putting out of fires that you just keep fucking lighting."

His words roll off his tongue like bitter poison and everything about him is pure hostility. The air between us practically crackles with tension as he dares me to contradict him.

Some fucking men can go fuck themselves.

"My fairytale is just getting started, Alan. I'm not going anywhere."

"If you don't leave him, he will never be president. I promise you that."

Alan knows how to press my fear buttons but I desperately scramble to stop him. To make it so those buttons can never be pressed by him.

Please keep letting Bradford choose you.

"That isn't something you can know."

"Knowing these things is why men like your husband pay me well. It's why they listen to me and do the things I tell them to do. It's why they're in power now." He clenches his jaw. "Your husband, though, is too fucking enamored with your pussy and can't see straight. He won't listen to a word I'm saying, and *that* makes it fucking hard for me to do my job."

"You seriously think Bradford would just let me go? Come on, Alan, use your brain. There's no way he's letting me walk out of his life."

"It doesn't matter what he does behind closed doors. I only care about the optics of it. He's got more chance of having a political career if you're no longer in the picture the public sees."

"Do you know what I think, Alan?"

"I don't give a flying fuck what you think."

"I'll tell you anyway." I take a step closer to him. Push my shoulders back a little further. Hold my head fucking high. "I think he's got more chance of having a political career if *you're* no longer in the picture. I think the fairy-tale is over for *you*. And now, please get the fuck out of my home."

The ferocity and rage swimming in his eyes is on a level I've never seen. Not even from my father. "You will regret this."

"Oh, I don't think so. My only regret is not saying those words to you sooner."

I'm shaking by the time he leaves. And I've reached the point where I can no longer honor the promise I made my husband this morning.

With trembling hands, I tap my phone and go online.

@thetea_gasp

Here's the facts, girlfriends, our girl @kristenblaise (who hasn't been online for some time now and really needs to update her handle so we all know she's @kristenblack now) has the moves. A video was posted of her last night where she shows us all how to really get a man's attention. In a public club #gasp We're not even lowkey obsessed with this video. We're

loud and proud obsessed. But did you guys do the math? Check her haircut in that video. She was grinding all over her zaddy nearly two years ago and he was a total simp for her. We are shook. Like, why did they not go to Elvis back then? Why did he get engaged to someone else? Why, why, why? These are the questions we need answers to! Sign us up for the reality show of their life, please and thank you. We will stan #Bristen forever!

Oh. My. God.

My heart almost beats its way out of my chest.

Someone filmed me begging Bradford to fuck me in that club.

And someone got hold of that video.

This is why people should never have sex in public.

Never, ever, *ever.*

I scroll for five minutes and see that this video has hit everywhere. Right alongside story after story about my wild and loose ways. Photos of me with all my previous boyfriends plaster the internet. Doctored photos of me doing very sexual things to other men in public have also flooded the net. Men I have never even met. Headlines scream "Do You Want Her To Be The First Lady One Day?" and "She Will Corrupt Our Country."

No wonder Bradford asked me to stay offline today.

Before I can think about what I'm going to do next, Jenna calls.

"Oh my, God, Kristen, are you okay? I just saw the news. Do you need me to come over?"

"I just saw it too. I also just had a visit from Alan."

"Shit. What did he say? And wait, why was he visiting you?"

"He told me my fairytale is over and that I need to get the fuck out of Bradford's life."

"That fucking asshole! I hope you told him where to go."

"I did."

"Good. Where's Bradford?"

"He's gone into the office."

Her voice softens. "Do you need me?"

"No, Mom's here. She'll fuss around me."

"I know. That's one reason why I asked if you need me."

I laugh and am so grateful to her for giving me that moment of respite. "I love you, Jenna. I'm okay." I take a deep breath. "I think I'm going to take charge of the narrative."

"That is a great idea."

"Okay, I have to go so I can get to work."

"I love you, Kristen. And I'm so fucking proud of you."

There's something about your sister telling you she's proud of you. It adds to the self-belief I've been digging deep for and helps me make my next phone call.

"Kristen," Gage drawls when he answers my call. "I imagine you're having a hell of a day. What can I do for you?"

I'm really glad I asked Bradford to key all his family members' phone numbers into my phone after I met them. It will make what I want to do today easier.

"Cecelia. What have you got on her?"

"Does Bradford know you're making this call?"

"No."

"I don't think you want to go there, Kristen."

"I'm not sure either, Gage, but I have to do *something*."

"You don't think Bradford's got this handled?"

"I don't think he should be burdened with this job alone."

He turns silent for a moment. "He made the right choice when he married you, that's for damn sure. But while I'm one of your biggest supporters, I'm not going to get involved. Not like this. You want to help him, you go to him."

While he doesn't give me what I'm looking for, I respect the way he looks out for his brother. I also like the way he looks out for my marriage.

After our call, I text a friend who might be able to help me.

> Anthea, I'm calling in that favor.

I watch the blue dots go up and down, up and down, and then stop. Anthea does not want that favor called in because she knows it's going to hurt.

The blue dots go up and down again a few more times before she finally sends the text.

ANTHEA
> Okay.

> I need something that will convince Cecelia Aniston not to pursue politics right now.

She calls me. "James will kill me for this, Kristen."

"I'm aware. But you owe me."

Anthea and James do owe me. I saved them from

financial ruin years ago when I gave them a heads up to get their money out of an investment that was actually a Ponzi scheme, information I'd put together from various whispers I'd heard.

Anthea told me back then that she'd repay the favor whenever I wanted. And since I know that she and her husband have dirt on everyone, I know she's the person who can probably help me now.

There's only one problem: Cecelia is her husband's cousin.

"I know, but I didn't think you'd want me to give you information that will hurt his family," she hisses.

"She won't know where I got the information."

She exhales a long breath. "I fucking hope not."

"So, what do you have?"

It turns out Cecelia has some skeletons in her closet. I refuse the first skeleton: the fact Cecelia has had an abortion. I don't care to use something like that against a woman, so I tell Anthea that doesn't work for me. She gives me something else I'm not really interested in because I don't think it's enough to convince Cecelia to stop vying for the senate seat. Then, she shares with me that Cecelia has had multiple allegations of sexual harassment made against her at work. Five, in fact, all from women she's silenced in one way or another.

After I finish with Anthea, I call Callan and ask him for Olivia's phone number. He's intrigued as to why I want it. I'm honest with him and tell him I need a crisis manager.

Five minutes later, I've got Olivia on the phone.

"Kristen." She sounds surprised to hear from me. "What's up and why aren't you and Bradford coming skiing with us? I was looking forward to getting to know you."

I fill her in on everything happening with me and Bradford. She listens carefully and when I'm finished, she says, "Holy fuck, that woman. I've seen a lot of shit in my line of work, and this is some *real* shit."

"Yes, it is."

"So, how do you want me to help? I know Bradford already has a PR team, so I'm not sure what I could contribute."

"Yes, he has a team, but I don't. I want you to be my PR team."

"Oh, I like that. Yes. Let's do this. I've got some time now to go over ideas if you do."

"I would love that. Thank you."

An hour later, I get off my call with her and think about Adeline's advice to listen to my gut. She was right; I had to stop thinking so hard in order to hear what my gut had to say. I just had to let how it feels guide me. Today, it's speaking so loudly I can't not hear it. And what it's saying is that I need to run as far in the opposite direction from Alan as I can. I need to have a conversation with my husband and share with him what Alan said to me. I really don't want to have that conversation because I don't want to put Bradford in that position. But the thing I've had to remind myself over and over this morning is that I can do hard things.

I promised to let Bradford worry about me and now I will uphold that promise.

But first, I will remove the burden of Cecelia from his life.

I find her at her condo. Anthea advised me of her

address before telling me that was the absolute last bit of information she was sharing with me and that I should consider the favor paid in full.

Cecelia looks at me with all the condescension she has for me when I arrive. She lets me step off the elevator into her condo but that's as far as she allows me in. Crossing her bony arms, she says, "Why am I looking at you?"

"Because you and I are going to have a little conversation. One in which I tell you why you should not run for senator, and one in which you agree that my idea is a very good one. After this conversation, we will never need to speak to each other again."

Her steely gaze freezes on me as icy fury swirls in her eyes. "I told you that you're dumb, Kristen. You really should listen to me. You're wasting my time."

"Did you treat all the women you sexually harassed at your work as awfully as you treat me?"

She stiffens. I see her try to hide that but she fails. "What are you talking about?"

"You know what I'm talking about. And I think Senator Hale might like to know about it too. I imagine he'd think that your brand of skeleton is worse than Bradford's. Good PR can polish me up, make people forget the video you made sure they all saw. But not even good spin can polish your kind of filth."

The veins in her neck strain against her skin. "Do you have any idea who you're messing with? What I'm capable of?"

"Yes, I know you're a bitch who goes out of her way to play dirty. But I've been in this playground my entire life and I also know how to play dirty. And I will, Cecelia, if I have to. If you think this is the only skeleton I have of yours, you're fooling yourself. I may not want to use your abortion against you, or the other things I know, but if you force me to protect my husband in that way, I will."

She glares at me for a long moment, her breaths coming faster with every second. Her fury is restrained, but only just. Finally, she spits, "Get out! And watch your back, because this is *not* finished between us."

"Oh, I think it is. I really think it is. And I don't wish you well. I wish you everything you deserve."

As I step out onto the sidewalk, I pull my winter coat around me tightly before walking the short distance to one of my favorite coffee shops. I've decided it's a good day to have a glazed donut. And a coffee with two sugars.

43

BRADFORD

"HE'S FUCKING FIRED!" I jab my finger at Alan as I let my anger surge out of me. "He's been reporting back every day for three weeks with the wrong fucking information, and thanks to his fuck up, my wife has had her private life smeared across the fucking internet. Get rid of him today. *Now*. I don't ever want to have to look at him again."

Fuck.

I force air from my lungs and yank my tie off while working like hell not to smash my fist through a wall. I've just spent the last hour with Alan and our team to get to the bottom of why our efforts to control the smear campaign haven't worked. And the fucking reason is that the team missed the fact it was Cecelia behind most of it all along. We were working with incorrect information and it has cost Kristen dearly, which isn't something I will tolerate.

"You're being unreasonable, Bradford, and making a rash decision. Yes, he screwed up, but anyone would have with the information he was being provided."

I see fucking red. "I don't pay you to share your opinion of decisions I make regarding my wife, Alan. I pay you to get me elected, so how about you get me fucking elected."

His brows knit together as he glares at me. "Here's an opinion for you. Your wife is your only weakness. Before she showed up, I saw the road to the White House. There were no obstacles in the way that we couldn't have dealt with. You were the best candidate I've ever worked with, but then she came along and fucked that all up. And now you can't see what I'm seeing. I actually don't fucking know what you're seeing anymore, and that's a massive problem for me. The guy giving us the wrong information is the least of your worries while Kristen's in your life."

A call comes in from Jenna, distracting me from Alan. I'll come back to him, but first I answer Jenna's call.

"Jenna." She's never phoned me and I'm instantly on alert.

She doesn't bother with social niceties. "Kristen will likely throttle me for this, but you need to know that Alan went to see her today and took it upon himself to tell her to get the fuck out of your life, and I quote him exactly. And further, he's been awful to her for weeks and she hasn't wanted to tell you because she knows you already have enough on your plate, but it's gotten to the point where I can't hold my tongue any longer because she's also got enough on her plate and the last thing she needs is to be constantly criticized for doing everything wrong." She takes a breath. "You need to keep that man away from my sister, Bradford. Please."

I stare at the man she's referring to and every cell in

my body wants to do damage to him. I've wanted to hurt people before, but I never knew what it felt like to want to inflict the kind of harm I now want to.

"Thank you for telling me. I will take care of this."

"Good."

I end the call and place my phone down on my desk, controlling my movements carefully because I'm concerned that if I don't, my body will take over, and I'll beat the shit out of him to the point he may no longer be breathing.

Calling on restraint I barely have, I say, "You went to see my wife today."

He doesn't bother denying it. Instead, he squares his shoulders and replies, "Yes. I gave her the honest truth that you never will."

Every muscle in me tenses and I fist my hands by my side. "You told her to get the fuck out of my life."

His face contorts with unchecked anger. "I told her what she needed to hear. And she does need to get out, and you need to let her go. You should have just fucked her in Vegas and left it at that. We'd all be a lot fucking better off if you had."

My self-control snaps and I'm around the desk before Alan sees me coming. I grab his shirt with both hands and jerk him to me while breathing fire all over him. "You are fucking done! I will make sure no one works with you again." I wrench him closer. "And if I ever hear that you've said a bad word against Kristen again, you will fucking wish you hadn't."

His breaths come hard and fast between us as he tries to push me away. "Get your fucking hands off me!"

I tighten my grip, still deciding if I'm going to punch him or not.

He shoves at my chest, pushing me back, and still I don't let him go.

My eyes bore into his, hating everything I'm looking at. I was a fucking fool to keep him around. From that very first meeting with Kristen, I should have known to get rid of him and I will regret for a long time that I didn't.

I thrust him away from me with so much force he lands on his ass. "Get out of my sight."

When he picks himself up off the floor and makes a move like he's going to come at me, I arch my brows and fucking challenge him to. My fists are itching to inflict pain. In the end, he snarls something at me about pussy that I don't care to hear and storms out of my office.

The second he's gone, I snatch my phone up and call Kristen to make sure she's okay. When she doesn't answer, I leave a message for her to return my call.

Then, I call Gage who answers almost immediately.

"I've got that information on Phillip," he says, "and fuck me, that guy is into some shit."

Last night, I asked Gage if he had anything on the guy who fucked with me and Kristen by sending me that text that kept us apart for nearly two years. He didn't but told me he'd look into it.

"Good. I need whatever you've got on Cecelia too."

"I wondered how long it would take you."

When Cecelia made it clear she intended on destroying me, I assumed she'd target me, not Kristen. And since there's nothing in my life that she could have used against me, except our fake relationship which I knew she wouldn't because that would hurt her too, I wasn't too worried. I had no reason to go to my brother for help. Now, I do.

"What have you got?"

"I'll send you a file. There's some juicy stuff in there that was buried so deep I almost didn't find it. She won't be a threat once you're finished with her."

I scrub a hand down my face. "Unfortunately, the damage has already been done. I shouldn't have let it get to this point."

"You couldn't have seen this coming. No one expected Cecelia to go after Kristen like she has. Besides, your wife has some grit. She's not going down without a fight."

"You've spoken with her?"

"Yeah, she called this morning looking for this file." He chuckles. "I learned a valuable lesson. Don't fuck with you because your wife will fuck with me back."

"Jesus."

"Okay, I've just loaded the files into our drive. Have fun with the dragon. And enjoy taking Phillip down."

We end the call and half an hour later, I'm standing in Cecelia's condo, file in hand, ready to tear her to shreds.

She assesses me with that cool gaze of hers I hope never to lay eyes on again. "Let me guess, your wife sent you because she knows she didn't actually get the job done."

Fuck, Kristen came here? It's troubling to me that I'm turned on by that. By her fierce desire to protect me. "I'm not here to discuss my wife." I jab the file at her. "I'm here to make it very fucking clear that if you continue attacking Kristen, I will begin dismantling your life, brick by brick until you have nothing left."

"Oh, Bradford, you dumb fucking man. Do you really believe you have that power?"

I lift my chin at the file she's yet to look at. "Open it. See for yourself just what power I have. I think you'll find that I don't issue idle threats."

She takes her time before opening the file, eyeing me like she doesn't believe one word I've said. Her tune changes the second she begins skimming the document inside. Her jaw tenses and her fingers grip the file like she wants to crush it into a million tiny pieces. "I always knew you were an asshole." She lifts her face to mine, the lines on it carved into angry slashes. "And now I have proof."

"I will do whatever it takes to protect my wife, Cecelia. Don't ever doubt that. The only reason you've managed to hurt her as much as you have is because I trusted the wrong person. I won't make that mistake again." I pause and look at her in such a way to let her know to pay very close attention to what I say next. "I won't ever stop watching you. One wrong step and I will make good on this promise. Are we clear?"

She does not want to give me the acknowledgement I'm looking for. When she doesn't answer me, I step forward and roar, "Are we fucking clear?"

She jumps, which pisses her off, and I receive a filthy glare as she snaps, "Yes, we're fucking clear."

"Good. And one last thing, you should expect a visit from the DOJ about that fraud mentioned in the file." At her wide eyes, I say, "You didn't think I'd ignore what you've already done to Kristen, did you? This is for that."

I stalk out of her condo and am on my way to my car when Kristen calls.

My phone is to my ear in seconds. "Where are you?"

"I'm in my favorite coffee shop eating my second donut for the day. I wish you were here."

"Tell me where and I'll be there."

"No, Bradford, I know you're busy today. I shouldn't have said that."

"You should always tell me when you wish I was with you."

"You sound a bit wild. Is everything going okay?"

"I fired Alan. He won't ever harass you again. I also just saw Cecelia. Her campaign against you is over. Although, it seems I was late to that party."

"I can't tell right now if I'm in trouble or not."

"You're never in trouble, Kristen."

"This is a good piece of information to have. And now that I have it, I'm going to tell you that I hired Olivia today to help me take charge of the narrative."

Fuck, I love my wife. "She'll get the job done."

"Also, as part of that, I'm considering doing an interview with Marlee James."

When it comes to respected journalists, Marlee is one of the most recognized in America. "*You're* doing it or *we're* doing it?"

"Olivia suggested an honest and vulnerable interview with just me, and I think she might be right. But I won't do it if you don't want me to."

"I trust you and Olivia to do what you think is best."

"I have something else to tell you, Bradford."

"What?"

"Actually, two things. First, we're not going to my class

reunion. I'm done with them. And second, we're bringing strawberry jam into our home, which means you should prepare yourself for my sugar comas and the fallout of those comas."

"What does a fallout entail?"

"It can be anything from excessive retail therapy to deal with the emotions of all the sugar I unwillingly consumed, to a hardcore exercise plan that I'll likely force upon you too, to long movie rewatching marathons while I wail about all the sugar I ate, to me removing any kind of fun food from the place, to me blaming you for my consumption of all that sugar."

"All this from strawberry jam?"

"Well, strawberry jam is the gateway drug. You do know about gateway sugar, right?"

I chuckle. "I did not, but consider me enlightened. Also, consider me prepared. I can deal with the fallout."

She's silent for a beat and when she speaks again, I feel her smile. "I know you can. I think you can deal with all my small things."

"Where are you, Kristen?"

"You really have time to come and eat a donut with me?"

"I do. Although, first I have to take care of something, so you may be onto your third donut by the time I arrive."

"It'll be a hardship but I'll take one for the team."

She gives me the address of the coffee shop and I end the call as I slide into the back seat of my car.

"Where to, boss?" my driver asks.

I give him Phillip O'Rourke's address and settle back against the seat while thinking about the conversation

I'm about to have with the asshole who kept Kristen from me.

As a general rule, I don't go out of my way to hurt people. It seems, though, that where my wife is concerned, I will go far and fucking wide to hurt those who hurt her. And this particular asshole is one I will enjoy taking down.

@thetea_gasp

@KRISTENBLACK STEPPED out in S.T.Y.L.E. today, girlfriends. Yeet! It's been three months since the release of her sex tape. Okay, okay, so it wasn't a release as such, but honestly, she should have released it herself. Everyone, and we mean EVERY.ONE. inhaled that shit. We're all still hanging for the Real Housewife of Bradford Black to be announced. Anyway, we got slightly off track there, which seems to be a #Bristen thing. Too many shiny things and all. Okay, so our girl is the new #girlboss since she did that interview with @marleejames and made us all swoon over her zaddy while respecting the hell out of her for being real and honest with us about their relationship, and now she's making her own moves. Today, she announced her very own foundation to help women rise. This girl ain't relying on her senator hubby for anything. She's out there slaying on her own. Periodt. And that @adeline-andpearce dress she wore today? All we've got is a hell yaaasss. We wish her besties were our besties.

45

KRISTEN

"WHERE ARE WE GOING?" I ask my husband as he rushes me into our elevator early one Saturday morning in May.

He's been bossing me around all morning.

First, he forced me to wake before 5:00 a.m. so he could fuck me before going for his run. Seriously, I told him next time to run first and then wake me for sex, to which he told me he wouldn't shower in between because he couldn't wait that long, to which I told him he'd have to suck his own dick then...I think I got my point across. After he returned from his run, he bossed me into eating my breakfast faster so I could get dressed sooner. Then, he bossed me into not spending long styling my hair or applying makeup. And that was right before he bossed me into the elevator.

He selects the button for the lobby. "Somewhere special."

I gape at him. "You're taking me somewhere special and you wouldn't give me time to style my hair properly? What is wrong with you today? How do you not know I am not a woman who doesn't look her best when she goes somewhere special?"

That entertained look of his settles on his face and he moves into me, backing me against the wall. Sliding his hand through my hair, he brushes his lips over mine. "You're fucking perfect, Kristen."

I smack him away. "To you, I am. I'd like to have the choice in how I present myself to everyone else."

He grins. "Have I ever told you how much I adore your grumpy moods?"

"No, and I don't care to hear about that adoration now."

"Because?"

"Because you're being excessively bossy today. And you wouldn't let me do my hair."

"I'll make it up to you today."

"How?"

"It's a surprise."

"You know I don't like surprises."

"You like fun. Think of this as fun."

I take in the earnestness in his eyes, the depth and sincerity of what he's saying, and decide I'm being a little hard on him. "Will there be sugar involved?"

"Yes."

"Donuts?"

"Yes."

Okay, we're getting somewhere now. I'm beginning to narrow our destination down. And if there's one sure way to get Bradford to give me what I want, I know what that way is.

I press my body to his and shamelessly rub myself against him. "What about cakes? Will there be cakes?"

He groans. "You don't play fair, baby." Then, he takes hold of my wrists so he can keep my hands from his dick. Because he knows from experience that that's where they were going next. "And we're done with this interrogation. All you can know is there will be donuts and it will be special."

The elevator reaches the lobby and he holds my hand as he leads me out of the tower onto the sidewalk. He then turns right and we begin walking down the street.

"You're making me walk there? In these heels?" God, I sound grumbly even to myself, but honestly, he could have given me warning that we'd be walking. I would have chosen better shoes.

"It's not far."

Okay, so there goes most of my theories about our destination. None of my favorite donut places are close.

"Bradford, I feel the need to educate you on what it's like to walk in these heels. *Not far* would be from the bedroom to the kitchen. Or from the elevator to the car. I mean, we have a fancy new car. Why are we not using it?"

He tightens his grip on my hand and practically pulls me along the street. "Consider me educated."

I don't believe him. I think he's on some kind of mission and isn't really paying too much attention to anything I'm saying. Which is highly unusual for him.

We cross at Seventh Avenue and walk down to Central Park. It's a beautiful sunny day. Some of my grumpy mood disappears simply because of the sunshine. Children are laughing and parents are chasing them. There's something infectious about a child's laughter and it improves my mood some more.

We cross to the entrance of the park where people

take horse and carriage rides. Bradford surprises me when he stops near one of the carriages and speaks with the man there. Then, he really surprises me when he ushers me toward a beautiful white carriage, making motions with his arms that indicate he wants to help me into it.

"We're going for a ride?"

"Yes." When I look at him with confusion because this is not what I was expecting when he said there would be donuts, he leans in close and says, "Hurry, before it turns into a pumpkin."

There's something in the way he says this, or in the way he's looking at me, or just *something*, that stirs all my butterflies. And those butterflies always make it so that when Bradford tells me to do something while under their influence, I do it.

I let him help me into the carriage and sit on the gorgeous red velvet seat. It's at this point that I really look at the carriage and see the flowers on the front of it. Flowers that look very romantic.

When Bradford takes the seat next to me, I say, "If I didn't know better, I'd think you were proposing to me today."

He looks at me and there's *something* in his eyes, but before I can think more about that, and before he can respond to what I said, the carriage driver passes him a box that is wrapped in exquisite cream and gold paper and finished off with a beautiful gold bow. He thanks the driver who then takes his position on the seat up the front.

And then we're off and within a couple of minutes, I'm in love with this way of experiencing the park. The rhythm of the horse, the gentle breeze brushing my face, the proximity of my husband.

I turn and find him watching me closely. My body lights up with the desire that has only increased since we were married. I didn't think I could want Bradford more than I always had, but I was wrong. I want him in ways I'm still comprehending.

"What's in the box?" I nudge my shoulder against his. "Is it a donut?"

His mouth doesn't smile but his eyes do. He has a way with that kind of smile. I don't think anyone else ever knows about half the smiles he gives me like this and that makes me feel so special. They're just for me. For us.

He passes me the box. "Open it."

I run my hands over the gold embossed wrapping paper and touch the bow. "It's a big donut."

Now his lips lift. "It's not a donut."

I pretend pout. "You promised me sugar."

"Have I ever let you down?"

No, no he has not.

I carefully undo the bow. I sense I'm going to want to keep this ribbon. I don't know how or why I feel that, but my butterflies are whispering very loudly to me, and if there's one thing I've learned this year, it's to listen to those whispers.

I place the ribbon on my lap and remove the wrapping.

It's a shoebox.

A cream shoebox that has "B&K" embossed in gold on the lid.

My butterflies are going wild now.

I look at him and every inch of my skin blazes with anticipation at what I see in his eyes.

Love.

So.Much.Love.

"You bought me shoes with sugar on them?"

He takes the lid off the box and I almost stop breathing when I see what's inside.

The most perfect glass slippers.

I reach in and take one of the shoes in my hand, admiring, *adoring*, the diamonds that are layered from toe to heel, the pointy toe, the spike heel, and the cluster of large clear crystals affixed to the top just above the point.

He leans in close, bringing his divine scent with him and driving me a little bit wilder when I would have thought that impossible. He cups my cheek and kisses me, taking all the time in the world to show me without words just how much he loves me. His tongue slides over mine and I almost forget we're in a carriage in a park. I *want* to forget that so I can slide onto his lap and get even closer to him. I will never get close enough to this man.

When he ends the kiss, he keeps hold of my cheek and stares into my eyes. I'm breathless as we escape into this moment together. I think I could *live* in this moment.

Finally, he says, "Will you put those glass slippers on and marry me, Kristen?"

I would crawl across glass to marry this man. Putting these shoes on to marry him would be my greatest privilege.

"Yes," I breathe.

He still doesn't let me go. "Today."

I stare at him. "You want to get married again today?"

"No, we *are* getting married again today." At my

confused expression, he lets my cheek go and says, "We're on our way to meet the girls. They'll help you get ready so you can marry me this afternoon."

I blink. "I don't have a dress."

"Yes, you do. Jenna and Adeline designed it. It's the only reason why this wedding didn't take place months ago. I had to wait for the fabric or the lace or something to arrive from Paris or Italy or somewhere."

His clear frustration at being hindered makes me laugh. I place my hand to his cheek. "Look at you getting good at being patient." *This man.* "Where are we getting married?"

"In our ballroom."

"And there will be donuts?"

He smiles and this one is spread right across his face. "Yes, there will be many donuts. You don't think I'd plan your wedding and not have sugar for you, do you?"

"Our wedding," I correct him.

"Our wedding."

I never imagined the day I'd be okay with not planning my own wedding, but that day is today. And I can't wait to see what Bradford has planned for us.

I glance down at my Cinderella shoes. "Will you carry me to bed on your back after you marry me?"

He eyes the shoes. "It was my stipulation when I ordered the shoes. The heel had to be so high that you would beg me to put you on my back."

I meet his gaze again. "Okay, I'll marry you today. I've got a dress, shoes, and donuts. And my girls will make sure my hair is done because"—I make wide eyes at him —"my husband didn't allow me to style it for a special occasion this morning."

"Your husband knows you're beautiful without your hair styled."

"My husband is being very reckless right now. He should know that styling my hair is a top priority of mine."

He kisses me again and I *feel* his recklessness. I feel how close he is to losing control. "You make me reckless, Kristen. You always have and always will."

I had no idea that the night I met Bradford would be the night I'd find my prince. I had no idea we'd spend the next decade falling for each other. And I had no idea just how well this man would love me.

I may have been searching for a prince, but I found a king.

"I love you, Bradford, and I will let Elvis put your ring on my finger anytime you want him to."

EPILOGUE

@thetea_gasp

OMG GIRLFRIENDS, did you see the photo @kristenblack posted last night?! The caption read: "He bought me glass slippers and asked me to put them on and marry him. I said yes, but only because he also promised me donuts." The photo was of two sugar-coated donuts, a set of wedding bands, and one diamond encrusted shoe. We die. We also die because our girl is now our new bestie! We opened our DMs this morning and FOUND ONE FROM HER #gasp. Our new bestie said we could share all the deets with you, so put your feet up and prepare to #swoon. The wedding dress was designed by @adelineandpearce and inspired by vintage Dior. A cap-sleeved coatdress crafted from scalloped Chantilly lace and vintage buttons was layered over an elegant strapless column gown. Kristen shrugged the coatdress off on the dance floor or maybe her bae did. We don't know because no one thought to stream the wedding for all of us #Bristen stans. We would have died to see Elvis serenade them for their first dance to "Love Me Tender". Our bestie shared that it was the same Elvis who married them in Vegas last year. #Swoon at zaddy flying him in. And the diamond shoes! Bestie didn't spill the tea, but Senator Black is for sure gonna have to tighten the budget for a while to make up for that expense. All the happy sighs for our girl finding a man to love her sweet. No news on where he's taking her for the honeymoon. All we were told was a cryptic "he's taking me dirty dancing" so really, that could be anywhere in the world. If you spot them, send us pics!

Thank you so much for reading Bradford's and Kristen's story.
I hope you loved it as much as I do!

Want more?
Download their Bonus Epilogue here:
https://www.subscribepage.com/asybonusepilogue

The next book is...

Yours Actually

Callan & Olivia's story
a friends to lovers romance
COMING 2023

ACKNOWLEDGMENTS

Jodie, "dude, me and you are a forever deal. I will always stay up." You may never know what it means to me that you always stay up for my deadlines. That you set alarms for every hour of deadline night to check in and see if I need you to read something. That you wake early to see if there's one last thing I need you to read. That you get snacks for release day because release day is as special to you as it is to me. *That you support me like no other.* Thank you, Phanie. I promise in our old age, you can go to bed at a much reasonable time every night of the year because contrary to your Misery plans for me, I will retire at some point. And yes, I'm sorry that means you may never get your love triangle from me.

Riana, thank you for letting me call on you for help with some of the American things in this story! I truly appreciate you being just a message away. I also truly appreciate your amazing support. I value our new friendship so much and can't wait to meet you one day (hopefully next year!).

Rose, thank you for being so freaking patient with me. For working to my crazy deadlines. And for adding just the right word here and there in my book. You always help make my story shine.

Letitia, this cover is everything and I am so grateful to still be working with you eight years (EIGHT!) after we did our first cover together. I can't wait to see what you design for the next book!

Andrea, you may never read this book but if you do, thank you for helping change my life. Parts therapy has been so much more than I ever imagined it could be. I never want to send you to outer space.

To my amazing readers, thank you for waiting for this story. For waiting so long! I hope you loved it and I hope that it touched your heart. If you're interested to know more about parts therapy (the therapy that changed Kristen's life), search for IFS therapy. I've been working with an IFS therapist for over a year now and I have found it to be the best form of therapy I have ever done.

To everyone who helps get the word out about my books, thank you! From the bottom of my heart, *thank you.*

ALSO BY NINA LEVINE

Escape With a Billionaire Series

Ashton Scott

Jack Kingsley

Beckett Pearce

Jameson Fox

Owen North

Only Yours Series

(The Black Brothers Billionaire Romance)

Accidentally, Scandalously Yours

Storm MC Series

Storm (Storm MC #1)

Fierce (Storm MC #2)

Blaze (Storm MC #3)

Revive (Storm MC #4)

Slay (Storm MC #5)

Sassy Christmas (Storm MC #5.5)

Illusive (Storm MC #6)

Command (Storm MC #7)

Havoc (Storm MC #8)

Gunnar (Storm MC #9)

Wilder (Storm MC #10)

Colt (Storm MC #11)

Sydney Storm MC Series

Relent (#1)

Nitro's Torment (#2)

Devil's Vengeance (#3)

Hyde's Absolution (#4)

King's Wrath (#5)

King's Reign (#6)

King: The Epilogue (#7)

Storm MC Reloaded Series

Hurricane Hearts (#1)

War of Hearts (#2)

Christmas Hearts (#3)

Battle Hearts (#4)

The Hardy Family Series

Steal My Breath (single dad romance)

Crave Series

Be The One (rockstar romance)

www.ninalevinebooks.com

PLAYLIST

"Never Be The Same" by Camila Cabello
"When You're Gone" by Shawn Mendes
"Treat You Better" by Shawn Mendes
"Lights Down Low" by MAX
"Maroon" by Taylor Swift
"Delicate" by Taylor Swift
"Surrender My Heart" by Carly Rae Jepsen
"I Think He Knows" by Taylor Swift
"You Are in Love" by Taylor Swift
"Butterflies" by MAX, FLETCHER
"Lover" by Taylor Swift, feat. Shawn Mendes
"There's No Way" by Lauv, Julia Michaels
"Comeback" by Carly Rae Jepsen
"Labyrinth" by Taylor Swift
"I Don't Wanna Live Forever" by ZAYN, Taylor Swift
"Lean on Me" by Cheat Codes, Tinashe

Made in the USA
Las Vegas, NV
14 November 2023

80738422R00252